ROCKET QUEEN

JULIANNA MORGAN

DEDICATION

To Nissa—I bet you thought I wasn't going to give you this dedication, huh? Also to my Mom and Dad.

ACKNOWLEDGEMENTS

Writing acknowledgements is a daunting task. What if you only ever write one book? You gotta get everyone in! And that's impossible, though I'll try my best. To start, I can't forget to acknowledge the people who had me kicked me out of my past ballet school, honestly I don't know if this would've been written otherwise. I should also probably acknowledge poor mental health, without it I might not be such a tortured soul and everyone knows tortured souls are great for creativity. Yeah?

Oh, and now for the real acknowledgments—I thank all my friends who helped me through my hard times, including those I was once close with and no longer see, and to those who continue to help me, no matter what—special thanks to Bella, Liah, Ty, Michi, Darren, Ginny, Nadya, Connor, Charlotte, Benny, The Common Room Gang, and my best friend, my sister, Anissa (more on you later). Also, thank you to my wonderful publisher and editor, Michelle—you have really helped shape this book into what it is. And thank you to the teachers who believed in me and pushed me, never allowing me to give up—with a special thanks to my dance teachers, Ms. Linda and Ms. Melanie, and my high school mentor, Ms. Renazco.

And a special thanks to my family, the most important people in my life. To my dogs, Honeydukes and Gryffin, and my cat, Tiger—you've made me so happy. To Nana and Papa, who always believed in my dreams and continue to help me make them possible. This novel would not have been published without you. To Jesse, who's made me watch an excessive amount of 80s movies and Disney movies and with whom I've played more rounds of Mario Kart than anyone else. To Yaya, Tintin, Tristan, and Dorian—I love you guys so much. To Roger, my uncle and a brilliant writer and debater, who gave me life advice and challenged my ways of thinking while also helping me understand the world better. You have always been there for me.

And now, to my dad—I never stop learning from you. I really do think you're the coolest person to exist. You are kind to everyone, always going out of your way to help whoever needs it no matter what, and completely selfless. You are, in my eyes, fearless. Thank you for opening my eyes to the world of Rock N' Roll. I'm so glad we have the relationship that we do, how we can talk about anything, from music to philosophical discussions about life to how to catch a snake. I wouldn't be the person I am today if not for you. And to my mom—I look up to you so much. You work harder than anyone I know, it's amazing and I'm not sure how you do it. You are so intelligent, strong, thoughtful, and loving, and I always know I can come to you about anything. No matter what is going on, you can always fix it, you can always help me. And as you help me, you teach me and push me, showing me how to be independent, strong, capable, and kind. You are my hero. And now for my sister—Nissa, I don't even know where to begin with you. We've got such a close bond, unlike any other I've ever seen. It's kind of crazy. This story would be very different (especially the ending) if you hadn't been there with me, critiquing me and calling me out and giving me your full, honest opinion on everything. I can always trust you to be straight with me, you never say what you don't mean, and that means a lot. There is no one like you. I love you more than anything.

And thank you to the movies, TV shows, and music that made this whole thing possible. A special thank you to Guns N' Roses, for so much, but especially for giving me the inspiration I need. No one quite understands my bond to you, but it doesn't matter.

TABLE OF CONTENTS

CHAPTER 1

STAIRWAY TO NOWHERE

I WANT PEOPLE TO LEARN to think for them "freaking" selves. That's not so much to ask for.

Sometimes you feel like hitting everyone and watching as they fall down
Sometimes they hit you and you fall to the ground
Sometimes you wake up tired and just want to go back to bed
Even so, I can't find a place to go and lay my head
Somethin' big is coming, I can feel it now for sure
But I don't know what it is or why I should care anymore

Beginning of a song for my first journal entry, written by me
—Wren Evans

I look up from my writing to gaze out the window, noticing the murky blue of the sky and thinking about what it all means. Maybe it is all the same and every day we're wasting away. Then I look back down at the song I've just written and realize how stupid it is. "*It ain't worth fixing,*" I think, so I shut the journal and turn it over in my hands. It's a real simple thing, but pretty, bound in leather with the helm of a ship imprinted on the cover. It was a gift from my friend, Violet. I must say it is a very timely gift seeing as how I have been feeling more emotionally conflicted than usual and a journal gives me something I can put my troubles into. However, I've got to wonder what this gift means. Our relationship is not as strong as it used to be, and I have to consider the fact that this journal might be a sort of parting gift. You know, when someone is like "Yeah we've gotten along real well and I like you, but we got to move on now so here's this journal." Sometimes you're close with someone and then all of a sudden, you aren't so close anymore.

Thinking about it brings an aching feeling to my chest, and I try to tell myself not to take it so hard or so bad. But still I think it may be for the best—for Violet at least. Besides, nothing lasts forever except the Earth and sky. *And I think my past might finally be catching up to me.*

I turn off the lamp on my desk and stare out the window once more; it's getting dark, almost too dark to see. I should go to sleep so I can be ready for classes tomorrow, the first day back from fall break. It's going to be hard, I bet—all of junior year is—and I really don't want to keep seeing Bianca all the time. Just one more thing about school that freaking sucks.

But before I go to bed, I have to listen to my Rock Playlist—or else I won't be able to sleep. Seriously, without it, I would have gone insane a long time ago.

Despite my efforts to avoid doing so, I replay events from the summer and previous year in my mind as I attempt to fall asleep, making the aching feeling in my chest intensify.

I want something to punch or break—that would be nice.

Does everybody need somebody? I can only hope that in the meantime, there's still a way to change the road I'm on.

***

Come morning light, I wake up feeling particularly restless. There was some sort of a strange storm that began happening last night and it woke me up several times. It's strange because it's pretty damn unusual for Sunrise Heights to be getting such a heavy thunderstorm in early October, and now I'm thinking it might have been a sign, a warning that I shouldn't get up.

I want to throw the covers over myself and never leave, but I groan and reluctantly roll to my feet anyway. I sit back down on the edge of my bed for a few seconds, holding my head in my hands before standing up, getting dressed, putting on my leather jacket, and packing up my dance attire. Even though I really don't want to, I have to force myself to go to dance today. So far, I have missed a total of eight classes since the last time I went—and in the ballet world that's like missing seventy-two years worth of training. Seriously, dance people are extremely sensitive about this kind of stuff, and by avoiding class and rehearsal I have managed to piss off probably everyone in my damn studio.

Whenever I talk to people about stuff like this they usually ask me why I don't just quit because they don't get it. When you're good at something, it doesn't much matter if you enjoy it or not. People will expect you to do it anyway. It's freaking annoying, and it'll make you feel trapped as hell, but that's the way it is. And while at times I'd like to quit out of spite, trust me when I say it is never that easy.

After packing the stuff I need in my backpack, I make my way downstairs and cook up some breakfast for my sister, Cara. Cara's 12-years old now, and I know she can make her own scrambled eggs, but I just want to make sure she's taken care of before I leave. She's my younger sister, by roughly four years, and she's someone I would do anything for. Really, she's amazing, not rude and selfish like some 12-year-olds can be. And sure, she's a bit overly emotional at times, but it's only because she cares so much. I mean she *really* cares, not just in a fake way like so many people.

Cara means more to me than anything or anyone else on the planet, even though we aren't talking quite as much these days as we usually do.

After scrambling the eggs I write a funny note and put it in her backpack before saying goodbye to my mom and dad and driving myself to school. My parents are good people, and we get along real swell. I'm lucky that way, I know it, because a lot of kids my age don't even want to talk to their folks, that's how bad their relationships are.

***

I don't mind the drive to school. I enjoy the freeing feeling driving gives me. And I like my car, it's a black 1980 Camaro (named Nightrider) that used to be my dad's but was given to me on my sixteenth birthday this past year when he decided to get a new car. At first, I couldn't believe it when he told me he was planning on getting a new car. I don't understand how anyone would prefer some regular new-age vehicle instead of Nightrider's sweet wheels on a 1980 Camaro. Thankfully he decided rather than getting rid of it like some piece of junk, he would give it to me as a gift.

I suppose you might be thinking that you don't need all this information about my car, and you'd be right, but it's important to me so I'm giving it to you anyway.

It's cool when you feel a connection to your car; I mean it. It makes driving even more fun. Though I must admit, no matter how much you like your car or driving, a lot of the fun gets sucked away when you know you're taking yourself to school.

I pull into the parking lot of Sunrise Heights High and rest my head against the steering wheel. Everything is still pretty damp from the storm last night, and I'm starting to wish I had worn a warmer outfit.

This school is an all right place, there's nothing extraordinary or terrible about it. It just sort of exists. The one real good thing I have to say about Sunrise High is that it has a perfect campus for escaping. Like if you want to get out of going to class and need to go home, and you know what you're doing, there's an excellent chance you won't be caught. Other than that, well it's like I said—nothing special.

I wait there in my car for a little while longer. I watch groups of friends go by laughing and talking together as they walk toward the school. Everybody seems to have somebody.

I'm not feeling so well anymore. Maybe I should go home. No, that's a stupid idea, then I would have to make up all that schoolwork—and I'd start feeling even more overwhelmed and depressed.

In the long run, it's better for me to suck it up and take whatever comes my way right now. At least, that's what I say when most of the school day turns out to be rather "soul-suckingly" disappointing. So far, I've gone through my classes mostly unnoticed and ignored, except for math in which I got in trouble for having my earphones in during class time. I never understand why teachers give such a damn about stupid rules like that. Having my earphones in doesn't hurt anybody, and should therefore be my business and mine alone. It's not my fault *Use Your Illusion II* is more interesting than AP Statistics.

I've only gotten through roughly half of my day when it's time for psychology, perhaps the only class I am actually somewhat interested in. I walk into the classroom and take a seat at my table alone, slumping down in a chair and looking across at the seat that should be taken by Lena, my only friend at school now since Bianca won't really talk to me. I'm not super close to Lena or anything—she's much more popular than I am. We just like each other's company and hang out is all. Unfortunately, Lena decided to drop psych right before fall break. Now who's going to be willing to be my partner? The pit in my stomach is getting deeper and deeper.

I fold my arms on the desk and close my eyes as I lay my head down and wait for the rest of the class to file in. I'm so tired and bored; I almost doze off completely, as I allow my mind to wander. I imagine going back in time to the Wild West and becoming the Sheriff of a town overrun by bandits. Man, that would be something.

Deep into my fantasy, I vaguely hear the teacher ask everyone to pay attention, which I don't, as she introduces some new student named Aidan Grey. Then she tells him to take a seat next to me because I no longer have a partner or something.

I hear the sound of a chair being pulled out and raise my head to see what poor soul is stuck with me for the rest of the year.

He's tall with dark, somewhat messy hair and unusually bright eyes.

"Hey," he says flashing a smile as he sits down, "my name's Aidan."

"I'm Wren," I respond with a nod. "*He looks familiar,*" I think. He might have been in my English class this morning.

"Nice to meet you, Wren."

"So you're new here, huh? Where are you from?" I ask, making friendly conversation.

"Why do you want to know?"

"If you're going to be a jerk about it, then I guess I don't."

He hesitates, like he's debating what to say, and then answers. "I've been around to a few places. Most recently, I was in Sacramento."

"Why did you choose Sunrise High?" I'm pretty sure there are loads of better high schools somewhere around this area—then again, maybe not.

"My mom and I moved down here for professional purposes and, well, I had to go to school somewhere."

He seems nice enough. I don't get a super-insincere vibe from him, meaning he's probably someone I can get along with pretty good.

But even with a good partner, the assignment in this class is still lame. It's a questionnaire that is to be filled out with your partner and meant to gage your current mental state—and I am not looking forward to answering it.

"Ok," Aidan says, clearing his throat and taking the paper, "first question: on a scale from one to ten, how are you feeling at this moment?"

What am I supposed to say for this? "Uh, I don't know, a four I guess."

"What? A four?" he asks incredulously, looking across at me over the paper in his hands.

"… Yeah."

He shakes his head and shrugs as he continues. "How many hours of sleep did you get last night?"

"Maybe five, tops. You know how it is, sometimes I sleep, sometimes not for days." I smile at my own reference.

"Damn, well you're totally healthy," he mutters under his breath.

"Right, 'cus I'm sure you are just *so* great."

"Ok, anyways, what has prevented you from getting an adequate amount of sleep?"

"Thinking and remembering, I guess. I mean, I've always been a terrible sleeper but it's been worse lately…" I trail off.

"What sorts of memories haunt you?"

"Is that a real question?"

"Yeah, totally—sort of."

The mischievous glint behind his eyes tells me otherwise.

"Oh really?" I say, putting my hand out for the questionnaire paper.

"If I'm going to tip you, you're going to have to do something for me first," he grins with a wink.

I tilt my head, feeling my eyes narrow at him. "You think you're very charming, don't you?"

"Of course not, I know I am."

"Well, maybe you don't know as much as you think you do."

"So are you going to give me an answer or…" He points at the questions on the paper.

"No, give that to me," I command and take the paper from him.

I look over the questions and see that there is nothing about "haunting memories" on there. However, I also see the questions that are on the paper become increasingly less pleasant and more specific.

I adjust myself so that I'm straddling my chair with my hands resting on the back. "I don't want to do this anymore."

"What do you want to do then? Not finish the assignment?" He appears genuinely confused, which I find really humorous.

"I don't care, just check off all the boxes randomly," I say, shoving the paper back at him.

Aidan flips the pencil in his hand and glances at me sideways before taking it. "Is this how you usually complete your work?"

"Only when I've got an annoying partner." He's not really that annoying, I shouldn't have said that.

"Is that so?" he challenges. "At least I'm capable of answering simple questions."

"Those questions were *not* simple."

"Fine, since you've already had to answer some, how about you ask me a question instead then? One that you come up with."

"All right…" My mind begins racing through the infinite number of questions I have at all times before finally settling on one. "What's the one thing you want most?"

"Jesus, you really just skip everything and go right to that?"

"You asked for it."

"I'm not sure how to answer. If I'm being honest, I don't think I really know what I want yet. Do you?"

"Not in the slightest." Suddenly, I don't feel so well all over again.

"Hey, Wren, are you good?" Aidan asks after I've stared off into space for a solid minute.

"Huh? Of course, I'm fine," I say quietly.

But really I want to get out of this class, this school, this planet.

Why am I here? I can't quite remember.

At the end of psychology, I notice a few girls glaring at me as I'm packing up my things. At first I don't understand—I've never really noticed them before if I'm being honest, and I don't think they've ever really noticed me—but then I see the way they look at Aidan as he leaves the room and I no longer have any questions. One even whispers to me on my way out something about how lucky I am to have him as my partner. Another begins whispering to her friend about ideas for how to begin talking to him. Girls are so funny.

***

In the hall on my way to lunch, I run into Bianca, literally.

At first she begins to go off about hating when people don't look where they're going, but then she sees it's me that has run into her and for some reason she stops.

"Oh, hey Wren! I didn't see you there. How are you doing?" She smiles brightly at me and goes in for a hug.

I reluctantly embrace her back, and man does it feel weird. I have no idea why she's so comfortable and happy right now. What's her angle? That's the thing with people like Bianca Davis—they've always got an angle.

"How is Violet do—oh wait, that's right. You two aren't really talking anymore." *And there's the angle.* Bianca barely knew Violet, but she still likes to bring her up to me whenever the opportunity arises.

After this, we make small talk, damned if I don't hate small talk, and she suggests that we get together soon.

This is very strange; she's sort of acting like we are all buddy-buddy. It's weird because she hasn't talked to me for pretty much this whole year so far, not that I am complaining. It's hard to talk to Bianca. For one, we are pretty different—she comes from one of those old, wealthy families, something that she doesn't like to let people forget—and then there's also

the fact that seeing her reminds me of being kicked out of my ballet school. Oh yeah, did I not mention that? I got expelled at the tail end of last school year. And then I got sent away over the summer to New York to go to some special year-round academy of dance, but that's a whole other story about how I messed up.

Regardless, do you know how troubled you have to be to get kicked out of a freakin' ballet studio? Me neither. Though to be fair, it was mostly someone else's fault. Not to be one of those people who can't take responsibility for their own actions, but without Seth—this real "asshat"—I bet I would still be there. Seth always disliked me, but then things really exploded once he realized he would never be able to get me to go along with whatever he said.

He wasn't used to that because he always did whatever he wanted and no one ever stopped him. Guess that's what happens when the son of the school's director is a bully.

You would hate him… probably.

Anyway, Bianca, Violet, and I used to go to the same dance school, but that's all changed now. After I was expelled, Violet quit dancing and Bianca decided to stay behind. She told me it was because "that place had been her home for so long that she could never imagine life without it" or something. It still kind of pisses me off how *she's* the one who convinced *me* to go there in the freaking first place, and yet she still wouldn't stand up for me. She knew the truth, I told her the whole story the night after it happened, but when the time came, she said she believed Seth over me.

Lucky me, we still get to go to the same high school together.

I can't help but wonder what sort of a plan she's coming up with.

I consider hanging out with her at lunch, just for curiosity's sake, but then I decide nah. I also think about finding Lena and sitting with her, but she usually sits with her girlfriend and I don't want to intrude on them. It can be real uncomfortable to be hanging around people when they're a couple and you're just sort'a there on the outside.

As I'm trying to make up my mind, I notice a boy from my grade sitting at a table alone. His name is Eric Coleman. I used to be real good friends with him back around third grade but, like I've said before, things change. Probably because that was around the time I began to become friends with Bianca. She's never liked him, for some reason.

He's pretty much always sat alone, but for some reason it affects me more today than usual. It's always kind 'a heartbreaking to see someone

sitting all by themselves; it'll make you wish to God they would find someone to be with. Usually, I think about going over to them and talking, however I never know if that's what they would actually want. I'm not sure if my company would make the person feel better or just annoy the hell out of him. So I'm always wishing someone else would get up and do it instead. They almost never do.

As I'm passing him I suddenly decide that what the hell—I'm going to do it.

"Hey Eric," I say as I sit down across the table from him. Hope I don't mess this up.

"Wren?" he says, looking a little startled.

"Do you mind if I sit here a while?"

"No, of course not."

We get to talking and it turns out Eric's actually still a pretty cool guy. I think I've just made my old friend a new friend.

Why is it always the good ones that have the hardest time?

The rest of my day trudges on slowly and I feel like a soldier marching in a field of sorrow toward the end. And the rest of my classes make me feel pretty stupid. Class will do that to you on occasion. I'll get asked questions and I never seem to know the answers, or if I do, I'm not sure I do so I don't say anything. Then I end up feeling even stupider.

And I don't like having to work with other people for group discussions and stuff. Most of them make it seem like I don't know anything or that they know so much better and I hate them for it. Worst thing is that you'll go through the whole damn class thinking, "Wow! These people know so much more than me—they must be real smart," only to find out that they don't know crap about crap. They just act like they do while putting you down. I'll tell you what; it's the most annoying thing in the goddamn world.

This school sucks.

I really wish Violet was here. She'd get it.

Without anyone, I keep losing my beat. All of my dreams pass before my eyes and crumble into nothingness.

I need to hit something.

***

After school, I head straight to my car and lean against the door, closing my eyes and squeezing the keys hard in my hand. The metal scrapes into my palm, sending a biting pain shooting through me. I squeeze harder.

"Are you ok?"

I open my eyes to see Ella, one of Bianca's pretty friends who are in my English, psych, and history classes, standing right next to me. My God, this day just won't let up.

"Oh, I'm fine. Just tired and not looking forward to getting home to do homework," I respond casually. Although apparently not as casually as I had wanted because Ella doesn't go away.

"It's ok, you can talk to me," she says, catching hold of my arm. I want her to go away.

"No, seriously, it's no big deal—"

"I'm not leaving until you tell me what's wrong." Man, I forgot how nosy this chick could be.

"Come on, Ella, cut me some slack. Things have just been a bit tough. That's all." As soon as I say this I get the sense that I've made a mistake. But now it's too late, she's already taken an interest.

"Oh no, what is it? You can tell me."

Here it goes.

"It's… I think there's something wrong with me." The words begin tumbling out of my mouth. "Like I keep going to bed later and later and being able to get up is getting a lot harder. At the same time, nothing really matters anymore; it's all going to fade away anyhow. It feels like there's a piece missing inside of me, one I'll never find. And I just don't get what it's all for, you know? I mean, what is the goddamn point?"

"Ok, I didn't ask for your whole life story," she says with a laugh. "Honestly, I think you just need to go to bed earlier."

Thanks, Sherlock.

"Yeah, I know, I was thinking that too. Anyway, it's no big deal."

"Seriously, you don't need to worry. You're just overreacting a little."

"Ok Ella, I'm going to leave now."

"Bye then. Hope you sort yourself out."

Me too.

***

I skip dance, get home, and go straight upstairs to my room to collapse on my bed. I knew it was stupid to think Ella would understand anything I said, so why did I try? Maybe I should contact a real friend, like Lena or Violet, and tell them about… well, I don't know. It's probably not a good idea. I can't even explain it to myself, and I don't want to put my crap on anyone else.

It sucks though. I remember a time when Violet and I could tell each other anything.

We would lie out under the stars for hours sometimes, just listening to music and talking. Thinking about it allows me to relive it, even if it hurts a bit. I can bring down a wall in my mind and, suddenly, I'm right back there again as if I never left.

The stars were especially bright that night as we lie under them listening to the radio.

"This song is terrible," she says, laughing, her warm brown eyes shining clear in the moonlight.

"No, no it's not! Vi, you gotta learn to appreciate good music—'Night Moves' is great!" I insist, turning on my side to look at her.

"Fine, the lyrics are weird, but it's kind of fun."

I raise an eyebrow, and she begins to smile. "Ok, it's great!"

We start singing along together, just the two of us without a care in the world.

I try not to dwell on the past, but sometimes I think I'm obsessed with it.

CHAPTER 2

UNCOMFORTABLY NUMB

"AIDAN. AIDAN! I need you to get up and I need you to move quick."

Aidan sat upright and found himself staring up into the worried eyes of his older brother who was now standing over him as he hurriedly stuffed things into some sort of bag. While he could tell something serious was happening, Aidan was still pretty annoyed because he'd just finally managed to fall asleep on the hard, damp floor as soon as Noah had woken him up.

"Are you paying attention? This is important, I said to get up!"

"Ok, ok. God damnit, Noah, it's like 2am. I'm—" He was cut off *suddenly by a loud banging on the front door. For a moment, he thought it was the sound of a harsh crack of thunder, for there was a violent storm raging outside, but he quickly realized it was something much worse.*

"Crap! It's too late. Do you know where Mom is?" Noah asked as he *pulled Aidan up by his shirt and shoved him back from the door. It was then Aidan noticed his brother was completely soaked and breathing heavily as if he'd been outside in the storm, running from something...*

"No, I don't think she came home last night. Now, I want you to tell me exactly what the hell is going on," Aidan demanded.

The banging on the door became deafening, this time accompanied by aggressive shouting. The sound of rainfall pelting the roof was making it hard for him to concentrate.

"Who are they, Noah?"

"It doesn't matter."

"What do you mean it doesn't—"

"Go out the backdoor, head over to Sebastian's. I'm not asking."

"But what do they want?" Aidan's heart began to pound even harder *than the fists on the other side of the door.*

"Me. Now go!" Noah shoved him back again. *"I'll be right behind you!"*

Aidan turned around and ran, bursting through the backdoor just as he could hear the hinges come flying off the one at the front.

Once outside he stopped, looking up at the dark, rumbling night, suddenly unable to move. Lighting sparked, sending out bolts that shot across the sky like veins pulsating with electricity. It was strangely beautiful.

But it was also loud.

It was so loud, it hurt, as if the storm was inside him—claps of thunder knocking against his skull as hot streaks of lightning cut into his brain. And it wasn't going away—

Aidan sat upright, gasping.

"It really was all in my head after all," he thought, trying to catch his breath and calming himself down as he wiped the sweat from his forehead.

However, there was indeed a storm going on outside. He noticed when he looked out the window—and a pretty bad one, at that.

With a heavy sigh, he collapsed back down on his bed, knowing he wouldn't be able to go back to sleep for the rest of the night. Not after that dream. Not with that storm. And not after remembering what tomorrow had in store for him.

Tomorrow was his first day at a new school. Aidan knew starting up at a new school was going to be hard; after all, he had already had the experience of it a total of seven times, having lived in a multitude of states ranging from Kansas to Indiana to Texas and on. But this time, things would be different.

This time, the town they'd moved to was one they had already lived in before—and for a quite a while. In fact, it was the place they had stayed in the longest, five years to be exact. And, on top of this, it marked the first time he would be moving without Noah.

It had been a while since Noah lived in the house with him and his mom, seeing as he started college right after they began living in Sacramento, but it was still hard to make a new transition without him. When they were younger, they did almost everything together. Aidan looked up to Noah more than anyone else—especially since he was the one to get Aidan through all the tough times before their dad finally left them. He didn't care that Noah wasn't perfect or that he had begun picking up a string of bad habits so nasty those things put both of them in serious danger on numerous occasions. He didn't care about the broken bottles, the scattered needles, or even the people who would come banging on their door in the middle of the night. He was his brother, and that was all that mattered.

But now, things were different. A few years ago, Noah's struggles from his past finally caught up with him for good, changing their lives for the worse. Suddenly, Aidan was more estranged from his brother than ever. What really killed him about it all was how hard Noah had always worked to protect Aidan from all the things that eventually consumed him. While he had been able to save his little brother, he couldn't save himself.

This was what Aidan had been thinking about before starting his first day at Sunrise Heights High, making him sick to his stomach. Not to mention that he was coming in partway through the school's fall quarter, which made everything even worse. He just hoped people didn't ask too many questions about where he was from.

His first few classes went by in a sort of dazing whirlwind, and the whole time he couldn't wait for the day to be over. Sure, there were a few pluses to moving this time—like how he was going to be close to some of his old friends, like Sebastian—but he wasn't really focused on any of that at the moment. Instead, he focused on how girls would turn to their friends and whisper things to each other as he passed them by in the halls, making him feel even sicker. You see, Aidan had the sort of looks that turned heads, but he didn't particularly know it. And because of this, he never really understood the way girls would stare at him, or the way they would act around him.

He got the same sort of reaction the moment he stepped foot into his psychology classroom. Well, except for one girl, who kept her head resting against her arms on her desk. He curiously watched her, as he was given the standard new kid introduction, trying to figure her out. While he was doing this, the teacher said to sit down next to his new partner for the class—someone named Wren…

"You know, Wren," my lab partner says, "we could be doing this in a much more efficient way if you would just let me do some of the work."

I've been completely engrossed in the worksheet where I am currently jotting down answers.

"Sorry," I say and glance up at Aidan while continuing to finish up a question. "I'm not used to working with people who actually want to participate in the assignment."

"I can see that."

This Aidan Grey kid has only been here a few weeks, and he's already getting snarky. I hand the worksheet over to him and scoot closer to the glass wall in front of me, curling my knees up to my chest as I examine the creatures on the other side.

I haven't been to the aquarium in a long time, so this field trip has been a most welcome one for me. Also, the demonstration on animal cognition was relatively interesting—though the note taking and questions that followed have not been so stimulating. But, high school worksheets rarely are.

I like to watch the brightly colored fish swim in and out of the coral reefs, like little splashes of sunshine dipping between this world and the next. I especially enjoy watching the sharks. There's something about the clear coldness in their eyes and the way they swim through the water in such a gracefully predatory way... and though they're far from my favorite animal, I still think they're interesting.

I get up from my seated position and start walking around the corner when Aidan looks up from the assignment and asks where I'm going.

"I'm just going to check out some of the other exhibits. Do you need help?"

"What? No, I..." He stops speaking and waves me off as if he's changed his mind about something. As he focuses back on the work, I direct my attention on how the combination of dark lighting and water movements behind glass create the illusion of small ripples of deep blue moving across his face in fascinating patterns.

He notices me staring and raises an eyebrow. "Do *you* need help?"

My cheeks heat up and I quickly avert my eyes. "I wonder that same question every day," I mutter, stepping out of the room.

Wandering down the halls of the aquarium, I pass by numerous rooms housing different exhibits, nearly all of which are close to, if not all the way, empty. In fact, this whole place is far emptier than an aquarium ought to be. If I were a regular person, I might be "creeped" out.

I stop when I see the entrance to the sea turtle exhibit. I really like sea turtles.

Once I step inside, I immediately notice how particularly dark the room is. Someone's turned off all the lights. Instead of over thinking the meaning of this, I sit down in front of the largest glass window and quietly stare up at the turtles, taking in the peacefulness for a few moments.

Out of the corner of my eye, there is a subtle movement from a dark shape—just barely enough for me to notice it.

The intense feeling washing over me snaps me out of my trance-like state of tranquility, causing my blood to run cold. I am no longer alone in this room. Or perhaps I never was… Yes, I am sure of it now—somewhere lurking in the shadows is another person.

While it is not unusual for there to be multiple people in the same room of an exhibit, their absolute silence and careful positioning in the dark tells me that they likely do not want me to know they are here. And if it was solitude they wanted, they would have simply left as soon as I came in, but no, this person stayed; however, they did not confront me, which means they planned on watching me.

What to do now?

Unable to contain the impulse any longer, I snap my head around. But there is no one there.

I scramble to my feet and dash out of the room. Now which way to go? Left leads back to the front and right leads to the back exit. This person went through some trouble to go unnoticed, so they wouldn't go past everyone to get to the front, I decide, quickly running in the direction of the back.

As I'm slipping around another corner, I smack into Ella.

"Ow. Wren, where are you going in such a hurry? You're supposed to be filling out the worksheet with your partner."

"Yes, I know, but—" As I am speaking, I catch a glimpse of a tall figure in a long, black coat move behind Ella before disappearing once again. "Sorry," I say as I push past her.

I race around the corner into the hallway I saw this person disappear into, but by the time I get there, he or she is gone.

I don't talk much on the bus ride back to school. Because the aquarium is only a mile or two from Sunrise Beach, our teacher lets us pull over so everyone can have some relaxing fun in the sun for a bit—but I don't even bother to get out of the bus, claiming to have a terrible headache. While everyone races down to the sand, I stay inside my head and completely ignore my surroundings.

I ponder a new burning question: Who the hell was that?

The more I think about the dark figure at the aquarium, the more idiotic I feel. In truth, I am not interesting enough to bother spying on—it seems my inflated sense of self-importance has gotten the better of me yet again.

Another part of my problem is that I am always looking for something new, something exciting—something to distract me from the boring, depressing realities of life. So, in the face of an unknown situation, I took what at the time appeared to be the most interesting possibility and ran with it. Now without mystery or excitement, I feel like nothing matters. And I wish I could reach inside myself and rip this feeling out of me, but it's not going anywhere. I'm stuck with it.

My mom once told me that when I feel this way I should try writing it on paper. I thought it was stupid at first, but what do I know? Maybe she's right.

So I crack open a cold one (a Sanpellegrino) and grab my journal. I hold it in my hands and run a finger along the leather binding to the cover, tracing the ship helm engraved on the front. Just holding it makes me feel like a pirate, and man do I love pirates. If I could, I would run far away to become a Pirate Captain and sail off to wherever the hell I want to go. Either that, or I'd want to be an outlaw in the Wild West. Maybe I could be both: an outlaw on the seas and on the land.

I pull myself out of my fantasy and back to reality. I got to take this writing stuff at least a bit serious. With this in mind, I start my next entry:

October—A Wednesday
I'm sure I'll get over this whole being moody-as-hell thing soon. I'll be fine; all I need is a little patience.
At least I've got my music...

Little did I know, things were not going to simply get magically better all of a sudden, patience or no patience.

October seems to go by like the slowest month I've ever experienced while still managing to go by way too fast. I hate it when months do that to you.

All this time, and I still haven't reached out to Violet. Fact is, every time I think about maybe calling her my stomach gets tied up in painful knots, and then I no longer feel like thinking about her at all.

I know you probably want to hear about why exactly I miss Violet so damn much, but the truth is I'm not ready to tell you yet. I don't even think I *could* explain if I wanted to. I just don't like talking about her very much. Or thinking about her. Or thinking about what her laugh sounded like. I remember this one time, when we were exploring out in the woods near her house, we came across a creek with an old bridge going over it and, because I thought it would be cool, I stood up on the railing of the bridge and balanced on one foot while lifting the other into an arabesque. But, out of nowhere, this squirrel jumped on me and I jumped back. It had startled me so then I fell straight down into that goddamn creek. I had never heard her laugh so loud before. But it wasn't an obnoxious laugh or anything; it was real sweet—like the feeling of fresh air across your face. She laughed about it all the way back home, and anytime I would bring it up or anytime we saw a damn squirrel, she'd start giggling again like a madman.

It was something special, that's for sure.

Usually I was the one that made her laugh by doing something stupid like that or like falling out of some tree that I'd try to climb. If she started to smile, then so did I. So I guess you could say I used to smile a lot.

There are some other things I also don't usually want to talk about. Like I get the same painful feeling in my stomach whenever I try to get myself to face up to things that happened last year and over the summer. I'm probably just being overdramatic. Though every time someone mentions Seth's name I can't stop thinking about how he got me kicked out and how that led to other, even worse problems.

I don't know how I'm supposed to make it through.

And not only is my life a mess, my whole room is a mess too, especially my closet. I need to clean my stuff up and get it together—it makes me upset to see it this way. Though I don't think it's just my messy closet that has me unsettled. Things have been difficult this whole week, and I can feel the aggression inside me building up. I keep wondering about who the stranger at the aquarium could have been—despite having already decided that they were a creation of my own imagination—and it's driving me insane.

To calm myself down, I go for a walk through the park near my house. The sound of birds singing makes me happy, and the fresh air flows through me, cleansing me of dark thoughts. The trees are in the process of changing leaves, going from shades of bright green to warm orange and red. It's amazing to watch, but something about it has always bothered me. The reason the leaves are changing is because they are dying, losing their natural color and eventually falling to the ground. I don't know why, I've just always thought about that. Still, I can appreciate the beauty of it and enjoy hanging out here. By the time I have looped around the whole place twice, I feel some inner peace has been restored.

But back at home I want to scream and punch something. Or maybe I want to run and hide away somewhere that no one can find me. I don't know. I don't know anything. Except that Lena, my only friend left at school, is no longer in any classes with me except US history. And in English, I'm supposed to write a personal paper about myself and my feelings and experiences and all that crap. I thought about sugarcoating things, but I'm too tired to right now so they're going to get more or less the truth—whether they like it or not.

As I'm typing up the paper, the noise inside my brain gets louder and louder, making it hard to concentrate. While I really want to throw my computer across the room, I push through it and finish writing. After I'm done with the paper, I return to listening to music and journaling to calm me down.

It's amazing how much the music you listen to affects your mood. It's crazy. It can make you go from feeling happier than you've ever been to making you realize life is depressing and meaningless. I don't want you to think I'm some sorry, overemotional sap, but it's true. Try it.

Oh yeah, journaling can affect you too. It lays out your open wounds right in front of your eyes, forcing you to see them.

I don't remember the date now; I'm about to crack. My head is spinning and humming and it won't go away. Everything depresses me.

Looking at my messy closet depresses me, thinking of my friends depresses me, going to the park depresses me, going to dance depresses me, drawing and reading depresses me, seeing myself in the mirror depresses me, having a conversation depresses me, looking at anything depresses me. Even this goddamn journal reminds me of Violet and therefore depresses me. Thinking of her makes me feel like a heavy stone is inside me, dragging me down beneath the waves, slowly drowning me. It's the burden of guilt.

If I'm being honest, I think a small piece of guilt follows me everywhere I go. If not about letting my friendship with Violet die, then about all the money my parents were forced to pay my old ballet school in reparations. Our family doesn't really talk about it anymore, but I still think about it sometimes. I can't help it.

I guess it wasn't really my fault, but I feel guilty anyway. It makes me sad.

If I'm not sad, I'm numb. And that's no fun either.

Also, as I wrote this, I listened to "Don't Cry". But guess what? I cried.

Life—it's a long nightmare that goes by too quickly.

I turn in my personal paper. At the end of the school day, my English teacher approaches me, holding it in her hand. She tells me that she's noticed a difference in me these past few months. The paper I wrote has only deepened her concerns. We talk for a few minutes, and then she asks me if I would be open to seeing the school counselor? She thinks it would be good for me. I don't know what to say so I shrug and follow her to the counselor's office. Once there, she brings me into a room with a lone couch in the middle and introduces me to the counselor, a pretty woman with sharp features and cold, dark eyes. Not exactly a lady you'd feel like confessing your deepest, darkest thoughts.

We start off with the basics, like my name and age, and quickly move into more difficult questions.

"So tell me, Wren, why are you here today?" she asks.

"Guess I'm depressed or something."

"Or something?"

"Yeah." I don't know what else to tell this woman. Maybe I should let her know straight up that I might not be all the way right in my mind. I mean, I *was* dropped on the head as a kid so I suppose it makes sense. Really, I was. It was pretty serious, if I remember correctly. But, then again, I was only about two-years old and had just had my damn head smashed in, so my recollection of it may not be the most reliable if you know what I'm saying.

"Do you keep a journal?" she asks, directing my attention back to her.

"Yes."

"Ok, good, I want you to keep that up. And this is a safe place so you can tell me anything you want to—just pretend like you're writing another journal entry."

"I'm not sure exactly where to start. I just came here because a teacher suggested I should."

"And why do you think she wanted you to come here?"

Oh, I don't know—how about *you* take a wild guess? "Um, because she's—she's worried about me, I think."

"Do you know why she might worry about you?"

I fight the urge to roll my eyes. "Not really. I think maybe because I just look sadder now than I did and stuff. And she read my paper and thought it seemed like I was in a bad place."

"Do you know why you might be in this bad place? And how are things at home?"

Holy hell, this lady asks a lot of questions.

"Uh, I mean I don't even have bad parents or anything that I can blame for this stuff. I just sort'a suck all on my own."

"I see… So it seems you may have some self-confidence issues." *No, you don't say.* "Have you ever thought of hurting yourself?"

I wasn't expecting this question. My heart begins beating faster and faster and my breath quickens. I swear her eyes are blazing into my soul; I can't even look at her straight on. I wish I could get up and leave.

"Wren?"

"I, uh…" Why can't she just tell me I'm depressed and have anxiety and about three years left to live and then let me out? This whole thing seems a bit excessive.

"It's ok, you can talk to me. I'm here for you." I hate it when people say stuff like this.

I shut my eyes closed tightly. "It's hard for me to say." *Because you suck.*

"Deep breaths. Do you know what you were thinking of using to do it?"

I feel like I'm going to throw up. This can't be how these things are supposed to go.

"You know what, darling? How about I schedule another appointment with you for a later date? I think it would be good for me to check in with you again when you're feeling more comfortable. Perhaps we could even start regular sessions if need be. I'll tell you what; I'll give your parents a call about it and explain to them the situation here. Would that possibly help?"

I nod my head, and get up from my chair.

"Yes…" I manage to say as I make my way to the door. I can't tell if she's serious or not.

"All right, Wren. Just know you'll be in my thoughts."

I fake a smile and nod at her again before leaving, still feeling sick. I don't know what the hell just happened, but I know one thing—my parents are not getting involved in this if I have anything to do about it.

***

That evening, I want to ask my parents right away if they got the call. But I know neither of them will be home for quite some time, so I listen to music and read to occupy myself. My dad is working practically all the time, and my mom's job is just about as stressful. Both of them don't usually come home until around 9:00 pm every night, and by then they're usually so exhausted that it wouldn't be fair for me to put any of my problems on them. I'm used to it though. It has been this way ever since I can remember.

I suppose when you've got parents that work a lot there's quite a few things you learn that can end up being pretty handy. Like how to make all your own food and how to deal with hard stuff on your own.

That's why it's a little silly of me to need a school counselor to call them and tell them all about my struggles, but this time I think I might really need help. Then again, like I said, I don't actually want them to have to get involved at all. They don't need this burden put on them. And I don't need the guilt that would come from putting that burden on them. Besides, even though I know my parents would want to help, I would probably just end up going to a doctor who would shove a bunch of pills down my throat and call me cured.

When they come home, I ask if either of them received a call from someone from my school. I got to admit, I'm pretty nervous. But my nerves turn out to be for nothing when both tell me they haven't had any such calls. They ask me what it's about, but I tell them just to wait. Problem is, the counselor never calls. Not that night, not the next, and not the one after that. It gets to the point where I have to wonder, is there a part of me that does actually want someone to help me? Or am I just confused as hell? I've never been one to want anyone getting involved with anything to do with me, but things are so different now. Unsure of what's going on inside of myself, I even email her to try and set up a time for when we could meet to talk again. I get no response; she's forgotten about me.

Yeah, this seems about right. What's-her-face acted all like she cared, but it was just a front. And what's worse is I think I almost fell for it. But it's all bullshit. Does she get paid for this? To sit around in her stupid office pretending to be concerned for about 20 minutes per troubled kid? No wonder they don't pay school counselors much—a lot of them are pretty useless, in my opinion. Adults and the "system"—it's all a bunch of crap if you ask me. But no one ever asks me.

Luckily, my parents forget almost immediately that I ever brought it up to begin with.

I'm still thinking about why she would have forgotten me when I go to dance this afternoon. I'm in the highest level at the studio, but I still suck

pretty bad compared to the rest of my classmates. Ok, maybe I don't suck, but I mainly hide in the back of class and attempt to stay out of the teacher's eye.

I'm not even doing *The Nutcracker* this year. I was supposed to—actually, I was originally offered the role of the Snow Queen, but then I was told I wasn't coming to class enough to keep the part. I do get that I need to be going more—my technique has definitely suffered these past few months. I just don't have any interest in it anymore. But to be honest, my dance company would be better off without me.

Toward the end of the class, the instructor stops me mid-combination, looks me in the eyes, and says, "Wren, you were a very talented dancer, but a lack of confidence has held you back from progressing. If you were to apply yourself, you could become truly amazing. But you have no confidence, and it shows in your dancing. I need you to work on that." *What the hell am I supposed to do with that?*

So, I actually respond, "What the hell am I supposed to do with that?" Which gets me sent home early.

Getting back, there's no one home so I jump on my bed and throw punches at my pillow.

No one really gives a crap. They pretend to, maybe to make themselves feel better or to look good in front of others like some sort of an act, but deep down there is no concern, no desire to help. They just don't freaking care. So why should I?

I begin screaming into my pillow. My fists clench so tightly it feels like my nails are drawing blood as they cut into my palms. Hot, angry tears burn my face, making my skin sticky and raw. I scream until I can't anymore. But even then, the tears keep coming, soaking my soul with each drop. When I finally finish, I'm left with a stabbing headache and my entire body drenched in a sick, cold sweat.

Every day is just another day.

Meaning escapes me.

Love will never find me.

And hope is lost on me.

I curl up into a tight ball and stay awake, eyes staring off into nothingness until I eventually fall asleep—shaking. All the while hoping that by some miracle I won't wake up when the morning comes.

It really is all a drop of water in an endless, black sea.

***

The next day, I show up to school a bit late feeling extra frustrated with the world. My head still aches and my restless sleep didn't do anything to relieve my pain. It doesn't help that Ella keeps talking at me about stuff that I don't give a crap about. I never should have tried opening up to her that one time. It seems in doing so I've also made her think I'm someone who wants to hear everything and anything she has to say.

She's just barely left me alone when psych class starts, and Aidan immediately begins with questions of his own as soon as I sit down next to him. It is not his fault that I am not in the best mood, but I still don't want to talk much.

"If you could only listen to one music group for the rest of your life, who would it be?" he asks.

"What's it to you?"

"Just trying to make conversation, partner. Do you not want me to know? Is it because it's some pretty boy band? Come on, I won't judge."

"Jesus Christ! If I tell you will you leave me alone?"

"Maybe," he responds cryptically.

I feel a bit bad after snapping at him. It doesn't have anything to do with him that I woke up on the wrong side of the Earth. Besides, I usually love talking all things music.

"My favorite is Guns N' Roses. Hands down," I say, already feeling my mood lighten up just by mentioning their name.

"Oh, a Classic Rock fan? That's my favorite music as well."

"Classic Rock, especially the hard rock, is my life; there's nothing better. But I also really like straight-up classical music, though not just Mozart and Beethoven. I'm talking *Pirates of the Caribbean*, *Star Wars*, *Avengers*, *Two Steps From Hell*, you know—the epics," I ramble. I think I love music a little too much.

"Awesome," he whispers.

I'm very happy that he hasn't asked me if I really like GN'R and rock or if I'm just saying I do, like a poser. I shouldn't care so much, but it bothers me a whole lot when people don't take me seriously about the things I like. Sometimes, I'll be talking to someone about it and they'll look at me like "yeah right." The freaking worst is when they say I only like a certain band or movie because they have hot guys in them, and that I "must have a crush on them." Screw that, I don't care about that crap. I just want good music and good movies, so they can take their stupid biases and shove 'em up their asses.

Anyway, Aidan doesn't seem that way at all.

We don't talk much the rest of the period, but it's still pretty nice to be near someone who shares some of the same interests as me. It makes me feel—well, I don't know.

Later that day is independent study, during which I put my earphones in and listen to music while "studying". I barely begin my first song when a voice above me makes me look up.

"What are you listening to?" Aidan asks, standing next to me.

"A clip from the Live at the Ritz 88 performance—'Sweet Child O' Mine'," I answer, somehow knowing he'll know what I'm talking about. "My favorite song ever from my favorite concert ever."

"My favorite guitar solo is from 'Sweet Child'!"

"Oh yeah?" I turn and face him. "Good taste. What's your favorite song overall?"

"I'm surprised you want to know."

I roll my eyes and look back to the textbook I had pretended to study before he interrupted.

Just when I think he's gone, he leans down over the side of my chair. "Probably 'Simple Man'."

I nod my head in agreement, once again impressed, and look over my shoulder—but he's already walking back to his seat.

We haven't talked all that much since we've known each other, and I wonder why. After all, we are partners in psychology, and he doesn't even annoy me. I'm pretty sure he's wondering the same thing. Neither of us said anything, but after this small exchange, something feels different between us. No, more like now there actually is something between us— and that feels good.

I wonder if he knows if everybody needs somebody, or maybe he feels estranged from the whole planet like I am.

***

In-between classes, I see the counselor lady walking in the halls. She gives me one of those fake, warm smiles as she passes by—and I can't even tell if she recognizes me. She seriously did forget about me, or at least she doesn't think I'm worth her time. What the hell man? I suppose there could be some sort of other reason—so maybe I ought to refrain from harsh judgment. Perhaps she's in the middle of a divorce, or starting her second mid-life crisis, or maybe her goddamned dog pissed on the carpet. Hmm, actually she seems more like a cat lady.

I guess I won't ever really know why she didn't come back to me.

I almost go up to her, but then I decide that I don't need that kind of a person in my life anyhow. I'm better off on my own.

Since I was feeling *kind'a* good for the rest of the school day, I told myself *I'd go to dance today*. So guess what? That's where I'm headed.

I drive myself over there and sit in my car, just staring at the studio from across the street. I *watch* some of my classmates *walk* in and duck *down to hide every time someone* begins to look my way. For some reason, I don't want anybody to *know* I'm here. Though now that I think about it, hiding in Nightrider really isn't going to do the trick—a 1980 Camaro is just *a little bit recognizable*.

After sitting out front for a good twenty minutes doing nothing', I get out of my car and start walking. But instead of walking on inside, I go around the back of the studio and jump the fence between the back lot and the train tracks. The fence is about seven-feet tall and has sharp things poking out of it all over the place. As I'm hopping over, my leg catches on one of the poky things and slices me up good, causing me to wince and swear. But I don't stop, I go all the way over that stupid poky fence, cutting myself up a few more times, and man does it feel good once I'm on the other side of it. Now it's like I can't really be going to dance anymore because I've got this big, dangerous fence in my way that I shouldn't try jumping 'cus I could hurt myself.

Now it's just the train tracks and me.

I walk along them, shivering slightly in the breezy air, and I think about where I'm going. Maybe I should head over to Riverview, a town that's about an hour out from here; it's very pretty, and it usually makes me feel better being there. As the name would suggest, it has a beautiful view of the water. It's really peaceful to sit out in front of it. Then again, I'm too lazy to drive all that way and back.

I remember what I told myself in October, that it was all ok and I would be getting better soon for sure. It's November now.

The clouds above darken and rain starts falling as thunder begins to crack. The world around me seems indifferent and cruel, growing darker by the moment. But I suppose darkness never scared me anyway.

Rather than returning to my car, I stay here in the rain getting myself soaked, staring down the open tracks imagining what it would be like to jump aboard one of the train cars as it rolls by. You could go anywhere, be anything.

I make my way over to the edge of the tracks that look out at the river below them and sit down on the railing, my legs hanging over the side.

The disappearing sun kisses the horizon—and its fading light shimmers on the water's surface. It's beautiful, watching the sunset as the storm above slowly overwhelms the oranges and pinks in the sky, replacing them with black clouds.

I feel so sad.

Sitting there, with my head tilted up, I let the rain pour down on me. As the cold droplets fall upon me, so does an equally chilling realization:

I'm not getting better. I'm never getting better.

CHAPTER 3

SWEET WAYWARD CHILD

November—a Tuesday

I would like to believe in the best in people, I would. But I don't know anymore.

Yesterday, a girl from stats class asked me if could give her Aidan's number, and when I said "no" she called me selfish and mean and told me to "go to hell." God, I hate everyone.

To get my mind off things, I sat down at the piano—for the first time in about a whole year—and began playing. I don't know why or how, but for some reason my hands played the beginning chords of "November Rain," and I suddenly knew what song I'm going to learn next.

I pulled up several YouTube videos, searching for the one closest to the actual piano playing from "November Rain". Once I picked one, I wasted no time in getting started. Finally, I have a project to be excited about.

Side note: this journaling thing has been helping I think, so I'm going to keep doing it.

***

November Again

I'm a terrible person. I hate everything about myself. How do I keep going with that?

Maybe if I follow my heart and nothing else I can find myself, but right now it doesn't feel like I've got one to follow. I'm too selfish. I don't want to say goodbye to her. I don't want to say that it's been nice and to wish her well. I don't want to be moving' on. I suppose one could say I'm stuck looking behind me and because of this my troubles will be many. But even so, I just can't let go of her. Poor Violet, she deserves a better friend than me.

Side note: I am seriously wishing something unexpected would happen or that the stranger from the aquarium would return and make things interesting—life has become so dull. The one thing that doesn't completely bore me is psychology class with my lab partner, Aidan Grey—isn't that a cool last name?

Even then, he can still be a pain in the ass.

***

Still November,

I need to start picking my battles more carefully. My stubbornness got me into trouble today because I refused to use a crosswalk. Well, I had already started across the parking lot without it, and then a school staff member began yelling at me to go back and use it but I refused. They told me again and I told them no again. Then they told me I've got myself a damn demerit. Oh well, what do ya do? Not say no to school officials with power complexes, I guess.

Side note: I need to get Cara more into Marvel. I told her I was going to watch Spider Man and she told me she had no interest. The horror was almost too much to take.

On the plus side, Aidan does like Marvel, and we've been talking about it a lot. You could almost say we're sort'a friends now.

Oh, and I wrote this song. It might look like a poem—but it's not.

If we could make it through, what would you say?
The people, they all seem so happy
With their lovers and friends
Leaving you alone and broken, though it's not all as it seems
Many are lonelier
Than all of your dreams

And when you feel like dying, don't give away your hope
I'll be standing by your side until the end

How you've been so lost there's
Something to be said
It can seem like you're the only one
Still looking at the people laughing away their pain
Thinking you're not the same

If there's just one thing you wanted

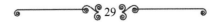

You just want to feel better
As you slip farther away, know it's never too late
Your heart has never been one
To be ruled by fate

So tell me
Where will you go now?
After you fall down
It might take a while
But all I want
Is for you to be free

* * *

I look over my last three journal entries and have to laugh at myself. Damn if I can't be dramatic sometimes. Though to be fair, I have been feeling quite depressed—which absolves all blame, right?

Shaking my head, I pick up my phone and put my headphones on as I press play on my playlist. Thank God for music.

If I could only give one piece of advice to someone at this time, it would be to give Classic Rock a shot. A lot of people my age don't even know that they're missing out on it because, well, maybe no one exposed them to it. Or they only tried it when they were younger. Or they're too caught up in the current stuff to realize it's there. Whatever it may be, I'd tell 'em to listen to "Stairway to Heaven" or "Estranged", to *really* listen, and see if it doesn't change them on the inside at all. I know it's not for everyone— but my God when it is, it's like nothing else. And if they don't like rock, that's ok. If their music is alternative, or jazz, or rap, or even pop—all that matters is that they have that music.

After this, I'd want to tell people that they have the free will to do any- thing or not do anything they want. With this, I'd tell them to open their eyes to their own views so they can make free choices based on what they truly know deep down is right. There's always a choice, and there's always a way. I'd put this first, but I believe the music inspires this idea and more.

A few days go by and I start withdrawing more and more. I thought I could perhaps just focus on my music, and then I'd be ok, but stuff always comes up. I do think I was doing all right not that long ago, but now I am at the lowest of the low.

I look in the mirror and see a pale face with dark circles that have worsened. My eyes are red from crying and the heated color contrasts with the deep blue of my irises, like blood seeping into water.

I see the face of a person who has given up—a person whose light has gone out.

I want to punch the reflection.

I imagine doing it, pieces of glass getting stuck in my hand as I push my fist through it, the blood running down my arm from my knuckles. For some reason, this does not make me want to do it any less, but I don't.

Instead, I back up into the wall of the bathroom and slide down it, staring at my hands. I sit there feeling the cold tile beneath me and imagining thousands of cuts appearing all over my body until there's a pool of blood around me.

I sit there a long time.

I think the world has the possibility to be a wonderful place, I do. I just don't think I'm meant to be here though. I'm ready to move on and what that means, I can't say.

Guess I don't know just what I am supposed to do.

I could try talking to someone about it, but people my age don't get it, and if they do, they most likely won't know how to tell me about it. And if you tell an adult that you don't know what you're doing, they'll probably tell you that you can do anything if you put your mind to it and work hard.

I like that people encourage you to do what you want and all, but if I really did what I wanted all the time the only thing I would ever hear from adults is "Ms. Evans, what the *F*— did you just do?" Kind'a like how I got kicked out of my old dance studio. I did what I wanted and got the axe because of it.

Now you might be wondering, "Hey do you ever do anything other than complain?" And the answer is, no. No I do not.

However, I manage to refrain from complaining today when, for some reason, our psych teacher decides to switch up the seating arrangement and instead of being partners with Aidan, I'm put with Ella. In case I haven't made it clear enough already, I don't care much for Ella. But I still know I need to give her more of a chance. Her parents just got a divorce, she's an only child, and she had a rough break up over the summer with some kid that she still has to see in about half of her classes. Besides, the teacher said these partners would only be for this one class period, just to get us to experience something new for a while, so I suppose I can get through it.

"Wren, we get to be partners!" she exclaims as I approach her table.

"Yes, lucky me." I wryly smile back.

The assignment is to pick a classic book together and psychologically evaluate the characters.

I want to write a classic book. The thing I never got though was what constitutes a classic? How do you get there? A lot of times I read a classic and think to myself that yeah it's good, but I could do it too. Then I lose all confidence because I can't put all my ideas out fast enough in any coherent sort of way.

I reach out to grab the worksheet in the middle of the table and I accidentally brush hands with Ella, who is also reaching for it. I mumble out a quick sorry and immediately kick myself for doing so. I apologize all the time for things that I don't need to apologize for. It's very annoying and I should stop. Problem is, it's a habit. Like if someone runs into me, I say "sorry," which isn't terrible or anything but it doesn't make much sense either—and I do it all the time.

I make a mental note to stop doing this.

"So, what book do you want to do?" I ask.

We end up going with *Pride and Prejudice* at Ella's insistence—she apparently finds the romance in it magical. I really couldn't care less, so I agree.

"Guess what!" she says as I am finishing up the worksheet for both of us. I don't know why she grabbed the paper to begin with if she wasn't going to do any of the actual work.

"What?" I say just to humor her.

"I have a date this Friday with Rob."

Who the hell is that?

"Rob King?" she adds in an exasperated tone. I guess she can tell from the look on my face that I have no idea who she's talking about.

And what kind of a last name is King? I wish I had that last name; it would be so much cooler than Evans. It might even be cooler than Grey… hmm, but maybe not. Still, maybe I can ask this Rob guy if I can steal his name.

"Cool, a date, huh? Where ya going for it?" *I wonder what a date is like?*

"The movies."

"Oh, great choice—I love the movies." It's true; I bloody love the movies. "But I haven't been in a while."

"How come?"

"I've just been a bit off lately so I haven't exactly thought about it much. But maybe going would get me out of my head for a while, that'd be good. Right now it's like a piece of me has been taken out and there is no replacement. I'm just never going to be as good as I was. But I don't know, maybe I'm just crazy."

Ella looks at me like I really am crazy. I turn the subject around.

I want to talk about somethin' with substance. Thing is, you don't always get to talk to someone that can talk about somethin' with substance.

If you my loyal readers were here, I bet we'd talk well together.

I'm packing up my things after the bell rings when I accidentally drop the pencil I was holding. My hand shoots to catch it, but Aidan beats me to it.

"I think you dropped this," he says, the corner of his mouth pulling up into something between a smirk and a smile.

"Nah, doesn't look familiar."

"Ok." He shrugs and sticks the pencil in his pocket.

"Hey, that's mine!"

"You just said, five seconds ago, that you didn't recognize it."

"Give it to me."

"No, let's call it a trade," he says and then reaches into his backpack, pulling something out. He hands it to me and expectantly looks at me. It's a CD labeled *Aidan's Classics*.

"It's a mix of my favorite tracks. I had meant to give it to you earlier, but I figure late is better than never. I thought you might like it," he says casually.

"I—thank you," I breathe, still looking down at it.

"You're welcome."

When someone shares his music with you, it means more than almost anything else. Seriously, what a person listens to can tell you so much about them. Like when someone gives you a necklace or a card, it's nice because then you have something that looks into their minds—but when a person gives you their music, it's like you've got something that looks into their soul.

Funny thing, people are. Just when you think you get 'em, they do something that changes your whole mind.

***

I'm tempted to play Aidan's CD on the way to ballet class, but decide against it. I have to make sure I've got my full concentration before going into dance. Why do I have to do this? Well, because every time I step foot in the dance studio, if I'm not at a certain level of calm, I'm bombarded by past memories. Memories that technically don't even have anything to do with this place. For the most part, they revolve around the experiences I had at my old studio with Seth.

The bastard locked me in a studio one time, and took my phone so I couldn't contact anyone. And there was no one else there because I had stayed late to practice for auditions the next day and everyone else had already gone home. He kept me in there for over an hour and turned off all the lights. But when he finally flipped them back on, he still didn't let me out. Instead, he came in and locked the door once again behind him. Not to mention that he's a pretty strong guy, and a few years older than me, so I probably couldn't have even fought my way out too successfully if I'd tried.

I don't like to admit it, but I was pretty scared. He made it seem as if he could have done anything he wanted to me. And, at the time, I thought maybe that was true.

Then, of course, not that long after, he did something else. Something even worse… But I can't go into that now.

I can't.

Seth also had a habit of intently watching our classes when he had no goddamn business doing so. The first few times he did it, I figured he was just curious about the art of ballet or had to do it because he was the artistic director's son or something, but after a while I realized there was something more to it.

Even after class, he would just hang around at the front desk by the exit and call out numbers for how well we did that day. Some of the girls ate that crap up, trying their best to impress him. He almost always gave me a zero. It pissed me the hell off, though I'm starting to see now that was the point.

For the longest time, I couldn't for the life of me understand why any of the other dancers were so captivated by him—especially Bianca. They all cared so much about what he thought, and it just didn't make any freaking sense. Of course, the fact that his father is the director gave him a certain air of importance, and with his tall and muscular frame he seemed even more intimidating. His strong jaw line, jet-black hair, and icy blue eyes also made him what some would consider an above-average-looking guy. And, well, for *some* girls that's all you need.

Midway through class, my instructor pulls me aside and begins talking to me in a low voice. I swear, if I had a dollar for every goddamn time a teacher pulls me aside to talk, I'd be able to pay my way out of stupid situations like this.

"Wren, you've seemed more distracted recently. I know moving studios can be hard, but you're doing very well here. I just need you to put in one hundred percent of your effort every class," she tells me.

I swallow and nod my head that I understand.

She then lists off some different auditions she'd like me to do once I get my head back in focus. All the while, the other dancers in the class pretend to mind their own business as they eavesdrop.

At times, I can't stand other dancers. Some are nice and cool, but there are so damn many who are not. I remember when I did all those ballet auditions for summer-intensive programs and other stuff; the toxic feelings in those places—all filled with those kinds of people.

It's like hundreds of girls (and one or two guys) in a confined space. Everyone wants the same thing. They will mostly put themselves before anyone else if they think it means they're going to be chosen. You can practically taste the disgustingly self-absorbed competitiveness. And most of the directors and people who audition are not very nice either. They're just there to see if you have the body they want or if you've got a lot of talent or potential. They sure as hell play favorites, and if you're not exactly what they're looking for, they don't care about you.

I used to be able to get into anywhere I auditioned, and I'm guessing that's what my teacher wants from me now, but I'm not sure where I stand. I haven't been to an audition in over a year. I don't feel an overwhelming urge to get back into them. Thing is, I used to *like* auditions. I thought they were fun. I enjoyed the rush of adrenaline you get from them. I liked being competitive and able to get into any school or intensive I wanted, which made me feel good—for a while at least.

Now I'm not satisfied with anything.

On the way home, things bubble up further in me.

Life and all its mysteries gone before it begins. I shouldn't hang on. It all slips away anyway.

At home I eat dinner quietly, my head miles away. Then I play a card game with Cara, and she asks me why I'm acting so weird. I tell her she's the weird one, and we continue playing for a while. Both my parents happen to get home early tonight so they want to do something with us, but I'm tired. They ask how my day was, and I tell them that school was fine and dance was fun but that I have a headache so I need to go upstairs and rest.

Back in my room, I start going deeper and deeper into my thoughts when suddenly I remember something.

I reach into my backpack and take out the CD Aidan handed me today of his favorite "classics". Holding it makes me smile a little. I think he's just excited to have found someone who likes rock as much—or more—than he does. I might as well give it a listen since I'm not doing anything besides depressing myself and avoiding my homework (two of my favorite activities). I got to admit I'm more than a little curious.

I take the CD from its case and find a little note stuck to it. It's kind of crumpled and written in messy handwriting, but it's clear what it says.

Hey Wren,

Don't go skipping through ok? Just listen to the whole thing for the full effect. Also, I think you're really going to (or already do) like the last one.

I put it in my CD player and sit back on my bed, wrapping a blanket tight around me as it starts to play. I have to smile when the first song to come on is a Bob Seger tune. Of course that's something he would like.

I listen, as the note requests, all the way through. So far, my favorites have been "Sweet Child O' Mine" (as always) and "Simple Man". I close my eyes and tilt my head back, laying it against the headboard. The last notes of the song I listen to fade out and the next begins. As it comes on I sit upright and my eyes open.

The breathtaking beginning of "Carry On Wayward Son" immediately sucks me in.

I know without a doubt this is the final song.

CHAPTER 4

SPRINTING WITH THE DEVIL

BIANCA CARED ABOUT WREN. She really did, but sometimes they just didn't get along the best. Though she supposed this made some sense, seeing as she was practically her opposite. And while they weren't good friends anymore, Bianca found it rather amazing just to think that there ever was a time when they *were* close.

It now seemed like forever ago, but really it had been less than six months since it all happened and while she never admitted this to anyone, she had a sense of relief after Wren was expelled from their school of dance—one that she sometimes felt guilty for. The truth was, Bianca had always held a bit of jealousy toward her—some of it having to do with her looks and talent and some of it having to do with the school director's son, Seth.

From the moment she first laid eyes on Seth, a part of her was in love with him. She'd never met anyone so charming and powerful, and before Wren showed up, Bianca had always believed he preferred *her* above the rest of the girls at the studio. She didn't have any proof of this, but she truly believed it, and it made her feel special. It gave her a sense of superiority that she liked. This superiority was then shot with insecurity the moment Wren had walked through the front doors.

But their friendship wasn't simple enough for her to break things off with Wren just like that. Whether they both liked it or not, they had a complicated bond that ran much deeper than the superficial insecurities which had begun to come out. After all, Wren had been the one to help Bianca through the hardest time in her life: her dad leaving. It wasn't that Wren had ever gone through something similar, she just understood some-how. That was something Bianca always admired about her; she could under-stand just about anything you told her. And when you told her something, you knew she wouldn't ever tell anyone else—that's just the way she was.

Bianca often thought about what their lives would be like if she had never asked Wren to come over to the same dance school as her. The competitive side of her would always have found a way to drive some form of a wedge between them, but she doubted their relationship would be nearly as strained as it was now.

The funny thing was that Bianca had to do quite a bit of convincing before Wren even considered the idea of moving over to the studio. In fact, if her other friend Violet didn't also go to the studio at the time, she probably would've said no. But when she did finally say yes, Bianca wasn't thinking that much about the reason behind her agreement. Instead, she was just thinking about how wonderful it would be to have her old elementary school buddy in dance with her. And she certainly never foresaw the happenings that were to occur only a few years later.

But, the results weren't all bad; for it wasn't long after Wren got kicked out that Seth began showing interest in Bianca again. In fact, by the beginning of October, he asked her on their first date. Upon this change, she finally had what she wanted and there was no longer any threat to it. She then suddenly had a desire to reconnect with Wren.

Nevertheless, with Bianca Davis, there was always at least some ulterior motive at play, something Wren would do well to remember.

Tonight, I feel like going to the movie theater. Hearing that Ella was going there on a date made me miss it. I thought about asking Bianca if she wanted to come—because it seems like she genuinely wants to start being friends again—but then I decided maybe not. I really do want to reconnect with her and all, we were good friends back when we were younger, and we've helped each other through some real tough times. But I'm just not feeling it at the moment, is all. So I think it'd probably be best if I just don't go with anyone.

One of the things I love most in life, besides music of course, are the movies. Anything can happen in a movie. You don't have to worry about it turning out a certain way because no matter how it ends, it always means something. Even if it seems to mean nothing then that's what it's there to mean.

I take myself to the movies all the time, sometimes going to watch the same one multiple times over. There's just a special feeling in the air at movie theaters. Other than seeing the movie on the big screen, a unique feeling comes from experiencing it with other people.

I also love getting inside characters' heads.

It doesn't happen often, but once in a while you find a character from a book, TV series, or movie that you can truly see yourself in. It's one of the few things that can help me to open up after I shut myself off from the world. Unfortunately, it hasn't happened to me in a long time; but I'd really like to find them, that one character that I just know is someone like me. It can be empowering and sad at the same time. Empowering to feel I'm not alone and sad to see how broken I am through another person.

I sure would like to be a movie character. Even if the filmmakers didn't get me right at all, I would still like to see people's interpretation of me. It would be interesting.

***

While I'm buying my ticket, the guy behind the ticket booth gives me a wink when he tells me to enjoy the movie.

Man do I love it when people wink. I've been trying to wink at people more often; I'm pretty sure it makes them happy. And it makes sense, doesn't it? If you're having a not-so-good day, and then out of nowhere a person comes along and gives you a nice wink it'll make you feel better.

Smiling to myself, I settle down in the back row, the only row completely empty, and take out the snacks I hid in my jacket pockets. Chocolate and sour gummies really heighten the enjoyment of the movie experience.

Once the credits roll, I notice the people sitting in front of me discussing the movie, and while maybe I should try not to eavesdrop, I overhear them talking about the plot and—more specifically—how it correlates to "feminist bullshit".

I don't see a goddamn difference between this movie and all the other movies that have been released this year, except oh wait—a woman fronts it. Well hell, someone call the newspapers and authorities, there's a woman in this and she's more than a supporting character. I see these types of reactions a lot.

What a bunch of jackasses.

Other stupid reactions I hate—people who think a woman who wears a dress on screen isn't tough enough. For the love of God, femininity and strength are not discrete variables. Why do so many people still think that in order for someone to be strong they have to have masculine traits? You can't ever please them all. If your character is a girl, there's a good chance she's going to come off to some asshats as too strong or not strong enough.

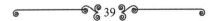

Sometimes if I talk to someone about my views on this stuff, they'll just respond with something like "Yeah, I hate men too," which really pisses me off. They're missing the whole point. Truth is, I'm not a big fan of when people say that sort of stuff at all; and by that I mean I hate it. I get what you're getting at, but it's a pretty un-cool statement if you think about it. It sucks when guys say something like that about women so, while it may not have the same meaning behind it, it can still hurt if you say such a thing to a guy. I mean, can't it? It wouldn't make sense otherwise.

I say screw all that.

***

Then I leave the movie theater feeling pretty good. Those "bucketheads" in front of me didn't get it, but it doesn't matter. I got something out of it. So I go home and know that is enough.

Tonight, I take a break from playing "November Rain" on the piano and try out "Knockin' On Heaven's Door" instead. After a while, I stop playing and stare at the reflection in the shiny black piano. So what? No matter what happens to me, "the wheel in the sky will keep on turning."

Perhaps I ought to start a band—to give me something to do so I could stop being such a dejected brat. Problem is, who would be in it? Well damn! There goes that idea. A lot of my ideas turn out this way. I feel so strongly about them for about five seconds, and then I realize I'll never make it happen. It's crazy kind'a, 'cus for those five seconds, I seriously thought I would put together a real rock band.

There just isn't enough time in the world—well, that and there's *too* much time in the world. Thinking about it can make you freeze up—too much time not to do anything and not enough time to really do something. At least that's what it can seem like, depending on my mood. It's one of the things to toss my insides upside down. I swear, I over-think everything. What I would give to have a quiet mind, if only for a little while.

Still, even with a loud mind, I can't put myself in the moment anymore. I'm always far away, and the times I can manage to get back down on the ground I only feel sadness. It overwhelms my whole being. Then I'm not walking or talking so proud anymore. But what's it all for?

This makes me think of writing a song. And I know I should really be going to bed now, it's just that I can't.

The song doesn't have a name but it's getting there.

Making it home again no more

Been through Heaven and Hell as the years roll over

40

I can't stand to see you go by
I'm here to keep you safe all right
But you can't see how you give me pain
Take it and leave me in the rain
If there's something you need from me
Know I'll always be there
If that's what you want then I'll make it right
I must give in a little longer
It's ok, I'll be there soon
You won't have to make it through

A few days later, I notice that my skin appears to be getting worse, along with my temper. It's almost as if getting no sleep causes irritation and dark circles. Who knew? And now I'm so tired, but I just can't seem to get the frustration out of me. No matter what I do, I always end up here.

I can feel it all over my body, stopping me from getting any rest. So I turn up my music and try to let it all go, but sometimes that doesn't work. Sometimes piano playing and self-indulgent songwriting can't fix every-thing—as much of a shocker as that may be. Sometimes the only thing that calms me down is to get my anger out inside my head. It works kind of ok to be honest. I first learned to use this technique when I was little. Growing up, I always had more problems expressing myself than my peers, and it got to the point where my teachers made my parents come in for almost weekly conferences. Apparently, it wasn't normal for kids to throw chairs across the room or curl up into a ball under their desks while refusing to come out.

So, my parents took me to the doctor's kind of a lot and, well, I don't want to bore you, but upon taking a bunch of tests they found that I suf-fered from some different issues, including anger problems. No one really knows where these problems came from, though they tried their damndest to figure it out. But hell—I don't even know. All I know is I had them, and if I didn't do something to mask it, I was probably going to be put in some psychiatric facility. At least that's what my parents made it seem like. I can still remember accidentally overhearing their conversation with a doctor over the phone about it. He told them there was a darkness inside of me—one that might be helped through more extreme measures of treat-ment, like going to a rehabilitation center for troubled youth. Afterwards,

I ran to my room and cried myself to sleep, vowing never to let that happen. Hence this is where the keeping-it-all-inside method came from.

I continued to perfect this technique when I began going to my old studio. There was something about Seth that just tore down all the walls I had built to keep my darkness back. He brought out the worst in me, I think; but finally I learned to deal with it. So whenever Seth would come around to get me in trouble or make something bad happen, I would put myself up in my head where I could cause as much damage as I wanted and no one would ever know. Then I began doing this more often after I was expelled. It was like being kicked out had torn down another wall, allowing even more darkness to leak through.

I don't think I'm depressed in the way that most people get depressed—there's something more to it—like I'm really not right in the head. I don't know why, I just feel constantly torn between sadness and paranoid anger. And whenever I'm sad, I get mad at myself for being sad—which continues the cycle.

I picture myself punching the wall, kicking in a door, breaking through glass, punching myself, banging my head against the wall, slamming into things, pounding my fists against my head, screaming, stabbing myself again and again and again. It usually begins with violence and ends with violence.

Sometimes this violence turns real, even though I try to stop myself.

I feel calmer after.

But I'm done with being angry all the time—I mean it.

I listen to *Appetite For Destruction* while I burn some of the pointe shoes I used at my old studio. The album comes in like a hard punch to the face and ends with a knife through the heart; there's nothing better.

***

Next day at lunch, Bianca comes and sits down beside me.

"Hey," I say.

"Hey," she says back, bringing out a bottle of sweet tea from her bag.

If this conversation becomes any more stimulating, I'm going to die of excitement.

"The homework from English today is brutal, isn't it?" I say, trying to dissolve the uncomfortable feeling in the air.

"Oh yes, it sure is."

"But I still think I'd rather be writing a ten-page essay than working on a ten-page math assignment."

"Me too." Hmm, talking to her actually isn't so bad. In fact, it seems pretty normal.

"How are things at your new studio?" she suddenly asks.

Uh-oh, here we go. "They're pretty good, you know. Things have been good." I don't even sound convincing to myself.

"I'm glad to hear it," she says, setting down her tea.

"So, what's going on with you these days?"

"Nothing much, though I've got a boyfriend now."

"Oh really? Good for you, Bianca. I'm happy for you," I respond. Really, it's good she's been able to find someone. Everyone deserves someone.

"Yeah. I'm dating Seth."

She's doing what? "Seth?" *One sec, let me just go slam my head in a car door real quick.*

"Uh-huh. It happened pretty recently, actually."

"Oh." I can't believe she would do this. I know we aren't the best of friends anymore, but I don't get why she would go after someone so mean—the person she knows is pretty much responsible for my expulsion. Not to mention he's a freakin' asshole, through and through.

I'll admit, this feels pretty rotten. For a split second, I'm almost worried for her, for what he might do to her, but then I remember: he never *really* hurt anyone but me.

She looks at me, smiles, and goes back to sipping her tea.

Wait a minute… Oh. Oh, I see what she's getting at. This is some sort of game for her to see how uncomfortable she can make me. *Well guess what honey? I ain't that naive.*

"I've got to get ready for my next class, but I'm glad you two are happy together. I bet you make a great couple." I could've gone with the spiteful "you-two-deserve-each-other" line, but I don't feel like it. Nonetheless, I stand up and walk away. I don't need to stay around and take that crap from her.

***

I start a song when I get home.

Staring at the Separate Suns

Where do I belong?

It's too weepy. I need to start a new one.

You don't want me

You don't want my love

Good, because you're not getting it

Better.

I stop there, not bothering to go further. Maybe I'll finish it later, maybe I won't.

Instead, I begin reminiscing about the days when Bianca and I weren't so apart. Though even at our best, our relationship was nothing like the one I had with Violet—something I think Bianca was always resentful about. She never did like Violet much.

Now I'm really thinking about the days of old.

I close my eyes and can see it all now. It's like I'm watching my memories as someone else, looking in on the scene just as it actually happened.

I sit on the bench and look at her. She's got a smile, and it seems to remind me of so many other memories.

"Violet, there's no one like you."

"Please, you put me on far too high on a pedestal," she says, shaking her head at me.

But I didn't; she's better than me, than everyone. Even now, that thought has never changed for me.

I need to stop thinking about her.

Today, while I was at the supermarket, I saw one of the dancers from my old studio. She walked and laughed with two other girls that I've never seen before. She looked really happy. We used to be sort of friends, but seeing her so happy made me feel self-conscious all of a sudden. So I hid in and out of different aisles until they left the store. Not that I wasn't happy for her; it's that I still picture her in my head as the same girl I was friends with last year. But truth is we haven't talked since I left.

It's hard to see people getting along just fine without you when you haven't yet moved on. It hurts a lot too. That's why getting close to people just hurts in the end. I see people that I used to think were my friends, and yet they're fine without me. I'm drowning and they're getting along just fine—just damn fine.

Well, don't I sound self-absorbed as hell? I shake my head at myself and kick my door. Time to drop this self-pitying crap and get my brain together.

Even still, I'm so lonely I could die.

***

November

I keep feeling so angry and then so depressed. I go from wanting to hit something to wanting to disappear. I get sparks where I feel like punching and kicking and killing, an overwhelming push for destroying things. And then I go back to a calm darkness of pure misery. No desire for violence, only the paralyzing pain of helplessness.

It's terrible. I don't know how to describe it more than that. Like I'm flipping my brain upside down and backwards, inflicting self-torture, but I can't stop.

Talking to anyone about it makes me want to rip my own head off or stick my fist through a wall.

Then I'm in pieces, and there's no one to pick me up.

***

Because I am so "in pieces," I decide not to go to dance class. I haven't told my parents yet, even though I know they've talked to me recently about why it's important for me to go as much as I can. But they'll just have to deal. Instead, I'm staying home to watch my favorite film and practice my snake-hip moves. I plan on getting them down perfectly so that I can put my new dance move together with singing "Welcome To The Jungle".

It's much more interesting than bar warm-up, and hopefully my ballet teacher will understand. *"I'm sorry I couldn't be at class today, I was too busy being delusional while pretending to be an 80s rock star—you know how it is."*

After I finish off "Welcome To The Jungle", I feel as though I've finally been able to get some of this stuff inside of me out. To be honest, this is the most fun I've had in a while, almost like I'm on some sort of high. In the heat of the moment, I pick up my phone and message one of my old friends, the one I saw in the Supermarket, telling her that I'd like to get together some time. I also send her a link to a song I think she'd like, just for good measure, and then I throw myself back on my bed and wait, humming "Patience" just to humor myself.

A few minutes later I get a response that makes my stomach drop: *Sorry, I can't.*

I now remember why it is I've stopped asking people to do anything. It's always a no, and it always hurts like hell.

The rest of the night I spend staring out my window.

I wonder what it would be like to shoot myself dead.

This thought sticks with me for a while before twisting into other questions, causing me to go a little silent.

***

I haven't spoken in class for three days straight now. The one time a teacher called on me I choked up so bad they decided to move on to some-one else. I'm really that bad.

Today, I'm doing ever so slightly better. Though it's nothing' to brag about, trust me.

My statistics teacher pulls me aside after class. I immediately can tell he's going to go on about something I don't want to hear anything about. At first, I think he's going to go off on how I'm going mute, but it turns out to be much worse.

"You have always been a straight A student," he tells me. "Last year, you managed to maintain a 4.1 grade point average. What is happening this year?" His eyes are filled with a false concern that makes me mad.

"Just realizing nothing matters is all," I answer honestly, looking down at my boots.

"I have no idea what you are talking about."

"What else is new?" I say under my breath.

"Excuse me?"

I look back up at him with a fake grin. "I said, 'What else can I do?'"

"Very funny. You do realize you'll have to get your grades up if you plan on going to college, right?"

Huh, college. Now there's an interesting discussion point. But I don't tell him as much. I just say that I've got to be getting on now. He nods and lets me leave. Little does he know that the thought of college is now stuck in my damn brain.

College is too goddamn expensive. I hate the system of it so much that if I could, I would just bail on the whole college experience altogether. I mean you often pay over a hundred-thousand dollars just to go to a school so that you can say you went to it. In my opinion, the idea of higher educa-tion is great but the reality of it sucks ass. They all want you to go because nowadays you can't seem to work anywhere without twenty-seven bachelor degrees, but I still think it's stupid as hell. A lot of them are institutions built on greed that don't give a damn about me, they just want me to come and give em' money till I'm buried so deep in debt that I can't ever get out.

Well guess what? They can suck me.

I'm still absorbed in thoughts about college when I slam my locker door shut and find Lena standing behind it.

"Are you going to the game tonight?" she asks.

"There's a game? No, I'm not going. Are you?"

"Yeah, it's the football game silly. Rose and me are going together with a few friends. I think it's going to be really fun, and I haven't been to one before so I figure I might as well check it out."

"Maybe I'll check it out too then. Who are we playing against? Are there assigned seats? How does it work?" I ask too many questions.

"No assigned seats, but we are planning to sit in the far right section of the bleachers so everyone can find each other easily. And we're playing against the Riverview team."

I tell her I'll probably come.

I probably won't.

***

Later on in history class, we have to work in groups on a small project of our choosing. The catch is our groups are assigned, and we only have this one class period to finish the whole thing.

Naturally, with my luck, I get placed in a group with a bunch of people I don't know and don't particularly like. However, maybe this is my fault because I don't seem to know or like hardly anyone. Either way, I slump into my seat at the table and bite my lip so hard that my teeth might go straight through it.

As we begin brainstorming project ideas, I make a suggestion, but no one responds or even reacts. I shrink further into my seat. I think I need to speak louder.

Toward the end of the period, we still haven't made any progress, and eventually one of my group mates asks me if I have an idea to share.

I start to answer but the boy sitting across from me talks over me and everyone's attention turns to him. They forget I'm even there.

As we're packing up to go to our next class, one of the girls looks me up and down. "You're shy," she says with an expressionless face.

My cheeks burn. I don't say anything. What could I say to that? "Uh, no." That'd sound even stupider than I feel. Perhaps I could ask her if it makes her feel good to say things like that to people. Or I could say, "And you're a dickhead."

Before I can decide on a response, everyone has left the room and I'm late for environmental science.

I decide right here and now that I won't take any crap from anyone. I mean, if you want to say something snarky or piss me off, then do it, but I'm not going to roll over and die. I'm going to kick you in the ass.

And when I say this, I don't mean for it to be taken lightly.

I'm true to my word, and in order to stomp on my shy image, it turns out that I actually do want to go to the football thing tonight. At least I'll know a few people there. It won't be too bad.

***

Before I leave the house to go back to school for the game this evening, I peek my head into the family room to check on Cara. I haven't spent a whole lot of time with her, and I want to make sure she's doing ok.

I find her watching a *Scooby Doo* cartoon and laughing. It reminds me of when I was a kid and used to watch *Scooby Doo* every weekend. Thinking about it makes me sort of sad-happy. Happy because I love watching how my sister enjoys them just like I did and sad because it makes me think of how I'm growing up.

Growing up is terrible. Lots of teens want to be older, to be more experienced, but not me. I know better. Not to say being a teenager is all peaches and cream. Adults go from treating you like some five-year-old to suddenly expecting you to have your whole damn life figured out soon as you turn eighteen. That's why being an adult is no good thing at all.

I remember not that long ago while I was boarding the plane from New York to California last summer, the flight attendant told someone to get behind me in line and they said, "Sir, please stand behind this woman." They were talking about *me*. Right then and there, I hated how it sounded—it made me feel wrong. The only good thing I can think about becoming an adult is more freedom. Even then, there are still so many other restrictions that come with growing up that I don't even know if it's worth it.

All I know is that I never want to become a grown-up.

***

I arrive at school right before the whole game is about to start. I wasn't sure how to dress for this thing, so I came in our school colors, blue and white, and painted those weird dots on my face above the side of my left eyebrow that I see girls sometimes do on TV shows.

There are so many people here. I guess football games really are as hyped up as they appear on screen. It's also loud. I expected it to be loud, but not this loud.

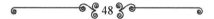

I enter the stadium and begin searching the bleachers for Lena and Rose. They're supposed to be on the far right side, which is on the opposite end of the stadium from where I am. The lights from above blind me as I make my way across the front of the bleachers. I use my fingers to pull hard at my hair. By the time I reach the right side, my bottom lip is sore from me biting it.

I scan through the seats and finally find them. All the air I've been holding is released in a single breath.

Lena waves at me and then turns back to Rose as she laughs at something she says. I smile and start to walk up the stairs to them and then stop.

Oh no. No, no, no, no.

There are no seats left in that row or the row behind it or the one in front of it. I want to call out to Lena, but she's absorbed in a conversation and likely won't hear me, so I climb passed them on the stairs and go all the way up to the top of the bleachers.

It suddenly occurs to me that perhaps Lena was not inviting me to go with her to this game, but that she was in fact just telling me she herself would be going.

I sit there at the top for a while, wringing my hands and twisting my hair as I wait for the game to begin. I want to get up and leave, but since I've been sitting here, more people have filed into this row and are blocking my way out.

The friends, who sit in front of me, begin speaking, more like shouting, loudly about a party they will go to after the game. Then the girl to my right elbows me in the ribs as she scoots further in to make room for another friend.

That's it. I'm done here.

Down below, the teams come out onto the field and the crowd begins roaring wildly. This is my chance. No one notices as I climb over the side of the bleachers and onto a steel pole that will take me to the ground. I feel like a spy making a daring escape after being captured by the enemy.

Unfortunately, I do not have the skills of a spy and the pole is harder to grab onto than I imagined so I slip down it more than climb. I end up making it halfway before eventually losing what little grip I had and falling completely from it, landing hard on the ground beneath me. My fingers curl into the dirt as I cough and struggle to breathe.

When I can finally suck in air, I roll onto my back, clutching my hands to my chest. Still lying on the ground, I close my eyes and take in the empty space around me as the cheering of the crowd becomes louder and louder.

I've got no one. It's just me, all alone, like always.

As I lie there, the sound of a branch snapping nearby startles me. But I sit up too fast and immediately get overtaken with dizziness while I try and search for the source of the snapping sound. Everything is dancing in and out of focus, and I'm starting to wonder if maybe I hurt my head as well as my ankle. Hmm, nah, I'm fine.

Right when I am about to give up and lay back down in defeat, I see a dark figure slowly moving farther away. This person has the same build as the stranger from the aquarium…

I jump to my feet and begin moving to them, but have to stop when I feel the earth sway beneath my feet. I nearly fall and have to grab onto the very pole I fell from in order to stay upright.

As I am stumbling, the stranger turns around and looks almost as if he is about to come and help me. But I still can't see his face, for it's shaded with a goddamn hood.

***

Back at home, I stay held up in my room over the weekend. I feel completely numb except for a sharp pain in my ankle. I must have twisted it on my fall. No matter what, feeling anything is better than feeling nothing at all. If you've ever been there, you know.

I'm thrown out of my dark inner monologue by a soft knock on my door.

"Hey, Wren?" I hear Cara say on the other side. "I know you don't want to hear from anyone right now, but you need to get out there again. It's been a while and you haven't gone anywhere since that game on Friday. All you've done this weekend is lock yourself away, blasting metal all night long and then staying completely silent all day. Would you please just talk to me?"

She's trying to reason with me and I get it, I do, but I really don't want to have to deal with anyone right now.

Time goes by and she returns, knocking more forcefully this time. When I still don't open, she slides something under the door. It's a piece of paper with one of our codes written on it. We have a bunch of different special codes we've made up for when one of us is in trouble or when something important happens.

I pick the paper up and turn it over in my hands. I have to answer; it's one of our rules. So, I write my response and slip it back under the door. After that, I unlock the latch and let her in.

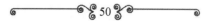

Cara smiles at me and runs in and jumps on my bed, grabbing my teddy bear.

We then open up my laptop and watch *The Lion King* together. It's a whole lot of fun, I must say.

Spending time with her is nice, but the fact is that Cara has a more active social life than me, so the next day she goes off with some friends while I stay at home alone.

It's quite depressing, really.

And while I'm here alone, I all of a sudden really want to go an adventure right now, but I don't.

Do with that what you will.

Instead, I sit down on the stairs with my chin in my hand and begin pondering things I could be doing. I haven't played piano in a little while, and my dad did tell me it seemed to put me in a better mood. I ought to play.

I get up from the stairs and go over to sit on the stool in front of the piano. I pause and sit there in silence for a few seconds before finally beginning "November Rain". I'm nearly halfway through learning the song now. How exciting is that?

Now it's time for a pizza break. Pizza generally makes me feel a bit better.

While I'm eating, I feel like writing another song, so I do:

It hurts so bad now
Oh I know
I'll tell you tomorrow, if I'm still around
Take it slowly, and it's gonna be ok
There's no need to be afraid

Making it alone never felt so lonely
I'd like to know what happens next
Oh if only

Something's broken inside me, please get it out
I'm bleeding through my heart
But I can't find the knife
I'm filling with doubt
What's wrong with me?

Why won't you let me out?

Making it alone never felt so lonely
I'd like to know what happens next
Oh if only

I would take you with me, but I know you wouldn't come
I'm running out of freedom here
So give me a chance before I'm done
If it all comes down to it, I think I'll slowly drift and die

Making it alone never felt so lonely
I'd like to know what happens next
Oh If only
Only

Huh, reading my song back to me it sounds a little lachrymose. But I'm not changing it.

I forget about it and lay down on the living-room floor, staring up at the ceiling.

Why is everything the way it is? What an original question, I know, but seriously nothing makes sense. I'm alive, obviously, but for what purpose? I feel like deep down I already know the answer—but I still want to bash my head against a wall until it all stops.

CHAPTER 5

COME AS YOU AREN'T

I SIT ON THE EDGE OF MY BED, head hanging low and eyes unfocused. My jackass of an ankle still hurts from my fall at the football game, and both Aidan and Lena weren't at school today. Basically, I was by myself all day while Bianca gave me weird glances every now and then. I haven't really talked to her since she told me she was dating Seth.

I'm skipping school tomorrow. I don't want to deal with classes and people.

I want to belong somewhere. I want this hole inside me to be filled. I'm tired of waiting. I'm tired of trying. I don't feel I'm getting anywhere; every day is the same—not what I want it to be. The more I think on it, the sadder I am. But if I don't think on it, the hole just sits there getting wider.

I've never come close to finding somewhere that really fits me, and I think the only way I could get what I need would be to jump out of this world and into a fictional one.

The few people I have found a connection with in my life seem to have all left me. And I'm still alone and drifting.

Does everybody need somebody? If so, I think I'm screwed.

As I'm sitting by myself at lunch, I pull up the music videos for "Don't Cry", "November Rain", and "Estranged". I've heard it said that they tell a story. Watching and listening to them now, I can see it. They do tell a story, and I don't think it's one I would have understood before this year.

There is something both freeing and frightening about having Rock music be my only relief.

At the moment, I do believe my "stairway lies on the whispering wind."

While I'm sitting here listening to my songs, I like to think that some-where someone else is listening to the same song. And then it's sort of like we're listening to it together, and suddenly I'm not so alone anymore. It's that way with all songs, really. You're not so alone anymore.

Thinking things like this makes me want to create my own music to share with people. Having my own band, that would be great. Problem is, again, you've actually got to have talent to make that stuff work. So I've got to stop thinking about this dream or it's going to kill me. Wanting something you can't ever have, that's dangerous stuff. If I did have the talent to create a rock band, I would make it the grittiest, dirtiest, hardest band around.

As I'm thinking about this, Bianca comes up to me.

"Hey," she greets, sounding a little *too* friendly for my liking, "do you want to come sit with us?" She motions toward her table of friends across the quad.

I hesitate for a second, unsure if I want to subject myself to her company, or Ella's company for that matter—I nearly forgot that they're good friends and sit together all the time. But maybe I should give them a shot. I know it's kind'a messed up that Bianca likes someone like Seth enough to date him, but I can't always be mad at her. I have to let the past be the past.

"Sure," I finally answer.

As we walk over to her table to join her friends, I see Eric sitting alone. I haven't seen him in a while. Part of me wonders if he's been avoiding school. I almost stop and ask him to come sit with us but I know Bianca would never let that happen.

I'm not the biggest fan of Bianca's friends, especially Ella, though they all seem to take to me well enough. And I'm getting along fine with Bianca. She even asks if after lunch I could hang out with them again tomorrow.

"I'll think about it," I reply and pause. "Nah, I'm just messing, sure."

But, the next day at lunch, I notice Eric sitting alone again and this time I can't shake the feeling I get when I see him all by himself. For some reason, I haven't been talking to him pretty much at all, and I'm feeling kind'a guilty about it now. He's another person I've let down, another relationship I've let slip through my fingers. I remember when we were kids how I used to hang out at his house all the time—we played together and then his mom would make us mac n' cheese and we'd eat it as she read to us from this old fairytale storybook. Just reminiscing about it gets me feeling depressed.

So, I get up from the table I'm sharing with Bianca and her friends and start making my way over to him. As I'm walking, Bianca runs after me and grabs me by the hoodie, pulling me back.

"Wren, what are you doing? You can't just get up and leave like this without saying anything."

"I'm going to sit with Eric." I really haven't spoken to him in a little while, so I hope he's been doing ok.

"Seriously?" Her eyes narrow and her voice raises.

"Yeah, seriously," I respond nonchalantly.

"You're unbelievable, choosing some random guy over your own friend," she mutters in disbelief, her hazel eyes darkening.

"Please, you don't need to see it that way, that's not what this is about, Bianca. He's alone and sad, I think, and if I can do something about it, then I got to. Besides, you know he's not a *random guy*, he's Eric." Her friends were sort of annoying me today anyway.

"Whatever," she shakes her head, "are you at least still doing the Ms. Sunrise Heights thing?"

Oh crap. I completely forgot that we signed up for it together last year, back when we were still kind'a close.

"Uh—"

"You forgot about it, didn't you?"

Yep. "No, no course not. How could you think such a thing?"

"Whatever, I'll see you there tomorrow," she says over her shoulder as she walks back to her table.

The thin tether keeping our friendship together is definitely fraying. I don't doubt it will break soon.

"Hello, Eric. How are you doing?" I ask once I reach him.

"Wren, why are you doing this?" Eric seems genuinely confused. He must have witnessed my exchange with Bianca.

I take a seat on the ground next to him. "Because I want to, that's why I came over here."

"But why do you *care*? We're pretty different, you know."

"I know what it's like to feel strange." Maybe that was too forward, I basically just called him strange to his face. But, in today's day and age, it's much more of an insult to call someone normal than it is to call them strange. Everyone wants to be unique—so much so that they're all ending up the same.

"Really?" he pushes back. "Because to me that doesn't make sense. You're real smart, funny, and... beautiful."

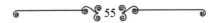

"Hey," I playfully punch him in the shoulder, "you're not so bad yourself."

He shakes his head and stares at me for a moment before sighing deeply.

"You are definitely not normal, Wren. That much I can tell."

"Oh, please, no need to flatter me," I laugh.

But he just looks at me sadly with big, dark eyes and I stop. "Do you remember when you used to come over to my house after school every day?" he asks.

"Was it really every day? Wow, yeah I remember."

"Did you know you were one of the only kids that would talk to me all throughout elementary school?"

"No..."

"I've always been *that* kid, with the stupid-looking glasses and bad skin—but you never seemed to care. I always wondered why." I stay silent as he continues. "If only I hadn't switched schools during junior high, maybe we would have remained friends. I don't know. But—" The sound of the bell cuts him off.

"Maybe we can talk again some other time," he says, standing up.

"Wait!" I stop him. "What were you going to say?"

"It doesn't matter. Have a nice day, Wren."

I wake up feeling pretty good, but then I think about how I have to go to the first Ms. Sunrise Heights candidates meeting or something. Is that what we're called? Candidates? Man that doesn't sound right, I really don't know anything.

Anyway, in order to be able to force myself into going, I decide I need to do *something* to boost my goddamn confidence. Time to go to *PsychologyToday.com*. Let's see, "10 Things You Can Do For Confidence"—that sounds about right.

I skim through most of it, not bothering to read anything on all the self-affirmation crap. It's like the only advice they can give is "Tell yourself you can do it," to which I respond, "Ah yes, now all my problems have been solved."

I'm about to give up completely when my eyes settle on number 9: "pretending to be someone else"—now that I can do. I need to channel a persona that can make me confident. So I head over to my closet and fling

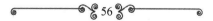

the doors open real dramatic like. Too bad I don't give a damn about fashion, or I might just have a little fun with this.

Still, for a person who claims not to care about fashion, I sure take my sweet time picking out something to wear. In the end, I put on my leather jacket, Rolling Stones t-shirt, black-coated jeans, cowboy boots, and a bandana. Suddenly, I feel like I could take on anything and anyone.

Time to get this freakin' show on the road…

***

I pull into the parking lot of the Sunrise Heights convention center, listening to *Appetite For Destruction* perhaps a little louder than need be. I begin to wonder if I've come to the right place. Oh well, guess I'll just have to check and see for myself.

I get out and lock my car and begin walking to the entrance when a voice calls out behind me.

"Hey, Wren!" My heart jumps and I turn my head, half expecting to find Violet. "I didn't know you were in this!" I watch as Lena runs up to me. Of course, Violet isn't here.

"Lena? I didn't think you were doing this either."

"Yeah, well my mom thought it might look good on college apps. Is that Camaro yours?"

"Uh, yep."

"Awesome car! Also, nice bandana. It's kind'a unusual, but it suits you well."

"Thanks," I smile. Her bubbly personality is a bit infectious and suddenly I am no longer feeling quite so anxious about being here.

We walk in together and greet some of the other girls, all of whom seem nice enough. Then, I see Bianca talking to Ella out of the corner of my eye and decide to walk up to her. After all, I'm pretty much only here in a last ditch effort to save what's left of our already-strained friendship. Even now, I can't explain exactly *why* I feel the goddamn need to fix this friendship, only that I do. It's like we're that one annoying couple with a long history that keeps breaking up and getting back together no matter how much they swear they hate each other. It doesn't make any sense, but that's the way it is.

Anyway, we have a small conversation. I ask her what the heck this whole thing is about? Unfortunately, before I can get any clarity this lady named Ms. Wood, who is in charge of the event, interrupts us. After her

long and rather boring speech about how important the rules are for the *contestants*—there's the word I was looking for—we are brought into a small studio space where we learn the basics of dancing.

First thing she does when we get inside the studio is tell me to please take off my bandana. I hate her already. Yet, as surprising as it is, it turns out Ms. Wood really likes me and even asks me, much to my discomfort, to show the class several of the steps. However, she does criticize my choice of outfit and labels it as inappropriate. Also, my ankle still hurts. I want to go home.

At the end of that class, Ms. Wood tells us to head to the ballroom to eat the lunch they have provided for us. We are also told to stay in there and not go anywhere until she comes back to get us for the next lesson.

The ballroom is huge, full of fancy chairs and tables. And there is one especially long table in the middle of the room loaded with elegant food and plates. I immediately walk over to it and plop three of the delicious-looking creampuffs right into my mouth, which earns a few dirty stares from some of the other contestants. I stare right back at them and shove two more puffs in my mouth. *What are you going to do about it?*

While those cream puffs are extremely delicious, I cannot say the same for the rest of the food. In fact, despite how expensive it appears, it sucks. And no one, except a few goody-two-shoes, eats any of it. Instead, Lena suggests we all sneak out the backdoor to some little, nearby coffee shop she knows about. I gladly oblige and start to follow the rest of the girls, but not before grabbing a handful of creampuffs—those things are freakin' good. Yet just as we reach the backdoor and are about to make our escape, the door at the front bursts open.

Aw crap.

In walks Ms. Wood and one of the other contestants, looking very smug. Obviously this girl went off and told on us in hopes of sucking up and seeming like a better choice for Ms. Sunrise Heights. At the moment, I'd like nothing more than to punch that smug expression right off her annoy-ing, punk-ass face. I wonder if that would get me in trouble.

Wasting no time, Ms. Wood immediately begins yelling at us about being bad, disobedient girls with no sense of responsibility. Then she tells us we have five minutes to give up whoever's plan it was to leave. Naturally, Bianca rounds us all up and says something about how it's unfortunate but that for the greater good of the group, we should let Lena turn herself in. *Yeah, I'm not about that.*

I clear my throat and pull Bianca aside for a second.

"Dude, they're trying to get us to turn on each other, to give each other up," I whisper quickly.

"Yes, but I guess we have to..." she begins to mutter, but I can tell she's unsure.

"No, no we don't. Come on, this is Lena you're talking about selling out, and I know we haven't always gotten along, especially lately, but seriously."

"It's not that big of a deal—you're acting like they're going to execute her or something. I doubt she'll even be in that much trouble. Besides, they told us to—"

"Yeah, so what?" I ask, cutting her off.

"You're too stubborn. We should do what they ask of us," she says pointedly, taking a step closer and crossing her arms.

"Only if it's the right thing to do. Does this feel right to you?"

"Not every little thing someone tells you to do is some big evil you need to fight against! You can be so paranoid about these things—and, I don't want anything to do with your little rebellions, no matter what they're for. Remember what happened last time you pulled a stunt like this? It's not our place to question the rules all the time, Wren."

"Of course it is. If we don't, who will? And you know what happened last time is... complicated, but a little questioning of authority is healthy. After all, free will is one of the most important aspects of humanity." I can feel myself going off on a tangent, but I can't stop.

"Technically speaking, free will doesn't exist," Bianca says, probably trying to antagonize me.

"That just sounds like a lame excuse not to do the right thing. I mean, truth is you can do whatever the hell you want whenever the hell you want."

"Is that what you really think?"

"Yeah, Bianca. It is."

At this point, we're standing only about a foot apart and the tension between us is reaching nuclear levels. Just then, right on cue, Ms. Wood returns.

"I'm only going to ask one last time, whose idea was it to leave?" she seethes, her face the color of a cherry. This lady is crazy.

I just roll my eyes, praying silently that everyone else will keep their traps shut as well. But, alas, this is not the way of the world, and Lena tentatively begins to raise her hand. I take one look at her fearful doe eyes and know immediately that I am about to do something I'm going to regret.

"It was mine. I asked them to leave for a bit with me, it was my fault. So… well I guess that's all actually," I blurt out.

"You 'guess that's all'?" Ms. Wood utters, sounding comically horrified. "Oh Wren, I am so disappointed in you." Never heard that one before.

"Sorry."

"You are such a beautiful girl too and an excellent dancer. You could have made the perfect Ms. Sunrise Heights."

"Don't worry, it won't happen again." It's like she's trying to antagonize me. *Oh please let me stay calm.*

"You're right, it most certainly will not. The ability to listen is very important for our contestants. When an adult tells you to do something, you do it—without question. Do you understand that?"

I can feel my temper rising, soon I won't be able to control it. "Not really," I respond through gritted teeth. *There it goes.*

"It seems you have some authority issues."

"You don't say."

"You listen here—"

"No, you listen. I'm not falling for your crap, so you can take your dumb rules and shove them right up you know where."

"This is unacceptable behavior! I'm—"

"Oh, cram it with a creampuff sweetheart."

Her eyes are bugging out of her head now, and her face is so red it seems like she's about to boil up from the inside out. I may have taken it too far.

"Also, I quit!" I add quickly, wanting this thing to be over already.

With that, I throw one of the creampuffs in my hand at the snitch girl's face and run out the door as fast as I can, no looking back. As I run to Nightrider and speed away, the only thing I can think of is the dull ache in my ankle that seems to be spreading throughout my body.

Getting my ass kicked out of things is starting to seem like a real talent of mine.

Friday, November somethin' (I never know the dates)
Aidan asked me why I was so grumpy looking today, and I told him about the Ms. Sunrise Heights contestants convention center disaster (say

that three times fast). He couldn't stop laughing and made me tell him twice more. I guess, from an outsider's perspective, it is pretty funny.

Also, apparently that incident took all my confidence because I feel right back to not being able to speak up about anything again.

(On a not-so-related note, I brushed Aidan off when he asked why I skipped class the other day. I mean, he technically also skipped class the day before that, so I don't see why he is acting like it was a big deal. Then again, I suppose I have begun doing it more frequently as of late—my grades are already being affected...)

***

Over the weekend, I go to the public library and borrow a ton of old murder mysteries. Just for fun. If I were to be murdered, I'd want my murderer—

"You're still reading those stupid creepy-killer books?" Cara questions out of nowhere, standing behind me with her hands on her hips.

"Fudging Christ, Cara!" I say, now fully turned around in my seat on the sofa. "I think you just gave me six heart attacks!"

"You have been extra-sulky all weekend. It's annoying me."

"Cool, I'll make it a point to be less annoyingly-sulky next weekend. Don't you have a soccer practice to be at right now or something?"

"No, it got canceled. So I'm going out to pizza with some of my team-mates, if you want to come."

"Thanks for the invite, but I think I'll pass on the preteen soccer kids get-together."

"Suit yourself."

"I always do," I call after her as she heads out the door.

Once Cara is gone, I set down my book and go upstairs to my room. I put on Aidan's CD—the one he gave to me—and suddenly get a great idea: What if I made *him* a CD? It'll give me something to do.

I managed to avoid Bianca all of Friday, knowing she'd be pissed as hell. I almost forgot about it for the entirety of Saturday and Sunday, but today I am not so fortunate. Toward the end of the day, she corners me, as I'm at my locker—the bastard.

"You really messed up with what you pulled at the convention center. And you've been ignoring my calls."

I groan internally before turning to face her. "Not in the mood, Bianca."

She disregards this and continues. "It seems like you have some deep personal issues to deal with. You should really consider apologizing to Ms. Wood, and then maybe we could start being friends again."

"Great! I'll put that right on my to-do list after jumping off a cliff and telling you to go to hell."

"You been saving that one?"

"Yeah, how was my delivery?" I say, swinging my locker shut. "Because to be honest it felt a little flat. How about we have a redo? We can start at the part where you stick your nose in my business and go from there."

"Whatever, Wren. If you want to be a loner with no friends, then that's fine by me. I've noticed you talking to Aidan Grey more, but if you think he's still going to want to have anything to do with you if you keep these sort of screw ups going, you're kidding yourself."

I shrug my shoulders and turn away, walking out of the hallway and outside. From there, I continue walking till I'm at the school gates. I still have US history class, but I no longer care very much. I doubt anyone will even notice I'm gone.

As I am about to push the gates open, a familiar voice stops me in my tracks.

"Where are you going?"

I spin around and find myself face to face with Aidan. *Well isn't this perfect timing.*

"Nowhere." Hey, this could be a good opportunity to give him the CD I made—I begin searching through my backpack. Ah there it is!

"'Nowhere'. Really?"

"Yeah, but Aidan," I begin to outstretch my hand with the CD in it, "I have something for—"

"Because it looks like you're trying to skip out on school."

My hand drops. "Ok…"

He crosses his arms, and my arms automatically cross in response, my body turning slightly stiff. "If I were, why would it matter to you?"

He sighs and pushes a hand through his hair. "Because… we're partners. We got to look out for each other."

We're… oh yeah, we're psychology partners. "I'm ok, Aidan." As I say these words, the air in my lungs suddenly feels heavier.

He gives me a look, but I can't tell what it means. All I can tell is that I can't stick around for another class at the moment.

"I don't know what's going on with you, Wren. But maybe I could help you, if you'd let me."

I stuff the CD back in my backpack. "I don't need help."

"You say that, but then you go around school sulking and acting out, and it doesn't make sense. I mean, look at what you're about to do right now—"

"Aidan…"

"Something is not right. If you don't want to tell me about it, fine—but don't act like you don't know what I'm talking about, because I know you do."

I can feel my eyes stinging as he begins to walk away.

What am I doing?

It feels like a bullet has gone straight through my heart, and a pool of blood is beginning to form around my cold, dead corpse.

***

Back in my room, I take out the CD and throw it across the floor, watching it slide under the dresser.

Tonight, December

GN'R is right; it is hard to keep an open heart when friends seem out to hurt you. But then does that also mean it's true everybody needs some time on their own; some time all alone? I know I sure do. I could live alone forever, just me, and be fine. To tell the truth, I'm already kind'a estranged from—well everything.

CHAPTER 6

IT AIN'T SO EASY

GOING THROUGH HER PARENTS' DIVORCE had been hard for Ella, but going through her breakup over the summer was even harder. Lucky for her, as both a pretty and sociable girl, she didn't have to wait all that long before she met Rob. Some might call her superficial for getting over her boyfriend so quickly, but Ella didn't think so. She knew that love was a battlefield and in order to win the war you had to be able to let go of any past feelings the moment you found someone new. And this someone new came in the form of Rob King, an attractive baseball player who also happened to be a wonderful singer. Yes, he met up with her standards quite nicely.

Just like she had high standards for romantic partners, she had them for friends. She was always one of the more popular people growing up, and that was the way she liked it. It's also how she found her way to Bianca and her friend group when they all began high school together.

It was around the time she started hanging out with Bianca that she first met Wren. From the very beginning, Ella found her strange, almost like she was out of place at Sunrise Heights High and should be somewhere else. She found it even stranger when Bianca told her that they were friends. She knew they danced together or something, but it just didn't add up. Even so, Ella didn't question it too much. In fact, Ella didn't question much of anything; she generally went along with things and the way they were supposed to be.

But Wren wasn't like this. She wouldn't just go along with anything— she pushed back. At first, this both confused and irritated Ella; and combined with her antisocial tendencies, general aloofness, and weird tastes, Wren just rubbed her the wrong way. It seemed Bianca felt the same toward Wren too, as she was frequently on the receiving end of her temper during their turbulent on-and-off again friendship.

Then, one day, Ella got on Bianca's bad side for a change. She couldn't even remember what for anymore, but that she had nearly been ready to cry at the time.

And there was one other thing she could remember about that day—just as the tears were about to start falling, Wren stepped in-between them and told Bianca to leave her alone. She could still picture the look of un-wavering determination in her dark blue eyes as they stared into Bianca's brown ones. It was like she wasn't afraid of anything.

The whole time, Ella was so shocked she almost couldn't believe it. But what shocked her even more was how Bianca actually listened to her. From that moment on, Ella couldn't help but see Wren in a completely different light—one that fascinated her.

This isn't to say that they began getting along well, though. There were still plenty of differences that kept them apart—such as Wren's absolute disdain for rules and regulations and Ella's constant need for control and organization. This is why suddenly noticing Wren sneaking around the back of the school office building made Ella dash out of the hallway to check on her as fast as she could.

She was up to something—that much she was sure of.

"Wren! What are you doing?" Ella calls out while she runs up to me. "You're not supposed to be doing this!"

The thing I am doing that I am not supposed to be doing is carving something into the back wall of the main office building using a switch-blade. You may wonder why I am doing this, well it's 'cus yesterday I got suspended.

It started in English when we were reading *Romeo and Juliet* and my teacher was going on and on about how great Shakespeare is and every-thing. She thinks he's some kind of God and told us that we should be grateful toward him because he made up a lot of the words we use today. But personally I think that's some BS right there. I'm supposed to be thankful because someone made up a bunch of words, but if *I* were to do the same thing it would be considered inappropriate and unprofessional. Seriously, I have a lot of ideas for new words, but if I were to ever use them in my writing my English teacher would flip out. So I told her my thoughts, which then got me sent to the Principal's office. But the real cherry on top of the whole mess was my conversation with the Vice Principal while I waited for the real Principal. He told me he didn't think

I was going anywhere in life with the way I had been acting. Then I told him that I didn't feel the same way about him because I thought he would go really far in life someday, and that I hoped he'd stay there. This got me suspended right on the spot for the next day.

At first, I was kind'a disappointed because winter break is almost here, and it would have been nice to get through the semester without any bad marks on my record—but now I couldn't care less.

Technically I'm not even supposed to be here today at all, but I figured I'd take the opportunity and do something productive with it.

"Wren, I asked you what you're doing!"

"Oh, hey Ella. Whatya doing out of class? Isn't English going on right now?"

"Yes, I have a hall pass to use the restroom though, and while I was on my way there, I saw you through one of the windows."

Damn. That means someone else could see me—I just hope Aidan doesn't... I better finish up as quickly as I can.

"Well I suppose you ought to be getting back to class then."

"You know you're not allowed to have a knife on campus, right?"

"Relax, it's just for my art project."

"What is—oh my God! That's absolutely vulgar—the worst thing I have ever seen! How could you write that?"

The side of my mouth pulls up into a smirk: exactly the reaction I was looking for—well, in a way. Though, I'm guessing she probably doesn't get it. If she did, she'd see the truth. No one ever sees the truth.

"Please go back to class, Ella."

Rather than going back to class, she goes on talking about school rules some more, and I go on carving with my switchblade, singing, "Don't Damn Me" in my head.

"You need to stop, Wren. Wren? Are you listening to me?"

"Oh, did you say something?"

"This is not funny."

"Couldn't hear you over me not paying attention."

"Seriously?"

"Seriously what?"

"Must you make such rude comments all the—"

"Ahem!" I interrupt her with an obnoxiously loud cough. I'm further risking being caught, but she's really getting on my nerves. "Sorry, could you say that again? Didn't quite catch it."

"I said—"

"Ahem! Sorry, go ahead."

"Wre—"

I cough again.

"I swear to God—"

I put up a hand to pause her. "Wait, you hear that?" Silence. "Yep, that's the sound I wish you were making."

"You're lucky I consider you a friend. Otherwise, I would already have called the Principal out here."

I don't respond, continuing to carve in the final details of my masterpiece.

"Done!" I say excitedly, flipping my switchblade shut. "See you tumorrow, Ella!"

New plan: anytime some asshat tries to tell me what to do, I'll have my phone ready so I can just press play on "It's My Life" and shove it in their face.

That'd be pretty funny, huh? I think to myself.

I crack myself up sometimes, I really do. And that's a good thing because if you don't crack yourself up, there might not be anyone else around who can.

***

Getting home, I still have four hours left of my mandatory day off before I need to go off to dance class.

I am sitting on top of the kitchen counter, swaying my feet, and opening up my phone, looking for somethin' to entertain my overactive mind. If I sit still without anything, I know that Aidan's words are going to begin plaguing my mind again. It's been over a week, but I can't stop thinking about it. I don't even technically know him all that well. It's pathetic.

I start to scroll through my social media, checking out friends' accounts and going through my own. Man, anyone who puts God before family in their bio is someone I do not trust. Honestly, I dislike a lot of stuff on here. I'm sick of seeing people pretending to have, or actually having, perfect lives. When I look at my page, I just get sad.

I've decided I'm going to delete my account.

Goodbye strangers, it's been nice—but I couldn't find my paradise.

***

I'm still sitting on the counter, now reading *The Outsiders*, when the house phone rings.

I jump down and go get it, immediately recognizing the number as Bianca's.

"Bianca? Why are you calling my house?"

"You weren't answering your cell. And I'm calling because Ella told me what happened this morning."

I roll my eyes. "Can you remind her that I own a switchblade?"

She ignores me. "I heard someone say you got suspended for the week, but I wanted to hear more about it from you."

"The week? My God, it's just one day! It's not so big a deal."

"Should I come to your place or do you want to meet me at the Ice Cream Shop diner?"

We haven't been to the Ice Cream Shop together since the events of last year…

"Uh, sure, let's do the ice cream idea." I mean, the thought of getting ice cream at this time in my life is a bit funny, but maybe it'll cheer me up, or something.

"Ok, see you there in twenty."

She hangs up. I'm left holding the phone in my hands and suddenly feeling very nervous. I suppose now that something interesting has happened to me, she no longer remembers the conversation we had after the convention center incident.

***

I get to the Ice Cream Shop and see Bianca in the corner booth, sipping on a strawberry milkshake.

"Hello," I say, sliding in next to her.

"Want some?" she asks, motioning to the shake and handing me a straw.

"Thanks."

"So what exactly happened?"

"It wasn't that crazy or interesting. I just got in trouble with the Vice Principal yesterday—didn't hold my tongue, you know—and got suspended for today." As I tell her, I stab my straw into the table and take off the wrapper. I begin to sip from it while Bianca stares at me with her chin resting on her hands.

I go into a bit more detail about how it happened. We soon start talking about some other stuff.

"Why didn't you stay at that year-round academy you started at this summer?" she asks, though I think it's possible she already knows.

"It just wasn't what I wanted it to be," I say with a shrug.

"Did things really go that badly?"

"No, I was fine there. There were other reasons that affected my decision to come home. But it was an amazing experience and while I was there, I did very well," I lie.

"Good to hear. And have you found anyone special lately?"

"Special?" She's acting like a scientist who has my life on the dissecting table.

"Yes, it's just that, in all the time I've known you, you have never dated anyone."

"I know," I shrug again, "but it's whatever. Guess people don't like me that way, I don't let it bother me."

"Hmm," her eyes narrow, "Anyways, I feel like I've finally found something real with Seth, and I want you to be able to have something like this too."

Things are about to get uncomfortable.

"We went out Friday night and had a really nice time. He asked about how you're doing."

I nearly spit out the milkshake. "I doubt that very freaking much."

"He did, he's changed—believe it or not. I told him you were doing fine, by the way."

"Seth is—"

"You never even gave Seth a chance," she snaps.

Is this the reason she asked me here—an ambush for her to guilt-trip me about her boyfriend?

"What are you talking about?"

"You purposely antagonized him all the time when you were at our studio."

"If by antagonize you mean not let him walk all over me then yeah, I suppose I did," I say, leaning across the table. "But hey, don't worry, you've done a real good job of never antagonizing anyone in your entire life."

"I remember some of the things you would say, 'I'll rip your head off, punk.' I believe that is a direct quote."

I start pulling on my fingers, making the joints pop. "Come on, that doesn't sound like anything I'd say."

"Or how about when you—"

"Ok, I get it, you don't like the way I talked to him."

"I just think you're a bit unfair. He saved your *life*. Or perhaps you've chosen to forget that. It's not his fault that you attacked him. I mean, clearly you have some issues—what with getting suspended and all—and now you can't handle that I'm with him because you can't stand to see both of us happy together."

"No, Bianca, I just don't understand why you would want to be with such a dickhead."

"No, you're upset because you were out of control and dangerous, and you got kicked out because of it!"

As soon as she says this she moves closer to the wall of the booth and her eyes have a shadow of fear and surprise in them, as if she can't believe she just said that. She's clearly waiting for me to blow up. I have to say, I thought I would feel something, but instead I just come up empty—nothing. My face stays blank as she continues to stare at me.

"Wren, I—I didn't mean that…"

Without a word, I get up and walk out.

At dance, I still don't say anything to anyone. The pain in my ankle is constant throughout the class, though I feel nothing but coldness in my heart.

When I get home the cold slowly builds until a hot rage rips through the ice, and I can no longer contain it. In my room, I scream and throw things, not caring what I break. I punch my wall continuously, bruising my knuckles, and likely jamming my wrist. But I just don't care. My parents aren't home yet anyway and my sister is still at her late night soccer practice—I can clean everything up before they all get back.

As I lay down to sleep, I feel like I've been strapped to a bed with my limbs tied down in each corner. I could scream and fight as hard as I can but it wouldn't make a difference. I can't break free. The cost is too high so I must stay low.

I'm pretty tied up as flashbacks bombard my brain:

"I'm not someone you want to mess around with, Wren."

"I'm not afraid of anyone, and I'm certainly not afraid of you."

Why must I be so stubborn? I ask myself questions like this as if I wish I weren't that way, but that's not true. Truth is, I know being so stubborn might not be the best thing, and it might lead to my downfall. Although it's unlikely I'll change that about myself anyway.

***

In the morning, I get up and can barely stand on my feet. School is going to be rough—but at least there is only a few days before winter break. It seems I've barely gotten out of my car when Bianca is already in my face, like she's been waiting for me to show up. It never ends.

"Hey, about what I said yesterday..." she begins, looking down at her feet.

"It's ok," I reply. "I get it."

To say the face she makes is confused would be an understatement, but I don't wait around, I get out of there and on to class.

Today in creative writing, our teacher talked about channeling what's inside you to fuel your stories. She said if it comes from a place of truth, it always comes out strong. I wonder if that's true. I must admit, after writing my story I felt a bit emotionally exhausted but also refreshed, like it had gotten something out of me that really needed to come out.

I've been writing quite a bit lately, coming up with new stories and whatnot, but I haven't found the courage to share them with anyone. Allowing someone to see into you, to catch a glimpse at who you are, terrifies me. I always worry they won't react the way I'm hoping they will and that my desire to continue writing will be destroyed. I'm not sure why, but after someone's read something I'm working on it just feels... tainted. Like it's not the same anymore.

As for right now, the story piece I'm working on could use revision, but at least it comes from an honest place:

Wren Evans
December 16th
Creative Writing

Uncertainty hung in the air, making each of her movements difficult and strained with fear. The heavy morning fog consumed the cemetery and rolls of curling mist trailed eerily, all the way to the outskirts of the surrounding forest. Every one of her senses told her that she shouldn't be here, it wasn't safe. Yet still she trudged on, forcing each foot to move in front of the other as an unseen force pulled her farther into the empty graveyard. She came into a small clearing where the branches of the tall hickory trees hung low and blocked out most of the gray sky. A certain unsettling stillness in the area made everything seem ever so slightly off. There were no birds chirping, no soft breeze blowing, and the air was quiet, too quiet.

Suddenly, a powerful wind began blowing wildly, brushing the heavy fog aside and sweeping the fallen leaves off the floor and hurling them at her. She frantically brought her hands up to her face in an attempt to shield herself from these attacks, but the gusts of tempestuous, freezing air persisted. The wind continued to pick up even more and became harsher and colder until she was sure she'd be swept away. Then, as quickly as the gale came, it stopped. The air was dead silent again; all she could hear was the pounding of her own racing heart.

As she stood there, struggling to compose herself a soft, compelling whisper from the shadows sent a shiver down her spine. At first it was so faint she couldn't make out what it said, but then it became unmistakable—it was her name. The darkness called to her, coaxing her to come to it, and a part of her wanted to answer it. She turned slowly, almost as if in a trance, toward the source of the whispers. She looked deep into the gleaming blackness of the twisted woods and saw nothing but darkness. Still, she could feel it. There was a powerful energy there, amongst the shadows, and it wanted her.

Suddenly, her feet floated off the ground as the unseen force pulled her closer. Fear was her immediate reaction, but soon the fear melted away leaving behind an unnatural calm. The force gripped her tighter and tighter, suffocating her near to the point of death, before abruptly dropping her to the ground next to an opening into the woods. She lay in a crumpled heap, shaking. After a few moments, she forced herself back onto her feet and looked into the opening.

She felt herself begin to step forward toward it, her mind no longer in control. There were no thoughts running about her head, only a feeling. An intense feeling that consumed her very being, she must reach—

Another cold shiver ran down her spine, as if to warn her, and she fell out of the mesmerizing trance. She could now sense the presence of danger in the cool twilight air. It's beckoning tug continued but she no longer gave into it. Instead, she began to run as fast as she could out of the cemetery. The looming black entry gate became visible as she raced in-between graves and tombs, but would she make it? Finally, she reached the gate and pulled it open, slamming it shut behind her. She stood there a moment, on the outside of the cemetery gate, with her breath caught in her throat, choking her. Slowly, the fear that had consumed her began to fade and her breath returned, allowing her racing heart to calm itself.

What was that? she wondered.

But even now, she could sense it, the power. Though it was distant, and somehow she knew it could no longer bring her harm. Still, she decided it was time to leave and go back home to where she knew safety could be guaranteed. But just as she started away, she heard it. A new surge of horror coursed through her as she realized what it meant. It was distant, just like the dark power, and didn't seem to be coming from anywhere, but the message rang out clear in her mind.

The storm is coming.

Humans, man—yeah, they can annoy the hell out of me, but they sure are something special aren't they? And for all the bad they do, they do an awful lot of good. I'd like it if people could see this side of each other more. There is so much good out there, but it can be hard to see sometimes. Even still, you can't ever give up.

When all you've got to live for is the fight, you keep fighting.

CHAPTER 7

DR. FEELBAD

SO MUCH FOR FINISHING OFF a relaxing winter break—three days until I go back to school and my parents are both gone for business-related trips. Cara is sick with what she claims is the flu (though I'm not so sure it isn't just a regular fever).

"Hey, Cara," I call as I get my keys and open the front door, "I'm going to the store because I'm out of Cocoa Krispies. Is there anything you want me to get you?"

"Yes!" she shouts from the sofa. "I really need you to get me some more orange juice. I love orange juice."

"Yeah, ok."

"I mean it! This OJ is very important to me—it'll help me get better."

"Don't worry, kiddo. I'll get it," I assure her.

But, once I get to the store, the problem with this is that it turns out I *can't* actually get it.

"No, god damnit! How can they be out of freakin' *orange juice*?" I place both hands on the outside of what is supposed to be the orange juice section, pressing my head against the glass. Damn this small supermarket— and there isn't another one for miles.

"Everything all right, Wren?"

Please, not right now. I freeze and then slowly bring myself upright and turn around. "Hello, Aidan." He's carrying two large grocery bags and is wearing a leather jacket. Hmm, I wonder when he got that? I've never seen him wear it before, but it looks used...

"Is there a reason you look like you're about to have a breakdown in the juice aisle?" he asks.

"Not one you need to worry about."

"Hey, maybe I can help out," he says, stepping closer and placing his bags down.

"I doubt it."

"What are you here for?"

"I came here for one thing—well, other than Cocoa Krispies—and they don't have it. I don't understand, what kind of a supermarket doesn't have orange juice?"

"So that's what you're looking for... this?" he reaches into one of the bags and pulls out a carton of OJ.

"What, how did you get that?"

"It was the last one." His eyes are practically dancing with mischief.

"Can I have it?"

"I already paid."

"You already bought it?"

"Yeah, but then I saw you come in and thought you looked kind of upset so I followed you and found you here."

"Look, I *need* that orange juice. Obviously I'll pay you back."

"Hmm, I don't know... OJ seems to be a rare commodity in this town, I think I might have to keep it."

"Aidan! I'm serious!"

"What, and you think I'm not?" Damn it all to hell. This kid is going to drive me up a wall.

"Aidan, I don't—"

"Hey, hey, I'm just messing you around. You can have it."

I tilt my head at him. "For real?"

"Yeah, so long as you now refer to me as the Juice Box Hero."

"This juice isn't even in a box."

He makes a face and shrugs. "Close enough."

"How much was it?" I ask, taking out my wallet.

"No, please, I don't want that."

"Come on."

"I'm not gonna take your money. Now, do you want this or not?" he says, holding out the carton.

"Thank you." I take it, and he begins to walk away.

"Wait! Isn't there anything I can do for you?"

He looks over his shoulder, smirking, and then shakes his head. "I'm all good, Wren. Enjoy the OJ."

After getting the Cocoa Krispies, I check out and go back to my car.

I can't say I understand why he ended up giving me the juice, but I know it's going to make Cara happy—and that makes me happy.

A few blocks away from the store, I do a double take as I spot Aidan walking down the street holding his two very heavy looking bags.

I roll down my window and pull up beside him. "Hey there."

"Hey." He looks surprised to see me.

"Where are you walking to?" I ask, continuing to drive slowly next to him.

"Home."

"How far is that?"

"A couple miles."

I slam on the brakes. "A couple miles?"

He stops and sighs. "Yes, but it's no big deal."

"Get in the car."

"What?"

"You heard me—in Nightrider," I say, motioning into the car.

"You named your car?"

"Course I did."

"Yeah, course you did." He rolls his eyes but gets in anyway. "Is this to pay me back for the juice thing?"

"No, now tell me where you live."

He hesitates a moment, but gives in. "Fairbrook Drive."

I believe I've heard of it before, but I don't know how to get there, so Aidan has to give me directions as we set off.

It's very weird having him in my car. I can't help but glance at him—and I notice him doing the same. We make eye contact a few times, but I just keep reverting my eyes to the road.

I should be playing music, why haven't I—my phone suddenly begins ringing. What if it's Cara?

"Could you do me a favor, Aidan, and check who that is?"

"It's someone named Cara."

"Son of a bitch. That's my sister."

"Do you want me to answer it?"

I swallow hard and nod.

"Hello, Wren's phone. This is Aidan speaking." He puts his hand over the speaker and looks to me. "She wants to know who I am, and she wants to talk to you."

"Just tell her I'll be home soon."

"Your sister will be—what's that? An emergency?"

"What?" I practically shout.

"She said she needs you to come back as quickly as possible."

"Ok, Cara, just hold on! I'm coming!" *Her illness must be more serious than I thought.*

"She hung up."

"I'm sorry, Aidan, but I have to go straight over there."

"It's ok, I understand."

I get home, going about 20 miles over the speed limit, and jump out of the car faster than lightning. As I move to the door, I notice Aidan follows.

"Cara? Where are you?" I call as I burst through the front door.

"Wren!" I follow her voice and find her still sitting on the sofa in front of the TV. "*Scooby Doo* is starting! You already missed the beginning of the episode and I don't know how to record it."

"Wait, I raced all the way here for a *Scooby Doo* episode?"

Understanding washes over her face. "Oh… sorry. I didn't realize…"

"Next time, think before you say you're in an emergency, ok?"

"Ok but—Who is that?" she asks, pointing behind me at Aidan, just now noticing him.

"This is my… friend, Aidan," I say as he steps forward and waves.

"Hello, Cara. It's nice to meet you," he smiles.

Her cheeks go a little red and I have to bite my lip to stop from chuckling. "You can thank him for your orange juice. Which is—oh, I left it in the car—"

"I'll get it," Aidan says, already moving toward the door.

"He's your friend?" Cara whispers once he's gone.

"Yes."

"Oh."

Aidan steps back in with my cereal box and the OJ, setting them down on the kitchen counter.

"I suppose I ought to be getting you home now," I say as he walks back over to me.

Before he can answer, Cara shouts from the living room asking for a cup of juice.

"Sorry, she's not usually like this—but she's feeling sick right now. That's why I got so worried so easily…"

"If you need to stay here and take care of her for a bit, I don't mind. And I can always walk home—"

"No! I mean, please don't do that. I said I would drive you home and I'm going to."

"Wren, my juice!" Cara calls again.

"We better get that, where are the cups?" Aidan asks.

"In there," I answer, pointing to the cabinet behind him.

He proceeds to pour a glass and takes it in to Cara.

"Here you go," he says, handing it to her. "Anything else we can do for you?"

"You can finish this episode with me."

"Sure, anything you say." To my surprise, he sits down on the sofa and leans back, putting his arms behind his head.

"Aidan, you don't have to—"

"Wren, I *have* to figure out who the bad guy is before the episode ends—I can't leave before I do that."

"Yeah, Wren," Cara adds, "he can't leave until we know who did it."

I shake my head but I sit down as well.

The entire time, Aidan continues to make ridiculous accusations, suspecting everyone but the actual culprit. And I spend more time watching him laugh n' joke with Cara than I do the actual program.

When it ends, we walk back out to my car. "Thanks for being so helpful today," I tell him as we get in.

He smiles and I smile back. "I had fun."

"Me too."

After I drop him off, I go straight back home and curl up on the sofa next to Cara once again.

"I like your friend," she says, turning on a new *Scooby Doo*. "You should make him come back again."

I guess my break had a pretty nice end after all.

Today is depressing because winter break is over and now everything is back to normal and I'm back to school.

Some girls that I haven't really spoken to before come up to me in between classes and begin chatting with me. At first, I'm very happy to finally have people who want to talk to me, but that quickly changes when they only start asking questions like what can I tell them about Aidan? They assume I should know him pretty well since I'm his psych partner.

I should have known that no one would actually want to talk to me for me. After a while, they appear to forget that I'm even there. They just continue to go on about how some guys at school are attractive.

"I mean, he's cute but he's not Aidan Grey cute."

"Yeah, I've never seen such green eyes!"

I walk away before I have to hear anymore.

Am I blind or am I losing my mind? I swear I've seen it all a thousand times.

By the time I make it to psych class, I am planning different ways I can get out of school and back to bed.

"Evans, are those leather pants?" Aidan asks, startling me out of my head. "And cowboy boots?"

Since when do we call people by their last names?

"Yes, Grey," I answer. I got these pants last year for my birthday, but I've never put them on until now. I almost forgot I was wearing them. As for the boots, well, I wear them all the time—I'm surprised he hasn't commented on them before.

He shakes his head and laughs. "You're crazy."

"Tell me something I don't know."

"'Immigrant Song' is the best Led Zeppelin song."

"What? Now *you're* crazy, everyone knows 'Stairway To Heaven' is unbeatable."

He shrugs and then winks at me. "Hmm, just telling you the truth."

"Whatever, you're just messing with me," I say, shaking my head in mock distress.

"How's your sister doing?"

"She's not completely over it yet, but she's doing better over all—still watching a lot of *Scooby Doo*."

"That's good to hear."

"Yeah. We should probably start this assignment."

"Ok, I'll read off the questions and you answer them while I write down the response. First question: What is it like having such an amazing, funny, attractive partner for psych?"

"I've never had a partner like that, but if I ever do I'll make sure to tell you what it's like. Then again, I suppose you would already know." Now it's my turn to wink.

The rest of class passes by pretty quickly, with Aidan asking stupid questions that are definitely not part of the assignment and me giving him equally stupid answers. It's silly moments like these that help to lift the darkness, even if just for a moment.

Later on, in creative writing, we begin working on a new story that's supposed to be a complete free write—no outlines, no rules, just writing. It's too bad the class is only two days a week. I'm starting to like it a lot.

I put my pen to the paper and stuff just starts coming out:

I've got to never mind the darkness. I mean nothing lasts forever anyways, right? I can feel the hangman coming down from the gallows and I don't have very long.

I just need some time on my own—all alone.

I then start writing about specific events that come to mind. I don't stop writing for even a second all the way until the bell rings.

We are now supposed to turn our ramblings into a real, coherent story. To do so, our teacher asks us to please get some outside advice by having someone else look over our writing.

I'm freaked out that the person reading my story is going to think it's *me* in the story. But it's not. I made it all up, just writing random stuff that I could think up. During free study period, I find Eric sitting peacefully, reading a history textbook. I feel bad about interrupting him, but at the same time I don't know whom else to ask.

"Eric, could you read over this writing and give me your opinion on it?" I ask him, shoving out the paper.

"I'd be happy to."

"Awesome, uh, just so you know, the story doesn't have anything to do with me, ok?"

He looks at me kind'a funny but he nods and takes the paper anyway.

I sit down next to him, twisting and pulling a strand of my hair, as he thoughtfully looks it over.

"That was very good," he says after he's finished reading.

"Really?"

"Yes, but, Wren… my impression from it is that you are in fact the person in this story."

"Why do you say that?"

"Because it really seems like you're the person in the story."

I take the paper back from him and head to the bathroom, where I wash my face with cold water. Then I rip up my story and throw it in the trashcan.

A group of girls come in, giggling and talking loudly amongst themselves. They stop when they see me and look me up and down. People seem to do this to me a lot.

"Nice pants," one of them snickers.

I say nothing, brushing past them and out the door.

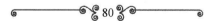

In the hallway, someone bumps into me, knocking me sideways into the lockers. They don't say sorry. I don't think they even notice. A few bystanders laugh and continue on walking to their next class.

Man, just when you start to feel ok, humanity comes along and disappoints the crap out of you. Or maybe I'm just confused and can't tell when I'm ok and when I'm not. To be honest, I can be quite an oxymoron.

Sometimes I'll be sitting alone thinking, "*Wow! I'm so cool. How could no one like me?*" while also thinking, "*Wow! I freaking suck,*" at the same time.

I just want you to enjoy life.

I wish I could, but I'm starting to think it's too late.

***

After my last class of the day, Lena comes up to me and taps me on the shoulder.

"Hey, I was wondering if you could drive me home. My usual ride, Rose, isn't here today and I don't know if I'll make it all the way back walking in these shoes," she says, looking down in dismay at her pink heels.

"Sure thing, I can drive us," I answer. I'm pretty sure Lena lives not that far from me, so it should be an easy drop off.

She says goodbye to some friends and then we walk to the parking lot and get in my car. The ride starts off smooth enough, but pretty soon I'm speeding, which spooks Lena.

"God damnit, Wren! Just because you drive a cool-looking Camaro doesn't mean you got to go this fast! You are going to get us killed or pulled over!"

"Relax, I got this under control. Besides, I can't help it if Nightrider's such a fast car."

I am an excellent driver. While I hardly ever go the speed limit, I never take it so far as to drive recklessly. I know my way around the road. I know what's too fast and what's not.

"Lena, if you're going to drive with me, you can be certain of three things: we're going to be safe, we're going to listen to rock, and we're going to go fast."

"Fine, Speed Racer. I'm putting my trust in you."

A few minutes later, we pull into her driveway. We sit there for a bit, talking about different things, when suddenly Lena asks me who I think I am? Not in a rude sort of way, in a genuinely curious way. But, this is not a question I expected to be asked, especially not by Lena.

"Well," I begin cautiously, "sometimes I'm all leather jackets and no personality."

She looks at me seriously before falling back into her seat and laughing.

"Better than all personality and no leather jackets," she grins.

We both laugh and relax back in our seats.

"Can I ask you a question?" I say after a few minutes.

She leans forward and her eyes widen in curious anticipation. "Yes."

"Do you think everybody needs somebody?"

"Of course."

"You think?"

"Without a doubt. Some people may be better at being on their own than others, but everyone has to have someone eventually. No one can stay alone forever." With this, she opens the car door and gets out. But just as she's about to close it, she pauses and smiles at me.

"Thank you for taking me home, Wren. We haven't hung out much, and I'm glad we got to spend time together today."

"I'm glad, too."

After that, I head on back home. I like Lena.

Even still, every time I looked at her smile, I could tell there's still something missing in my life. And I don't know if that thing is tangible or just something inside of me that I'll never find.

But I know it's not there right now.

I see her, the way she breathes in the air and looks out to the world with confidence and excitement, and know that is not a part of me anymore.

It's slipping away from me—further every day.

***

The next day at school, I feel myself slipping even lower when I find out that there's a huge test I didn't study for. We are only two days back into the semester, so having such a big test now doesn't make any sense. I mean, were we told to study over break? Sure—but that doesn't mean it's ok.

My original plan had been to cram all my environmental science stuff in the night before, but now that plan has been shot. I was too caught up in thinking about what's missing in my world to remember about something as stupid as a test. Of course, now it doesn't seem all that stupid. It seems pretty darn scary, actually.

I feel almost frozen as I stare blankly at the questions and bubble sheet lying on the desk in front of me. Who needs to know seventy questions worth of stuff about renewable energy? I get it; it's important—but shoving down my throat facts I can't ever use doesn't make sense. It'll be over soon. Just stay calm.

The whole rest of the day, my thoughts revolve completely around the test and, more specifically, how terribly I did on it.

Back at my house, I'm still going over everything I did wrong on it. I failed it; I know it.

I turn up the radio to drown out the noise in my head and "You Give Love A Bad Name" comes blasting through, projecting all throughout the house.

I run around from room to room like a crazy person, bounding up and down the stairs and jumping on tables, sofas, and beds, singing loudly with a hairbrush microphone. I then start sliding on the floor and spinning around in my socks. I slip a few times, but who cares? I just keep bouncing and thrashing my head to the music.

I abruptly stop singing and slump down on the couch, banging my fist into my forehead.

How could I fail that test? I knew it was coming, why didn't I do better? I suck.

I turn off the radio and head outside and into the park. All the while, my mind is spiraling out of control.

It's too big. It's all too much.

My head collapses into my hand as I slam into the tree beside me. I slide my back down it and sit on the ground. Shudders pulsate through me as the sharp sting of tears streak my face. I don't want this war people call life. I can't go anywhere I can't do anything I can't be here anymore. The world is a bloody mess that can't be fixed. Where's to go after that? Millions upon millions suffer and millions more do nothing because what can you do? I have no plans, just sorrow and a life that loses more meaning than it gains every day.

I sit against the tree late into the night, only bothering to get up and go back home once the biting cold begins to freeze the tips of my fingers and nose.

But even tucked away in my bed, I can't lose the chilling feeling that has now spread itself throughout my body.

I don't often feel super awesome, but right now I feel especially terrible. My forehead is sweaty. I'm feel both shaky and achy—cold and hot at the same time. I must be sick with whatever Cara had. I mean this is what having a fever is like, isn't it? I haven't been sick with one of these what seems like 37 years, but here we go, I guess. Am I being punished for failing that test?

I almost force myself to school, but my parents just got home from their trips the other night and stop me before I get to my car, telling me I look sick and need to go up to my room and rest. I could argue with them about it, but I'm too tired to fight, so I go to my room and crash down on my bed.

Man does it feel nice to lay down knowing I don't have to go anywhere. Though even when I get a glimpse of nice, there's always something ugly deep within me threatening to bubble up and explode.

I've just barely settled down with *The Body* when I hear a knock at my door and my dad comes in and walks over to my bedside.

"I wanted to check in with you before I left for work. How do you feel, honey?" he asks as he ruffles my hair.

"Not so great," I answer honestly, putting my book down and pulling my blanket in closer.

"Is that the fever talking, or is there something else going on?"

"I don't know."

He pauses and then sits down at the foot of my bed.

"Wren, you know your mother and I are here for you. If there's something bothering you, you can tell us."

"I know. I know I—" All of a sudden I can't talk so good.

He looks at me expectedly, and I try again but nothing comes out. I don't know what to say. How do I explain any of this?

Part of me doesn't want to tell my dad anything, but another part of me feels like a scared child that wants to be comforted. Both parts are horrible. Still, I should say at least something.

"Dad," I finally manage to get out, "the stuff that happened at the end of last year and over the summer, I think they really messed me up good."

He nods with understanding. "I know, they really did a number on you. Those were hard times."

I suppose he doesn't know that those hard times haven't yet ended.

"But I am proud of you for getting through them. You are stronger than you give yourself credit for. I'm late for work now, so I have to get going, but I want you to get some rest." With this, he kisses my forehead and walks out of my room, closing the door softly behind him.

He doesn't get it, but there's no way he could. I'm not strong; I'm dying inside. I hear the sound of his car leaving the driveway and then I am once again alone.

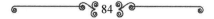

I haven't sobbed this hard in a long time. Everything hurts. But it doesn't matter anymore. This is the thought that repeats over and over in my mind as I fall into a feverish sleep.

I wake up a few hours later, still feeling sick, on the outside and inside.

I feel like crap: about myself, about where I am, about where I'm going. I don't know what to do.

I don't know what to do.

No one can help me now
I'm lost forever
Alone for eternity though that's not what they say to me
If I'm going then I just want to be gone
While they won't let me go, no one will bring me up
So then I'm drowning on my own
Too far to tell you what I need
I am just lost inside my dreams
You know if it's true than this must be
Be the end of me
N' I'm takin' this in stride
But there's nowhere left to cry
And there's no way to get out now
No matter what I do
We always end up right back here
All alone oh
Why'd you have to leave me
There was something great here
Now it's dead and gone
So what am I to do
If I really can't have you
Oh no one can help me now
Guess I'll have to make it on my own
'Cus no one can help me now
We take it all alone
No one can help me now
It's all passed away
Oh no one can help us now
Maybe we'll find our peace someday

CHAPTER 8

LESS THAN A FEELING

AIDAN HAD FOUND that it wasn't uncommon for Wren to abruptly go silent throughout class. But there was just something particularly off about her today, and it made him worry—she seemed legitimately sick. Of course, she wouldn't really let him help her and evaded all his questions. But, not wanting to push her away, he let her go.

Of course, this didn't mean he couldn't still *watch out* for her, though. They were psych partners, after all.

At lunchtime, he quietly walked with her to the school quad and stopped a few feet away as she continued toward a tree to sit under by herself. He considered sitting next to her, but a ringing sound from his pocket caused him to sigh in frustration and turn away. It was Noah—he felt sure of it—probably trying to figure out how his job at the record store was going, as in how much money was he making? His brother was flunking out of college and getting himself into some serious problems. Problems he had told Aidan not all that long ago that he had gotten rid of.

As he began walking to a more secluded area, he passed by that Bianca Davis girl and one of her friends. *Kate was her name*, he thought. *Yes, that was it.* He remembered her specifically because of the intense stares she had been giving him pretty much since the first day he arrived. And he remembered Bianca because she was Wren's friend and because she also frequently stared at him, though in a notably different way from that other girl, Kate.

While walking by, he caught a piece of their conversation—something to do with Wren and it didn't sound nice. As curious as he was to hear more, he shook his head and continued walking; he'd have to deal with that later, right now he needed to figure out what to do about his brother. Should he call him back or not?

But, when he did pick his phone up to dial Noah's number there was no answer. Resisting the urge to throw his phone on the ground and smash it, he made his way back over to go sit down next to Wren. However, she had disappeared. Or at least that was what it seemed like until he finally spotted her in what appeared to be a very intense conversation with Bianca and her friends. He immediately noticed that Kate stood particularly close to her, and Wren would have none of it. And then there was poor Eric, a boy Aidan didn't know personally well, who seemed to be caught in the middle of it all. Something was definitely up…

He left for less than five minutes, and she had already managed to go off and find trouble. Why was he not surprised?

Wasting no time, he rushed over to break it all up. But, even after everyone went separate ways, he could still sense there was something eating at Wren in a big way.

Upon following her to the school's back lot and finding her sitting on the ground with her head on her knees, his suspicions about her health were confirmed. She was, indeed, *not* all right. At least, that seemed a fair assumption to him as she slumped over unconsciously just as he managed to pick her body up from the pavement to carry her into the nurse's office.

I still feel kind'a sick this morning, but for once I don't want to be in my house right now. As I'm leaving, my mom asks me if I'm ok enough to go to school. I tell her I probably am even though I probably am not. She has to leave for work though, so she doesn't check to make sure.

At this point in time, I'm around eighty percent sure that my fever is mostly gone. I didn't sleep last night though so I have no clue what today is going to be like.

Still, nothing matters right now. It's all the same, and nothing matters. I don't even realize I forgot a jacket until I'm already at school.

I spend the majority of psych class staring at my hands as I play with the rubber bands around my wrists. We apparently have a mandatory field trip tomorrow to an old sanitarium. The teacher says she told us about it last month but I don't remember that happening at all. Anyhow, I don't want to go. Big surprise there, I know.

After class, Aidan comes up to me, wondering if there's something wrong with me.

"I'm fine."

"You seem sick."

"No I don't."

"Yeah, you do. And you're heating up too."

"Don't touch my forehead!"

"I think you should get some water and maybe go home."

"I think *you* should go home."

"You have a fever and—"

"No, I don't."

"How can you say that so surely?"

"I know everything."

Of course, that was a very bold statement to make and perhaps not entirely true…

At lunch, I don't want to talk with anyone so I sit by myself under a tree in the corner of the school quad, shivering in the cold January air.

I look up for a moment as I'm getting my earphones out and notice Bianca walking side-by-side with a friend. It's in this moment that I also notice Aidan passing by them as he does a double take, looking back at Bianca as though he wants desperately to say something to her. And as soon as he turns back around, Bianca turns over her shoulder to stare at him while he crosses to the other end of the quad.

It's interactions like these that make me hate school just simply for existing.

I put in my earphones and listen to the piano chords of "November Rain" for practice. I hear a fairly loud noise off in the distance. I look up to see a pile of books on the ground and an angry-looking Bianca, who is surrounded by a group of friends, going off on a tired-if-not-somewhat-anxious-looking Eric. I get up and take my earphones out as I start walking toward them—the "Queen" and her "Court", playing judge, jury, and executioner by the looks of it.

"Hey! What's up over here?" I shout.

Bianca rolls her eyes as she turns to face me. "Your assistance is really not needed right now."

I ignore her and put myself between Eric and the rest of them.

"Ok, so you wouldn't mind just moving along then," I say patiently.

"This idiot ran into me and didn't apologize."

"For the love of God Bianca, what are you, five?"

"Watch your mouth, Wren. Besides, why do you give a crap about this?" It's times like this that make me *really* glad Seth doesn't go to this school. He always was able to bring this side out of Bianca. Dating him must be rubbing off on her in a bad way. I'd say I didn't see this coming, but I did.

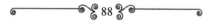

"They're both rude and weird. It's no wonder no one ever wants to sit with them," another girl says in an indifferent tone. I don't know who she is but she's annoying.

I look back at Eric and see him staring at the ground. I don't know what was said before I got here, but I can tell that it cut deep.

"In fact, you may be worse than him. You seem to just be a pointless maverick, inserting yourself into yet another matter that doesn't concern you," the girl continues.

"Careful," I say turning back around, "you shouldn't use your entire vocabulary in one sentence."

That really blows up her skirt, but I'm not interested in a big fight at the moment. Actually I think I might fall over right now if someone tapped me too hard.

"Just move along, ok?" I say.

"I don't think so."

"Look, I see you all standing here," I say, looking around the group of friends, "and you obviously think you're so cool, but how about you just… shove off?"

"Or what?" she asks, crossing her arms and stepping up uncomfortably close to me.

"Or I'm gonna punch you hard enough to break your nose," I say through my teeth. I'm talkin' big for someone who's starting to see in double vision. Guess my fever hasn't kicked the bucket just yet.

"Whoa, hey, what's going on?"

I look over my shoulder to see Aidan running up to us. As this happens, I motion for Eric to leave, and he does after giving me a small smile and nod. But there's something in his eyes as he leaves that makes my insides hurt.

"Is there a problem?" Aidan's voice is calm and collected but also authoritative. And with his tall, defined frame, serious expression, and leather jacket, he doesn't look like someone you would want to question.

Bianca's cheeks turn a rosy color. "Course not. Everything's cool," she grins nervously. "Come on, Kate," she hisses in a quieter voice as she attempts to pull her friend away from me. Oh yes, Kate. That's the girl's name.

Before she steps back, Kate leans in closer and whispers in my ear, "I'm not finished with you." And I know immediately this is just as much a threat as it is a promise.

Unsure of how the hell to respond to that, I start to walk away as a hand reaches out and grabs me by the shoulder. If he didn't have a firm grip I'd

probably have lost my balance. Then I'd fall down, down, down to the ground.

"Are you ok? What happened? What about Eric?" Aidan asks, leading me over to a more private corner. He sounds legitimately concerned, but even so, I don't want to talk to anyone right now.

"It's fine, Aidan." I wrap my arms around my waist.

"Why don't you have a jacket? And what was going on with you and Kate? Things seemed pretty tense."

"Like I said, it's fine." I have to get out of here.

"Fine?"

"Yes, I handled it."

"It doesn't exactly seem that way."

"Well, why don't you ask Bianca? I'm sure she'd be more than happy to tell you all about it."

His hand drops from my shoulder, and he looks at me sideways while I do my best not to stumble sideways. "What does that mean?"

I turn back around and continue walking.

"Nothing. Nothing."

I head to the back school parking lot and kick the fence blocking me from making an easy escape—*son of a bitch*. It's not usually locked. I feel like screaming.

School sucks, dance sucks, I suck. I'm lost inside myself, and I don't know how to get out. I reach a hand up to my forehead and feel the cold sweat on my burning skin. Should have gotten some water. I wrap my arms around myself and sit down on the ground, placing my head on my knees.

What more do I have to give?

"Wren? What're you doing back here?"

I don't look up but I can tell from his voice that it's Aidan. "Dying," I groan.

"Dying?"

"I really don't feel so well."

"Ok—"

"It all hurts, and I can't take it much more!"

"Listen to me, Wren. I think you're having a panic attack."

"Huh, really? Screw you, Aidan."

"It's ok, they're actually pretty common."

"No, I'm not having an 'attack', I just need to sit here a little while. I'll be fine. It's just some lightheadedness.

"You're shaking."

"Please stop talking."

"And having trouble breathing. I also noticed you're kind'a sweating and you seem nauseous…"

His voice is starting to sound distant. Like there is a veil between us and I'm floating farther and farther away—off to another planet maybe. I suddenly feel very sick, like if I open my mouth I'll surely throw up. My breathing quickens and my vision goes a little fuzzy as I begin to lower my head to the concrete.

"Whoa! What are you doing? Stay with me Wren, don't go passing out on me."

I vaguely hear Aidan continue saying things to me as I begin to close my eyes, but I can't quite process it. I probably just need…

***

I can see her now, only a few feet away from me.

"Vi?" I ask.

She doesn't answer; her back is turned away from me. She's watching something.

"Violet!" I call out again.

She can't hear me.

I walk over to her, to see what she's seeing. We are suddenly on a balcony, high above a stage. I peer down at the stage, desperately trying to understand.

There's a dancer, moving across it—jumping, gliding, turning.

I look to Violet, but now there are more people surrounding me, and I can't get to her. My parents, Cara, people from my studio, and Seth, are all watching the stage. I look at the dancer and then back to him, his hard eyes fixated on her as his mouth grows into a chilling smile.

Then, a bright light begins shining on me. I can't see anything.

***

I open my eyes and find myself lying on a bed staring up at the fluorescent lights of the school nurse's office. I sit up quickly and grimace. God, my head is humming like the piper's calling to me.

"How do you feel?"

I look over to the corner of the room to see Aidan lounging back in a chair.

"Like I've been knockin' on heaven's door. How did I get here?"

"Ok, good. Your ability to make references at any time is still intact.

And I brought you here. The nurse left just a second ago. She said you've got a fever and probably haven't eaten enough or something."

Oh, God, *he* had to bring me here? "Great. Can I get out of here now?"

"Sure. Do you want me to take you home?"

"No, I drove myself. Thanks for, uh, helping me and stuff..." My cheeks are beginning to flush. I need him to go away.

"Course. How about I come over, just to make sure you're okay."

I look down and try avoiding eye contact, but I can still feel the heat rising in my face. I can't believe I passed out. "No, that's all right."

"I'm serious, Wren—"

"Get out of my face, Aidan."

I didn't mean it to come out as harsh as it did and as soon as the words leave my mouth I regret them. I swear I see a flash of pain pass over his usually confident-looking face before being replaced by a crooked grin.

"Ok, Evans. See you later then."

Before I can respond, he gets up and walks out the door.

I slip down from the bed and start to follow him when I suddenly stop and notice what I'm wearing. It's a large leather jacket—much too large to be mine. And while it smells good, it doesn't have the same scent as anything I wear. But the scent is familiar—this is Aidan's jacket.

***

All the way home, still wearing the jacket, something is gnawing at my stomach, and I think I know what. I must be the worst person alive.

Once I get inside my house, I take off the jacket and examine it. On the inside is a name, but the name isn't Aidan—it's Noah. Noah? Who is that? Regardless, I'm still sure this is Aidan's jacket and I need to return it to him.

I consider playing the piano to figure out what's bothering me but, for some reason, I don't feel like doing that at all. Instead, I pick up my guitar and stare at it, trying to think of something to play. Suddenly, I get an idea. I grab my keys and run out the door, driving myself to Aidan's house. Good thing I already know how to get there.

I knock on the door and step back, waiting anxiously. He opens the door and looks pretty surprised to see me, and even more surprised when he sees my guitar case.

"Hey," I say, "mind if I come in for a sec?"

"Uh, hey, Wren," he mumbles as he adjusts his hoodie and smooths back his messy hair. "Yeah, please come in."

His neighborhood is rough, of course that doesn't put me off in the slightest, and his house is small. But the inside of his house is nice, not in like a fancy way, more of a "you-can-tell-they-try-and-take-care-of-their-stuff" kind of way. I like it.

Still, Aidan looks almost embarrassed as I step through his doors. He quickly kicks some things lying on the floor under a table.

"Here's your jacket," I say, handing it to him. "Can I show you something?"

"You gonna play a song for me?" he wonders, taking the jacket and eyeing the guitar case again.

"That's the idea."

He motions over to the couch and we both sit down as I get my guitar out.

"Okay, I haven't tried playing this in a while, so don't be too hard on me when I mess up."

"Wouldn't dream of it," he promises, a smile tugging at the corner of his mouth.

Before I can talk myself out of it, I begin playing the solo from "Sweet Child O' Mine". I mess it up—a lot—but Aidan still seems to enjoy it.

"Whoa! I didn't know I was psych partners with Slash," he exclaims when I've finished.

"Eat me! I know I'm not that good, but at least I learned it." I'm a bit surprised he could even recognize what it was supposed to be. Seriously, my playing is atrocious.

"No, I'm serious, you're good Wren. That solo isn't easy; you've got some talent. I would know because I also play guitar."

"I didn't know you played guitar, why didn't you ever bring it up?"

"There are a lot of things you don't know about me," he says seriously. "Anyway, thanks for playing it. That's my all-time favorite guitar solo."

"I know, I remembered."

Neither of us says anything for a few minutes until Aidan finally speaks first.

"Hey, if you could stay a bit, want to watch the *Live at the Ritz 88* concert? I managed to buy a VHS of it online a long time ago."

A warm feeling spreads through me when he says this. I freaking love that goddamn concert.

CHAPTER 9

TOO FAST FOR FEAR

TODAY, I'M SUPPOSED TO GO on that sanitarium field trip for psych class, but after yesterday's somewhat embarrassing event I am seriously considering ditching it. I know that Aidan doesn't think any different of me, at least I don't think he does, but I worry something similar might happen when he's not the only one around to witness it. Still, before I left his house, I told him I might possibly think about being there so I suppose I should go.

Weird psychology field trip here I come. If it's anything like the last one, then it's sure to be interesting...

I arrive at school a bit late and everyone is already on the bus, making me quite nervous to get on. I hate it when you're late to a thing and every-one stares. Yet I convince myself to get on it anyway, holding my breath as I climb the bus steps and begin looking around for somewhere to sit. I see Ella sitting with an open spot next to her. She motions for me to come over, but I do not want to do that at all. I'm trying to make up an excuse for why I have to sit somewhere else when a voice calls out to me.

"Wren!" I look to the back of the bus where I see Aidan waving to me. I don't know what he's waving for though because he's sitting on the inside of a booth with Bianca right next to him, leaving no room for someone else to sit. I make my way toward the back, passing straight by Ella, and pause by them to say hello.

"Hey, Aidan," I smile weakly. "Bianca," I add with a small head nod. "I'm going to go sit over here I think," I say, taking a seat at the very last empty booth.

"Wait!" Aidan turns around in his seat to look at me and then at Bianca, pondering a decision. He seems to have made up his mind as he begins climbing over his seat back.

"Mr. Grey! Sit back down this instant!" our teacher yells out at him from somewhere at the front of the bus. But he ignores them and takes the empty seat next to me.

"I thought you weren't coming on this?" he asks once settled in.

I shrug and look up at him. "Yeah well, here I am."

"And you're a rocket queen," he sings, finishing the lyrics with a smirk. "What?" he questions as he notices my wide-eyed face. "You're not the only one that listens to *Appetite*."

"I know, I'm glad you like it." I lean back, putting my arms behind my head.

"So what made you change your mind about coming here?" He changes back the subject.

"I don't know," I respond semi-truthfully.

"I thought you knew everything though."

"Yes, well if I claim to be wise it surely means I don't know."

"Ok, a Kansas reference. So that's the kind of day this is going to be?"

"Oh please, you love Kansas."

"Yeah, you're right, I do. Oh, and if you didn't want to come because you're worried you might pass out again, it's ok, I'll catch you if you do."

"Bite me, Aidan. I can handle myself."

"Could have fooled me."

"Yes, well that's not exactly a difficult thing to accomplish now is it?"

He stares at me quizzically for a second before breaking out into a large grin. "I'm just messing with you."

I glare at him and put in my earphones, pressing shuffle on my playlist. He immediately grabs my phone and starts pressing buttons.

"What are you listening to?" he interrogates curiously.

"A great song called none of your business."

"Come on, at least give me one earphone—I'm bored. Don't leave me here on this bus alone."

"Fine," I give in, taking my cell phone back and giving him my right earphone. "But if we're gonna do this, let's play a game."

"A game?" he asks, confused.

"Yes, I'll put on a song and then you'll put one on and each time we have to guess which song it is the other has chosen as fast as we can."

"You're on!"

The score ends up as an even fifty/fifty, with Aidan getting the songs "War Pigs", "Run To The Hills", "My Michelle", "Blaze of Glory", and "Fear Of The Dark" and me getting "Turn the Page", "Heartbreak Hotel", "Last Child", "Too Fast For Love", and "No One Like You". We decide to leave the competition at this and spend the rest of the ride with our eyes closed, listening to whatever comes on.

A few hours later we reach our destination, an old sanitarium with thick ivy growing all over it. Aidan gently wakes me up to inform me that we've arrived. At first I'm completely disoriented, but then embarrassment sobers my mind as I realize I've been leaning my head on his shoulder. I quickly sit up and mumble an apology.

Amazing how I have trouble sleeping in my own bed but can manage to nod off on a goddamn school bus to sleep on someone else. Aidan doesn't say anything, but he looks as though he's about to tell me something just as the teacher yells at us from the front of the bus to get out because everyone else has already filed off and into pairs.

We're supposed to be going around with our partners from class and taking notes on whatever we can. The whole idea is that we'll get an understanding of how mental health used to be thought of and treated. I'll be honest, it's pretty interesting stuff—though not as interesting as the aquarium field trip. I check out inmate cells, rooms for electroshock therapy, lobotomy/surgery rooms, and a few unlabeled places that look like they may have been used as laboratories.

Everyone, including Aidan, seems to be at least a little disturbed if not completely "creeped" out by the place. I feel more fascination than fear toward it all. The only thing that messes me up about it is thinking about how I probably would have been kept away in one of these places if I'd lived back in these times. I don't bother to take notes on any of the stuff; I just look around and read all the descriptions to myself.

"Hey, there you are! You went so fast, I lost you," Aidan calls as he runs up to me.

"Maybe you're just slow," I joke.

"Whatever. We've been walking around for almost an hour now, how about we call it good and compare notes."

"I didn't take any notes."

"Still, I'd rather be sitting than standing here looking at more creepy, musty insane people's rooms."

We find a corner that's kind of out of the way from where everyone else is and sit down.

"Man, doesn't this place give you a weird feeling?"

"I suppose, though I think I get more of a sad feeling from it."

"Yeah, it must've sucked being locked in here all the time. What do

you imagine it was like?"

"Hell, probably…" I say, staring at the cracks running along the old stone floor.

"Wren, is something bothering you?"

I shake my head.

"At least this isn't the way things are anymore," Aidan says.

"Not that they've got super great treatments now though."

"Maybe not, but some things do help a lot. Like therapists these days actually know what they're doing, and we have medication and all that stuff."

"I don't know how much I trust therapists…"

"What makes you say that?"

I reluctantly tell him a little bit about what happened with the school counselor.

"That sucks. But one bad experience doesn't define them all," he comments after I've finished. "Just trust me on this one, ok? It helps."

I look into his eyes and can tell he's being serious.

We then decide to get up and go walking through the rooms some more when, out of nowhere, I get a crazy idea. I won't get back on the bus and once everyone leaves I'll hang out here for a while. The teacher didn't even take roll or anything so if I don't go with them, she won't notice.

I tell Aidan that I am getting picked up from here by my ride and that I won't be there the rest of the school day.

While he and everyone else are boarding the bus, I hide in one of the dark inmate cells and wait there until they're gone. But, as they drive off, I'm having second thoughts about my decision to stay here.

My parents are going to be worried about me—I ought to let them know that I won't be home for a while because I'm stuck out in the middle of nowhere due to the fact that I purposefully chose not to get back on the one means of transportation that could take me back—but I won't. I know I should, it's just that I don't like that idea all that much because I bet they'll be kind of upset with me.

You see, my parents are some of the few people whose opinions I actually care about—I mean, even after what happened… when I got kicked out and when they had to pay all that money to the school for damages—they still listened to me. I can't say for sure that they know I'm telling the truth about it, but at least they listened. That's a lot more than most people did.

But the fact that I respect my parents sometimes surprises people. In fact, after finding out I had problems listening to authority, a lot of the psychologists I went to see when I was younger would ask my parents about what I would do to rebel against them. But the thing is, I never rebelled against my parents to begin with. Even now, I always listen to them, because I *respect* them. I trust them. Not liking being told I have to be obedient doesn't mean that I run around disrespecting people for no reason.

Sure I believe in fighting the system, but if someone has a good reason for doing the things they do, I will follow along. But if you're going be a dumbass, then I'm going treat you like one. Though, honestly, as I'm making this long walk back, watching the sky slowly get darker and darker, I'm starting to think *I'm* the real dumbass here. Why didn't I just get on the freakin' bus?

Too bad I don't have my switchblade with me. I'm kind of nervous for some reason, being out here alone in the night. I'm not sure why. I usually don't scare easy but right now my heart beats like crazy, and I keep waiting for something to jump out at me. Even if something did jump out or try to get me, I would probably still be fine. If they tried to catch me running—well then I really wouldn't have to worry. I am very fast. No one can catch me if I don't want to be caught.

Despite all this, my nerves don't calm. People usually tell me I should be scared of this sort of thing, because it's not safe to be a girl and walk around at night alone, and I usually tell them in my head to shove off. But, I don't know, maybe it's finally getting to me. You can't outrun the crap in your brain, I'll tell you that much. Doesn't matter how fast you are, it'll always catch you.

Even though it might be a little creepy out here at night, walking out here on my own gives me time alone with my thoughts. Because, you know, I need more of that.

Right now, the thing that pops into my brain, and I can't say why, is helping people. For some reason, that's where my mind goes as soon as I start thinking about thinking. It's not exactly a new thought, though, I mean I sort'a feel like I have to be helping people, somehow, all the time. Because if I'm not helping people, what am I doing? I should get in Nightrider, mileage be damned, and drive across the country hopping in and out of places like "Is everyone good here? Oh, there's a mean person? Let me take care of them for you" and then move on to the next place and go on like that until I help everyone I can. I'd just go around taking up people's pain and hardship while kicking bullies into next Thursday. Problem is, this isn't practical apparently, and also I haven't the confidence to do it anyhow. Still, I just want to do the right thing. I want to be *good*, but I need a sign. Something to tell me I can or that I'm on the right path.

Too bad the universe only sends signs very rarely—if at all.

***

I get home late, like the 'middle-of-the-night' late. But, somehow, my parents are both still awake and waiting for me as soon as I walk through the door.

"Wren, you cannot simply send us a message saying you'll be home 'a lot later than you are supposed to' and then not answer when we call you!"

"Sorry, I wasn't checking my phone while I walked back."

"You walked back? From where?"

"A sanitarium."

"A what?"

"A—"

"How the hell did you think that would be ok?"

"I think I want to see a therapist," I say abruptly.

CHAPTER 10

UNFORTUNATE SON

"AIDAN, I KNOW this is all really hard right now, but I'm going to try and come up to see you soon," Noah said from the other end of the phone.

"You always say that, but then you never actually do it. How can I take you seriously?"

"I'm your big brother, I—"

"Yes!" Aidan shouted, cutting him off. "You *are* my big brother! So I shouldn't be worrying about you getting arrested and about sending you money or anything like that. You were supposed to be looking out for me!"

"I do look out for you, more than you know."

"Save it. I'm going to be late for school if I don't leave soon. I need to go."

"Wait! I'm sorry, I just—just this one time, I need your help."

"Just this one time? *Just* this one time?"

"Aidan…"

"Fine! I'll send it all to you, just give me time to get it together, ok? I don't get this month's paycheck from the record store until next week."

"It's not just that. I've been having some…" Noah paused, "…other problems."

"Other problems?"

"Yes."

"Well, what are they?"

By the time Aidan's conversation with his brother had ended, he was already 20 minutes late to school. But it really didn't matter anymore.

He suddenly seemed very small, and the world around him, very dark.

What he wanted to do was go find his mother, but he already knew that she wasn't home and that she wouldn't be home for a long time. So, instead, he sat down on his bed and held his head in his hands. He sat this way until he was finally able to stand and walk himself to school. He would be extremely late, but going was better than staying where he was. In fact, anything was better than staying where he was.

On his way out the door, he instinctively picked up the old, slightly worn leather jacket Noah had sent him over winter break and began to put it on. Then, abruptly, he stopped and harshly threw the jacket across the room, watching it land on the coffee table. The hardness in his eyes softened as he spotted a VHS lying out on the table next to it. It was the *GN'R Live at the Ritz 1988* VHS. He walked over and picked it up, a slight bit of the weight on his heart lifting.

It hadn't been that long ago that he'd played this for the first time, and he could clearly remember the day he bought it. Aidan still wasn't sure *why* he ran out to buy a copy of it a few weeks ago, and he certainly wasn't sure why he told Wren he'd had it since "a long time ago."

Whatever the reason, he couldn't afford to think too much about it now. There was too much going on. If he did think about it, it would overwhelm him to the breaking point. That is, if he wasn't already broken.

I can't sit still. I keep squirming in my seat, rockin' back and forth.

"Wren Evans?"

I look up and see a young woman standing at the door. She seems a little too young to be a therapist, but oh well.

Let's get this damn thing over with.

After last night, my parents decided it was a good idea for me to see a professional, so they set me up with someone who specializes in teens and depression. They said they would come with me if they could, but both of them had to rush off to the airport this morning for business trips or something.

I walk into her office feeling shaky and disoriented. I hope to hell that things go better this time around than the last time I tried something like this.

"Hello, my name is Amelia," the therapist says as I sit down. She has a nice voice; I like it.

"Wren."

"I'm glad to finally get to meet you, Wren. I've talked with your parents a few times over the phone." Damn. I only told my parents like yesterday, when did they have time to set all this up?

"How about you start by telling me what's on your mind," she says.

"Like right now?"

She nods.

"Well, I guess I'm pretty nervous right about now. And I'm worried about my life at dance; my ankle has been hurting for a while; and about my friendships at school. I seem to lose people a lot, sometimes it seems like people like me real well for a little while and then all of a sudden don't want anything to do with me anymore. It always hurts no matter who does it, but there's one person that…" I stop myself before saying her name.

"One person that what?"

"Never mind."

"Wren, who are you talking about?"

"My friend, Violet. Or at least she used to be my friend."

"Can you tell me what happened?"

This woman asks a lot of questions too, but she asks them in a nice way, a way that I can tell is sincere, unlike that other counselor.

"We went to dance together for a while and… I'm not sure exactly what happened, only that now we don't talk so much these days. It began some time last year, right before summer, I think. I just finally realized that I was no good for her. It's for the best. I can't seem to feel anything right anymore, and I don't want to drag her down with me. Besides, whatever connection we used to have, I doubt there's anything left of it."

"Did you ever think that the reason you don't want to talk to Violet is because she is someone who can actually make you feel something, and that scares you?"

Jesus Christ. This is why I hate therapy.

"Uh, no." I can feel my eyes narrowing.

"Tell me about your relationship with her."

"With Violet?"

"No, with some other random person that we weren't just discussing."

Ok, I see how it is. "Ha, ha, ha, funny. And I don't know how to tell you about my relationship with her."

"Try."

"We were great friends, and now we're not. It just is what it is, ok? We met when we were like seven-years old, and our first interaction I can remember is when I pushed her down in the sandbox because she kept trying to play with me and I wanted to be left alone. But then later that day, I saw this other kid picking on her and for some reason it made me kind of mad. And then *he* pushed her down on the ground and before I knew what I was doing, I was sitting on him and punching his face yelling 'No one gets to push her around but me!'. And that was the first time I ever got in real trouble. But, from then on we were kind of like best buds, so it was worth it."

"It was?"

"Yeah. We started doing just about everything together. And the older we got, the closer we became, which isn't usually the case with friend- ships, in my personal experience. I think I tend to push people away 'before they can hurt me', according to my mom. But I didn't do this with Vi. She stayed with me, even when I was going through some rough times—times that kind of changed me, in some ways. At least that's the way it was until we got into a fight, a serious fight... and then, all of a sudden, it hit me that while our friendship was good for me, maybe it wasn't all that good for her. And after that, gradually things just seemed to deteriorate between us. I stopped coming over, and she stopped calling me until one day we just weren't talking anymore. There's some other stuff about it too that I... never mind." My eyes begin to burn. "I don't want to talk about it any- more, please."

"It sounds like you are experiencing a loss of one form or another. Might I give you an outside assignment to complete before our next meeting?"

There's gonna be another one? "I don't know, you tell me," I shrug.

"I want you to look into the five stages of grief."

"The five stages of—are you serious?"

"Yes."

***

In the evening, I sit down at the piano and begin playing, my fingers gliding across the keys as all my worries seem to drift away. I know the therapist said to look into the stages of grief, but we both know I'm not really going to do that.

So I keep playing.

There's just something about it that feels so right. "November Rain"— in the middle of January.

At the moment, my sister is sleeping over at a friend's and my parents are both away on business trips, meaning I have the house to myself. For someone so lonely, I sure like to be alone.

I haven't been to the movies in what feels like forever, and I kind'a want to go now. But at the same time, I don't want to go at all and I'd prob- ably die if I did. I just don't feel like being around people at the moment.

So, I end up staying at home on my own.

I eat a bunch of ice cream, bake a cake, work more on "November Rain", and dance around my house in the dark while blasting some good old-fashioned hard rock. I even get out my sketchbook to "draw out my feelings" like the therapist suggested at the end of our session. And after I do all this, I put on one of my favorite films ever. It's a Buster Keaton film, which means it's also black and white and silent. Still, I like it. I like his deadpan style and refusal to smile—after all, I don't smile much myself. But I find his movies pretty funny, so I guess I smile during them.

Ahh, what a perfect night... Keeping myself occupied with all these different activities helps me to un-cloud my mind and focus on the good things in life, even if it just lasts for a little while. I even manage to fall asleep before 1:00 a.m. and don't end up waking in the middle of the night as I always do.

***

Unfortunately, my good fortune does not follow me into the next day.

It's only second period and Ella is already getting on my nerves. She's one of those people who, in her second semester of psychology, think she can diagnose anything in anyone. Add "people who pretend to know things they don't know jack about" to the list of things I hate.

For some God-forsaken reason, I am her focus of the day. So far she's told me I have depression (which to be fair is probably correct) and possible bipolar personality disorder (definitely not) along with anxiety and maybe even some high-functioning antisocial personality disorder. Just when I think she's done, she follows me out of English class and down the hall while going on about some *new* disorder she just now came up with specifically for me.

"Hey, Ella?" I interrupt her. "No offense, but if you say one more word about how messed up you think I might be, I'm going to invert your ribcage before pulling it up through your throat."

"You hide behind a wall of dark humor," she says gravely.

"Oh, good one."

"You need to get more sleep."

"I'm sorry, is today 'list-things-that-are-real-freakin'-obvious day'?"

Her lips form into a pout, and she gives me a slightly pissed and offended expression before turning on her heel and heading back down the hallway.

Freaking high school kids, man.

I proceed to step inside my next class, environmental science, muttering things to myself and imagining what it would be like to kick Ella in the face. Caught up in my own head, I forget to be aware of my surroundings

and run into someone. I apologize and look up to see that it's Aidan.

"Oh, Aidan, I didn't see you."

"It's fine," he mumbles hurriedly while avoiding looking me in the eyes. Hmm—that's strange—no little, witty comment or annoying half-smirk.

I don't say anything else as we take our seats, but I notice that his eyes seem a bit puffier and have a red tinge to them. I try not to stare for the rest of the period, but it's difficult. He's just sitting there in the corner, tugging on the strings of his hoodie while he sinks lower and lower into his chair as the class goes on. Needless to say, I'm not used to this Aidan.

Once the bell rings, I pack up my things slowly, watching him as he leaves. I then follow him out to his locker to talk and internally groan as I see that Bianca has cornered him already. I consider leaving them be for a second, but I take one look at how *tired* he is, just standing there—running his hands through his rumpled hair—as if he would like to be anywhere else, and I know I have to do something. After all, he's been there for me before, now I'll be there for him.

"Howdy partners, what's up?" My greeting could have been a little subtler.

"Wren, so good to see you," Bianca smiles without a trace of warmth behind her eyes, "but me and Aidan are kind of in the middle of a conversation here so…"

"That's awesome, but uh I'm going to take him away anyway."

He gives me a puzzled look but doesn't resist as I grab him by the hand and pull him outside. Bianca makes another comment as I do this but I don't hear what it is, which is probably for the best.

"Ok," I say once we're out of the school hallway, "what is going on?"

"Wren, it's nothing you need to worry about."

"If you're worried about it, even if I don't know what *it* is, then…"

"Please, I can't get into this right now. Not here. Not now."

"All right, but you gotta understand that you can talk to me. When you're ready, I'm here."

Aidan looks up from the ground and into my eyes. He doesn't say anything, but his expression tells me more than words ever could.

After school, I offer to take him home (he always walks) and he accepts. I'm not sure if I should ask him about what's upsetting him or not. I don't have to decide because Aidan is the one who brings it up.

"It's my brother who's giving me trouble right now," he says as I pull out of the parking lot.

"I didn't know you had a brother, what's his name?" I swear this guy keeps so much to himself.

"Noah. I don't talk about him much because, well, I guess it's hard for me. He's older and already moved out and on to college, but he has a lot of issues."

"Oh," I respond, remembering the name from the inside of Aidan's jacket. Speaking of which, I can't help but notice he's not wearing it today. I'm not sure if I should be pressing for more information.

"Just some bad run-ins with the law and... other stuff. When he comes back home—*if* he comes back, I'm not sure how to deal with him. I mean I'm not sure how to deal with him *now*. I want to help but I just don't know."

"I'm sorry. Family is hard," I say, taking my eyes off the road for a moment to glance at him. He doesn't seem quite as sad anymore.

"Yes, it sure is."

We don't talk about his brother or other problems for the rest of the drive over; instead we focus the time on talking about homework and music. I tell him about this 10-plus minute version of GN'R recording "November Rain" way back in '86 with just a piano and singing. I'm not saying it beats the official version, but it's pretty damn good. We also go over which bands are our favorites. I list off Guns, Zeppelin, Sabbath, Crue, Iron Maiden, and others, and he names Lynyrd Skynyrd, Zeppelin, Kansas, Bob Seger, Elvis, and The Stones.

When we get there, he asks if I want to come in and I decide that, sure, I want to. I didn't exactly think about it until now, but he lives at least twenty minutes by car from school. That has be a long walk to make every single day.

Aidan makes us a snack of grilled cheese while I sit on a stool next to him and talk his ear off about different movies and albums. I'm usually not one for talking a whole lot, in fact I'm usually told I don't speak enough, but right now I sort of feel different.

After we eat, he starts telling me about a band that he's put together of him, an old childhood friend he hasn't seen in a while, and some guy they found by putting an ad in the local newspaper.

"That's awesome, Aidan," I say, genuinely impressed. I had no idea he was this involved in music.

"Yeah, it's pretty cool. We're actually trying to work out a gig right now, and we've been practicing for it for a while. Do you ever make your own music?"

"Not really."

"You don't do covers or anything?"

"I do a few covers and sometimes I write my own songs, but I just keep them away in the back of my mind somewhere. I don't actually use 'em or anything."

"Can I hear one?"

"I don't know if that's a good idea."

"Oh come on," he begs, looking at me with the face of a sad puppy.

"Wow! You are a hard one to say no to."

"It's a talent."

"Fine, but I need a piano then."

"You mean a slightly broken keyboard? Sure thing."

He takes me to his keyboard. I sit down, running my hands over the keys while taking in a deep breath. Then I begin playing.

"Tell me your hidden sorrows, n' I'll make it ok
Give me a place in your heart, and don't look back today
The past is gone and so it will remain
Sometimes people are there for you,
And sometimes only the winds of shadows can be blamed
If you don't give me your hand now, I'll be lost out here forever now
Searching for somethin' that I'll never find
So don't take that away from me 'cus I can't love without anyone to be mine
If I am the only one, then what does that make you
If I'm the only one
Isn't there another place, someday we'll find another way
The rains are coming down hard, telling me not to cry this time
But no one told me this would be and I won't fall away and die."

I hit the final chord and hold it until it fades out on its own.

"Wow. Does it have a name?"

"I was thinking Hidden Sorrows, then again that may be too soppy for my taste. Hmm, yeah definitely too soppy."

"Can I ask you a favor?"

"Course."

"Will you sing with me and my band at the end of the month for my friend's talent show? That's the gig I was talking about."

"What?"

"Well, you see, it's just me and two other guys but none of us are singers, and we haven't been able to go out and find someone to sing with us. I mean, my friend Sebastian found a guy to begin with, but then he left after only a few rehearsals. Anyway, I think you'd be perfect, and it would only be for a little while."

"What's the band name?"

"Renegades."

"What songs would we do?"

"We've been working on 'Rocket Queen'."

"Seriously? 'Rocket Queen'? Out of all the damn songs in the world, that's the one you decide to try and take to a school talent show?"

"Everyone would be high schoolers there, they can handle it. Besides, I know you love 'Rocket Queen'."

"I'm not worried about the high schoolers, it's the teachers that are gonna be a problem. Why not 'Sweet Child O' Mine'?"

"I was hoping we could keep that—well I just thought 'Rocket Queen' fit the band better."

"Okay, just know we might be chased off the stage."

"Yeah, maybe. Are you in?"

"Sure."

He smiles and pushes off from the wall he'd been leaning against and walks back into the kitchen saying he'll get some drinks.

"Hey, Aidan."

"Yes?"

"If you want, I could start giving you rides to school and back."

There's silence for a few moments. "Uh, thanks for offering, but I'm probably going to get my own car soon anyways…"

"Ok." I can't see his face but his voice tells me not to press further.

***

As soon as I get to my car, I sit there for a while and wonder what exactly I just got myself into. On one hand, I don't even know if I can sing the song, and on the other, even if I kind'a can I'll be terrified to sing it in front of people.

I am so screwed.

CHAPTER 11

BOYS, BOYS, BOYS

I'VE BEEN CONCENTRATING ON MY PREDICAMENT this week and have found that I don't have what it takes to get in front of an audience and give a performance. Even when I'm just dancing, I still get real nervous every time I go on stage, and I've been doing that since I was born. But singing is a whole other story. I have never really sung in front of anybody, except for my sister when we're just being silly together and now Aidan.

The pressure weighing down on me every time I think about it is stifling. I have to tell Aidan I can't do it. I've been avoiding him so I don't have to say it, but he needs to know.

Preparing to give him the news, I go over to his house and knock on the door. No one comes to answer. While I'm waiting there, I hear music coming from within the house. Sounds like he's blasting some rock and probably won't be able to hear me knocking. This being said, I take the liberty of trying the doorknob and find it unlocked. I call out into the house and when no one answers, I step inside. I follow the sound of music as it increasingly becomes louder. I find my way to what I'm pretty sure is the garage. I take a deep breath and open the door.

Aidan is in there along with two other guys, all of whom are in the middle of playing a song. Aidan quickly stops when he sees me uncomfortably standing in the doorframe.

"Hey, I had no idea you would be here today, this is great—we can finally practice full out!"

"Umm, about that, can I talk to you for a second?"

He walks over to me. I tell him that I can't take part in the talent show thing. He tries to convince me otherwise, but I turn him down. Even still, he keeps trying.

"You gotta at least meet the band though."

"Ok," I agree reluctantly as he leads me over to the other two boys.

Boys are something I find pretty interesting, but they can also make me kind'a nervous. I don't all the way understand them, but I'd like to understand them more, if given the chance.

"That's Tommy on the drums," Aidan says, pointing to a guy with a boyish face and long, reddish-brown hair, "and Sebastian on the bass," he nods to a tall, more serious looking guy with short, curly black hair. "He's the one who put the band together."

After he introduces his band-mates, he turns and motions to me. "Guys, this is Wren."

"And we are the Renegades!" Tommy shouts proudly, doing a little bow from behind his drum set.

"No, Tommy," Aidan puts his hand on his forehead and leans in closer to him, lowering his voice, "we've talked about this. There's no 'the', it's just Renegades."

"Why?"

"'Cus it's like Eagles and Scorpions and because it's— 'cus it just is! Ok?"

"Ok, whatever," Tommy says shrugging. Then he turns toward me, "Nice to meet you, Wren. We're real glad you're here, we desperately need a singer."

This makes me feel guilty.

Both guys are friendly toward me. Tommy seems genuinely happy that I'm there while Sebastian appears slightly unsure of me. I don't blame him. I'm just some weird girl interrupting their band practice. What's strange though is that he sort of reminds me of someone... but I can't place it.

We all talk with each other for a little while, and it doesn't take me long to deduce that Sebastian is the one Aidan has known longer. They all get along great, but there's a slightly different feeling to their friendship that comes with having known someone for a long while. It's something I remember having with Violet.

Then, before I realize what he's doing, Aidan goes over to where he left his guitar and picks it up. As he walks back to me, he scoops up the microphone and holds it out to me. *Aw shoot.*

"Aidan, you know I just came here to tell you I can't do it."

"Aw come on, Wren!" Tommy pleads, flipping his drumsticks up in the air. "We need you."

"It would only be a few practices and a one-night performance," Sebastian adds, though he still seems like he's suspicious of me.

"I don't think it's a good idea."

"Before you go, you have to try it once," Aidan says determinedly.

"No I don't."

"Evans, please—"

"No."

"Do you know the words?"

"Of course I know the words."

"Great! Then it's settled!" he exclaims, clapping his hands together.

Before I can protest anymore, Tommy kicks off on the drums and Aidan and Sebastian join in. *Well, this is going to be awesome.*

***

Here's the thing, I was going to *not* do it, but it went well. It went really well. In fact, singing that damn song made me happier than I've felt in weeks.

"Okay, okay! You win, I'll do it!" I tell them.

"I knew you could do it," Aidan smiles smugly.

"But, uh, what about the sounds that are supposed to be in the middle section?" I ask, referring to the interesting, and most certainly inappropriate, noises made around the halfway point of the song.

"What about 'em?" Tommy asks. "We don't have a problem with them."

"I figured as much, but how are going to swing that at a school performance?"

"I guess we'll just have to figure out how to put them in. I mean, is it really 'Rocket Queen' without them?"

I ponder this for a second and decide that if we're going to do the song, then we might as well do the *whole* song. "Yeah, the lyrics alone will be enough to get us tossed out of there, but keeping the noises in will send it over the top."

"Awesome, so it's decided," Aidan says, nodding in agreement.

"Hang on," I forgot about one thing, "who is going to *make* the sounds?"

"You of course," Sebastian states as if it's the most obvious thing. "Who else?"

"No," I deadpan.

"Come on!"

"I said no."

"I'll do it then," Tommy says happily, pumping his fist in the air.

"No you won't, you need all of what little concentration you have when playing the drums," Sebastian says dismissively.

"It's ok, we'll figure it out later," Aidan reasons.

Not feeling the need to stick around any longer, I decide to make my exit. As I'm getting into my car, Sebastian comes up to me.

"Wren, I know that you are new to all this, but I want you to understand that this band isn't just messing around. What we do is important to us, and I will always do whatever is necessary to ensure that the best interests of the band are preserved."

Sounds like a roundabout way of telling me to shove off.

"I understand, Sebastian." Guess I figured right about him not liking me. I mean, I had already noticed him glancing at me strangely while we were all talking, but this seems to confirm my suspicions.

"I just want to make sure that things are going to go well because I don't want it to end after the talent show, our plans are bigger than that. And 'Rocket Queen' is a hard song to pull off—"

"I get it, thanks," I say, leaning back against my car door wishing to God that I didn't show up today.

Before he can say anything else, Aidan comes over.

"Can I talk to you for a minute before you take off?" he asks me.

"Sure."

Sebastian shakes his head and walks back inside.

"Don't mind Bash, he's just a bit slow to warm to people sometimes," Aidan tells me once he's gone. "He's a bit older than me so he was actually a friend of my brother's before he knew me, and it still took me almost half a year to get him to consider me an actual friend. Of course, now we're closer than he ever was with Noah," he adds as though he is thinking about something as he says it.

"I hope you're right."

"So, anyway, are you going to the Spring Formal? It's a long way off, not until May, but I was just wondering."

"Me? No, I didn't even know we had one—school dances are not my thing. Are you going?"

"Umm probably not, I was just wondering—trying to figure out if dances here are worth going to or not."

"Hey, if you're curious, I think you should go. And who knows, maybe it'll be fun."

"You think so?"

"Yeah, for sure."

"Ok, well see you Monday."

"Yep, see you then."

It's the weekend, and I feel like going out and doing something. I don't have a clue what that *thing* is, but I do not want to sit around all day today. If I did, I'd probably drive myself crazy stressing about singing with Aidan's band—or Renegades, I mean. Yeah, sure, it's just a high school talent show—and not even for my high school—but when you don't know anything about singing and performing this kind'a thing it's crazy scary to think about.

Also, there's the fact that Sebastian definitely hates me and thinks I'm going to screw up. Maybe he'll get to be ok with me because he knows they won't have a singer otherwise. He would rather have me than no one.

Regardless, I want to keep my distance from that guy.

I would hang out with Cara, but she's gone away on a weekend camping trip with friends. Wait, I just got the best idea—I can go down to the record store and look around at stuff. I might even be able to find an older record of *Appetite For Destruction*.

I decide to ride this idea and go down to the downtown area of Sunrise Heights.

After I get out of my car, I see a woman handing out pamphlets on the street. She's stopping people as they try to pass by her, forcing them to take one. Stuff like that always makes me uncomfortable so I make sure to cross the street before I get to her.

Once I make it safely inside the record store, I begin looking around to find what I need. But now that I'm here, I don't feel like getting anything. Great, I came out here for no reason.

As I'm about to turn around and leave, I see Sebastian skimming through albums.

Son of a bitch.

Now I'm really wishing I hadn't come. Just then, he turns around and sees me staring at him. He frowns and I realize I must look like a total creepy stalker. I avert my attention, pretending to be interested in the guitars hanging on the wall next to me, but it's too late, he's already coming over this way.

"Wren, what are you doing here?" he asks once he reaches me, raising

an inquisitive brow. "If you're looking for Aidan, he doesn't work here on Saturdays."

"Aidan works here?"

"Yes, he has for quite a while. If that's not why you're here, then what *are* you doing?"

"Checking out some music stuff, what are you doing?"

He laughs dryly and lifts up the *Mob Rules* album he has in his hand. "Just checking out some music stuff."

"Oh, cool. Um, good seeing ya. I'm going to get on my way now," I say while backing up toward the door.

"Wait, I wanted to talk to you about what I said after practice," he calls out after me.

"Some time later, I really have to get going. I'll see you at band practice." With that, I wave goodbye and step outside.

I am so caught up in thinking about what an idiot I must've sounded like; I don't even notice that the pamphlet lady has crossed streets. As I'm making my way toward my car, she grabs my wrist while I'm walking by, startling the hell out of me.

"Jesus lady—"

"You have a darkness inside you," she says abruptly with wide eyes. *Wow! No cordial formalities with her, she jumps right to it.* "Let God lead you to the light." She then hands me one of her pamphlets, an advertisement for a local church.

"Um, thank you, but I don't need this," I respond politely. I think she's kind'a a crazy person or something.

"Of course you do. What bothers you, child?"

God dammit, I should have just taken the thing and moved along.

"Nothing."

"I can see that's not the truth."

"You don't—"

"You are in need of help."

"Look, lady, you don't know me or what I need. If I'm sad and angry, then that's my business and nobody else's." I don't know why I'm talking to her, of all people, but all of a sudden I don't care too much.

"Don't worry, God has a plan for you. He has a plan for us all."

Oh here we go. "Bullshit."

"Excuse me?"

"No one's deciding what I do or where I go but me. All that responsibility falls on me just as it falls on everyone else. So even if there is some sort of a God, they've never stepped up to help before and I doubt they're going to start now. Honestly, I don't give a crap anymore if there is or isn't a God. Either way we're all screwed."

She stares at me blankly before sighing deeply. "I'll pray for your soul, I will," she promises as she turns and walks away.

I stare at her while she disappears down the street, haggling more people to take a pamphlet.

Guess you could say I'm not the God-fearing type.

CHAPTER 12

DON'T GO AWAY SAD (JUST GO)

TO SAY THAT SEBASTIAN WAS UNSURE of using Wren Evans as the lead singer for their performance would be an understatement. There was something about her that made him uneasy. There was something that just felt not-quite right—something that made it hard for him to understand her.

Sebastian didn't like things he couldn't understand; and there was no way he would let anyone, especially this girl, disrupt the band. You see, the band, consisting of him, Aidan, and Tommy, was currently all that meant anything to him. He had worked hard to see it come together, and he wanted more than anything for it to *stay* together.

What was lacking in real life, he was able to find within music. So, this band gave him something to hold onto. It gave him a purpose. Sure, this upcoming gig was only a high school talent show, but at least it was a start. If it went well, it could prove that they might have what it takes to go the distance. It could open up new doors to new opportunities. And, because of this, he took it seriously.

But, he knew that the others did not exactly share in his professionalism. Tommy rarely took anything seriously, Aidan was preoccupied with family troubles and his job. Wren—well, he wasn't sure about Wren, only that she caused an unwelcome feeling of curiosity to burn inside him.

As for Aidan, though, Sebastian *was* sure that if he could somehow get Noah to come back for a while, things might shape up for him. Aidan hadn't seen his brother in quite some time and, as a good friend of both his and Noah's, Sebastian knew a reconnection between them was much needed and long overdue.

But such a task was far easier said than done. For one, despite more than a few questionable jobs and favors, he still didn't have enough money required to get the plane ticket for flying Noah out here. Also, convincing Noah, in his current state, to do much of anything would be nearly impossible.

Still, Sebastian couldn't give up. He didn't care what it took. He *would* see this band take off, and he *would* make certain that Aidan saw his brother. And, he felt sure that he'd figure this Wren girl out—no matter what.

I want you to understand so badly—and I'm not sure how to do that. I can try to tell you with words, though that will only get me so far. If you really wanted to get to know me, you could just listen to my playlist and that'll tell you more than anything.

It's like my music is a part of me. And that's why it really bothers me when this jackass comes up to me in the Ice Cream Shop diner while I'm reading a book and scoffs, "Nice shirt, have you ever actually listened to the album?"

He's referring to my *Use Your Illusion* t-shirt.

"Yep, and I know more about them and their music than you ever will," I reply calmly.

He looks like I took him back a bit.

"Oh yeah? Name ten of their songs."

I set down my book and stand up so that I'm eye level with him. I could knock his ass out of the park and list fifty songs right here on the spot, and I almost do, but instead I shake my head.

"No. If you need help knowing what ten of their songs are, you can look them up yourself."

I pick up my book and brush past him and out the door, not caring to hear what he has to say next.

Punk.

I had been waiting inside for Aidan to finish up on a call so we could get some ice cream before band rehearsal, but I'm just going to go find him now anyway.

Outside, Aidan is still on the phone. He is pretty tense from what I can tell.

"No, Noah. I don't have any—I'm sorry. Can you just wait till I get back? That's not on me, that's not fair." He abruptly swears and hangs up, jamming his phone into his pocket.

"You all right?" I ask him.

"Yes, it's just my idiot brother."

I'm unsure of how to deal with broken family stuff, so I turn the conversation topic toward something a bit lighter.

"Want to start rehearsal early?"

"I thought we were getting ice cream," he says puzzled.

"I don't feel like it anymore, but if you want it I'll wait out here for you."

"Nah, that's ok. We can leave now."

We leave the Ice Cream Shop and head back to his house. Tommy and Sebastian come over not long after and we all hang together for a while. I'm still not feeling cozy with Sebastian. I think he may, hopefully, be warming up to me. We go through "Rocket Queen" a few times, perfecting the song and letting our worries escape us for the time being.

When we finish, I head inside from the garage to get a drink. Sebastian follows me in, and I roll my eyes as I see him coming toward me. I back up against the wall, cracking open my lemonade can and waiting to hear what he has to say this time.

He leans against the wall next to me, looking down at me with a serious expression. "To be the lead singer, you have to be able to carry the show."

"Get your panties out of a twist, Bash. It's not like I'm planning on becoming your front man. It's just this one performance."

His cheeks redden. "That's not what I was going to—never mind. I'm just saying your singing is fine. If you work on your stage presence a bit, you can make it all work."

***

My heart feels heavy as I go back home.

You know when everything around you seems just fine, but on the inside you still feel like crap, like you could fall apart at any second? It's awful. And knowing that you have no *reason* to be so down will only make you feel worse about yourself. Then you get stuck in a place you can't seem to get yourself out of.

You know what it is? The "reason," I mean. Well, personally I'm starting to theorize it's that I'm constantly searching for something, and I don't know what for. I think it may be an illusion—my illusion. And I'll never really get there because I can't ever really get there. So, I'll never be satisfied. If I could get my head out of the clouds and land my feet back down on the ground, maybe I would find my way out. I just don't know that I'm ready to lose my illusion. If I do, I think I'll lose my will to live, too.

So, maybe one day I'll learn to *use* my illusion. To test this theory, I try working on that song I started a while back.

Honey you can't see
What you don't mean to me
'Cus I've moved on but you're still here
Why are you still here?
Try and keep me under control
It's too bad
But I don't work that way no more

You never wanted me anyways
You know it's true
I'm fighting for change and you won't let go
I ask you what you need
But your answer isn't me
N' you never wanted me anyways

Things are gettin' crazy now
I'm picking up my pieces
You don't want my love
Good, you're not getting it

If my time is up
I'm taking you down with me
If you don't let me go
I'm gonna stab you through the heart
Trouble is rounding the corner
Turn your head I'll kick you down
Try it, I can do this all day

Feeling in the mood, I make up another one. I know I write too many songs, but you're just going to have to deal with it.

I'm getting outta here, whether you like it or not
Try and stop me

I wanna see you try
Don't worry, if you can't feel my anger
You will

Touch me again and I'll kick you in the face
Do it one more time
I want out of this place
You think I'm so freakin' helpless
I know your arrogance makes me sick
I used to care
Now your name's just one to cross off my list

They talk about peace and crap like that
I'll talk about peace when I'm finished
I move forward
You pull me back
It was fun while it lasted
But now I'm done with this track

You think of yourself as an asset
Really you're just an Asshat

No more running, I'm here to stand and fight
I'll take down whatever comes my way
All right
You think I can't
I'm gonna punch through your throat

Screw you

Well damn, that sounds practically Shakespearean. I stuff my song notes away and am about to call it a night when suddenly my phone rings.

It's Aidan. "Hello?" I say, confused as to why he would be calling me at—I check my watch—2:00 am.

"Wren, I saw Bash follow you back inside after practice today."

"Yeah, and?"

"I just know he's not always the most *friendly* guy, so I wanted to make sure he didn't say anything stupid."

"Anything stupid? No, don't worry. I'm fine."

"Ok, but like—"

"Though I got to wonder," I begin, getting up from my bed, "why do you want me in this band anyway?" I pace up and down my room. "I'm not any sort of great singer, and I'm too nervous to be someone who can perform well, so what's the deal?"

"Oh come on, don't you trust me? I wouldn't ask you to do something like this if I didn't know you could do it."

"Please—"

"Stop. Don't worry. Don't ever think I'd bring you harm, or leave you out there in the rain."

"You better not be doing what I think you're doing."

"Just tell me you'll always be there because all I want is for you to know that I care."

"Stop paraphrasing 'Rocket Queen' to me."

"No one needs the sorrow and pain. I won't ever leave you strung out—"

"Aidan!"

"What?" I can practically hear his smirk from the other side of the phone.

"And you weren't even doing the lyrics in *order*!"

"Ok, well, I'm going to head off to bed now," he says, yawning.

"Yeah, you do that," I respond, laughing softly despite myself.

"Goodnight."

"Goodnight."

CHAPTER 13

EXIT SANDMAN

I'M FAKING CRAP ALL THE TIME. And I'm not even doing it well; people still think I'm a mess. This being said, I've made a list of what I think I could be. If I was one of these things, I probably wouldn't have to fake it anymore because I'd probably be good with myself, you know—all self-fulfilled and all.

A List of Stuff to Be

Songwriter
Dancer (if I get myself together and my ankle stops hurting)
Singer (not a very good one)
Train hopper
Superhero movie-maker
Dead in a ditch
Music/movie critic
Record-store person
Band shirt designer
Professional music listener
Cowboy
Radio-station person

There are some good options in there; and one or two of them might actually have the potential to work. It would be especially cool if I could be one of the slightly artsy things because once you're a well-respected-artist type, you can get away without following reason.

And even if I don't get to be one of those sorts of things, I don't need a Piper to lead me to reason. Either I'll find it myself or I won't.

Update:

I don't know what the hell I'm doing, and I'm never going to find reason. I feel like I've boarded the crazy train and there's no getting off. I can't be thinking about losing my mind right now, though. I need to focus on driving.

My dad texted and asked if I could pick up my sister from school and take her to soccer practice. Of course I said yes; it'll be nice hanging with Cara for a bit.

I get there a little late, because our schools get out at the same time, and see her talking and laughing with some friends out front. It makes me smile—she's always been better at making friends than me—thank goodness.

"Hey Cara," I begin once she's in the car, "I was thinking maybe we could go for some ice cream after school next Friday. I can't do it right now because I have to drop you off at soccer and I have to go to dance."

"Aw, I wish! You know how much I love ice cream, but I leave for my school trip that day."

I totally forgot she has that trip coming up, and she's only been talking about it since forever.

"How long is that thing again?"

"Two weeks. I'm gonna put on some music." She opens the glove compartment and begins rummaging through my CD collection.

"Whoa there! We're riding my sweet wheels, and I can tell you right now we ain't going to be listening to that Taylor Swift disc you shoved away in there last time I drove you."

"But maybe Nightrider would appreciate a change up from rock n' roll."

"I don't think so."

"Ok, ok. But then I get to pick from your CDs."

"Fair enough. Let me guess, Bon Jovi?" They're her favorite of mine.

"Would it be anyone else?"

I'm going to miss Cara. Her school trip may only be two weeks but when you think about it, that's a pretty damn long time.

I've had a recurring dream this week, or has it just been my imagination while I lie awake before falling asleep? Either way, it always ends bloody. A pack of monsters rip me apart, tearing into my flesh and slashing me to pieces while I watch from afar. Maybe there's symbolism in that, but I've never cared for the whole idea that there's symbolism in everything and anything. Maybe sometimes things just happen because, well guess what, things just happen.

My English teacher would kill me for saying this stuff, but I can't stand it when people are like "the curtains in this scene were blue because they represent the protagonist's depression in the second half of the novel." Um, no, they're blue because they're freakin' blue—end of story.

Not everything has some hidden deeper meaning.

If I wrote a novel and found out that schools were forcing kids to analyze the whole thing for symbolism, I'd probably have a flip-out. Then they'd put it on the "banned books" list, and I don't know where we'd go from there.

"Ms. Evans?"

Huh?

"Ms. Evans, am I boring you?"

I avert my attention from spacing out back to the front of the classroom to my environmental science teacher. He does not look happy and my cheeks begin to heat up; I don't like being singled out in front of people.

"No, sorry sir."

"Is there something more interesting going on that I should be aware of?"

"No."

"Then why were you not paying attention?"

Wow, this guy really won't let up on me.

"I promise you have my full attention. I have never been more interested in anything in my entire life." In truth, I have no idea what lesson is being taught right now.

"Ms. Evans, I want you to step outside right this instant and think about your tone."

"My tone? Well, I suppose you could say it's pretty pale right now, you see I haven't gotten much sun as of late—"

"Get out of my class right now!"

I grab my bag and skip out of there in a hurry. I don't like people that yell.

***

While I wait for the next class period to begin, I stare at the bricks that make up the wall of the hallway. Perhaps I really don't need an education.

***

At dance rehearsal this afternoon, I spend most of the time sitting in the corner thinking about what sort of a book I'd write and watching the other dancers perform their solos for our upcoming showcase. I may be in the highest level, but I'm the only one from it who doesn't have a solo. Though perhaps that's for the best. After all, in terms of physical health, my luck just keeps getting better and better; my ankle still aches and my feet cramp up so bad sometimes that I nearly fall over when I've been dancing too long. It's terrible, like my own body is attacking me from the inside.

I basically can't dance anymore, at least not like I used to. And if I can't be a dancer, what can I be? I've got to be on this goddamn planet for some reason, so if not for this, then what?

No matter what I do, I can't find it. I can't find my way. I have no way. I have nothing.

As soon as I come home, I see Cara sitting on the stairs, and it appears her eyes are red and puffy. If anyone messed with her...

"Cara, what's wrong? Do I need to kill someone?" I ask, half-joking.

"What? No, it doesn't have to do with anyone."

"Then what does it have to do with?"

"My school trip. I thought I'd be ok going, but I feel really scared now. But it's stupid, I'm acting like a crybaby."

"No, you're no crybaby. It's perfectly normal to be afraid of going away from home for the first time. I get a little scared almost every time, and I've been away a lot of times, like this summer, but I got through it— and it was not so bad."

In truth, last summer was *not* "not so bad." But, I am trying to think up some other past examples of going away from home that were actually successful.

Last time I went to a regular school associated summer camp that had nothing to do with dance was back in middle school. It was only two weeks long, but I got sent home early. The problem began when one of my bunk-mates told a camp counselor that I listened to my music too loudly. I told her I'd turn it down, but she wanted to confiscate it anyhow, so she tried to take away the Walkman I had brought with me.

It went like this:

"I need you to hand over your Walkman, and I'll keep it until the end of the camp."

"No, please, I need my music."

"I think your music is having a bad influence on you. I've heard you swear more than anyone else here, and if you get into an argument with someone you tell them to 'get in the ring.'"

"If I can't listen to Guns, I will kill someone! Or I'll die myself!"

"You're being dramatic."

"And you're being a pain in the ass!"

"I am your camp counselor. You cannot talk to me that way. Now hand over the Walkman, I mean it."

"Sorry, but you'll have to take it off my dead body."

Then she tried to grab it out of my hands, and I threw it on the ground and stomped on it, knowing I'd be sent back home.

So yeah, there would be no more recreational camps for me—and no more Walkmans.

"It changed you though, didn't it?" Cara asks, bringing me back from my blast from the past.

I look at her, confused.

"You just seem different since you came home this last summer," she mumbles.

"Hey, I'm fine—really I am. And you won't be going anywhere even remotely close to the place I went. You're only going to be gone two weeks, and it's a school field trip. Trust me, everything will be fine. You'll have fun, I know you will."

She wipes her eyes and looks up at me with a small smile. "Remember that time you caught a snake at a camp and brought it to the camp counselors because no one would believe you that it wasn't venomous?"

"Hey, that was a long time ago."

"And then you tried to let it bite you for proof, but it wouldn't so you let it go in the girls cabin and had to catch it again and set it back outside because no one else would touch it?"

"Yes, thank you for bringing that up."

"Just checking." She gives me a quick hug and starts walking away.

"Where are you going?" I call after her.

"To pack. I have to get my stuff together, the trip is in two days."

"You're all good now?"

"Come on, Wren, it's only a school field trip."

I laugh and shake my head. Cara can be funny, even when she doesn't mean to be.

"Hey, what if we did something tomorrow—before you leave?" I ask, getting an idea. "Just us. I can skip dance and we can go to Riverview to look at the museum or something. It'll be better than ice cream."

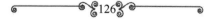

"Yes! Let's do it!" she says excitedly—she loves the museum in Riverview.

"Wonderful, it's a plan."

"Wait, but Wren…"

"Yes?"

"Um… do you think you could ask your friend Aidan to come? I haven't seen him in forever, and I thought you said you were going to bring him around more often." I should have seen this coming, sooner or later.

"I never said that."

"Still, please? Please, please—"

"Ok, fine. I'll ask."

"Yay!"

We talk a bit more while I help her pack and I continue to smile and laugh, but inside my mind is drifting. It shouldn't bother me so much to think about my summer in NYC but, well, here we are.

In case you are at all curious about what the hell exactly happened to me over there to make me so annoying and depressed, I got to start by telling you that it wasn't even hardly that bad. Whatever you think happened, it's probably not that bad. I'm not sure how to describe it without making it too boring or explicit—when you try to stay away from one it usually brings you around to the other.

I suppose being there mostly caused problems for me because I couldn't make any damn friends. So then I became "all lonely and stuff," and I started getting depressed. I held out just over one month, thinking that maybe things would get better, but they did not. They pretty much got a whole lot worse, and some of the teachers at the academy developed a pretty strong disliking for me. There are a couple of reasons for that, but let's not get into those.

Bottom line is they made me realize I no longer have the talent I once possessed, and that I was never going to be wanted by those who had left me. Then I got sent/taken home. But at least when I got back here I managed to get a job. In fact, I made quite a bit of money by working at the downtown bookstore. Course, then I got fired, but you know, shit happens.

Rather than driving myself crazy by thinking too much, I head over to Lena's. It's late and I didn't exactly give her a call or anything. I'm just sort'a heading there and hoping she's hasn't left or something.

Good for me, Lena is there. She is not upset with me for not giving her notice. She can be cool like that.

We are lying face-up in her backyard and talking about school stuff for a while.

"How come you don't care, Wren?" she asks all of a sudden.

Well that's a loaded question. "I'm sorry, that question came out a bit rude."

"It's just, you are so—I don't know—*whatever* about things."

"Because," I stop to think a moment, "everything is dust in the wind."

Lena looks a bit confused with my answer at first, but after pondering it for a moment she understands what I meant.

***

When I get back from hanging out at Lena's, I go out into the backyard and lay down in the grass. I like it out here, being able to hear the sound of crickets while taking in the feeling of fresh air on my skin. I'm just going to rest my eyes for a bit...

"Oh please don't do this," Bianca pleads.

"I'd listen to her, you're just going to hurt yourself," Seth sneers.

"The only person that's going to get hurt is you."

My eyes open, and I find myself lying in the grass in my backyard, staring up at the sky above me. I was dreaming—too bad I woke up, things were just warming up.

I sigh and sit up, trying to remember why I was sleeping in the backyard on the ground in the middle of the night. Oh yes, that's right, I didn't have a reason.

It was just another dream about the past; another look at my personal hell; and another reminder of how I got to be where I am.

One of the things I hate most is people trying to tell me what to do. And when push comes to shove, I know I'd die before letting anyone force me into doing something that goes against what I believe. I'm on the extreme side of things, but I do wish people would question and push back more often. We ought to question *everything.* Too often people get sucked into their family's beliefs or the beliefs of other people around them and begin to think exactly like them with little to no ability or willingness to consider other points of view. Not that you can't share in your family's views, but if people would step back and think about all the information and expectations they've been given, the world would be a different place. This

goes for any and all forms of authority and rules as well. Question them, and if you don't believe in something, push back.

I get that it can be scary, but if we don't fight for freedom, what exactly are we living for? If you aren't free, then what's the point?

I make a lot of grand comments about life, but you should probably take them all with a dash of salt. I mean, I do sort'a know what I'm talking about, but it's more complicated than that. I know what I'm talking about because I know I don't know what I'm talking about.

Still, the bottom line is I don't like being put in a box. I don't like being told what I can't do or say—I just want the freedom to work through my own nature, so long as I am not hurting anybody, without having someone on me about every little choice I make. Apparently that's a lot to ask.

But if I can't live my own life, then this is all a waste of time.

Life's so strange.

What'll happen to me? Guess I'll have to wait and see.

Despite giving him less than a few hours notice, Aidan agrees to come with us to Riverview to go to the museum. He doesn't get off of work until seven tonight though, so it'll be a late night drive there and back.

"Hi, Aidan," Cara greets him as he gets in the car. "How was your day at the office?"

"Hey, kid. I wouldn't really consider the record store an office, but it was pretty good—I sold a Metallica album to someone I know from school, which was weird, but cool I suppose. How are things with you?" he asks, turning around in his seat to high five her.

"Who was it?" I ask, interrupting them.

"It was Bianca, actually. I was pretty surprised, too," he answers, acknowledging the look of disbelief on my face.

"That doesn't make any sense." I know for a *fact* that Bianca does *not* listen to freakin' Metallica. But perhaps she was buying it for someone else?

"Yeah, I thought so too—but she said they're one of her favorites or something. Funny, right?

"Yeah, funny."

"Excuse me, Wren," Cara cuts back in, "but he was asking *me* a question. As for how I'm doing, Aidan, I am very well."

"Glad to hear it," he chuckles.

"Hey you two, any music requests you're dying to hear?" I ask them, opening up my CD stash. I'll have to get to the bottom of this Bianca-is-suddenly-a-metal-head thing later.

"Yes, Taylor Swift."

"Cara, how many times do I have to tell you—"

"I'm down for some Swiftie," Aidan says, catching us both by surprise.

I glance over at him, my jaw slightly hanging open. "What?"

I can see Cara's face lighting up in the rearview mirror.

"You can't be serious!"

"Why not? What's wrong with Taylor Swift? You don't like her?" he asks innocently, cocking his head toward me.

"I just didn't expect you—"

"Wren, the people have spoken," Cara exclaims, "give us what we want!"

"Whatever you guys say." I reach in grabbing the one Swift disc in the car, putting it in, and pressing play.

"One more thing," Cara adds, "skip to track number six."

Sure enough, "You Belong With Me" comes out of the speakers and—I'm not sure how—we start singing while Aidan smiles and laughs. I can feel the cold exterior around me melt as my heart warms. Now this, this feels right.

CHAPTER 14

TAKE ME TO THE BOTTOM

BIANCA DIDN'T HAVE AN APPETITE for breakfast or lunch today, and she barely spoke throughout any of her classes—all of which was fairly unusual for her. Fairly unusual, that is, except for when her father came around.

It had been several years since he'd walked out on his family, but it was only recently that he begun to come and visit. It was always for very brief periods of time, never more than a day or so, but it always hurt. It hurt when she'd see him appear on the doorstep, and it hurt even more each time that he'd inevitably walk away.

The first time he showed up, she felt ecstatic. She thought he'd finally returned, that he'd finally come back for her. But then he told her that he would be leaving again, and all her hopes shattered. She pleaded with him to stay, even if just for one more day but he left all the same.

Then, one day, Bianca overheard a conversation between him and her mother and she realized that all these visits had more to do with money than they did with her.

That was when she understood she was never really getting her dad back.

And today he would be here once more—for the first time in over a year. The reason behind this particular visit, she didn't know. But she knew it was going to be hard. And it made her angry because of this.

She ought to be happy right now—she was doing well in school, she was more popular than ever, and she'd just been cast as the lead in her ballet school's new production of *Sleeping Beauty* (a part which she'd wanted since all the way back to when she first became friends with Wren).

Ah, to go back to those times. Back before things blew up and everything became so complicated.

She could easily remember it—that first year when she and Wren began walking to dance together. Sometimes, they wouldn't even go to class or rehearsal, choosing to ditch and head down to the nearby forest instead—a forest Wren nicknamed The Black Forest.

Bianca was always unsure of it, but Wren always managed to persuade her. That was the sort of dynamic of their friendship. Once they got to The Black Forest, they'd go straight to the old, abandoned tree house they found together—and sometimes stay up there for hours and just talk.

And now, just as Bianca was in her greatest need of having someone to talk to, she had no one...

Shaking her from her reminiscent daydream, she suddenly spotted none other than Wren from across the school parking lot.

Wait... perhaps Wren could help her.

Yes! After all, she was the one she always used to turn to when it came to these sorts of issues. Why not now?

Of course, things were different now. Bianca was no longer sure if she was keeping Wren close because she was her friend, or because she had too much potential to be her enemy. Either way, she needed *someone* to speak with. So, she stood up tall and began marching across the parking lot. But, with each step, she could feel her false confidence slipping further away. By the time she reached Wren, she no longer knew what to say or if she even *could* say it.

"Wren," she sucked in a deep breath, their eyes locking, "I have something I want to talk to you about."

This morning was a real bitch, and it looks like this afternoon is going be the same. Nightrider got a flat tire, which means I had to walk all the way to school, and now I'm going to have to walk all the way back to my house to change the damn thing.

As I'm making my way through the parking lot after school, grumbling to myself about not having my car, Bianca blocks my path—she likes to catch me off guard. But this time, there's a slightly serious expression on her face that kind'a freaks me out.

"Wren, I have something I want to talk to you about."

"Hello, Bianca." I'm already feeling tired just looking at her. "What's up?"

Suddenly, her serious expression breaks into a wide smile. "You'll never believe what role I'm playing in the upcoming showcase." She's talking about the annual end-of-the-year ballet performance all studios do in the spring.

"I—"

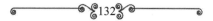

"I'm going to be Aurora! I'm the lead! Isn't that amazing? I've always wanted to do *Sleeping Beauty*, it's a dream come true!" She's talking unusually fast, I wonder if something is up.

"Yeah, that's amazing. Good for you." I remember a time when Bianca and I used to fantasize about playing parts like Aurora. Now she's climbing to the top of the ranks while I'm sinking to the bottom, my talent withering and dying.

"Any good news for you?"

"I'm working with a rock band now," I say, unsure of what else I have to share.

"A band?"

"It's just a one-time thing, but yeah."

"With who?"

"Mostly people you don't know—except for Aidan." I go into a little more detail about the band and her eyes widen at Sebastian's name—though she doesn't say anything about it.

"You're in a band with Aidan?"

"Kind of, we're working on performing at his friend's talent show."

Her nose crinkles a little.

"I thought you would be happy, Bianca. What with being such a big Metallica fan and all, it seems you would like the idea of me being part of a rock band."

I see a glimpse of her nervousness underneath the mask before it is replaced by her regular cool expression. "Oh, well, what about dance?"

"What about it?"

"How well are you doing at your new studio?"

Jesus goddamn motherfreaking Christ. "Super great."

"Really? Because I was talking to some of the girls that go there when I came to take a drop-in class, just to see what it was like there, and they said you practically don't even go to classes or rehearsals anymore."

"Does this really matter to you? Please don't go asking about me to them anymore."

"If you want to know the truth, you seem to be changing, and I don't think it's healthy. I mean, from getting expelled last year, to being suspended, skipping dance, and starting up in some rock band? You're lashing out at something. I don't know what but I think you should stop and go back to focusing on dance and school."

"Wow! Tell me what you really think."

"It's the truth."

"Why do you think I should care so much about your opinion? You don't know any better than me."

"If you would just let me talk to you for one minute without pushing back—I'm trying to help you god dammit!"

After this I go quiet.

"Listen, I'm not even saying this because I want to, but I've noticed the way you've been acting this whole year and, well, you have got to get your crap together, Wren. You just do."

How dare she?

"You're going off the rails, and honestly it's kind of scary."

"I'm not going off any rails."

"I'm sorry, but you are. Even before this year, you were always a little… difficult."

"Difficult?"

"You know it wasn't just Seth that had problems with you, right?"

"What?"

"Remember Maisie's parents?"

"I hardly remember who Maisie herself is."

"Yeah well—"

"Oh, is she that girl that always used to follow you and Seth around wherever you went?"

"Yes," Bianca sighs, "but her parents were considering getting a restraining order against you and your family."

"The hell? On what grounds?"

"I don't remember exactly, it was right after you left the studio. I'm just saying that there were other people you pissed off, other people that noticed the way you began acting."

"Whoa, back up, what did I ever do to Maisie? I can't even recall ever having spoken to her parents. Man, people really are crazy. Can you tell them I don't even remember who the *hell* they are? I mean, do they know that you actually have to have a reason to get a restraining order, or is that fact lost on them?"

"But you know what they *think* you did."

"That didn't have anything to do with them, though. Wait… you don't actually think I did anything to them, do you?"

"No! God, I know you better than that."

"Is this the sort of reputation that I have at your studio now, like they all think I'm crazy?"

"The truth has been twisted." She pauses for a moment. "It's not as bad as you think, though."

"Sure it's not."

"Anyways, I couldn't help but notice that you walked here today. Is there something the matter with your car?"

"Yes, a stupid flat tire. I'll fix it tonight."

"How about I give you a ride then. To dance."

"Oh, I didn't think you drove regularly?"

"I don't, if I can help it. Usually a friend takes me to school and my cousin picks me up from dance. But today I felt like practicing my independence as a person with a license," she smiles, flipping her dark curls behind her shoulders.

"Well, it's very generous of you to offer, but I don't want to trouble you. And it's a long ways back afterwards, so I'd rather not have to make that walk."

"It's no trouble, really. I would pick you up after, of course. Then I was thinking we could go to the movies."

"The movies?"

"Yeah—oh hey! Guys, over here!" Bianca suddenly calls out, looking past my shoulder and waving her arm.

I turn around and see a group of her friends coming toward us and quickly recognize one of them as Kate—the girl who gave me a hard time for intervening as they picked on Eric. My eyes narrow as my jaw tightens.

"I was just telling Wren about the movies idea we had. We can all meet up at the theater after I pick her up at—what time is your class over?"

"Uh, seven," I answer.

"Great, so we'll meet there between seven thirty and eight everyone?"

There's some talk about what movie we ought to see and about going to pizza afterwards. I don't catch most of it; my mind is a bit distracted due to the intense look Kate gives me. It's very clear that she has not forgotten about our last encounter. But that's not all—there's just something about her. Something that really rubs me the wrong way…

"What are you guys talking about?" Aidan asks, appearing right behind me, seemingly out of nowhere.

"Going to the movie theater downtown later tonight," one of the girls giggles.

"You want to come?" Bianca asks.

He shrugs with a small grin and turns to me. "Are you going?"

I look to Bianca, whose brows are now raised at me. "Yeah, I'll go."

Aidan nods and turns back to the group. "I'm coming too. Seven-thirty or something, right? I get off work around seven, so I should be fine to make it."

"Yep!"

"Great, see you all there."

The girls let out a few more giggles, even though nothing funny got said. People seem to be waiting to see if Aidan's going to say anything else but he simply smiles and begins walking away.

"Hey, why don't you go ahead and start the car? I'll be there in a sec, I just got to do one thing," I say to Bianca.

She rolls her eyes but agrees.

I run after Aidan, catching him before he leaves. "Hey, how are you getting to the movie theater?" I ask, walking beside him now.

"I was planning on walking, like usual."

"It's going to be pretty late when we get done though."

"Yeah, so? Are you going to give me a ride then?"

"Actually, Nightrider isn't working right now. Flat tire."

"Flat tire, huh? You don't know how to change it?"

"Of course I know—well, I can learn pretty quick I bet."

"I could help."

"I'm not going to change it right now, I'm going straight from here to dance."

"Oh, do you want me to walk you there?"

"Actually, Bianca offered to drive me there and then to the theater. But I know that she'd be happy to take you as well."

"Or you could ride with me, Aidan," Kate suggests. She's been lingering near us, listening to our conversation. "I live relatively close to school which, I believe, isn't too far from where you work." Hmm, so everyone just knows where Aidan works, huh?

"Sure... that'd be great," Aidan says. "If you give me your address, I can try and meet you at your house around seven-twenty?"

Kate nods and writes down her address on a piece of paper from her backpack, handing it to him. He sticks it in his pocket and begins walking once more. I watch him as he disappears out of the parking lot, feeling a little uneasy all of a sudden.

"Wren." I face back toward Kate who's now staring at me. "I wanted to talk to you for a moment."

"Yeah, I—uh, I'd been meaning to tell you, when I said I was gonna break your nose, I'm not really going to do that," I say, trying to sound as lighthearted as possible.

Still, Kate doesn't look particularly amused. "So, you and Bianca are back to being friends."

"Yes?" I'm not sure where she's taking this.

"Huh, we'll see how long that lasts," she mutters under her breath, but not quiet enough to where I can't hear. I'm pretty sure this girl would kill me without hesitation if given the chance.

"Yep," I nod after she doesn't say anything else. "Ok, I have dance, so I gotta get going."

"Where is it you dance again?"

"The studio on the North side of town, next to the train tracks."

"Isn't that kind of far from here? Why not go to the studio that's only a few minutes away? You know, the one Bianca goes to?"

I freeze up at her words. She cocks her head innocently at me, but I know deep down that she knows exactly what she asked and what the answer is. I can also tell that she's not going to let me off the hook, she's waiting for my answer.

I open my mouth, unsure of what is about to come out. "I really like trains." With that, I turn back around and walk over to Bianca's car.

On the drive to the studio, I tell Bianca more about the new band thing, and she tells me all about what it's like to rehearse for the main role of a production. She also asks me about what Kate and I talked about. But, I spin the conversation back around to her and she soon seems to forget her questions as she goes back to the topic of being cast as Aurora. She's still going on about it when we pull up in front of the studio.

"Ok, Bianca, I have to go in now or I'll get in trouble for being late."

"Yes, yes—have fun. I'll be back to get you when you're done."

I give her a smile and hop out of the car. Before I make it inside, she yells after me.

"And Wren, I'm really glad that we're doing this!"

"Me too," I call back. It's been a little while, but I think things might actually be looking up for me.

***

After dance class, I hang back in the dressing room to get changed before Bianca arrives to pick me up. The entire place clears out pretty quickly, leaving me as the last person in there. It's almost spooky.

I take off my dance clothes and throw them in a pile, grabbing my outfit for tonight in exchange. I've just barely gotten on my underwear when I hear a creaking sound toward the front of the studio.

"Hello?" I call out. There's no reply and Bianca hasn't texted me that she's here yet. Something is off. I quickly slip my t-shirt over my head and peek out of the dressing room door. All I can see is darkness. I walk back over to my stuff and grab my jeans when I hear another noise, this time closer. The only logical explanation is that it's Bianca. There's no reason to be afraid.

"Hey Bianca, could you just wait a sec? I'm just finishing getting changed and then I'll be right out," I say.

"Bianca's not here," a voice says from the other side of the door. "But I am."

The door then pushes open and Kate steps through it.

"Kate, I suppose the words 'wait a sec' are lost on you? Where is Bianca anyway?"

"She's at the movie along with everyone else," she states without looking away as I pull on my jeans. "I already dropped Aidan off as well."

"Oh... then I guess we'd better get going. Is your car out front?" Her unrelenting stare is making my stomach squirm.

"I said that you weren't coming, actually. Bianca was a little skeptical, but I told her that during our conversation in the school parking lot you expressed the truth that you don't really want anything to do with her or her friends."

"Why would you do that?"

"You don't quite mix with our group, and I think it would be best if you were to stay out of our business. Altogether, that is."

"Is this a joke?"

"Hardly. And it's also in your best interest if you were to stay away from Aidan from now on."

"Why do you care who I talk to?"

"I don't care about you, but I know that you're not a good influence. I've heard things about your past, about your... reputation. And I know what kind of a person you are now—you think you're good, but you're not. Aidan deserves better."

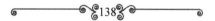

"You mean deserves someone like you?"

Her cheeks flush. "I never said—"

"That's it, isn't it? You want Aidan for yourself. And you want me, what? Out of the way? That's not going to happen, Kate. I'll talk to whomever I want to talk to. You don't get to control that just 'cus you're jealous or threatened."

"Is that what you think this is?" she scoffs with a laugh. "Why Wren, how positively self-absorbed can you be?"

"I don't know, but I could ask you the same question."

"Funny."

"Ok, if that's all you came here to say, then we're done."

"So I take it you won't be following my advice?"

I narrow my eyes in response.

"Then maybe I'll just have to tell everyone it was you that made that carving on the back of the school office building."

I raise an eyebrow at her.

"Ella told me about it."

Is she really going to pull *this* on me? I'm going to have to have a talk with Ella about keeping her cakehole shut.

"And perhaps I'll throw in some info about Aidan's brother, just to make things interesting."

I take a step back and can feel my nose and brows crinkle as I stare at her.

"After all, I've heard some *very* interesting things about him. My cousin was his roommate in college for a while; that is until he—you know. What's his name again? Ah yes, Noah. Do you even know about the things he's done? I bet Aidan would just hate for all that to get out. I mean, he makes even you look like an angel."

My muscles tense and my jaw clenches tightly. "Kate," I begin, taking a deep breath, "you really don't want to go down this road with me?"

"Why? What are *you* going to do?"

"Oh," I say in a restrained voice, "there are a lot of things I could do to you."

"But Aidan—"

She quickly backs up to the wall as I slam my hand into it right next to her face.

Leaning over her, I hold her gaze, forcing her look at me. I suppose I surprised both of us when my hand smashed the wall rather than her head.

"If you say his name one more time, the next thing my hand hits won't be the wall. That's a promise."

Her lungs seem to have stopped working almost completely until she finally draws in a shaky breath. She starts to say something, but I cut her off.

"How about you stop this whole threatening thing? It just doesn't work for you. You get what I'm saying?"

She nods frantically and I pull away, letting her back away from the wall.

She looks at me for one more second and moves to the door. Once out of my grip, her eyes go from frightened to a cold, hard fury.

She then leaves me with one last thing before disappearing out the door. "One day, Wren, I am going to hurt you."

***

There's no one to pick me up now, so I begin the long journey home by foot. On my way, I keep getting flashes of unwanted images as Kate's words ring through my mind. I see her lips form into a smile as she wraps her hands around Aidan's neck and he leans down to kiss her. Her fingers run through his hair and she pulls him closer.

I shake my head and pull myself out of those thoughts. But they keep coming back. Then the things Bianca was telling me about my "reputation" come back up as well. Now my chest is tight, making it hard to breath, and my stomach is in knots. My hands press up to my forehead and I feel as though I'm about to be sick.

Sometimes it really does feel like people are out to get you.

Friday, nighttime—

Worst thing about all this is the helplessness of a damaged reputation. Doesn't seem like it should be such a big deal, perhaps, but knowing that no one will ever really know the truth... that hurts. I could go around telling everyone what really happened, who I really am, but it's not like it would make a damn difference. I remember after the incident, the first time I tried to talk to some people I used to know, they looked at me with this look in their eyes that I never want to see again. It was horrible. I knew right then, it didn't matter what was real and what wasn't, they would never believe me.

So if anything, it would just feed the twisted lies: I'm a crazy person that can't be trusted—a threat that needs to be cut down.

And I don't even want to get into what Kate did today. I worry if I think about it too much. I really will break her nose. But with that being said, I'm

serious when I say there is something about her I find off... it almost scares me. And I don't get scared. I just think she legitimately wants to 'hurt' me. And I guess that's a little frightening.

I look up from my writing and my fists clench. Screw Kate—screw what those other people think, it doesn't bother me. It's not like she knows anything. It's not like any of them know anything.

I stare out at the night sky, the cool air flushing in from the open window, giving me chills. My eyes fixate on nothing and linger there a moment longer before pulling my consciousness back into the bedroom.

Everybody might need somebody. But I don't have anybody.

Truthfully, I've never had much in the way of friends. Mostly a few here and there if I was lucky. I'm not exactly sure why. I know, I can be tough to get along with but there's always seemed to be something more to it. I'm kind'a on the shy side of things, which makes it harder, and sometimes I think I'm boring and hard to understand.

So I get it that not everyone would want to hang around me, but I just wish I could have someone. And I have to say, it seems I have far more trouble than most, if not all, people in this area of life.

Whenever I changed schools or went to a new summer camp or ballet intensive, I usually hung out by myself the whole time. Not on purpose or anything, people just didn't like me very much. This last time I went away, to that year-round academy place, I didn't make one single friend the whole time I was there. Not even hardly a friendly acquaintance. I was just alone. I called my mom at the end of the first week about it, saying everyone already knew each other, and she told me that she was sure I'd make some kind of friend soon enough.

Turns out I didn't.

I didn't tell her about it though, because I wanted her to think I was ok and not worry or feel guilty about me being there. And before that, any friends I had from the old studio that expelled me dropped me like I never existed.

There's something wrong with me, I swear.

Right now, I guess I'm actually doing ok because I have Lena and I'm working on things with Bianca. But even then, there's a piece of me missing, a part of me that remembers nearly everyone I've ever cared about has left me.

Thinking about it makes me want to cry sometimes.

I shouldn't be crying right now though. I need to make sure Aidan made it home ok.

His picks up his phone almost immediately and says, "Hey, where were you tonight? Kate brought me and then left saying she had something she needed to do and just never came back. And you never showed."

"I'm sorry, there was a complication. But I need to know, on the way there, did Kate say anything to you?"

"She said lots of stuff. Why?"

"What did she say?" I can tell my voice sounds stressed.

"Just things you say in normal conversation," he laughs. "Do you want me to go over it word for word for you? There was no court recorder present so I'm not sure I'll recite it all correctly. Why are you acting so weird?"

"Sorry, just forget it. Did everything go ok?" I decide not to tell him about my dressing room encounter.

"It was fine, I guess. Bianca gave me a ride home."

"That's nice of her."

"Yeah."

After hanging up the phone, I go out to the road and sit down on my knees. I'm already dust blowing through the wind with no purpose, no place to belong. No one can help me. I guess I could say that I wish people would like me more, but I suppose if everyone likes you, you're not being your-self.

Too bad I don't know who I am anymore anyway.

***

I wake up early this weekend to work on my car and as it turns out, there's a bit more wrong with Nightrider than just a flat tire. Overall, it's a frustrating endeavor that leaves me very dirty. This is what I get for having an old car—but I wouldn't have it any other way.

Upon finishing with my tire trouble, etc., I take off to my appointment with Amelia. When I get there, we hit a few rough spots.

"I'm working with a band now, kind of," I tell her.

"How is that going?"

I'm thankful she's choosing to ignore the fact that I've got dirt and grease on my clothes.

"I can't tell yet, it just happened so I don't know how it's going to be. Do you think I'm going off the rails?" I did not segue into that question seamlessly.

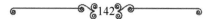

"Can you elaborate on what you mean by that?" She's always asking what I mean by stuff, but I don't know what the hell I'm saying either.

"What do people want from me? I don't get it. What am I supposed to do?"

"Well, there will always be others' opinions and expectations, but you have got to trust in who you are."

"If you say and nothing else matters..."

"I'm being serious, Wren."

"Yeah, I get it. Everyone is always being serious," I mumble, looking out the window. "But I just wanna know, am I a bad person?"

"What makes you ask that?"

"Just something someone said..." My thoughts jump to Kate. *I know what kind of a person you are now—you think you're good, but you're not.*

"You can't base your self-image off what other people think of you."

"Yeah, but if what people think of you doesn't matter than what exactly is the point of living? What matters? The fantasies in your head that you make up about who you are? Why don't I just go die in a ditch right now!"

Amelia just stares at me and says, "That's a negative response." She goes on to talk about things like mantras and positive self-talk and affirmations. I nod and listen, trying to consider what she's saying. Then our session ends with her suggestion I read some self-help books like The *Power of Now* by Eckhart Tolle. She writes it down, hands it to me, and bids me goodbye until next time.

***

Later that afternoon, we're in the middle of practicing "Rocket Queen" when Aidan gets a phone call and rushes outside to answer it. He's seemed more than a little distracted today, so I wonder what's going on.

"Must be Noah," Sebastian comments, tuning his bass guitar.

"Is everything ok with him?" I ask.

"He just got back to town the other day—did Aidan not tell you?"

"No..." I wonder why?

"Well, if you notice anything off about him, it's probably because of his brother."

"Speaking of being off," Tommy starts, "*you* seem a little off today, Wren."

"Hmm," is all I respond.

"He's right, actually. You must not be feeling well," Sebastian adds.

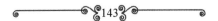

"Thank you for your observations, I feel much better now."

"You're welcome," Tommy says without irony. "Also, you've got something on your face. Your left cheek."

"Damn," I say, wiping my cheek. "I thought I cleaned it all off."

"Why did you have dirt on you to begin with?" Sebastian asks.

"Car stuff."

"Ever so specific."

"Noah is going to come to the show! He's gonna watch us perform!" Aidan announces as he comes back into the garage. He sounds really excited; it makes me happy. "I can't wait to introduce you to him, Wren. I mean, he can kind'a be an asshole but I think he'll like you a lot."

"Awesome, that'll be great."

"Did you hear that guys? Noah's gonna be there!"

"Hell yeah!" Tommy congratulates him with a high five.

Sebastian doesn't say anything. Aidan doesn't notice because he's busy talking excitedly with Tommy, but I notice.

"What's the matter?" I poke him on the shoulder. "Bash?"

"I don't trust him."

"Oh." He's talking about Noah. "I thought you two were friends?"

"We were, at one point," he says, shifting his weight and looking down at me. "But stuff like this has happened before, and every time Aidan thinks he's going to come, he doesn't. And every time it breaks his heart."

***

Over the next week, I try out Bianca's advice of focusing on dance a bit more. This means that I skip a few band rehearsals in favor of dance rehearsals.

At the moment, I am going over to Bianca's house to drop off some supplies for a party she's having and to hopefully talk to her about what happened with Kate. I don't think she totally gets it yet. However, she did invite me to her party so she must not completely hate me at the moment. Of course, I hate parties though, so I declined and instead offered to help her set it up.

I pull into her driveway and unload several boxes of soda into my arms. Actually, make that more than several. Rather than put any boxes down, I decide the smartest move is to struggle them up the stairs and into the house. As I begin to climb the first step, the sound of the door above opening abruptly startles me.

"Sebastian?" I say, nonplussed, as he walks out and slams it shut.

"What are you doing here, Wren?" he demands more than asks.

"I—" My drinks are about to fall.

"You weren't at rehearsal the other day. Do you think you don't need the practice? Because if so, I can assure you that you do."

"Bash, do you think you could stop insulting me long enough to help me carry in these goddamn drinks?"

"Oh, sorry," he mutters, rushing down to me and grabbing two boxes right before they fall out of my arms. "You know, it is possible to make more than one trip rather than attempting to take everything in one go."

"Why are you here anyway?" I ask once we've set all the drinks safely on the entrance table.

"I believe that's the question I asked *you*."

"I'm here because Bianca asked me to help her set up for a party."

"That's right, you're friends. Ok, well, I'm just heading out…"

"I had no idea you were friends with Bianca as well."

"We are most certainly not friends, Wren. Of that, I can assure you." The grimness on his face lets me know he isn't joking around. Of course, I'm not entirely sure Sebastian is capable of joking to begin with.

"That still doesn't explain why you would be at her house."

"Well, I'm not here by choice. Speaking of which, I think I'll get going now," he says, moving past me and out the door.

And just like that, he's gone.

When Bianca shows up, I don't bring up that Sebastian was here. Instead, we both continue on as though everything is normal. And we both know this is a lie.

By the time I say goodbye and get back into my car, I am left with a bad feeling in my stomach.

As I start the drive back, I am nervously drumming on my steering wheel—something that is usually not a good sign. On impulse, I make a wrong turn before reaching my street and head down the old Hollow Bridge (cool name, huh?) toward my old studio. Right as I get to the bridge, I abruptly stop the car.

What in the hell am I doing? This is insane, stupid even—no, it's *insanely stupid*. I can't go back there.

But I can pull off here and go into The Black Forest (ok, this isn't its official name, but it's what I've always called it). I haven't been here in a while; not since the last time Bianca and I wandered in here together— which was a *long* time ago. We used to go all the time, 'cus every time we'd skip class and rehearsal—something Mrs. Davis hated us doing, we'd go here, up to the freaky-ass tree house we found. Sometimes, Violet would even come with us.

But, again, that was a long time ago.

Making my way through the brush, I get caught on about 50 different branches and thorns before finally stumbling into a clearing. *The tree house should be close—ah, yes, there it is!*

I run up to it, my heart beating faster than humanly possible. Wow, it looks exactly as it did when I was last here—rundown, creepy, and possibly dangerous. Can't wait to climb up to it!

I place my foot on the bottom of the ladder and begin to go up. It's rickety and fragile, so I'll have to be careful as I—oh, I broke it. Well, that's just part of the ladder, maybe if I just keep going I can—all my thoughts are cut off as the entire ladder begins to shake like the whole thing is about to crumble. I'm almost to the top, so I quickly scramble up the rest of the way, catching onto the edge of the tree-house floorboards just as the entire ladder falls down, landing with a great big crash on the ground. I almost think I might fall down too, but somehow I manage to pull myself up and over.

Oh man, am I glad that's over. Now I just have to call someone who will be willing to come—*Wait, no. Dear God, no.* I left my phone in the car.

Sweet Jesus, this day could not get any better.

"Wren?"

Who in the hell? I peer down over the edge of the platform to see who just said my name.

Standing at the base of the tree and staring up at me is Sebastian.

"All right, what's going on here?" he questions.

"I should be the one asking you that."

"*I* come here all the time. You, on the other hand, I have never seen here before."

"Has it occurred to you yet that I have also never seen *you* here before? How do you even know about this place?"

"My cousin showed it to me, a while back. I've been coming to this tree house ever since. And I see on the one time I find you here, you managed to destroy the only way up to it."

"Yeah, about that... Wait, first, did you follow me out here to lecture me more about coming to rehearsals? Is that why you're here?"

"Relax, Wren. I was coming here to have a quiet place to think when I heard some loud noises and then found you."

"I see. Um, not to bother your 'quiet thinking time' too much, but I'm too high up to jump, so do you think you could go get me some help to get down from here?"

"No."

"*No?*"

"Hey, you got yourself in this mess, I'm just gonna sit here while you figure out how to get out of it," he says, sitting against a nearby tree and pulling out a book.

"You have got to be kidding me! Bash—"

"Yes?" He doesn't even bother to look up.

"I've been stuck up in this tree for less than three minutes and I'm already going insane. If you leave me here, I'm going to die."

"Don't you think you're being a bit dramatic?"

"Nope, not really.

"I'm not leaving, I'm just going to sit here, reading."

"Oh great—'cus I was just thinking 'Wow! I'm completely stuck up here in this tree, if only some guy would come along and start reading a book.'"

He snaps his book shut and jumps up. "Damn, are you difficult."

"You know what, I'm just gonna jump. I'm just gonna do it, and see what happens."

"Quiet, I'm thinking."

"Great, you can just stand down there and *think* at me."

"Fine," he comes closer, "I'll leave. And then you'll never get down."

"Wait! Sebastian—"

"Wren, careful!"

But Bash's warning is too late; I've already moved too quickly, making a wrong step and losing my footing as I tumble off the side of the tree-house platform.

I scream as I fall, expecting to land and break something. But instead of landing on the hard forest floor, I land on Sebastian.

As my body hits his, he falls backwards onto the ground with me on top of him. He lifts me off him slightly and we both make shocked eye contact before he whispers, "Well, I guess you're down now."

I roll off him and stand up hurriedly. "Wow, look at the time, I better be going before my parents miss me too much."

"Wren," he stands up, "you don't have a watch on."

"Well, I should probably go get one. See you later, Bash."

I run back to my car, get in it, and drive home—relieved never to have to go back into The Black Forest again.

Three days until the "Rocket Queen" Show. That's what I've decided to call it. It's not like we are the main act or anything, it's a high school talent show after all, but I'm going to keep my name for it anyway. Thinking about it sometimes makes me get a little sick in the stomach. But Cara is coming home from her school trip tonight, which is taking most of my attention away from being nervous.

Once she gets home, we have a good time catching up together. She tells me all about the adventures she experienced over the past two weeks. Then I fill her in on what I've been up to. She thinks it's cool that I've joined a band. She says she likes the name Renegades.

But not everyone feels this way. Bianca still thinks the whole idea of it is stupid. To be fair, at the moment she hasn't quite gotten over what Kate had told her about me. We got along well enough while setting up her party, and she says she believes me, and that she always knew Kate was up to no good. But I'm pretty sure it's going to take some time for her to really forget about the whole thing. Regardless, she thinks I should focus my energy on dance rather than messing around in a band.

To be fair to myself, I did try this advice out all of last week and it didn't help me hardly at all. Despite this, in all seriousness, she may very well be logically correct. But since when have I ever let logic stop me?

CHAPTER 15

ROCKET KING

THIS IS IT. The time has finally come.

I've straightened my hair and put on eyeliner, leather pants, a black top, my cowboy boots and hat, and a red scarf tied around my waist. To finish the costume off, I add a streak of black eyeliner to each of my cheeks as well.

Backstage, my body is shaking and I can't get it to stop. My stomach is upset and my head hurts. If I'm going to do this, which I am, I have to calm down and play it cool. Everything is all right.

"Hey," Aidan taps me on the shoulder, "are you ready?"

I feel like I'm about to fall over and die; I swear my stomach is going to jump out of my body.

"Yes."

***

After the show, I find Aidan sitting out on the steps in front of the school parking lot. It's dark now and stars are shining high in the sky like something out of a movie.

"Hey," I say, sitting myself down next to him.

"Hey, Evans," he says back, his voice sounding a little off.

"So it went pretty well, huh?"

"Yeah, it did."

"I mean, they tried to get us off stage, but we kept going. We finished it."

Aidan doesn't say anything.

"You should do 'Out Ta Get Me' or 'Anything Goes' next," I say.

"Hmm, those would really get us in trouble."

"Yeah, can you imagine people's reactions? They'd flip." Aidan still looks pretty down. I wish I could make him feel better. "You know," I say, nudging him, "once you guys find a real singer, I think you're really gonna take off. You'll be amazing, and nothing will stand in your way."

He sighs and looks at me. "Thanks, Wren. That means a lot."

"So what are you doing out here? Shouldn't you be celebrating with the rest of the guys?"

"Noah was supposed to drive me home. He didn't come."

Now it makes sense.

"Aidan, I'm so sorry."

"I should have expected it." His eyes are starting to glisten as he looks to the sky.

I put a hand on his shoulder and stare off into the stars with him.

A few minutes later, Tommy and a group of other teens come out and grab Aidan, taking him into their car. They're going to a party back at Tommy's house. He invites me to come with them, but I really don't feel like it, in fact I feel kind'a empty, so I say I have to go home and finish up homework. He gives me his address anyway, telling me I should change my mind.

But the only thing on my mind now is how I feel like I'm missing something.

I begin driving around aimlessly, the pain in my heart welling up to an unbearable point. I don't know what happened, a few hours ago I felt absolutely over the moon and now I'm so down I can barely think straight.

Where do my illusions end and the truth begin? I can't tell anymore. Or maybe I never could. I really think my reality is blurred, completely twisted within my own mind. My illusions *are* my truth now.

A buzzing noise from my phone takes me out of my head and I pull over to see what it is. It's a message from Aidan reading: *Hey Wren, sorry. I really need to get out of this party n I don't think I can walk myself anywhere right now. Please pick me up?*

I can tell from the text alone that he is drunk. Well, at least it gives me something to do.

I pull up to Tommy's house and walk up to the door. It's very loud inside; there must be a lot of people. I ring the doorbell, but, unsurprisingly, no one answers. So I open up the door myself, but before I can come in, Bianca comes stumbling out.

Her eyebrows raise as she sees me. "Wren, what're you…"

"I'm here for Aidan. Is he in there?"

"Maybe," she shrugs, "maybe not."

I go to step around her but she reaches out and grabs my shoulder.

"How did the show go?"

"It went well."

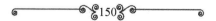

"Of course it did." She huffs and rolls her eyes.

"Did you really care to know?" I ask. "Or did you just want to be able to roll your eyes at me?"

"No, I didn't really care to know. You have the prettiest eyes I've ever seen; you know that? So dark and blue at the same time..."

"Bianca—"

"Your whole face, with your cheekbones and everything—it annoys me sometimes that you're so pretty."

"You're pretty too," I say awkwardly. This might be the most unpleasant conversation I've had in a while.

"Save it, please. I used to envy you, I suppose I still do, but you seem to have fallen so far from where you once were—now I mostly feel pity."

My eyes threaten to well with hot tears.

She continues on. "It always amazed me how little luck you've ever had when it comes to romance, but maybe it doesn't anymore... Oh, don't cry Wren. I'd hate to see that pretty face of yours in pain."

"Evans!" I turn and see Aidan coming toward us. His dark hair falls in his face and he can barely walk without stumbling. I grab him by the arm and take him to my car. I don't look back at Bianca. I don't think I can.

"Wren, you'll never believe it," he says as soon as we get in the car. "I met this guy tonight, Rob, and man can he sing! I heard him doing karaoke and I knew I had to talk to him, so I told him about the band and then guess what—he said he'd be our lead singer!"

"That's great." Rob, that name sounds familiar. Well, I guess it's not exactly very uncommon though.

"I know, right!"

I start tapping my fingers on the steering wheel and biting my lip.

"You just gotta know," he says abruptly.

"Know what, Aidan? You're drunk," I say pointedly.

"You're drunk."

"No I'm not. You are. I should get you home."

"You want to take me home?" he asks with something between a snort and a giggle.

"Amazing, your humor is just as stupid drunk as when sober."

"Someone spiked all the punch at the party."

"No they didn't, that stuff only happens in movies."

"No, it happens for real."

"Not around here it doesn't."

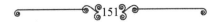

"You did good today, Wren. You did really good."

"Thank you. I'm gonna get you home now."

"No, that's bad." He shakes his head and looks out the window.

"Ok... what am I supposed to do with you?"

"Noah is here, and I don't want to be around him."

"Ok, I get it. But I still need to take you somewhere."

"Where is that?"

"I don't know, I'll figure it out."

I begin driving back to my house, but then it hits me.

"Hey, was Sebastian at the party tonight?"

"Bash? No way, he hates parties."

Figures. "How about I take you over to his place? Where does he live again?"

"He lives close to my neighborhood."

"Ok, but you have to tell me where specifically."

"Twenty-nine eighty-eight Newbury Lane."

I'm surprised he actually remembers that right now. "Got it."

A few minutes later, I notice Aidan has gone completely silent and I start to worry.

"Aidan? Aidan, are you ok?"

He turns toward me, his face twisted in pain.

"He didn't come. He said he would come."

I glance over at him, unsure of how to help. Sebastian said Noah would do this, and he was right.

The hurt in his expression suddenly morphs into a sizzling anger. "I don't want this anymore," he growls, taking off the leather jacket that used to belong to Noah.

"You might want it when—"

"He said he'd come. How could he do that?"

"I don't know, Aidan."

"I hate him, Wren. I hate him." Tears begin streaming down his face, and he puts his hand up to his forehead. He turns away from me, but I can see his body shaking out of the corner of my eye.

We are both silent the rest of the way there. I can't pretend to understand exactly what he is going through, but I can feel his pain. He falls asleep by the time we reach our destination, so I leave him in the car as I go up to the door to get Sebastian.

He opens it before I even knock.

"Wren?"

"Uh, Aidan, he's in my car. I think he's a bit drunk, and I wasn't sure what to do with him. He said he didn't want to go home."

"Noah's there?"

"Yes."

He nods like he understands and begins walking toward my car. "He can stay here for the night. I'll make sure he's ok."

Sebastian helps me wake up Aidan and walk/carry him inside. We lay him on the sofa. I look down at him for a second. I hope he's going to be ok. But what does being ok even really mean?

Wait, the jacket! I run back to the car and grab it, taking it to Sebastian. "Make sure he gets this."

He nods, placing it next to the sofa.

"Thank you for doing this, Bash," I say as I step back outside.

"Hey, wait!" he calls after me. He almost looks nervous. "I wanted to tell you that you did well tonight, with the performance and all."

I nod and give him a half-smile. I used to think I really wanted to hear Bash say something like that to me, but now—even though it's nice—I don't feel I need it anymore.

"Bye," I wave as I get in my car.

"Goodbye, Wren."

Truth is, I don't much feel the need for approval for anything anymore.

After leaving Bash's place, I sit in front of my house on the steps and look up at the stars. The wind blows my hair across my face, and I breathe in the air around me. I can feel it all. I can see past everything, see it for what it truly is: the beauty, pain, love, anger, understanding, freedom, and hope. For this moment in time, I've found myself. I am where I'm meant to go, and I know peace. But it's fleeting and almost as soon as I feel it, I lose it. Even so, the ghost of what it was remains tattooed on my soul.

CHAPTER 16

HIGHWAY TO HEAVEN

SINCE THEIR FIRST DATE, Lena knew Rose was the one. They just had that special connection—the kind of connection written about in poetry and movies. But, this didn't mean they didn't have their share of hardships.

At the moment, things were going rough for them, which made Lena's life a lot more difficult than usual. She still put on happy smile and continued to pretend to be the bubbly, joyful girl people liked to see—but this really just seemed to do her more harm than good.

On top of this, she'd just gotten her driver's license and now her parents were beginning to pressure her into driving herself everywhere, no matter what—something Lena did *not* enjoy doing. And while Rose had been giving her rides to help her out, that had pretty much stopped by now.

She kept her relationship troubles to herself since she had recently found an unlikely confidant in Wren. As strange as it was, she knew she could tell her anything without worrying about gossip or judgment. The one thing that bothered her about Wren was that she rarely ever shared anything back with her. She would listen carefully, and give advice when she could, but she never talked about her own difficulties. Lena didn't understand it.

She also didn't care much for Wren's other friends. Aidan was ok, he seemed like a good, charming guy, but Bianca, Ella, Kate, and all the rest of them—they rubbed her the wrong way. However, Bianca came up to her the other day telling her that she wanted them to become better friends; so perhaps she would come to see her as Wren did.

And besides, regardless of whom Wren hung out with, Lena knew she could trust her. So, when Wren *did* choose to share something, she knew it was the truth. All this thinking about Wren made Lena want to see her; so she picked up the phone and gave her a call, asking if she wanted to go to Riverview to visit her favorite museum there.

Yes, a nice relaxing day with her friend was exactly what she needed right now.

This evening, my parents are both still working and Cara's with a friend watching a musical, so I watch a horror movie by myself. I've been told before that this is not a smart thing to do, but I don't have anyone to watch it with, so what am I supposed to do? Besides, I don't scare like most people.

So, I hop over the back of the couch and curl up with my blanket and some popcorn. Just as things are heating up on screen, there is a loud knocking sound on the window behind the couch. Not going to lie, it makes me flinch. I look over my shoulder, ready to fight someone and see Aidan standing outside. I turn off the TV, open the window latch, and he climbs through it.

"Why didn't you just knock on the front door? Are you still super hung over or something?"

He frowns. "I tried, but your movie must have been too loud because you didn't hear me. Anyway, I'm here because I don't remember much of last night, but Bash told me that you were the one who picked me up and took me to him so I just wanted to say thank you."

"You don't need to thank me."

"And I want to make sure that you don't think that I'm, that I would usually—I'm not—"

"I understand," I reassure him. I know he doesn't have a habit of going to parties and drinking. He's not like that.

His cheeks flush slightly. "I also… I wanted to talk to you about what we talked about in the car. Do you think we could go outside?"

"Sure."

***

"What do you remember from the conversation we had?" he asks once we sit down on the front steps.

"You talked about your brother."

He nods like he already suspected as much.

"He means a lot to you," I say.

"My parents, they split a long time ago. I haven't seen my dad in three years—and when he was around, he was mean. My mom never did anything, I don't think she knew what to do, and I'll probably always resent her for that. To be honest, that hurt me more than any of the stuff my dad did. It's ok though; she's barely ever at home now. But Noah was always there; he would protect me. He was all I had." His brow furrows deeper as he continues. "I can't give up on him. It doesn't matter how far he goes or—" his voice breaks for a moment, "I just, I have to be there for him now. He needs me."

I look at him as he squints into the setting sun. "Aidan, you're a good brother. He's lucky to have you."

He lets out a deep breath and turns to face me. "I do what I can."

After Aidan leaves, I can't help but feel stupid for ever feeling so sad for myself. I've got a family; I get along with my parents and my sister; I can afford to go to dance lessons; and I get a nice house to come home to. There are so many people who have it so much worse than me—so many *good* people. Aidan may not see it, but he deserves the world. I only wish I could give it to him.

If nothing else, at least I am able to keep Kate away from him. She still stares at him from time to time, but it's nothing compared to how she stares at me. At school, I stay out of her way and she stays out of mine, and for the most part this seems to work—but I have noticed her looking at me in a way that really gets under my skin. It's like she's constantly thinking of ways to torture and kill me—or something. I'd like to get her to stop, but I don't think I can, and I figure that just being able to get her to leave Aidan alone is enough. I don't want to push it.

The next day, I get a call from Lena asking if I want to go to the museum in Riverview with her—the one I went with Cara and Aidan to a while back.

I don't want to go anywhere right now, but I know she's having some problems with her girlfriend, and I think she just wants to get away for a while, so I say yes. Also, Riverview is one of the most beautiful places in California so anything over there strikes my interest.

***

I walk into Lena's house and immediately the scent of lavender over-whelms me. Not sure why, but that's what her house is doing to me. Though for some reason it's messing with my head and I can't wait to get out of here.

"You ready yet?" I call out.

"Almost!" Lena yells back.

"Yeah, ok. In case you forgot, we're only going to a museum, not a freak-ing red carpet event." This girl is a lot of things, but fast is not one of them.

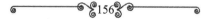

And I forgot my phone at home, so I can't even do weird Wikipedia research to occupy my time and keep me from boredom.

"I'm ready, are you?" she asks, coming out of the bathroom with curled hair and a red dress.

"Only for the past ten years since I've been waiting for you."

She gives me an innocent smile and we head out.

"I just got my license pretty recently, that's exciting, isn't it?" she chirps as we walk toward my car.

I turn around to face her, walking backwards. "I didn't know you knew how to drive."

"Usually Rose gives me a ride, that's why you never see me on the road." I forgot her girlfriend's name was Rose until right now. I should pay attention to these things more—after all, she's only talked to me about her a *thousand* times.

"Awesome, so you can drive us."

"Actually, I'm not totally comfortable with driving just yet."

"Aw come on, it'll be good for you."

"I'm serious. I don't think I'm ready yet."

"You're good enough to have gotten your license, you're good enough to drive the straight road to Riverview. It's not like it's a real complicated route."

"I don't know."

"You'll do great."

"I really don't think—"

I hold up my hand to stop her protests. "No more excuses. I'm taking shotgun."

"Ok, fine," she says while grabbing out her keys, "I'll do it. But you know that means I get to control the music and you're in charge of directions."

"Well like I said, it's basically a straight shot, so deal."

***

"How are things with you?" I ask once we're out on the road.

"To tell you the truth, me and Rose are in a difficult spot in our relationship."

"Oh. I hope you guys work through things all right."

"Me too," she sighs. "Wren, are you ever going to get with someone? In a relationship, I mean—I've just never seen you with anyone in that way."

"Probably not. I can't see myself ever finding someone."

Lena shakes her head. "Someday you'll find someone you can call your own."

"I really don't think so. Who would ever want me?" As the words come out of my mouth I realize just how true they are. I have nothing to offer someone as a real partner in life. I'm neurotic, stubborn, antisocial, temperamental, narcissistic, obsessive, and sad as hell.

"To be honest," I begin, "I'm not so focused on that sort'a stuff right now. I kind'a just want to be good, like a good person."

"What does that mean?"

"I'm not sure. I just wish I didn't think about myself so much. I want to put others first, and when I don't, then I feel like I'm letting everyone down, you know?"

She doesn't answer but I can tell she's thinking about it.

After what seems like a rather long time of driving, we reach Riverview and begin crossing over the bridge. I look out the window to see the horizon against the water. It's beautiful.

Suddenly, I see something out there that makes me sit up and press my hands against the windowpane. I lean forward until my nose is almost touching the glass. Birds, what appears to be hundreds of birds, begin flying over the water in our direction. They seem to pick up speed the closer they get, and I cock my head to the side as I squint at them.

My gaze follows the birds as I turn my head back to the road. While they captivate my attention out of the corner of my eye I notice a truck on the other side of the road up ahead, the first vehicle we've seen this whole time. I start to look away but then I notice that it's driving exceptionally fast and unusually jerky, especially for a straight road. They must be drunk or on drugs.

This isn't…

I look to Lena but she's so engrossed in looking at the birds that she doesn't even realize what's happening. I open my mouth to point it out to her, but as it approaches us it suddenly swerves into our lane. Then, as they say in the movies, everything happens so quickly.

Lena screams and turns the wheel harshly, steering us out of the path of collision. We start to head straight for the edge of the bridge, and I grab the wheel as she lets go of it. I turn it left but it's too sharp, causing the car to flip and roll off to the side.

The force of the airbag hits me like a wall of steel, knocking the wind out of me on impact. As we flip, my head slams against things multiple

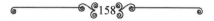

times and I almost black out completely. I can barely make out anything besides the near-blinding pain, everything else just appears as a whirlwind rushing by until the car rolls over the edge and down into the river.

By some miracle we land upright, but we're still going to sink to the bottom in a matter of minutes.

As I struggle with my seatbelt, I look to Lena to see if she's ok, but the throbbing in my brain as I turn my head causes my vision to go sparkly. My chest is on fire from being unable to breath and water begins to fill up the car.

We are going to die.

What is happening? My conscience is slipping and I can hardly tell if this is real.

No, what's real is we're in a car that's about to go to Davy Jones's locker.

I have to pull myself together enough to get us out of here.

I reach over to Lena, fighting the banging pain in my mind, and find her motionless with her head tilted to the side at an unnatural angle.

No, it can't be.

I undo her seatbelt and grab her, pulling her toward me. The water in the car has filled up to our waists now. *Crap. I have to break a window. How the hell do I do this?*

I quickly scan the windows, mine is the most cracked looking. The last time I tried something like this, it didn't work so well, but I have no other choice. I lean back and kick it as hard as I can. Nothing happens, we're sinking more rapidly.

"Come on!" I scream.

I kick again, this time the glass seems to crack a bit more. The water in the car continues to rise. I pull back my leg for one final kick—if this doesn't work it's going to be too late, we'll be too far underwater to escape. I kick my foot into the window with every last fiber of my strength, driving it straight through the glass. Immediately, more water begins pouring in, making it nearly impossible to get out. But I grab Lena and pull her along with me, forcing us through the opening.

Holding onto her, I begin swimming to the surface. For a moment, I don't think we're going to make it to the top; my lungs are on fire and my legs are giving out. After what seems like an eternity, we finally break the surface. I want to collapse now, but I'm still hanging onto Lena, trying to hold her deadweight while keeping her head above water.

I whip around, looking for help, but there is no help. We're alone out here. And I'm not strong enough to get us to shore.

No, I can't let her die.

I don't know how I made it there, but I did by heaving Lena out of the water before crawling ashore myself. Lena's body looks like that of a doll, as she lies crumpled in a heap on the ground. Once I reach her I fall to my knees and desperately grab for her. Wrong—it's wrong. She isn't moving. There's no rise and fall of her chest. No moans of pain—absolute silence. Her skin is covered in dark bruises and some of her limbs appear to be pointing in the wrong direction.

"No. Lena, please… please. We made it. You're ok. Just—you're gonna be ok. It's ok. I've got you."

I cradle her head in my lap, rocking back and forth, my surroundings blurring together more and more.

"It's ok. I've got you."

Everything aches and black spots dance in my vision.

"I've got you."

I pass out, unable to hold out any longer.

I've got you.

CHAPTER 17

SYMPATHY FOR THE ANGEL

I WAKE UP IN A HOSPITAL BED with a nurse fiddling with something by my bedside. I quickly sit upright and immediately my hand shoots up to my head as I groan involuntarily. I feel like my brain has been whacked with a sledgehammer. I make moves to get up but the nurse rushes over to me and tries to force me back in bed.

"Honey, you can't get up right now. I need you to lay back for me, ok?"

"Where's Lena?"

"The other girl from the crash at Riverview?"

"Yes, where is she?" I push the nurse's hands off me and swing my legs over the edge of the bed.

"She's all right, you can see her soon, just not now."

"Where? I need to see her now."

When she doesn't answer me, I stand up and start for the door. If she isn't going to help me, I'll find Lena myself.

"Miss, please, you need to get back in bed! You may have a concussion!"

She grabs me by the arm and I shove her off me, a little harder than I mean to, and run out into the hallway. I can hear her calling after me, but I keep going. I turn my head over my shoulder to see if I'm being followed and then suddenly, bam! I run smack into a doctor. Fortunately for me, she turns out to be a nice doctor and after talking to the nurse for a while, she comes back over to me.

"Hello, Wren. I understand that you're looking for your friend?"

"Yes, her name is Lena."

"She is with her family right now, so you won't be able to see her for a few hours most likely."

"Is she all right?"

"There was some minor internal bleeding, but it's nothing too serious. She'll be fine."

"What about all her broken bones?"

"Broken bones?"

"Yes, when we got out of the river her limbs were pointing in the wrong direction." It's like these people don't know anything.

"There were no broken limbs, the shock of the crash may have caused you to see certain things that weren't real."

Huh?

"I mean that you may have been having hallucinations. It's probably best for you to go home and rest, after you have a CT scan, that is. We will give you a call when Lena is ready for visitors."

I let them give me a CT scan—no concussion, thank God—and then I have to talk to some police officers. Apparently the truck we almost hit took off as soon as they called 911. They've got quite a few questions, but I can't even remember what color the truck was or much of anything else. If I can't see Lena, I want to go home.

My parents come with Cara to pick me up not long after, and they all also have a million questions. After answering them, I go up to my bed and lie there, staring at my ceiling while I wait for the phone to ring. Cara tries to come in and stay with me, she's definitely been crying, but I tell her I need to be alone.

While I wait for the house phone to ring, I check through my cell— lucky I forgot it here—and find that I have quite a few missed messages from a couple different people like some relatives, Aidan, and—surprisingly—Sebastian. I don't get back to any of them, at least not yet.

Then, the house phone begins to go off, and I nearly jump at the sound of it.

"Yes?" I say, picking it up.

"Wren, please tell me you're ok! I heard what happened—"

"Violet?" I can't believe it.

"Yes, tell me how you are." It's really her.

"I'm fine. You don't need to worry about me. I'm really fine." I haven't spoken to her in so long.

"How could you be fine? What happened was terrible! You're mother told mine all about it."

"It wasn't as scary as people are probably making it out to be."

"I'm coming over."

"No, you don't need to. I promise Vi, I'm all right."

"You're all right? How is that possible?"

"Just because things aren't all right doesn't mean they're not *all right*."

"That doesn't make any sense."

"I'll come to you some time, you don't need to come over here."

"I can get my parents to take me to you right now."

"No, no that's ok. I'm all-good right now. I've had lots of visitors so it would be best I think if I were to just get some rest at the moment."

"Are you sure?"

"Uh-huh." My throat is getting tighter.

"Ok. But, if you need anything, please let me know." She sounds kind of sad.

"Yep, I will. Goodbye, Violet."

"Bye, Wren."

I hang up and throw the phone across the room onto my bed. Then I decide it's time I changed clothes—they're still damp and extremely dirty. As I slip my jeans off, I notice something strange sticking out of one of the pockets. I stick my hand in and pull out what appears to be a crumpled piece of paper; but smoothing it out, I see that it's something much more. It's a note and says:

I'm coming for you.

Ah, well that's cheery.

I wonder who wrote it? And why are they "coming for me"? Are we going to dinner? A movie?

There's only one creep I know creepy enough to do something like this: Seth. He can come for me if he likes, but I'm not going to let him get me.

***

It seems like an eternity before the hospital gets back to me, but as soon as they do, I have my parents take me straight back there. Though I'm greeted with even more waiting once I get there because her family decides they actually want some more alone time with her. And then Rose shows up with tears streaming down her cheeks, and I have to wait some more.

My dad tells me that they may not want anyone else around today and that it might be a good idea for us to leave for the day and try again later.

We're about to leave when Rose stops us and says that Lena has been asking for me. She then leads me to her room and goes off to get some coffee or something, saying she'll be right back.

I take a shaky breath and step inside the room, closing the door behind me.

"Hey, I'm here," I whisper.

"Wren, I can't believe you're finally here! I feel like I've been asking about you forever!"

"I feel like I've been trying to see you forever. Lena…" Her usual olive-toned skin looks pale, and her face is visibly tired. My stomach drops.

"It's ok, please don't cry. I don't want to see you cry, please."

"I'm trying. It's just, for a while there, I don't know…"

"Don't you cry tonight. Isn't that one of those songs you love?"

"Yeah—yes it is." I sniff and wipe my eyes, a small smile appears on my lips.

"Oh! And look at this! My dad brought it in for me, he said it could keep me entertained while I spend the night here," she says excitedly, pointing to a small and rather old radio on the nightstand next to her bed.

"Awesome," I say, examining it before turning it on.

After it begins playing, I hesitate and then sit on the edge of the bed. "I'm so—I'm so, so sorry. I never should have pressured you to drive," I choke out. "I wish I could go back and change everything—this never should have happened to you. I'm sorry."

Lena stares up at me with wide eyes and smiles sadly. "I know. Things just happen sometimes."

I turn my head and look out the window at the dark-gray sky. "Not to you. It shouldn't have happened to you."

"What's done is done."

I know Lena is going to be ok, but it's still my fault she's here. I'm to blame, and perhaps, subconsciously, she knows that too.

She could have *died*, and it would have all been because of me—because I made her do it. She never would have gotten behind the wheel if I hadn't pushed her to do it. And after all that, I couldn't even warn her fast enough.

***

I don't leave her side all night. Even after Rose is gone and her parents kiss her goodnight and go home to bed, I'm still here. My own parents try convincing me that it would be for the best for me to come home as well, but I don't listen.

Long after Lena falls asleep, I'm still sitting there in the dark, head in

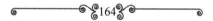

my hands, listening to the radio softly play as the rain pours down outside. The last notes of the song playing fade out and, whether it's fate or something else, "Don't Cry" comes on. The soft melody of the song's beginning is more jarring than anything that had happened earlier today. My head shoots up and the tears I'd been trying so hard to keep away suddenly become unstoppable.

"No, no, no, no, no—" I begin whispering over and over until I no longer realize what I'm saying.

CHAPTER 18

HOME SWEET NOTHING

SETH WAS NEVER LIKE THE OTHER KIDS AROUND HIM. He saw things differently, felt things differently. He didn't really understand people's emotions, and he definitely didn't care about them. All he knew was what he wanted.

And when he wanted someone, he didn't just want the person; he became *obsessed* with her. The thing is, he was always so good looking and charming that no one ever really had a problem with his behavior. And, these obsessions were generally short-lived because not long after they started, he would become bored of the object of his fascination and throw that girl away, no matter who they were.

Boredom became his worst enemy. And while he was stuck, never knowing what he was really looking for, no one he knew could seem to help him. Sometimes he really hated life and wished desperately for something, *anything* to relieve his apathy.

As he grew up, he became increasingly restless and angry, to the point where some might have even said he was dangerous. Seth had learned to mask his true nature, with the ability to force himself to appear calm and controlled at a moment's notice. With this ability, combined with his muscular physique, he became very successful in both school and extracurricular activities. He always got good grades, possessed great athletic ability, became popular, and had a girlfriend—just never one he particularly cared about. However, it wasn't like he actually considered any of them to *really* be his girlfriend in a serious way. These girls were more like toys he could use and manipulate as part of a continuous game he got stuck playing. And because his father was the director of a large school of dance—a profession he found rather stupid—there was a seemingly never-ending selection of girls to pick from whenever he wanted. Yet even this overabundance of girls soon became dull, because it was all so *easy*.

Then, one day, while he watched people at the dance studio, he spotted a girl he hadn't seen before. Her body type was unusually slender, almost boyish, and her hair fell down over her shoulders in waves of dark brown. She had headphones on and listened to something, swaying slightly to the beat as her fingers adjusted her shirt—*a Led Zeppelin shirt*, he noted.

He knew immediately there was something strange about her, and then she looked up at him with large, deep blue eyes, and something in him clicked.

My birthday is coming up, but seeing as how so much craziness has been going on, I haven't thought about it. It's been two weeks since the accident and Lena has long since been back at school her usual perky self, seemingly good as new. Her injuries weren't nearly as serious as I had seen them in my head—thank goodness.

While she appears to be great, I'm still having trouble sleeping, waking up in a cold sweat after visions of her dying on the road, in the hospital, in my arms. My therapist has asked me about it, but to be honest I haven't said much to her. Finally, though, it's showing signs of getting better.

Sometimes no matter how much I feel like crap, I thought I'd feel a whole lot worse. For one, I expected to be scared of getting in a moving vehicle for a while, but I've had no trouble jumping right back in Nightrider and driving myself around as usual. In fact, if anything, I've been driving a bit faster than I used to, like I need to get somewhere. Once I allow myself to let go, I'll feel better just like Lena. Till then, I just have to suffer with my feelings.

It's been a bit annoying at my therapy sessions, all Amelia wants to talk about is the accident. And it's all my parents and people at school want to talk about. It's all anyone wants to talk about—and I don't want to have anything to do with talking about it.

In fact, I don't much want to talk about anything at all.

***

April

I have not written anything in forever. I'm writing this because I probably should be getting some stuff out and onto paper. If I'm keeping it all inside, silence isn't the way.

Still, I haven't spoken to Aidan—beside what few conversations we have to have in psychology. I thought about telling him about the note I received,

but then I'd have to explain some things... some things I don't ever want to explain. Besides, he's usually busy with his work anyway.

I haven't even talked to Lena very much and I've mostly avoided Ella and Bianca altogether.

The last interaction I can think of is:

Ella: "So, you were in a crash."

Me: "Yes, thank you for reminding me. I almost forgot."

The only person who doesn't bring up the damn accident is Eric. He can tell that I don't want to talk about it.

And Aidan—though he's just not talking to me much in general. For some reason, this is what hurts me the most.

I don't want to be here. I don't know where I want to be, but it ain't here.

I'm alone, my heart has been ripped from my body and my mind is so far gone no one will ever find it.

I am Iron Man.

Not the movie one, the Black Sabbath song one. Staring alone at the world, and no one wants him.

The memories just keep coming for me. I can't escape them. That's the problem with having dark things in your mind, there's nowhere to run and nowhere to hide. The monsters are a part of you.

The words *my fault, my fault, my fault* are like a virus in my brain.

To keep myself from completely falling apart, I put my headphones on and play "Knockin' On Heaven's Door". But it doesn't work. I still end up with hot tears streaming down my face as I fall into a restless sleep.

The sky is a dark, inky purple that mixes in with the clouds and hides the stars. Something feels off, like I'm up in the strange-colored sky looking down on something. Upon closer inspection, I see there's a figure crouched on the ground—no, two—and one of them is holding the other in their arms. I look closer and see that it's Violet and, she's holding... me? There's blood on her face and all over her hands from where she had tried to stop the bleeding from a wound in, well I can't tell where it's from because it appears there is blood everywhere. It's seeping out of my clothes and running down my face from my eyes. She bends her head down to whisper something to me and suddenly I am in my body, looking up into her eyes.

"Why? Why'd you have to do it?" she asks softly, her voice cracking slightly.

I try to speak but can't.

"You're all alone now," she says. "All alone."

I wake up gasping as my eyes bolt open.

To punish myself, I listen to "Stairway to Heaven" while replaying bad memories. I know this is something I shouldn't do, but I do it anyway.

I'm hurting. I'm really hurting.

I feel more alone than anyone seems. And the pain—I can't take it anymore. I lie in bed in the middle of the night, crying to the point that everything turns to nothing—everything. I can't think or else I'll fall back into my ever-fading world.

Lying there, I might as well be dead.

And no one knows.

After this, I watch the "Sweet Child O' Mine" music video over and over to give me some comfort.

Where do I go now?

Maybe I could just run away and become a rock star. Why haven't I done this yet? Oh yeah, I forgot—I have no talent. Guess I'll have to stick around and get some normal-person job. How lame is that? Actually, nah, if I were to end up living a normal life I would blow my goddamn brains out. Regular living is never enough for me. I'll have to find something else—or die trying.

In the morning, I'd like to stay home all day and do nothing but play my records and figure out how I am going to live my life. Too bad I have to get my butt off to dance. Last time, after class, my teacher told me I need to come to rehearsals more often because I have too much talent to throw it all away. I think it's a load of crap though. I think my technique and ability peaked about three years ago, and it has been downhill from there.

After dance, I go to the theater and watch a movie.

I think I've said before that you haven't got to worry about the way a movie is going to turn out, but I think the truth is more complicated than that. Say all films and their endings do mean something, what about if you don't *like* what they mean? Then what, you're stuck with that? No thanks. Then I have to sort of make my own ending up as I leave the theater. Sometimes I'll spend almost an hour simply daydreaming up ways to continue or end a story from a movie.

I'd like to make a movie someday—make things the way they're supposed to be.

When I get back home, I turn my light off but my brain is still very much on.

Tomorrow is my birthday. I will officially be one year older.

Lying here in the dark, my mind comes up with unwanted visions I can't shake. This time, I see my parents at my funeral, crying. But the worst was definitely imagining my sister, the one person I know I couldn't live without, and how she would be. I continue to watch the aftermath of my death unfold and see how my family fares without me. It's not a pretty sight, but my head is so wrapped into it, it all seems real. When I do finally escape, a new pit has formed in my stomach.

***

April 17, middle of the night—

I technically just turned seventeen a few hours ago, and I don't like it. I thought going to the movies would relax me, but I still can't fall asleep. Can not getting sleep cause you to be delusional? I swear I'm seeing things in the night now. Shadows that come to life while I'm lying in bed trying to fall asleep and failing miserably.

Thing is, even so, I'm not afraid. Not a bit.

I imagine them leaning over me as they whisper things in my ear and reach out shadowy hands to suffocate me.

Live and let die.

***

Getting out of bed the next morning is really hard. I just want to fall back into a deep sleep, part of me returning to the dark feeling of wishing to never wake up—but I do it. I pull myself together, put on my leather jacket, and walk right out the door.

I actually completely forget it's my birthday until my parents stop me to say "Happy birthday" right before pulling out of the driveway. Oh yes, that's right, I turned seventeen today—one year closer to death. I feel great.

At school, the only one who remembers it's my birthday is Bianca. But I don't blame 'em or anything—this sort of thing can be hard to remember.

***

At dance this afternoon, I mess up everything I try to do—no longer surprising yet still disappointing. Apparently, being seventeen doesn't give

me more skill. And I can tell from the look in my teacher's eyes that she's tired of this, of me. Well I'm tired of me too.

Coming out of the studio, I consider hopping over the back fence to the railroad tracks again. Instead, I go to my car and sit there without moving.

"I'm going to die alone. I'll never have anyone to show me the things in life that I can't see," I say to no one. When you're in a not-so-good place, sometimes you talk to yourself.

I'm a failure at everything. Anything I do, I mess up and there's always going to be someone who can do it better. So then what's the point? What am I doing? How is it worth anything?

No one ever answers.

I just want to be really good at something and then I can be confident, and say, "Yeah, this is what I do, and I'm really good at it." Maybe if I make this my birthday wish it will come true.

That ain't the way things work though, and I know it.

***

Back at home, my family sings me "Happy Birthday" and gives me some more art supplies and *GN'R: Lies* in CD format. Also, it turns out Violet sent me a card in the mail, which was nice of her.

I go up to my room after we eat cake and put my new CD in, turning up the volume. I'm going to sit here and listen to this forever. You know how a lot of singers' voices are pretty and smooth and sweet? His voice is more like a hot, grated knife, slicing straight through your heart—or like fire burning ice. I've never heard anything more amazing.

***

Next day at school, while I'm sitting with Eric during lunch, Lena comes up to us and sits down next to me. She looks very nice today, wearing a yellow sundress with her hair all done up and everything. I wonder if Rose is taking her out somewhere.

"Can I speak with you alone for a sec?"

I look at Eric and he nods.

"How are you holding up?" she asks after we walk over to some trees a few feet away.

I lean against a tree and tilt my head back on it. "Swell." I thought she was going to wish me a belated happy birthday, but I guess not.

"Is that the truth?"

"Doesn't matter."

"Yes it does. Whenever you want to talk—"

"I'm sorry, Lena. I don't think I can do this right now." Every time I look at her face…

"We were both in that accident together. If anyone understands, it's me."

"You think I don't know that?"

"I didn't mean it that way. But if you want—"

"I just want to wake up and not hate the person I see in the mirror every day." What a dramatic thing for me to say.

"What are you talking about? You're beautiful, Wren."

No, she doesn't get it. It's—whatever is inside me, I can't stand it.

"I really am sorry, Lena. For all of it."

"I know, but that doesn't change the fact that it happened, does it?" Her words sting, but I know they're true. "The least you could do now is *talk* to me."

I knew it. There is a part of her that blames me.

***

Back at home, I turn on the TV and stare blankly into the screen. Some time later, while I'm still sitting in front of the TV, I get a call from an unknown number. Before I even pick up, I get an unsettling feeling. I could choose not to answer, but the desire for a distraction from the pain I'm feeling makes me pick up.

"Hello?"

"Hello, Wren." My stomach drops. "Happy birthday."

"Seth. My birthday was yesterday."

"I know."

"Why are you calling? Are creepy, handwritten notes not enough?" I say, thinking of the one I found after being at the hospital. There's no doubt; it must have been him.

"I can assure you I don't know what you're talking about."

Sure you don't. "How do you have my number?"

"How do you think?"

"Bianca gave it to you," I deduce. Whatever he asks for, I'm willing to bet she gives him. "But that doesn't explain why you would want it." I know I should hang up, but I need answers.

"I've been watching you—"

"What do you mean 'watching me'?"

"To see if you were ready."

Watching me… "Wait a moment," I say—pieces beginning to come together in my brain, "was that you at the aquarium? And again at the football game?" The silence at the other end lets me know I'm correct. "Oh my God! I thought I was crazy! How did you know I would be there? And why would you need to watch me to begin with?"

"It's complicated, but Bianca had mentioned you'd be there, and I thought perhaps it would be a good time to discuss—"

"That was months ago. Why wait so long to contact me?" My patience is wearing thin.

"Don't interrupt me again. I went there to see if you were ready, but after seeing you, I decided more time was needed. And, I've been rather busy myself—not everything revolves around you, Wren."

"There is an 'end call' button, and at the moment, I am pretty inclined to use it."

"I wouldn't do that if I were you."

"Why? Are you suggesting that you might actually get to the point of this conversation within this lifetime?"

"You ask far too many questions."

"All right, then I'll hang up."

"Wait!"

I pause and hear nothing but silence on the other end for a moment.

"I want us to meet—in person," he says finally.

"Not a chance," I retort, holding in a scoff.

"You don't know why I want to meet," he challenges.

"No, but I know you won't tell me."

"Can't you just trust me?"

I feel my body go rigid. "You will never have my trust again."

"Still," Seth continues, "I find it hard to believe you don't have anything you want to say to me. After all, you've always had so many things to say."

"I'd like to say that you're a jerk, but I figure I can get that message across over the phone."

"That's not very kind of you, Wren."

"Kindness is something you have rarely shown me."

"And respect is something you have rarely shown anyone."

"Well, when it comes to people like you, it's never been one of my virtues."

"You have no virtue," he snarls. "You lost it long ago."

"You don't know what I've lost. You don't know anything about me," I whisper.

"Oh, but I do."

If I wasn't so dead right now, perhaps I would be more frightened. "No, you don't. But I know about you. And I know you'd like to hurt me if given the chance."

"We will meet again, whether you agree to or not—it's only a matter of time. As you know, I *always* get what I want."

I hang up and curl into a ball on the couch, feeling more lost than before I picked up that call. I'm too tired to really make a sound, so I scream in my head until I feel I may burst. Then I drag myself upstairs and grab my journal, desperate to write it all out and make it better.

It doesn't get better.

I shut the journal and raise it up, smashing it over my head. Bang, bang, bang. It doesn't hurt that much, and I feel almost calmer now.

But by the time I sit back in front of the TV, I feel just as depressed as I did before. Maybe I really have lost my virtue. Maybe my soul is fading to black and there's nothing I can do about it. I no longer feel there is anything more for me. I mean I can hardly even get myself to get out of my house these days. I'm falling farther and farther down into a steep pit and can't crawl my way up the sides. Every time I try, I slip a little more.

There's no end in sight.

What do you do when you no longer have anything to hold onto? I know I have my family and some friends, I'm not an idiot, but there's nothing inside me that wants to keep going. It's hard to force yourself to get up every day when things aren't what you want them to be, day after day. Emptiness grows and my heart feels darker and... I'm not sure how to explain it to you.

My nails begin digging into my wrist.

I can't get a handle on what anything is for. The world seems void of meaning and every day I wake up with my heart broken into another piece. When there's nothing left, maybe I'll understand, but by then it will be too late. I used to think about this frequently, now it's relentless. My mind won't let me rest.

I'm so tired.

My nails push harder into my skin, leaving red marks behind. I try concentrating on the TV show I'm watching, but I can't.

Just then, I hear a knock at the door.

I open it and there's Aidan. He looks serious, more so than usual at least.

"I was thinking," he begins before I say anything, "that we haven't had a real talk in a while." He walks inside and I close the door behind him.

He turns to me abruptly as soon as I do this. "How come you didn't tell me it was your birthday?"

"Didn't think of it."

"Well, I got you something. If I could have had more time to prepare something, that would be better, but this will have to do," he says, handing me a small box.

Inside is a silver pendant of a rose. It's simple and beautiful. I love it—but I barely have time to appreciate it before he switches subjects entirely.

"Why didn't you call me after you got out of the hospital?" There's something in his voice... anger?

"I'm sorry, Aidan," I say, setting the gift down. "I should have. I didn't really talk to anyone..."

"But why didn't you talk to *me*?"

"I'm sorry."

"You seem like you're hiding something."

"I'm not hiding anything."

"I just want the truth."

"The truth?"

"The whole truth."

"That's a bit more complicated than what you're looking for."

"Try me."

"No."

"Wren..."

"Stop pushing me."

"No I—"

"The truth is I try not to put my problems on other people or need other people to help me with my problems because I always seem to need and want people more than they'll ever need or want me! And I've been through that before, and it hurts—a lot. So sometimes I just deal with things on my own." I say it all so fast, before I can stop myself.

"God, Wren," he laughs and runs his hands through his hair, "you can be so blind sometimes. If you would just get your head out of the clouds for a minute, maybe you could see. It's almost like you *want* to be alone.

But despite what you may believe," he looks me in the eyes, "you're not the only one."

I hadn't ever looked this closely at his eyes. They're beautiful. An intelligent, bright emerald green unlike any other I've seen before.

He reaches for my hand and holds it tight for a second before abruptly letting go, as if he's touched something hot that burned his skin.

"I want to show you something," I say.

I finally finished learning all eight minutes and fifty-seven seconds of "November Rain," and this is the first time I will ever play it for someone. I don't tell him what it is, because I think he already knows. So I just start playing.

"Let's do it," he says after I hit the final note.

"What do you mean?"

"I mean let's play it, as a band."

We speak for a bit more, but I'll spare you the details. We've decided to try and learn all of the "November Rain" parts together. It's just for fun, nothing serious, but he thinks the rest of the band will enjoy it, so it's settled.

As he leaves, he tells me to try listening to the tracks he gave me when we were just getting to know one another.

I heed his advice later that night as I close my eyes and think about what I am going to do. When you don't know what else to do, you carry on. Because there's nothing else you can do.

I put the rose pendant around my neck and clutch it close to my chest.

Maybe now my life is no longer empty, but does heaven still wait for me?

I'm knock, knock, knockin', but nobody's letting me in.

CHAPTER 19

EVERYBODY'S FAULT

MY LAST THERAPY SESSION WENT SOMETHING LIKE THIS:

"Would you like to talk about what happened with you and Lena in the car accident?"

"No."

"All right, do you have anything specific on your mind at the moment you'd like to bring up?"

"No."

"What about particular feelings that you've been experiencing? Anything stick out?"

"No."

Before I left, she handed me this book on teens and depression and what not.

And I guess I ought to skim through it a bit—blah, blah, blah, boring, stupid, blah, blah, more boringness.

You know what? I'm going to write a story—one that people like me can actually connect with. And my story's going to have a playlist attached to it that will be all movie soundtracks, Zeppelin, and Guns N' Roses. Well, there'll be some other things in there too, but that's the important stuff. I smile thinking about it but almost immediately my smile fades. I'm never really going to write this damn thing. And even if I did, it wouldn't make any sense.

I set down the book and pick up my phone. I notice there's a missed call from Aidan. His message says to meet him at the public library in one hour. Going by when the message was sent, I have about fifteen minutes to make it over there.

I arrive a few minutes late and begin looking around for him.

I find him hanging out on the floor with his earphones in, reading *Pillars of the Earth*. He looks up and waves me over.

"What are you listening to?" I ask as I take a seat next to him.

"'Stairway to Heaven'." He offers me an earphone.

"No thanks, I can't listen to that right now."

"I thought you loved Stairway?"

"I do, it's just not a good idea for me to listen to it in the middle of the day around other people."

He's confused probably, but he doesn't ask for clarification. I suppose it's obvious I don't want to go into it.

"Hey," he says a while later, "remember that song you wrote that you sang for me?"

"Sure."

"Could you write a song for the band? We're trying to make a single before putting on a concert, and I remembered how good you are at writing songs."

"What would it be about?"

"Something tough and interesting. Like a rough-tortured-soul type of thing."

Man, that is my specialty. "No problem. Though you sure you want me writing your single?"

"Yes."

"When do you need it by?"

"We'd like to film the video sometime in the next month, so just whenever you can would be great."

"I'll see what I can do."

"Awesome."

"Hey, are you still planning on going to that school dance thing?" I ask, completely switching the subject in a very non-discrete way.

"The Spring Formal?" The tone of his voice is suddenly different.

"Yes."

"Yeah, I am. I'm actually going with Bianca to the dance. We got to talking about it a while back and one thing lead to another..."

Well son of a *bitch*, I didn't see this coming.

"Isn't she dating Seth?" My breath is shallow, and I can barely get the words out but, somehow, I manage to keep a blank expression.

"No, they broke up a while ago. So, uh, yeah we're going together." He's staring at me in a strange way, looking for a reaction.

"That's great, I uh—that's great," I say. I feel like someone just slapped me across the face.

"Uh-huh."

No, more like someone punched me in the face 50 times.

I don't understand.

I don't understand.

"I have to go," I say quickly, scrambling to my feet.

"Wait! That's it? Wren, I—"

"Sorry," I mumble over my shoulder as I dash out of the library as fast as I can.

***

I go home that night and try to get comfortable so I can begin my process of coming up with song ideas.

I am calm and apathetic.

I don't have feelings.

I don't care.

First, I get into my most comfortable bedtime band shirt and wash my face, and then I sit down on my bed, staring at the wall. I can feel my body begin to shake, so I close my eyes and breathe in deeply.

Five seconds later, my eyes bolt open and I jump up—unable to sit still another second. In one rash movement, my hand grips the rose pendant from around my neck and rips it off, throwing it on the ground as I suddenly lose the ability to stand and slump to my knees.

After a long time, I crawl over to the dresser the pendant slid under—at least, I think it's here. I stick my hand under it, searching. *Where is—oh.*

Right as my fingers close around the pendant's chain, they brush against something else. I hesitate and then pull the pendant out, grabbing the other object with it. It's… the CD—the one I made for Aidan.

I leave the pendant on the floor and slowly stand up, holding the CD. I remember when I made this. Seems like forever ago. Maybe it was forever ago.

My heart begins to bleed just looking at it.

I set the CD aside and reach back down, picking up the pendant—feeling the pulse of my bleeding heart quicken even more at the cold necklace lying in the palm of my hand. How can a piece of jewelry have this much effect on me?

Before I can throw it again, I hang my head in defeat and carefully place it on my bedside.

I broke the clasp; I'm going to have to fix it somehow if I ever want to wear it again—which I don't.

I'd started wearing it kind of often, but for some reason I tended to wear it under my clothes. I wonder if Aidan thought I didn't like it. My mind

begins racing, going round and round the tracks, never reaching the finish line. I'm driving myself insane.

I reach over to my blanket and pull it in, draping it over my shoulders as I snuggle back against my pillows. Once satisfactorily comfortable, there's nothing else I can do but start scribbling out songs. They just keep pouring out of me, my pen pressing into the paper so hard that it rips through it and few times.

I only stop when I get a call from Ella, who tells me she is going out on another date with Rob, the new singer the band found, and that she needs me to watch her new dog, a pit-bull puppy named Tony. There's no way I could be her first choice for this favor, so she must be resorting to asking me because all her other friends turned her down. Ella gets on my nerves, but from what I remember of her dog, I like him a lot so I say yes in a heartbeat. Besides, helping other people is good. Right?

Naturally, when she comes over she wants to talk before leaving.

"Wren, you're the greatest! Well, when you're not being mean you are. Too bad I can't stay longer though."

"Oh yeah, real bummer."

"We should hang out more often. Don't you think?" Ella asks.

"Only on occasion," I joke back.

"What?" She doesn't get it, but that's sort'a my fault because I can see how that'd be confusing.

"I mean, yeah, we should hang out more often. Sounds super."

She smiles at me, looking pretty happy with herself. Then, she begins talking about the date she's going to go on tonight and how cute she thinks Rob is.

I don't much care for this sort of talk, but I don't want to offend Ella, so I act like I'm interested, and she takes to it well.

Once she leaves, I run around with Tony for a while, and then I tackle him to the ground and roll around with him. Despite my protests, he licks me all over my face before I push him off me, laughing. Then we curl up on the couch while he sleeps and I watch *Iron Man*. We make a great team.

There's something comforting about his presence for me, like looking at his cute, little face makes my problems not seem so big or important anymore. I sure wish I had a dog.

***

It's late when Ella comes to get him, and I almost forgot I was going to have to give him back.

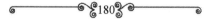

After a long time of her talking and me pretending to be at least somewhat interested, Ella finally leaves.

I then go to the front yard and sit on the steps.

I get a feeling when I turn to the West, and while part of me truly wants to give up, there's another voice in my head pleading for me to hold on a little while longer. What I really want is that feeling when you just know you're home. Nothing ever did feel so sweet as that, though I can hardly remember what it's like.

I want to go inside now, but then I reach into my pocket at take out the necklace. I don't have any idea how it got there; last I remember, I put it on my bedside—but I must have grabbed it at some point without realizing. So, I keep sitting on the steps, looking down at this goddamn necklace. And it takes me until around 4:00 am to finish fixing it.

Maybe sleeping would have been a better use of my time, but if I know myself at all, then I know there's no way I would have been sleeping anyway.

***

In the morning, Cara comes running into my bedroom, startling the hell out of me.

"Wren! Come on, get up! Let's go!"

"Holy Mother of God, it's a freakin' Saturday, man. What're you even going on about anyway?"

"Don't you remember?"

"Do I look like I remember?" I ask, throwing the covers up over my head. "What time is it?"

"It's already 9:00 am!"

"Son of a bitch, I've only been asleep for less than five hours then. Can't you let me be?"

"Language, Wren. And no, no I cannot. Because you promised we would do something today."

I pop my head back out of the covers. "When on earth did I do such a thing?"

"Sometime after the crash, when you wouldn't really talk to me."

"If I wouldn't really talk to you, then how did I promise you we'd go somewhere today?"

"Because you said you needed space but that you'd make it up to me by doing something fun with me. And I asked when, and you said you didn't know, so I suggested Saturday, April 20th, and you said yes."

"Ok, ok. I got it. So what exactly is it you want to do?"

"Well..."

As it turns out, Cara doesn't just want to go for a walk or a drive or to ice cream or anything—no, she wants to go to the freakin' *amusement park*. So, I force myself out of bed, put on my favorite boots, and pray to the Lord above that I have enough strength to get through this day without acting like a depressed bastard.

"So, I was thinking we could get Dippin' Dots first and then go to the Shark Land area or maybe head over to ride The Scrambler," Cara says excitedly as we finish paying for our tickets and walk through the gates.

"Sure. Whatever you say, kid."

"Or we could go on Cobra Coaster and then walk to the Butterfly Gardens and get more Dippin' Dots."

"Cara, I am good with any of those ideas. Just pick something."

"Ok fine, Dippin' Dots it is."

We make our way over to the Dippin' Dots stand and begin to wait in the unreasonably long line ahead of us. As we stand here, I look around at all the thousands of people bustling about, listening to the screams from the roller coasters, and taking in the unmistakable scent that only amusement parks have.

I used to love this place more than anything. I would come here as much as I could. Now, I'm sort'a just wishing more than anything that I could leave. But I promised Cara I would take her here today, and I don't break my promises. Besides, it could be fun... I think.

After eating our birthday cake and cookies n' cream flavored Dots, we decide to go to Shark Land—which is really just a large, dark building with some shark tanks. Its saving grace is its shark tunnel—a long, see-through tunnel that you can walk through as sharks swim above and right next to you.

I must say it's a weird experience.

Cara moves through the tunnel quickly, eager to see the next exhibits, but I linger behind, staring up at the moving creatures overhead. I am surrounded by sharks; each of them moving closer and closer, coming straight for me.

"Come on, Wren—you're holding me up!" Cara yells to me from up ahead.

This whole place is kind of eerie and reminds me of that psychology field trip to the aquarium I went on with Aidan at the beginning of the year.

What a strange time that was.

I turn my head to look back at the sharks in the tunnel; I could swear one of them is staring at me. Is that even possible?

My head is still turned as I suddenly go around a corner and smack into something hard.

"Ow! Jesus Christ!" I shout.

"I'm so sorry! I didn't... Wren?" There is no doubt who that voice belongs to.

I look up to see Aidan looking back down at me.

"What the hell are you doing here?" I ask, confused.

"Well, you see, I'm—"

"Wren, fancy seeing you here!" Bianca cries, coming over to give me a hug.

"Ok, what are *both* of you doing here?" I ask, this time even more confused.

"Aidan!" Cara runs up to us and wraps her arms around Aidan's torso.

"Hey, kid, it's good to see you too," he smiles, ruffling her hair.

"I haven't seen you in so long!" she exclaims, holding onto him tighter.

"Hey, Cara," I pull her back toward me, "how about you keep going through the exhibits and I'll catch up with you in a bit, yeah?"

"No way, I want to stay with Aidan."

"It's ok, I'm happy to have her hang with us," he says, looking at me.

"No—Cara, please." I put a hand on her shoulder.

"Are you serious? Fine—but you owe me for this."

She begrudgingly runs ahead, and I look back to my two friends standing before me.

"Aidan took me here, isn't that sweet?" Bianca tells me once Cara is gone. None of this makes any sense.

"It's adorable," I say through slightly gritted teeth. "Well, I shouldn't leave Cara on her own for too long, so I'm going to get going."

"Hang on, you could stay with us? All four of us could do something—" Aidan begins to say.

"That's all right. I think I'd rather spend time with my sister, alone."

"Wren—"

"And you two seem to be getting along just fine by yourselves. I'd hate to come in between that."

A dark cloud hangs over us for the rest of the day, and we end up coming home early. I feel guilty for letting Cara down, but I just couldn't do it.

So much for not acting like a depressed bastard.

I want you to understand. I want you to understand so badly, but I can't rip these feelings out of me and into you. I wish to God I could, but I can't. And that kills me. Sometimes I really hate life.

The date no longer matters—
My therapy meeting went strangely this afternoon. It started like this:
Me: "I was so selfish the other day, I couldn't even let Cara get through a full day at the amusement park." Then I explained what had happened there.
Amelia: "Is that selfishness? Or jealousy?"
Me: "Are they not the same thing? Besides, there's nothing to be jealous of. Anyway, things just sort'a suck."
Amelia: "Yes, there seems to be a lot wrong with the world at the moment."
Me: "Guess nothing's doing ok then, huh?"
Amelia: "Yes and no."
Me: "What?"
Amelia: "Everything may not be all right, but that doesn't mean everything's not all right."
Me: "Funny, I've said that same thing to someone I know."
Amelia: "So what are you then?"
Me: "What?"
Amelia: "All right, or not?"
Me: "What?" I sounded stupid repeating myself, but I didn't understand.
If you would have heard it, I bet you'd be confused too. Though maybe you'd get stuff better than me.

I stop writing and put on my headphones, ready for a change in mental scenery.

I have a choice right now, I think to myself as "Stairway to Heaven" comes on from my playlist. I can listen to it and remind myself of that which I never want to think about, or go to sleep and wake to another worthless day.

I make the wrong choice.

But truth is, I can't sleep anyway. I'm too disappointed in life. I don't want to wake up the next day. And so, I do not sleep.

When I do sleep, I can hardly get myself out of bed. Sometimes I don't. On these days, there's not much that can make me see the light of the world. Everything is dark and cold, the way I must want it to be.

To warm myself, I take a shower. The hot water makes the air steamy and the glass fog over. I use my finger to draw a heart. Then I cross it out.

Sometimes, as I let the water pour over me; I like to imagine myself saying certain things to a bunch of different people. Of course, I know I'll never really say that stuff to them. It's still fun to picture, though. Not sure if that's healthy or not, but I do it.

This time, even though I try my hardest to think of *anything* else, I imagine myself saying something to Aidan. It's like he's stuck in my head. He's inside of me.

I sit on the floor of the shower and continue letting the water come down on me. I try not to do this for too long though. I try to be conscientious about wasting water. If I spend any longer than ten minutes, I start to feel guilty.

I step out of the shower and onto the cold bathroom floor. I stand there while drops of water on my skin turn ice cold, sending a shiver down my spine.

Outside, it's raining now. I enjoy listening to the sound of rain. It calms me, momentarily washing away my guilt and anxiety, offering an unstable peace.

Out of all the feelings, the one I hate the most is guilt. Sometimes I feel it even when I don't know why I feel it. But it's often there, eating away at me, whether I'm aware or not. My thoughts keep me prisoner in my own mind. I may not deserve to get better.

After a long period of self-indulgent self-hatred, I get an urge to go out into the storm. I'm already wet anyway. Without pausing to question my desire too much, I run outside and look up at the rain as it falls. I'm not even fully dressed.

"What do you want from me? What am I supposed to do?" I yell up at it.

Naturally, there is no response.

No wonder everything is such a chaotic free-for-all. It's either chaos or captivity, and there's no help in navigating either. Which is worse and which is worth it? It reminds about the question: do I want peace or freedom? I know which I would choose. Do you?

When I go back inside, I sit down on my bed and think back to this past summer. Back to what it was like when I tried to stay away from home for good at a professional academy for dance.

I've been trying to tell myself I don't remember it at all, that it's all just sort of an unpleasant blur that I can forget about if I push it back far enough—but that's a lie. I remember it all: everything said to me; every lonely night; every impossible morning. Not being wanted anymore. I remember coming back from a day after barely having kept it together and wanting to do nothing but go home or disappear while knowing that both were not really options. I remember picking up the knife and staring at it before putting it to my wrists and then throwing it across the room as I screamed. But what was I screaming at? Myself? My family? God? Life? Everyone? Then I remember lying awake feeling numb as I had no one to turn to except for the stuffed bear I brought with me.

Even when I eventually did get on an airplane to return home after the summer ended, after everyone realized I wasn't going to make it there, I still felt there was a part of me that never made it home. And while this marks a particularly nasty experience that has left its scar, it only begins to scratch the surface of my true problems. Truth is, my troubles run far deeper than I had ever thought they did. I know that now.

Sometimes I think I'm a bad person. I'm trying not to give up on myself, but it seems most everyone else already has. Then sometimes I think bad things. I want to hurt them—those that hurt me. So, all I can do is pray to the Lord my soul to keep—or is it take? I can never remember. But I have no faith, so does it really matter?

That night, in my dreams, I see Violet's face. She tells me that I'll never find home again. Then I see Aidan's face and he tells me he doesn't want me—that he'll never want me.

My soul feels like it's being crushed.

"Don't you say that to me. Please. Not you," I plead.

And then I wake up.

There is no peace. And there never will be.

Lena finally got me to agree to go to lunch this weekend and talk about stuff with her.

She does most of the talking. I listen, staring out the window next to our table. Outside, the birds are singing and flying from the trees up into the clouds and back.

They fly free. I'm stuck down here.

I would say I want to be a bird, but they have to stay outside when it's cold, eat insects, have limited thinking abilities, and die early.

So I stay stuck.

After our lunch, I go to dance rehearsal. It bores me out of my mind and I get scolded for not being there enough.

Ironically, I will probably not go next time.

When I get back to my house, I rest on my bed and close my eyes, allowing myself to slip away for a little while.

There's a knock on my terrace door, and I get up to see who it is. Outside there's a storm, making it difficult to see, but I catch a glimpse of a dark figure each time the lightning flashes. It almost looks as if—as if it has wings.

What a strange dream, and it felt so real. Which is questionable in and of itself because, first of all, I don't have a terrace. Secondly, why the hell would an angel want to talk to *me*?

They did have a message though: there's a bad moon rising. Whatever that means.

***

New entry: Don't remember the date—

I just hope I can hold on a little longer.

No one can save myself except me.

So how the hell am I doing? Not so freaking good. There's all this shit going on in the world and it all freaking sucks. Life is lonely, hard, and boring. And it's nobody's fault, so you can't even be mad at someone for it. The anger is stuck inside you.

This makes me even more pissed off until I just want to destroy something, to rip it apart and watch it burn. I want to thrust my fist through a wall until blood runs down my knuckles and then scream.

It makes me so mad... I can't describe it.

And even though I know it's stupid, I can't stop thinking about Aidan and Bianca together. It just adds to the torment.

Here I am, fading away, and there's nothing I can do about it. I drift farther every day.

I'm in a dark hole and the sides are caving in on me but I can't get out. I reach for the light and no one pulls me up—so the dirt falls from the sides and covers me until no one can ever find me.

CHAPTER 20

TRAIN STOPPED A ROLLIN'

AIDAN WATCHED AS WREN BEGAN TO WALK AWAY, kicking himself for what he said. It was the truth, and he just wanted to know if she would react, but still, he should have found a better way to tell her. Or perhaps he should have found a different solution all around... He didn't know.

All he knew was that he didn't want her to go, so he quickly got up to catch her before she left the library. But, as he was about to run after her, he got a phone call—a phone call from Bianca.

"Hello, Bianca." Wren had already walked out the door—he was too late. "This isn't the best time—"

"Aidan! Please, don't hang up. I need you."

"Need me?"

"My dad, he's visiting tomorrow for some reason, and I just can't deal with that right now."

"I'm sorry, Bianca, but what would you like me to do?" Ever since the night she drove him home, months ago, she'd continued to come to him about the difficulties she had with her father. This is because, at the time, he'd opened up to her about his troubles with his own absent father. He couldn't remember why he did it, only that he did and that they now had a sort of bond because of it. In fact, after that night, Bianca had made it a point to frequently come visit him during his work hours at the record store. From then on, it wasn't long until she asked him to the Spring Formal with her. Though, in truth, he had pretty much forgotten all about it until Wren brought it up.

"It's just... I know you understand, and I need you to help me—to take me away somewhere."

"Take you away?"

"Yes."

"Where?"

"Anywhere!" Her voice sounded genuinely panicked, and Aidan felt for her. He knew he couldn't just turn her away—he would have to help.

"Ok."

"You mean it?"

"We'll go somewhere—tomorrow, all day."

"Really?"

"I promise."

The call ended and Aidan sat back down, letting out a conflicted sigh.

He would do as he said and take Bianca somewhere this weekend, just to help her out while her father was here, but then he would figure out a way to set things straight with Wren. He would talk to her, for real.

First, though, he needed to decide what he would be doing with Bianca. What would be a good, fun, full-day experience to take someone's mind off something troubling?

Screw this whole goddamn world. I'm done with it—all of it.

You can keep trying but it never turns out right. The stupid people always win. Their insanity cannot be penetrated by logic or the truth. None of it means anything. And so the wheel in the sky turns, over and over, people crushing people for a blind faith or a faith misplaced.

You can never win, but you still have to fight. Or else everything would be lost. A world so drowned by order that it twists itself into one destroyed by chaos.

I skip school today; I can't get out of bed. My dad is already gone off to work and I tell my mom that I'm sick.

She tells me to get some rest and kisses the palm of my hand like she used to when I was younger. Then she leaves as well.

I lie in my bed for a long time, holding my blanket close and staring at the ceiling.

I can't explain it. That moment when all hope has left you and the only thing inside you is an empty pain—just loneliness. Just knowing you're going to have to make it your own way, and you won't feel better in the morning. It's the kind of pain that makes you realize how jacked up you are on the inside—the kind of feeling that makes you want to die.

Every time I take a step forward, I do something that pulls me back two. It really makes me wonder.

The hurt builds up, and there is no tragic beauty to it. It's just sitting alone in my room, crying so hard that my whole body aches and I just want it to stop. I can't take it anymore. So I start breaking things, starting with my own mind, and I go on tearing myself apart to no end—because it never ends.

There's no way to spin it or sugarcoat it. There's no making this pretty. I'm too tired, too empty. I'm so angry and sad; I really could die. I need to get out of here, so I walk myself over to my dance studio, which takes about forty minutes. Once there, I climb over the back fence, making sure not to get caught on the poky things, and take off my boots as I lay down on the grass across from the railroad tracks.

A train begins to roll by and I sit up and stare at it, wondering where it's going. It's going slow, so it must not be in any sort of a hurry. Maybe it doesn't have anywhere to go, so it's just going.

I get up and start walking toward it, holding my boots in my hand. The ground is hard and unforgiving, hurting my feet. I don't stop to put them back on. Then I see an open boxcar and start running. I run faster than I ever have and make a giant leap, landing inside the car and almost rolling through out the other side. Once inside, I lay on my back, my chest heaving up and down. My heart is going to burst.

I notice a sharp, stinging sensation on the bottom of my feet and find that they are bleeding. I also find a lot of graffiti, including a few hearts with initials in them. One says *R.Q. & N.R. forever*, another says *D.W., I'll love you always. Man, what is love anyway?*

I curl up on the floor and rest my eyes.

I wake up a little while later, pretty disoriented, and I almost freak out before I remember. I don't wait any longer though, I jump off first chance I get, putting my boots back on, and walk a ways until I reach what looks like a little town.

Actually, this place looks more like a *ghost* town. Though maybe that's only because it's got to be like almost the middle of the night and all the people here are either asleep or out and up to no good.

In the distance, I see bright lights flickering from inside a large house. At least that's what I think it is. Not sure. But I'm guessing the people in there fall into the "up-to-no-good" category. Might as well check it out.

I get there and find that it has big Greek letters on the front above the door. It's a frat house. There's obviously a very big party going on right now, and I want to go in and see what it's all about. Soon as I go inside, though, I get the feeling that I should not be here. It's packed, the music is too loud, and everyone seems kind'a…

"Hey, I haven't seen you around before," a tall guy hanging near the entrance says to me while I'm staring off into the crowd of people.

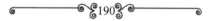

We talk a second, and he tells me to wait here while he gets something for me saying it will "take the edge off." *The edge off what?* I wonder.

He comes back and gives me a shot of something; a dark liquid that tastes like it's burning my throat as it goes down. I should not have done that. Someone else tries to hand me another, and I turn 'em down. Won't make that damn mistake twice; I'm such a freaking idiot.

No, I'm not an idiot, so I need to stop acting like one.

The guy who gave me the first shot comes back around to me and puts something else in my hand.

What the hell is this? "No thanks," I say, shoving it back toward him.

"If you're gonna stay, you gotta do it."

"Then I won't stay."

"Come on, just take it," he says, forcing it into my hands. "Everyone's—"

"I said no!"

I throw the thing at the floor and run out of there faster than you can imagine.

As I make it outside, my body feels like it snaps in half as I double over and throw up.

I don't think I've ever been so sick in my life.

I stumble through the street, looking for a place to lay my head. There ain't nothing here. No people, no food—and nowhere to go.

I think I've hit the goddamn bottom of the rock.

Seeing as there's nothing around, I wander real far off and make it to a little river with a bridge going over the top of it. It's kind'a high up, but I start climbing the sides of it anyway. I get up a long ways and look back down; I seem much higher than I thought I was. If I let go now, I'd never stop falling. And this time, I know I wouldn't be able to make it out of the river.

My hands almost slip for a second, but I catch back on just in time. I get to the top and stare out at the river below me. It's not so little after all.

Sometimes I tell myself I'm stupid for being sad, but why? Why am I not allowed to feel pain without feeling guilt? I've been ignored by most of my peers for most of my life. My parents sent me away from home by myself every summer since I can remember, and I never make any friends. I was thrown away from a school and blamed for something horrible that I didn't even do because I stood up to a bully. People, who don't know me, have spat on my reputation. I was sent away again to another school far away where the people there told me I was worthless. Then when I got back home because I couldn't take it anymore all the friends I had known abandoned me. I was nearly killed in a car crash. Any talent I once had has crumbled to dust before my eyes. The one person I thought I could depend on has chosen someone else over me, and every time I look in the mirror I want to kill the person I see staring back.

My hand pulls the necklace Aidan gave me out from under my shirt, and I stare down at it, my fingers feeling over where I had broken the clasp.

I start crying.

I won't bore you with what happens next, but the bottom line is I go home. Well, my mom picks me up and takes me home after a very tense phone call.

***

"I need you to tell me exactly what happened," she says as soon as we walk through the house doors. She then hands me a glass of water and sits me down.

She sounds upset.

"Mom—"

"I want to know what it is you're thinking you're doing."

"I don't know what I'm doing! I don't know anything! And I really don't want to talk about it!"

"Well that's too bad, because we *need* to talk."

Without thinking, I throw the glass in my hand on the floor, smashing it hard.

I hardly even notice I've done it.

"Wren Elizabeth Evans! What is going on with you?"

"Mom, please leave me alone!"

"Do you see what you just did?"

"Go away, please." My voice is now trembling.

"I'm not going anywhere." Her tone suddenly gets softer. "I want to help you, sweetheart. Let me."

"No one can help me."

"That's not true, there is always help to be given."

"I just wish I was better."

"What does that mean?"

"I want to be someone better."

"You don't need to be anyone else, you just need to be you."

"Mom, please—"

"Because you are enough, Wren. There is no better. You are enough."

"It's because of me that you and Dad are having to work more hours now than ever before. I cost you all that money last year, because of what happened. You try to tell me otherwise, but I *know*. If I hadn't of—"

"Oh, honey, I thought we had moved past this?"

Tears begin streaming down my face, and I don't even try to stop them. My mom pulls me closer and holds me while I cry. I feel like a child, but I don't care.

All of a sudden, a thought I haven't had in a very long time passes through my mind: *maybe I deserve to be saved.*

After talking with my mom, I go outside and sit on the back of my car hood, drinking a soda and watching the fading stars as the morning comes to take them away. I don't know why I'm drinking soda, I hate soda, but being here like this reminds me of good memories. I want to enjoy this moment. I want to stop worrying and feeling anger or sadness.

And I can see I'm avoiding what I really need to be doing, which is talking to my parents, telling them the truth, but it's only because I know that once I do, things are going to change.

A few minutes later, I get up and walk myself inside, heading straight to my mom and dad. I sit down across from them on the couch. It's about five am, so I hope they don't mind that I'm springing this on them now.

"Mom, Dad, I need to talk to you." I never thought saying words could be this hard. But I'm doing it.

I look back at my parents' faces. They must already know some of it or at least suspect something—after all, they set me up with my therapist. Also, I pretty much had a mental breakdown in front of my mom less than two hours ago. Still, it's hard for me to say, really hard. But I need to get it out, or we're all going to suffer for it later. I take in a deep breath and attempt to steady my heart before I say what I have to say.

"I haven't felt home in a long time." Once I say it, there's a definite weight that's been released. And as soon as it starts coming, it all falls out.

"I've been hurting, on the inside, and I don't know what to do." I'm already starting to cry. "The way I got expelled, and the aftermath of it, really got me. I still feel this, this *guilt* every time I even think about thinking about it. In fact, I'm still not sure if I'm really ready to go into that part of it—but then being left at that place last summer, right after being thrown out," I'm having trouble getting through a full sentence, "it hurt me. And I'm sorry that I messed it up there, I know you guys thought it would make a good fresh start for me; a start away from everything that had happened here. Things just didn't go the way any of us wanted them to and I messed it all up. Sometimes I don't think I'm ever going to get better. I've wanted to talk to you about it, though I never knew how. And I know there's more to say, but I can't right now."

They look at me and wait for me to say something else.

"I need help." The final words finally come out of my mouth. My face is wet, and my throat is so tight I don't think I could say anything more if I tried. I'm worried about what they'll tell me; if they'll think I'm messed up or overly emotional.

"Wren," my mother speaks first and I hold my breath, "I am sorry, honey." She gets up and walks over to me, pulling me into a long hug. My dad looks a little shocked, like he doesn't know what to do either. And, for a second, I think he's not going to do anything; but then he stands up slowly and comes over to me as well.

He kisses me on the forehead and hugs me. I didn't expect so much hugging to be involved in this process.

Then my dad stands back and looks at me. "Your mom and I have felt for a while now like something was off, and we too didn't know what to do. We should have done something sooner—just know that no matter what, we're *always* going to be here for you."

For some reason, this makes me cry harder.

There are some more tears, and some things said that I didn't expect to ever hear. But it all helps, and when it's finally finished, I feel like I can start breathing again for the first time in a long time.

***

The next afternoon, my mom takes me to the doctor's office to get a real check-up and to see if they can help me out at all. I've decided that I freaking hate the doctor's office, and this appointment didn't help alleviate that hate to any extent. Though there were at least a few good things to come out of the visit. For one, my doctor gave me a prescription for medication that should make me feel not so bad all the time and, secondly, I got actual medical confirmation that I have depression.

I just about knew on my own, but still, it's best to have for sure confirmation on this stuff so you don't think you're just going crazy.

Crap. Speaking of going crazy, I completely forgot about that damn song I said I would write—and it's already May.

I'm looking to write something that grabs you by the throat and knocks you off your feet. Thinking about these goals, I start writing.

CHAPTER 21

SHADOW OF YOUR HATE

"WHERE IS AIDAN?" I ask as I step into the rehearsal garage. I don't see him anywhere.

"Dealing with something to do with Noah," Sebastian answers. "Do you have the song ready? It's been a while."

"Here you go." I hand him the crumpled piece of paper with the song on it. He flattens out the paper while Tommy reads it with him over his shoulder.

It took me almost all of last week to write the thing, due to trouble concentrating, rewrites, and multiple versions of about ten different songs I tried to make up. In fact, I've barely slept—but on the flip side, I have been taking my new meds, so it'll all even out, yeah?

Anyway, this is the finished product, and the one I think fits them the best.

While I wait for them to go over it, I notice a vaguely familiar looking boy sitting on the couch and twirling a microphone. I go over to introduce myself.

"Hey, you must be Rob. I've heard a lot about you. I can't wait to hear you sing."

He sets down the microphone and stands up. "And you must be Wren, I've certainly heard a lot about you as well. It's wonderful to finally meet you!"

I reach out my hand to him, but instead of shaking it, Rob grabs it and pulls me into an unexpectedly tight bear hug.

"Ahem," Bash clears his throat. "If you're ready, we'd like to go over this with you."

"It's great, Wren! It just needs to be sexier," Tommy says as I come back to them.

"Sexier? Fine, just add in a few inappropriate innuendos somewhere, I don't care."

"I want to read it," Rob says, reaching for the paper, but Bash holds it out of his reach. "No fair, I'm the lead singer. I should know what songs we're thinking of doing."

"Where is the chorus?" Bash asks, ignoring him and peering up from the paper.

"It doesn't exactly have one…"

He looks back down at it, his brows slightly crinkled. "What's it called?"

"'Take It Down The Line'."

"Ok, fine."

"Good, I'm glad you feel so strongly about it."

He ignores me. "All right, everyone, just because Aidan isn't here at the moment doesn't mean that we can't still practice."

"You've got to be kidding, Sebastian," Tommy complains, throwing a drumstick at Bash's head. "We already went through our line up like 78 times today."

"More like three times," Bash corrects.

"Hey, that's still a lot," Rob interjects.

"Oh is it? If you—"

"Why don't you all just take a break for second?" I suggest.

"Yes," Bash says, eyeing me, "let's all listen to the person who showed up five minutes ago and hasn't had to do a single song."

"Hey, I'll do a song."

"Great, we can't start all the way, but we can go over some things about November—"

"No 'November Rain'. Not right now."

"Then what do you want?"

"To have fun."

"Have fun?" My God, this kid is too much. I swear, he wouldn't know how to relax if relaxation punched him in the face.

I take out my phone and press play on a song, wondering how long it will take him to figure out which song it is.

"Wren, Wren what is this?"

The words kick in and I immediately begin singing to it, loudly and dramatically, dancing around the garage space. By the chorus, both Tommy and Rob are singing with me—all three of us belting "Love Hurts" at a horrified-looking Bash; though I can tell a part of him wants to smile.

When it ends, we all burst out laughing.

After this, I decide to head out.

In my car, I turn the radio on and am hit with a huge surprise as "My Michelle" begins playing. It's a song that never gets airplay, so this is a miracle if I've ever experienced one.

I decide to sit in Nightrider for a while, simply enjoying the track as my hand mindlessly plays with the rose pendant around my neck. As I'm sitting here, a tap on my window gives my heart a swift kick in the ass.

"Mother fricker, Sebastian! What gives? Why the hell you trying to scare me?" I yell, opening the car door.

"You left before I could talk to you more about your song. I have some edits here for you," he responds, handing me a new piece of paper. "I want you to make them by next week, if possible. The concert should be taking place in June, so there's no time to waste."

"Yeah, ok, we'll see," I say, glancing over these new "edits".

"Why are you playing that song so loudly?" he questions, leaning in slightly as if he just noticed it.

"It's 'My Michelle', I can't *not* play it loudly."

"'First Love Hurts', and now this." He rolls his eyes and looks as if he's about to turn away when he stops and looks down at my hand, which is still holding onto my pendant.

"What is that?"

"A necklace."

"Oh really? You don't say," he counters, initiating a glare from me.

"It was a gift, if you must know."

"From who?"

"Aidan."

"Oh." At this, he breaks eye contact and straightens up. Suddenly, things feel uncomfortable again.

"Is everything ok, Bash?" I ask. I'll never understand why this kid acts so weird sometimes.

"They will be once you make these edits," he says, turning around and walking back inside. I then shut my door and pull away from the driveway, turning the volume up on my radio even higher.

Maybe if I turn it up loud enough I'll be able to drown out all the stupid shit people say.

Bash may not have been wild about my song at first, but it turns out that after a few edits and a load of rehearsals, the band can turn it into something pretty great.

After school today, I'm going to help them make the music video for it. They will be marketing it as their new original song so that they can get more exposure for the mini-debut concert they want to have. Then, they are going to make flyers for it and post them up all over town and on the Internet.

As for a performance venue, Tommy's uncle owns a club downtown and said they could play there so long as they play for free and the show lasts under an hour. Overall, the whole thing seems to be coming together surprisingly nicely.

While I'm setting up the cameras for the shoot, I notice Rob brought along a girl with him. Unfortunately for the rest of us, that girl is Ella.

"If we're going to be filming, are you sure you want to be wearing that?" she asks me, looking at my t-shirt and boot-cut jeans outfit.

"Hello, Ella," I sigh. "Don't worry, I won't be on camera—I'm the one shooting the video. And, just so we're clear, you won't be on camera either."

The door from the house to the garage opens up and the boys walk in. They've all got a full face of show makeup, teased hair, leather pants or ripped jeans, leather jackets, and a few bandanas thrown in here and there.

"How do we look?" Tommy asks, taking a dramatic pose.

"Like you're bringing back 80s glam metal."

"Perfect!"

"Dude, you look like a chick," Rob laughs, looking Tommy up and down.

"At least I'm gonna look prettier than you!"

"Will you two quit it, we have a video to film." This comes from Bash, who is looking less than amused at the moment—big surprise.

"Hey," Aidan steps in, "by today's standards, we all kind'a look like chicks. But it's all cool; it's a style and we'll be the ones to bring it back."

"So now that we've decided you all look weird, how are we doing this?" I ask. "Are you guys going to actually play the song or are you going to fake it?"

"Fake it and lay the track over," Rob answers.

"No, we gotta play it for real and then lay the track over," Aidan protests. "It'll look more authentic."

"Ok fine, let's get this show on the road then."

Aidan nods his head in agreement, but as the rest of the guys get their equipment set up, he comes over to me and pulls me aside.

"Are you all right? You look exhausted."

"Thanks."

"No, I just mean—I'd get it if you'd want to reschedule the shoot. We could do it tomorrow instead."

"No, I'm good. I want to do it now."

I start to turn away but he grabs my hand and looks me in the eyes.

"I mean it, I'm ok."

"Ok." He lets go and walks back to the rest of the guys, getting out his guitar.

Once they're all set up, I put on my headphones, press play on the side cameras, get behind the center camera, and give them the signal to start playing.

Two seconds in, Ella screams out that it's too loud and I have to cut filming.

"Ella, babe, we have to get this video finished," Rob tells her.

"But my ears can't handle that. It's too heavy and too loud."

"So get some earphones or go outside," I say.

"Excuse me?"

"Please, this is really important to us," Rob pleads.

We start rolling a second time and this time we make it through to the first minute before being stopped again.

"Those lyrics are not going to work, who wrote them?" Ella asks.

Tommy giggles and points to me with a drumstick.

"I should have known."

"Look, we're trying to film a music video here, ok? So if you're not going to help out, we need you to get gone."

Ella does not get gone. Instead, she stays the entire time, out of what I'm pretty sure is spite, and sulks.

I have to hand it to the band though, we went through the song multiple times for different angles and close-ups and each time they gave it their all.

"Well, that's a wrap on filming," I announce after finishing the close-ups on Bash. "Though you guys still need to take the promotional photos before you put the video out there."

"Got it. Thanks so much, Wren."

"Yeah, thanks a million."

I think their music video is going to turn out well. Not sure which one of them is going to edit it, but I hope they don't screw it up. And I'm a little nervous to have "Take It Down The Line" be heard by other people, but if they liked it enough to make it into a song, then it's probably ok. Plus, to be completely honest, the band sounds real freaking great doing it.

Before I leave, Aidan comes up to me.

"Can we talk a second?"

I nod my head, and we step outside.

"I know it's getting late, but can I run some possible album names by you?"

"I didn't know you were making an album."

"We're not… yet. But someday."

"Uh-huh. Fire away."

"Tumbleweeds—"

"Nope."

"Scallywag—"

"No."

"Watch The World Burn."

"Hmm, we're getting closer."

"I thought that one was really good."

"I bet you did."

"Renegades."

"No, don't do a self-titled debut album, that's lazy."

"Ok, so I assume you have some great ideas then if you're shooting down all of mine."

"You're in a real mood," I comment.

"What, I was in a fake mood before? Just tell me what you think the name should be."

"Never mind." He's just being mean now, which is not like him.

"Never mind… hmm, I like it."

"I didn't mean that as a suggestion. Besides, isn't that the name of a Nirvana album?"

"How about End Of The Line, in honor of the single?"

"Yeah, I think that could work."

We're both quiet for a minute before Aidan sighs and reaches a hand behind his head.

"Look, what I really came out here to talk to you about is that we want

you to help us open up our show by performing 'November Rain' with us. I know we've talked about trying it out as a band before, but now we're thinking of really working on it, in a serious way."

I'm a little shocked. "You guys have a great singer now, why do you need me?"

"Come on! It wouldn't make sense for Renegades to do a debut show without you involved at all. And it would just be the opening, Rob would sing with you and then he would do all the rest of the show solo. Besides, the band already knows the song, we've got it down, and I know you do too."

"I'll think about it."

"So you'll do it?"

"Yeah, I'll do it."

"November Rain". "November freaking Rain". *How are we going to pull this one off?* I think to myself as I twirl the straw from my chocolate malt shake. After school, I come to sit by myself in a booth at the Ice Cream Shop, just to think about my conversation with Aidan yesterday. I usually think these sorts of things to myself, tending to go straight for the doubt and pessimism.

I get up from my booth and walk over to the old Jukebox in the corner of the Shop. I need some music to clear my head, so I put in some money and select "Take Me To The Top", "Patience", "Wanted Dead Or Alive", "Come As You Are", and "Sweet Child O' Mine". I'm going to be here a long time.

I turn back toward my booth and am startled by Bianca. She sits there calmly, with her own milkshake in hand, sipping it quietly.

"Jesus Christ, Bianca. Where did you come from all of a sudden?" I ask, walking over to her.

"I've been waiting here for quite a while. It took you an exceptionally long time to pick your jukebox choices."

I frown and slide in across from her. "Ok, so why are you here?"

"Seth asked me to arrange a meeting between the two of you."

"He asked you? I thought you were broken up."

"We are… but that's besides the point."

"And Seth isn't going to just tell me this himself? I mean he already tried it with me before, but I said no."

"He asked me to do it."

"Tell him I have no desire to speak with him, please. Not now, not ever."

"He's not going to take no for an answer."

"Then what's the point of asking? If he doesn't take no for an answer, you can tell him that he's a little bitch, and I don't want to look at his dumb face ever again."

"Look, it might be good to hear what he has to say."

"And it might be good for me to stop listening to music until three am, but I'm sure as hell not going to do that either."

"Don't you think you need something to help you move on?"

"I moved on a long time ago."

"No, you haven't. You act as though you are ok but you're not. I can see it in your eyes every time I look at you."

"And for some reason, you think that talking to Seth would somehow help me be ok? If so, you're in need of more help than I am."

"Come on, be reasonable."

"I'll think about it, but 'reasonable' doesn't come naturally to me like it does to you."

"Well, being difficult seems to come very naturally to you."

"All right, I have had a really great time," I say standing up, "but this wasn't it."

"I'm not finished."

I slam back down in my seat. If I have to listen to one more minute of this, I'm going to lose it.

"Remember what I told you about how people view you at the studio now? Like Maisie and her parents?"

"The crazy restraining-order family? Yeah."

"Well, when you meet with Seth, just remember—"

"Remember what? Not to damage my reputation more than I already have?"

"You take everything so personally."

"It *is* personal."

"These feelings you're expressing only reinforce the fact that you need help moving on. So just meet with him. It won't kill you."

Shaking my head, I get up—and this time, I walk out.

Checking my watch, I see that it's time for my appointment with Amelia.

***

"Hello, Wren," she greets as I sit down across from her. "Have you been taking your medication?"

"Yes."

"Has it helped at all?"

"I think so, yes." My mind is a bit preoccupied with knowing that in less than twenty-four hours, I might be facing *him*. If I choose to, that is.

"And how do you feel?"

"Huh? Uh, I guess like the path I'm on has led me to a big, dumb wall. I'm stuck behind it."

"There's something you've been repressing, we've touched on the subject many times in previous sessions but never have we actually gone through it."

"Because I—I wouldn't know how to get it all out."

"That's just it, it doesn't all have to come out. We can take it slowly, piece by piece, and if there's anything you're not ready to share, then you don't have to."

"I punched him," I say abruptly.

"Oh, ok. Can you give some context to this statement?"

It's hard to say, but I feel like I have to talk about this now or I'll explode.

"I've been trying not to think about it, but it hasn't really worked. Truth is, I couldn't control my temper and I punched him, this person named Seth. But that's not the whole story—you see, *that* story is much more complicated. It started back, hmm, probably as soon as I began going to his studio. We had problems from the very beginning, he was a bully and did bad things, but no one was listening to me seeing as he was the son of the director and everything—nepotism is a bitch. Anyway, he was hurting people and I wasn't on board. Then he and some not-so-nice friends try to force me on board but I wouldn't give, and that made him mad. Like really mad. And then..." *Wow a lot more is coming out than I thought would.*

"Continue."

"And then, there was a... a fire..."

"A fire?"

I don't answer. I've barely spoken of this since it happened.

"Wren, what was this fire?"

"It, it doesn't matter." I begin talking faster. "Some more things lead to other things and I ended up being blamed for it all. Then, suddenly, I've punched Seth straight in the face. I got kicked out and banned from ever stepping foot on the school's property not long after, but I think I would've

been told to hit the highway sooner or later no matter what. Pretty sure people didn't like me there very much. After that, I was sent off to this other, 'more prestigious' school—but that didn't work out either. And by then I was so angry that I didn't even care that I had nowhere to go, but that didn't last long. My anger turned darker and deeper and sadder. Soon I was just plain depressed and alone. And this isn't the only thing going about my brain, but I still think it toppled some destructive dominos."

"Is there more?"

"What?"

"I'm not sure why, but I still feel you have something else to get out. Is there more?"

Of course there's more. There's everything more. "No, there's nothing more. At least not that I can think of right now."

There's no way in hell I'm ready to talk about all that stuff. I suppose this would be considered some of the big stuff, but it's not the deepest stuff. There's more, and it doesn't even really have to do with him or me getting expelled. But it's buried.

"Wren, these things you hold—"

"Things I hold?"

"Yes, you may not notice, but things like the hate toward yourself, guilt, things you don't want to feel, the experiences that have hurt you— the more you push them down, the more they get in you. This creates wounds within your mind and when they don't heal, they fester."

"Oh, please never say the word 'fester' again."

"I mean it, Wren. How much can one person take on? And how long until they break?"

***

I leave my therapy session with a lot to ponder. For one, I'm finally voluntarily and actively thinking about what happened when I was kicked out of my last dance school—something that I haven't purposely thought about in a long time. Some of it's been blocked in my mind, but it's all starting to rush back now—on the anniversary of the night it happened.

It's overwhelming—like it's all happening all over again.

***

It's May 13th, 2016. 9pm.

Rehearsal just ended 15 minutes ago and Bianca's already left, and I'm still inside the school. She was supposed to give me a ride home tonight, but Seth told her that he was going to drive me instead.

She had spilled her water all over the studio's Marley floor just a few minutes earlier, so I told her I'd run to the bathroom to get paper towels, and by the time I got back here, she was gone.

There are still plenty of other dancers around at the moment, but none of them really like me, so I don't want to ask any of them if they'll take me home. Instead, I just sit down in front of the windows inside the main studio that face outside, watching the cars all pull away until there's none left.

I'm alone, or so I think. At first, everything seems mostly normal, except for a strangely sweet flowery smell—it must be a new air freshener they're trying out—but then I start to get a pit deep within my stomach and the blood pumping through my veins runs cold.

By the time I dare to get up, the entire school is dark. I would call my parents, but they aren't around.

What I ought to do is start the walk back, before Seth decides to do what he said he would do. But I'm too late. I think a part of me always knew I was too late, and that's why it takes me so long to turn around.

When I do finally pick myself up and turn around, there he is. Standing on the other side of the observation glass, staring—as if he's been standing there since the beginning of time.

I can feel it, right down into my bones; something bad is about to happen.

Maybe I should just break the windows and escape out into the parking lot. No, that would be stupid—nothing is going to happen. Nothing is going to happen.

Holding my breath and forcing my spine to stay straight, I walk toward him. There's a thinly veiled animalistic gleam behind his eyes as he stares at my every step.

"Seth, what are you still doing here?" My voice shakes slightly as the words come out of my mouth.

"No, Wren. I want to know what you're still doing here."

"I'm—well I'm not exactly sure..."

Seth suddenly steps closer and leans his head down, kissing me.

Every part of my body is shocked to its core, and all I want to do is jump back—but his arms are firmly holding me in place.

I turn my head and pull away as best I can, but he just brings me in closer, his lips moving harder against my own.

Finally, I manage to bite down on his lip and push him back as he lets go in surprise.

"What the hell?" he yells.

"You son of a bitch—that's what I should be saying to you! What did you just do to me?"

He doesn't answer; instead he reaches into his pocket and takes out a cigarette. He lights it and looks at me like he's trying to decide what to do with me. Seeing as he's blocking the exit, I begin moving backward, toward the windows once again, in case I need to somehow use them to escape. Of course, he follows.

I sit down on the windowsill, trying to catch my breath and calm my mind. He sits next to me, still smoking the cigarette.

"Do you really need to be smoking that right now?" I ask, without thinking.

"Yes."

"I didn't know you smoked."

"That's because you really don't know much about me."

"And you don't really know me."

"I know you better than you think." He abruptly throws the cigarette past my shoulder and into the wastebasket behind me, making me flinch. I hate flinching.

"I need to go, my parents will be worried about me."

"Really?" He scoots closer. "Because I have it on good authority that both your parents are out of town this whole week."

I swallow hard and break eye contact, feeling my heart might pound its way out of my chest at any moment. Bianca must have told him.

"I can't be near you right now," I say as soon as I find the words.

"Why is that?"

"Because of what you just did."

"I didn't do anything," he says, relaxing back against the windowsill.

"You kissed me!"

Out of nowhere, far too quickly for me to react, his hand flies at my face and smacks me hard across the cheek, causing my whole head to turn to the side. I don't know what hurts more, the fear or the stinging pain from where I was just struck.

I just sit there, stunned, with no idea what to do.

I feel as though I am in some sort of a paralyzing trance.

"I shouldn't have done that," Seth comments. "But sometimes, you really get under my skin, and I can't help myself."

He gets up and begins pacing back and forth in front of me as I continue to sit still.

Then, everything breaks loose.

"Don't you ever touch me again, or I swear to God, I'll kill you."

Seth's head snaps in my direction. "What did you just say to me?"

"I said, don't you ever freaking touch me again, or I swear to freaking God, I'll freaking kill you!" I shout, jumping up.

The next thing I know, I am on my back with Seth pinning me down. Still holding me in place, he flips me over onto my stomach.

I cry out in pain, but then he just uses one of his hands to press my head down, grinding it into the floor. I struggle to get free, but he's too strong.

"Stop, get off of me!" I am barely suppressing the tears that are welling up in my eyes.

He releases my head and uses his free hand to get something from his pocket, but I can't see what.

I hear a click and the sound of a spark and see a bright light from the corner of my eye.

"Seth, what is—?"

He moves the bright light in front of my face and I can feel the heat radiating from it on my skin. It's his lighter.

"Why don't I just burn you right here and now?" he asks in a sinisterly low voice.

"Uh, because that would be psychotic?"

He moves the lighter closer and brings it right next to my eye as I realize that I need to learn to keep my mouth shut sometimes.

"God, if you're gonna do something horrible to me, can you just do it already?"

He's still keeping me pinned on the floor, and if I try to move, I might accidentally burn myself with the flame. I'm helpless—something I've never allowed myself to be before.

"Why are you doing this?" It's a stupid question, I know, but I'm running out of ideas.

There's a long silence. "I don't know."

He moves the lighter away from my face and throws it behind him,

standing up and letting go of me. I immediately push myself up and onto my feet.

I'm preparing myself to have to fight him, but then something catches my eye. Behind him, on the windowsill, there's smoke. The curtain is on fire. He tossed the lighter onto one of the curtains, and it caught fire!

He follows my gaze, turning his head toward the curtain. This is my chance, and I take it—sprinting for the door.

It's locked. How is it locked? Oh, no, I forgot that these old studios must be locked and unlocked by a set of actual keys.

I turn around and find him standing there, facing me, all the curtains along the windows behind him now completely engulfed in flames. In his hand are the keys.

"Seth! It's locked! We need to leave, now!"

"Looking for these?" He lifts up the keys.

"Uh, yeah, no shit!"

"What's wrong? You afraid of a little fire, Wren? And here I thought you weren't afraid of anything."

"It's not that, Seth, it's just that I'd rather not burn alive if I can help it."

"I don't think you understand yet. But you will."

"Understand—" The sound of my own coughing cuts me off.

Smoke is beginning to fill the studio space, and I'm wondering how long it will take before the whole place goes up in flames.

Not willing to give up, I start to kick the door in. But I'm far from being at my full strength and I tire quickly, unable to breathe as the smoke fills my lungs. I begin coughing even more violently as I look around the studio. Flames are everywhere. Even my eyes have smoke in them, making everything blur together.

I take a step, and collapse onto the floor, rolling to my back. I lie there, looking up at the ceiling, knowing that I am going to die here. I've never been so sure of anything in my life.

With the last of my strength, I turn my head to see a blurry, dark figure approaching me. He picks me up and begins carrying me in his arms—and that's when I finally black out.

I wake up to the sound of emergency vehicles. I am alone, lying on the ground outside—right in front of the burning school.

***

The loud blaring of another car's horn startles me out of my head and back to the present.

Quickly correcting my drifting, I pull off to the side of the road. I don't even remember getting into my car—how long has this been going on? I lift up a hand and see it trembling. I definitely need to sit here a little while before I start driving again.

I've never told anyone this story, not in full anyway. And I'm never going to. I try thinking about other things, but my mind keeps jumping back in time.

After that night, I was blamed for the fire. At first, I tried telling them what really happened, but everyone thought I had done it and no one would listen to what I had to say, so I stopped trying. People could barely look at me, and when they did, the contempt in their eyes was too much for me to bear. They might as well have been screaming "Guilty!" at me. To them I was, and probably still am, dangerous and insane.

My family had to pay the school a lot of money to make up for the damages. I was told I was lucky the disaster was put out before it spread from the studio it began in. I was told I was lucky Seth was there to pull me from the fire. Bianca still thinks he saved my life. A part of me thinks that maybe Violet believes this too.

This nearly drove me insane, so I confronted Seth and got into a big argument with him. Bianca was there, watching on the side, and I could tell Violet was unsure about what to do. He kept coming toward me—I told him to back off and he grabbed my arm hard; then my fist hit him straight in the face and he went stumbling back. He wasn't expecting it, and neither was I. I didn't even know I could hit that hard until I did.

And I remember thinking "take that you motherf—"

Course, right after I got a bit worried about what people would think of me; though not worried enough to apologize or anything. Besides, it probably didn't even actually hurt him all *that* much seeing as he's built like a goddamn ox.

Anyway, I had already been told I was no longer welcome at the school and, once this happened, I was told I was no longer legally allowed within one hundred feet of the place. I finally became the outlaw I always knew I was meant to be.

I might have even come out the other side ok, if it weren't for one person: Violet. My life wasn't the only one ruined that night. Not in the same way, but still, everything changed for her, too.

She was dating a friend of Seth's at the time, and he left her because of me. And everyone at the school gave her a hard time, also because she was so closely associated with me. It got to the point where she had to quit dancing altogether—and there went everything she had been working for, down the drain to be dumped into the never-ending black hole of lost hopes.

I should have talked to her directly after it happened, to explain my side to her before anyone else could mix her head up. But I didn't.

By the time I did go over to her, I think I was too late. When I looked into her eyes, I didn't see the same distrust as I did in everyone else's, but I did see a level of uncertainty that made me nervous.

Then she asked me that dreaded question: the one question that had been keeping me from coming to her—the one I hoped I'd never have to hear. *"Did you do it?"*

I couldn't believe it. And I completely lost it.

"How could you ask me that, Violet?"

"I need to know."

"You should know already!"

"You do realize that no one is talking to me anymore. Even the teachers are treating me differently."

"Wow, that must really suck for you."

"I'm being serious, Wren. I lost my relationship because of this. Seth told him—"

"You never should have been with that asshat anyway—he's Seth's friend, that should tell you everything right there."

"Is this all a joke to you?"

"Come on! Are you blind? Why are you falling for this?"

"I'm not—"

"Can't you see how they're manipulating you? Everyone thinks I did this, that's what they want you to think too, and you don't even know it! I knew most of the people at that school were idiots, but I never thought you would be one of them. I guess you learn new things every day. Like you've learned I'm a lying, deceptive criminal, and I've learned that our friendship never really meant anything!"

"I think you should leave, you're saying things you don't mean."

"Oh, I mean everything I've said. Everything."

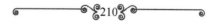

Things only got worse from there. This was the last time we ever saw each other in person. I seem to lose every relationship that means anything to me. The things you say, or don't say, can cost you *everything*.

***

I sit on the side of the road, thinking, until the sun begins to go down. This is when I feel the sudden need to go to Aidan's house. Not sure why that's where I want to be, it just is.

The whole ride over, I feel something deep inside of me pulling me there.

But when I get there, it's not Aidan who opens up the door—it's Sebastian.

"Hey, Bash," I say, attempting to sound normal. "I didn't know you guys were hanging out." The feeling I had is beginning to fade.

He's got a slice of pizza in his mouth so he just motions for me to come in.

"Who is it?" Aidan calls from another room. The moment I hear his voice, the feeling returns.

"It's Wren," Bash answers, putting his pizza back on a plate.

"Wren?" Aidan stumbles out of the other room, coming over to us.

"I can come back later," I suggest. I don't think this is going to work out like I thought it would... in fact, I don't even know what I thought I was doing here in the first place.

"No, we were just going over some band stuff, nothing important," he assures me.

I take a breath and look up into his eyes. I finally realize why it is that I came. It's funny I didn't know before; I want to tell him.

A loud buzzing noise cuts off my train of thought.

I look down at my phone and see that it's a message from Bianca. It says that she's at her dance studio and she needs me to come quick.

"What is it?" Aidan asks, confused by my sudden change in demeanor.

"Bianca." I notice a strange look appear on Sebastian's face when I say this, but it disappears so quickly I hardly think anything of it.

"What does she want?"

"My help," I say, backing up toward the door.

"Wait, that's it? You show up out of nowhere for five seconds and then leave?"

"I gotta see what she needs. Sorry."

"Let me come with you."

"No!" I say too quickly. I know going back to my old studio could stir up trouble that I don't particularly want him to know about. Hell, who knows, I could get arrested. "I mean, I think she'd rather it just be me."

"Are you at least going to tell me why you came here?"

"No."

I exit out the door and sit in my car, trying to figure out what to do. I text her back, asking for more information and, of course, there is no reply. Then I try calling and—surprise—she doesn't pick up.

This is just fan-freaking-tastic. On one hand, my friend needs help— on the other, I'll be walking into what could essentially be a personal deathtrap. If I'm caught, I will be tried for trespassing—a federal offense.

It'd be stupid of me to go, and it would be terrible of me not to. So, for this adventure, I'm gonna have to give in to my not-so-smart side. Guess it's good for me I happen to have a lot of practice with that.

CHAPTER 22

KNOCKIN' ON HELL'S DOOR

FROM THE MOMENT WREN LEFT, Sebastian had a bad feeling. Actually, as soon as she'd said Bianca's name, he had gotten a bad feeling. No, when she first showed up on Aidan's doorstep that was when the feeling started. Or was that feeling about something else...

He was probably just being paranoid. His mind was a confused mess. But then he remembered something Bianca had told him.

No, everything was fine. Wren was fine. She was going to be fine.

But what if she wasn't?

I pull up in front of the studio and gape at it for a moment. It is just as I remember, if perhaps more ominous looking. I see the renovations on the studio that burned down are still in progress, with much of the fire damage still visible. That part looks like something out of an old horror movie.

And then there's the gates that surround the whole place, which are the same as those that sit outside a prison; and I get the feeling that if I'm found, these gates used to keep me out would quickly become ones used to keep me in.

I park behind some bushes and take in a couple of deep breaths before checking my text messages again.

"Damn you, Bianca," I mutter, hanging up my phone after another failed attempt to reach her.

I then put aside my nerves and get out of the car.

"Don't worry, baby," I whisper looking back at Nightrider. "I'll be back soon."

Dusk is setting in, and it should be dark by the time I'm done, making sneaking out less of a challenge.

The gates are unlocked, so I walk straight through them and around the building until I find the back door. My skin is crawling as I go to open it.

It all seems too easy. Every fiber of my being tells me to get out of here while I still can. The door creaks open and I step through it, holding my breath.

As soon as it closes behind me, it takes me less than a second to realize the mistake I've made. This place is a lion's den, and I've walked straight into it.

The first thing I notice is the eerily familiar scent of—what's that? Lavender?

As I'm preoccupied with the studio's smell, a few dancers pass by me, looking at me with wide eyes. I don't recognize them, so I can only hope they don't recognize me. Regardless, I need to get moving.

I snake through the bottom level and work my way up to the second floor. No sign of Bianca anywhere. As I'm about to call bullshit on her and go back downstairs to leave, I hear some voices and footsteps coming around the corner. I quickly rush inside the nearest storage closet, leaving it open slightly.

"And you're sure it was her?" the first voice asks. It sounds like it belongs to an older woman, perhaps a teacher.

"Yes," says a younger sounding voice—must be a student. "I'm sure."

"If you see her again, Maisie, bring her to me. Tell the same to your friends. She is *not* welcome at this establishment any longer."

I want to hear more, but their voices fade as they continue down the hall. All I know is if I don't get out of here fast, I'm in serious trouble.

As I'm trying to come up with an escape plan, Bianca's words come back to me in a rush. She said I needed help moving on and that I needed to talk to Seth. Could this be her twisted way of making me see things her way—of making me see that I haven't moved on from this place? Could she do this to me?

When I'm sure there's no one there any longer, I come out of the closet and close the door very slowly so as not to make a sound. But as soon as I shut it, I hear people approaching me from behind. I turn around and find myself face to face with two dancers, both of whom look quite smug.

"Oh hey guys," I greet, my mind reeling, "I was just looking for the restroom. If either of you could point me in the right direction that'd be great."

"I don't think so," one of them says, narrowing her eyes at me.

"Yeah, sorry. We were told to bring you to our teacher if we found you," the other joins in.

"Look, I think there's been some sort of a misunderstanding…" Panic is starting to rise in me. I don't want to hurt them, but I'm not going to go quietly.

"Then how about you start by telling us your name?"

"Umm, it's… Axl."

"No, it's not."

"Yes it is. Would you please let me pass?"

"Well, just come with us first, and if we're wrong, then no hard feelings."

"I don't think so."

"Come with us."

"No."

"You have—"

"What part of the word 'no' are you having trouble getting through your brain?"

"Come, or we'll have to force you."

"Hah! You, force me? Sorry girls, it's time I get going. So before we do this thing, do either of you—" Something hard hits me on the back of the head, causing me to stumble and see bright flashes of light. I hear gasps as I fall to the floor.

"I'll take it from here," a voice says from above me. I can't make out who is speaking though, everything hurts too much.

"Oh my God! What did you do to her? Who are you?"

I stay curled up on the ground, clutching my head and trying not to cry out.

"I'm here to take care of this situation, so I'd appreciate it if you wouldn't get in my way any more than you already have."

"You just hit her! And we don't even know who you are!"

"Plus, we were told specifically by our teacher to let her know if we found this girl."

"And I was told specifically by Bianca and Seth to deal with this first before notifying any other authorities. So I wouldn't tell *anyone* about this if I were you, because they won't be happy if you mess this up. Do you really want me to go back and tell them that you two directly interrupted their orders?"

There's a bit more arguing, but I really can't understand any of it. Then everything goes silent, and that's when I know I'm screwed.

I feel myself get picked up off the ground and I attempt to push myself free, but I have no strength and the arms holding me don't let go.

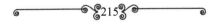

Helplessly, I'm half-dragged, half-carried into a dark room and slammed down in a chair.

"Do you know where you are, Wren?" my attacker asks, flipping on a dim light.

I answer with incoherent groaning.

"I asked you a question."

"If you were going to hit me over the head, couldn't you have at least bothered to knock me out properly?" I finally say.

"I was stopping you from being turned in. You should be thanking me."

"Right, remind me of that when I'm finally able to see straight again."

"Do you know who I am?"

The person's voice is definitely that of a female and it sounds familiar. I squint up at her, trying to get a better look at this person who is now tying my hands together. "No... what are you doing?" I should be stopping her, but my body is frozen.

Kate smirks down at me, tightening the ropes around my wrists. "We have unfinished business—I warned you this was coming. Didn't you like the note I slipped in your pocket?"

"That was you?" I recoil away from her and begin to stand up, but she shoves me down again.

"I wouldn't do that if I were you."

"Did Bianca and Seth really send you here?" Dizziness is beginning to set in.

She laughs—it's a cold and menacing sound. "No, but Bianca was telling me about her issues with you and how she wished you would just meet with Seth so I suggested she trick you into taking a little visit here to— you know—jog your memory or whatever. She thought it was a great idea, and I knew it was a great opportunity."

"So you tricked me here, knocked me over the head, dragged me into some sort of closet, and tied me up? Is it just me, or are you also seeing how crazy this makes you?" I look at her but she's not paying attention to me. Instead, she's admiring a jacket in her hands—a dark brown leather jacket, my jacket. How did she get that? I look down at my torso and see that I am now only wearing a tank top.

"Whoa, whoa, whoa. Physically abusing me is one thing, but taking my freaking jacket? That's a whole 'nother level of low, Kate."

"I don't particularly admire your fashion sense, but I must say, I like this jacket. I think I'll keep it," she says, slipping it on.

"Over my dead body."

"Don't be so dramatic, Wren."

"I'm the dramatic one? You're basically kidnapping me."

"So why don't you call out for help?"

"You know why," I say through gritted teeth.

"I'm just here to set a few things straight."

"No, I'm done listening to you," I rebuke, standing up. As soon as I get to my feet, my head pounds and my knees begin to collapse.

Before I can fall, Kate shoves me, knocking over the chair and sending me into the wall where I bang my head once again. I whimper in pain and she places a hand on my chest, holding me against the wall as she places her other hand beside my head.

"Remember this? Doesn't feel so nice, does it?" she spits.

"You talking about that time in the dressing room? You know this isn't the same." *I think I might be sick.*

"You always seem to find a way to get one up on me. Well not today. Today you're mine," she hisses, leaning in closer.

"Awe man," I laugh, "I always knew you were a psycho."

She gives me a glare that would terrify me if I wasn't already so out of it. Then she proceeds to stick a hand down my tank top.

"Hey!"

Her fingers enclose around my rose pendant that had been tucked away, yanking it from my neck in one swift movement.

"This is new. Who is it from?" she asks, dangling it in front of me.

"Give that back. Right now," I say in the calmest voice I can.

"You are in no position to be giving me orders, Wren."

"I said give it back."

"This is from Aidan, isn't it?"

"Why does it freaking matter?"

"Listen to me, right now, I could turn you in or I could let you go. If you do as I say, I'll help you escape this place. If you don't, I'll leave you here by yourself. I'll let all those dancers and teachers know exactly where you are. And I'll tell them you attacked me, just like what you did to Seth."

I begin to feel myself shaking. "Screw you."

"You shouldn't be so hasty—"

"I said screw you."

"Stop it!"

"Yeah, sure, just do me one favor first. I want you to walk out this door, head down the hallway, and go screw yourself."

"You don't even know what I want," she says, sounding almost confused at my apparent insolence.

"I don't *care* what you want. But I can bet it has to do with Aidan, and I'm not playing your jealousy games."

"If you would have just stayed away from him and Bianca like I said—"

"Let's be real here, the only reason you're so confident at the moment is because I'm basically half-conscious in the place I'm most vulnerable and my hands are literally tied. You might be fooling yourself now, but I remember the look in your eyes back in that dressing room, you were afraid. So I guess this is your idea of revenge, a way to make me feel the way you did. Thing is, there's one problem with your psychotically twisted plan—I'm not scared of you."

She abruptly grabs me by the hair, forcing me to my knees and yanking my head back so that I'm looking at her. I bite my lip to stop myself from making a sound.

"You've always got something to say," she seethes, gripping my hair harder. "What, no more smart comments?"

"Bite me, Kate." At my words, a look of pure rage appears on her face and she lifts my hands upwards.

"Hey—Ow! Freaking hell! You bit me. You actually bit me! You're crazy!"

"Shut up. Someone is going to hear you and then you'll be in real trouble."

I stare at my wrist, watching the blood trickle down from the teeth marks in my skin. The shock combined with my throbbing head makes me wonder if I'll pass out. At least then maybe this whole thing would be over.

"Do it," I mutter suddenly.

"Do what?"

"Get the authorities, get someone, for your own sake."

"What are you saying?"

I stand quickly in a rush of adrenaline and shove my knee into her stomach, sending her stumbling back. "I'm saying you better go tell some-one I'm here so they can come save you or I swear I will break out of these restraints and strangle you with them."

She's doubled over, holding her stomach and dramatically gasping as though I had just beat her with a club.

"You can't," she coughs.

"Yes, I can. And believe me when I say now you're messin' with a son of a bitch."

Kate straightens up and moves toward the door. "Have it your way. You'll never make it out of here."

She opens up the door and closes it behind her quickly. I rush toward it but the harsh click on the other side lets me know I'm too late. I try turning the knob, but it doesn't budge. I'm locked in. I look around for something to cut the ropes around my wrists, but I can't find anything. This means picking the lock is probably a no-go. Looks like I'll be getting out of this one the action movie way.

I stand back and kick the door. Lucky for me, its bolts aren't very strong and the whole thing comes crashing down. Stepping out, I look both ways before dashing down the hallway in search of my way out.

I begin running to the stairs, but the sound of more footsteps sends me running into a storage closet instead. If I never see another damn storage closet, it would be too soon. I hear the footsteps coming closer and move to get further away from the door, accidentally backing up into a bucket and mop, causing them to fall over and hit the floor with a loud bang.

"Crap!"

The footsteps get closer and I prepare myself. I'm not getting taken by any of these self-righteous dipshits again without a fight.

The door opens and a dark curly head pops in.

"Bash? What are you doing here?" I ask, almost more shocked than when I saw Kate.

"Saving you. You're welcome."

He ducks his head back out of the door and then opens it wider for me to come out.

"You sure there's no one there?" I whisper.

"No, I checked to make sure that there *would* be someone there," he replies sarcastically.

Regardless of his unfriendly tone, I step outside.

"I need to find something to cut through these," I say, holding up my hands.

His eyes widen. "What happened to you?"

"Doesn't matter. Can you get them off?"

He reaches into his back pocket and takes out a small knife, using it to slice through my restraints with ease.

"Why do you have a knife on you?"

"Why don't you? Seems you could have used one."

"Yeah, I suppose I could've..." I begin thinking about Kate holding me on my knees by my hair.

"Come on," Bash says, frowning at my unusually dazed expression.

He brings me back to the present, taking me by the hand and leading us toward the staircase.

As we are rounding the corner, he abruptly shoves me backwards.

"Hey girls," he calls out toward the end of the hall.

"Sebastian!" I hear some female voices yell back. I recognize them as belonging to the dancers that found me right before Kate did.

He waves and moves forward as I stay pressed against the wall behind the corner. I'm quite glad that I didn't shove him back.

"How's it going?" he asks them. He sounds uncharacteristically charming and happy—very different from the way he usually interacts with me.

"We saw that girl that got kicked out last year sneaking around. At least we're pretty sure it was her—she looked like she was up to no good," one of the girls responds.

"Yeah, she tried to tell us her name was Axl," another one chimes in. "It was all very strange and then this other girl showed up and—well— told us that she'd take care of her. But apparently that girl attacked her and escaped so now we're looking for her again."

"Wow, that's quite the story," Bash says with a laugh. "Has anyone else seen her?"

"No, but we were all told to keep a look out. She could be dangerous."

I almost scoff at their words, but I remind myself that my goal right now is to not be caught.

"Right, well, I'll let you know if I see anything suspicious. Come to think of it, I thought I saw someone that looked a little off..."

"Where?"

"Right down the hall, that way. You might want to check it out."

"Was it a girl?"

"Uh-huh."

"Can you help us find her?"

"Course. There's just one thing I need to do first. You girls go ahead, I'll meet up with you in a minute."

I hear the sound of people moving farther away. When they're gone, Bash comes back and grabs my hand again, pulling me around the corner.

"Someone that looked a little off?" I question as we both check over the side of the stairs before going down them.

"It worked, didn't it?"

"I guess. But how did they know you?"

He shushes me, and I glare at him.

We reach the bottom and I begin to walk toward the back door exit. I only make it a few feet before he jerks me backwards by the arm and pushes me against the wall, giving me flashbacks to what happened only a short while ago.

"What the h—" I start but he silences me by putting a hand over my mouth. He's lucky I don't bite him out of instinct.

He looks up at the staircase and then glances back down at me. Still covering my mouth, he uses his free hand to open up a little door to a closet space in the side of the stairs, ushering me inside. Under different circumstances, he would have a bloody nose right now.

He closes the door and I forcefully push his hand off me.

"Don't you ever do that again," I warn.

Just then, the sound of people walking right by our hiding spot startles me and I grab onto Bash—causing my cheeks to turn red. Good thing it's dark in here. When they pass, we step back out and he takes off his sweatshirt, handing it to me.

"Put this on." I give him a look and he gives me an exasperated sigh. "Just do it."

I pull it over my head and find that it comes down to my mid thighs. It's a painful reminder that Kate has my jacket, but I guess this will make for an ok disguise.

"Put the hood up," he commands. When I don't do it right away, he reaches out to do it himself but I swat his hands away.

"I got it," I say, flipping up the hood. "Would you please tell me what is going on now?"

"Would you please be quiet for just a minute?"

"If you tell me to shut up one more time—"

"This isn't the place for you to be throwing around threats, Wren."

"What's that supposed to mean?"

He ignores me, taking my hand once more as we set out down the hallway toward the front of the building.

"Why not use the back?" I ask.

"We can't, you came in using the back and some girls saw you. You

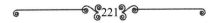

weren't exactly Ethan Hunt about the whole thing, you know. And now there's a bunch of people over there."

"So we're just going to waltz out the front like it's no big deal?"

"Yes."

"That's insane."

We stop for a second and he turns to face me, looking me in the eyes. "Just trust me."

My eyes search his and I nod. He wouldn't bother doing any of this if he wasn't really trying to help.

We continue walking down the hall and finally I can see the light of the exit sign at the end of this nightmarish tunnel. But just as I think we are home free, I spot a woman reading a paper at the front desk, which happens to be right by the door. I elbow Bash in the ribs and motion toward the lady. He nods calmly and keeps walking. This is where I would make a run for it, but he seems to have a different plan. I told him I would trust him though, so I'll go along with it.

We reach the desk and the woman looks up from her paper. Oh man. I definitely recognize her, which means she will likely know exactly who I am. This should be exciting. But rather than focusing on me, she looks to Bash and a smile spreads across her face.

"Sebastian, how nice to see you! If you're here to pick up Bianca, I'm afraid she already left over an hour ago."

Pick up Bianca?

"I figured as much. Thank you Mrs. Gayle."

"And who is this?" she refers to me. I promptly turn my head and let the hood hide my face.

"This is… this is my girlfriend," Bash responds, wrapping an arm around my waist.

"Ah how nice. What's your name dear?"

I just cough in response, unsure if my voice would give me away.

"Sorry, Michelle's not feeling well and she's terribly shy around strangers."

I give her a slight smile and turn back around to face Bash, using my eyes to motion toward the exit.

"Strangers? Interesting, I could have sworn I've seen her before. You said her name is Michelle?"

To stop her inquiries, I collapse suddenly, pretending to faint, and Bash catches me immediately as if he knew what I was going to do.

"Oh my! Is she all right?"

"Yes, this happens quite frequently actually. Nothing to worry about."

"I'll call—"

"No!" he cuts her off. "It's perfectly normal for her to do this, especially when she's not feeling well. I can handle it on my own."

"Are you sure?"

"Yes." He picks me up in his arms. "Could you just do me the favor of opening the door for me?"

"Of course!"

I hear the door swing open and can feel the fresh air hit me as Bash carries me outside.

"I do hope your Michelle feels better!"

"I'm sure she will—thanks so much, Mrs. Gayle!"

The door slams shut and I open my eyes and peer up at him. "Why Michelle?"

"It's just what came to me first, because of that song you like. But, honestly, no matter what name I chose, anything would be better than what you were trying to tell people. I mean, Axl? Seriously?"

"Oh. Can you put me down now?"

"Not yet."

About twenty seconds later he checks over his shoulder and sets me back on my feet. We then run out the gates as quickly as we can, the darkness of the night cloaking us in shadows.

When we are a safe distance away, I pull us to a stop.

"All right, time for some answers."

"I would say so. Want to tell me why I found you tied up with a bloody bite mark on your arm?"

"It's a long story, sort of."

"We've got time."

"Well, I want my answers first."

"Fine," he snaps, "but before we get into all that, I have something to say to you."

"Ok, go for it."

"Stop sticking your neck out for people who wouldn't do the same for you."

"What are you even talking about?"

"You risked coming here to help Bianca, yeah? And she didn't even show. I'm not sure what she was getting out of it, but I'm willing to bet

none of it was for your benefit. Is that the kind of person you think deserves your time and energy?"

"How did you know any of this?"

"I could tell something was off right when you left, and I knew it had to do with Bianca, so I followed you. When I realized this was where she was leading you to, I knew it was going to be bad if someone found you. But I thought there was no way you would be stupid enough to actually go inside so I started to leave. Then, as I was leaving, I saw you sneak around back and found you hiding in that storage closet like some sort of wanted criminal."

I dismiss his rudeness and continue with my questions. "How do you know Bianca?"

"She's my cousin."

"Oh, so that's why you were at her house that one time. Why didn't you tell me before?"

"You never asked."

"She has never even mentioned you, I don't think."

"I'm not surprised. We're not exactly close."

"Wait, you said you knew it was going to be bad if someone found me. Do you know…"

He doesn't say anything.

"Bianca told you, didn't she?"

"I had heard a bit about you before I met you for the first time."

"Is that why you were so suspicious of me?"

He shrugs.

"How come you didn't ever say anything about it?"

"Oh right. And what was I supposed to say? 'Hey my cousin told me you were kicked out of her dance studio for setting a fire and assaulting someone, welcome to the band.'"

"Truth is better than silence."

"Sure it is."

"Still, if you're her cousin, and everyone here knows you so well, how come I never knew you while I went here?"

"My parents just started paying me to pick her up after dance classes a few times a month, since she hasn't had you to go with this year. Before that, I never set foot in this place. She has her own car too, as you probably know, but she doesn't like to use it all that often."

"And what do you think of me now?"

"What do you mean? And why must you ask so many damn questions?"

"Well, I figure if you bothered to come after me you must not hate me anymore, so what do you think of me now?"

"I think you're bad at choosing friends that are good for you. And I think you need to do everything you can to stay far away from this place. Especially seeing as Seth could come around the corner at any time. And yes, I know Seth—a bit. From what I know of the guy, you shouldn't be anywhere near him. Ever."

"Seth doesn't scare me."

"He should."

I spot Nightrider just as I left it, tactfully parked behind some bushes, and begin walking toward it. Bash follows.

"So, are you going to go home now?" he asks.

"Maybe. Not sure yet."

"Just don't get yourself into anymore trouble."

"I couldn't even if I tried."

"Yeah, right."

We make it over to my car and I open up the door, resting my hand on it.

"I suppose this is where we part ways," I say.

"Before you go, I just wanted to thank you for making me carry you out of there. It was a great way to make things more complicated than need be."

"Hey genius, if you had given me a few more seconds before picking me up you would have known that I was going to run outside to fake being sick."

"Oh, well apologies for disrupting your stellar plan. I should have known from the moment I found you tied up and knocking things over in a closet that you had everything under control."

I frown and pull his sweatshirt off, balling it up and throwing it at him. "Here, I see I've annoyed you enough for one day. I wouldn't want to cause you any more trouble by failing to return your sweatshirt."

He looks down at it in his hands and shifts his weight, looking to the black sky before focusing back on me. "Wren, just so you know, I never hated you." The tense energy between us softens at his words.

What do I say? "Oh, good."

On that articulate note, I get into the car and roll down the window.

He places a hand on my car and cocks his head at me. "You're not leaving until you tell me how you got bitten and ended up with ropes around your wrists."

"Please, Bash. I don't want to go into it all."

His hand doesn't budge.

"Son of a goddamn bitch. Fine." I begin telling him, starting from the first time Kate threatened me and then jumping to Bianca's message and going up until when he found me. For some reason, I can feel my cheeks flush uncomfortably during different parts of the story. His expression, on the other hand, remains mostly neutral and calm throughout my retelling.

"So, she hit you, tied you up, and bit you," he says, more to himself than to me.

I nod slowly, the pain in my head returning.

"I know you don't want to hear this right now, but you need to understand what will happen if you try to press charges or even just tell someone about this."

"I know, Bash. If I do anything about it, Kate is going to tell everyone I was at the studio and I could get charged with trespassing."

"She did have witnesses, but those witnesses also saw her hit you over the head which could be used to your advantage."

"Yeah, and those witnesses are also under the impression that she was acting on orders from Bianca who directly correlates to Seth—the one person everyone in that damn place seems to be terrified of above all else." I lean forward and rest my head on the steering wheel, shutting my eyes tightly and willing the pain to go away.

"Can you even drive right now?" he asks.

"Hmm, I hadn't thought about that." I suppose I shouldn't, but I really want to get out of here. Right now.

"Yeah, no. There's no way I'm letting you drive yourself anywhere. Not in this condition."

"Let me? Sebastian, you are mistaken if you think you could ever 'let me' do anything."

"That's not what I mean and you know it."

"What are you going to do, huh? Drive me yourself? You came over here in your own car and there's no way I'm leaving Nightrider in this place."

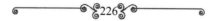

"Yes, I'm aware of that. Wait, Nightrider?"

"My car."

He shakes his head and swears, brushing his fingers through his curls. "I'll call your parents, they can come pick you up."

"You will do no such thing. I don't want to explain all this to them."

"Ok, then I'll..." he takes in a long breath, "I'll get Aidan."

"Get Aidan?"

"And he'll drive you in your car to wherever it is you decide to go and I'll go back in mine."

"Ok," I sigh in agreement.

"Just wait here, keep your doors locked, and don't do anything stupid," he says.

"All right, don't do anything you would. Got it. And Bash?"

"Yes?" He raises a brow, unsure of what I'm about to say.

"Thanks."

CHAPTER 23

I COULD BE YOURS

I WATCH AS BASH DISAPPEARS into the darkness of the night to get his car. Suddenly I am very alone. I curl up in my seat, hugging myself. I feel exposed and vulnerable—and I hate it. To distract my mind from these horrible feelings, I focus on what tomorrow may hold. I know what Bash said about Seth is true, but I can't stop thinking about my conversation with Bianca. I think I may finally be ready—ready to face him. And if I'm not, then I probably never will be, so there's no harm in trying.

I know Bash won't like this decision, but it's my decision to make.

As I remain sitting alone in my car, I message Bianca and tell her to set up the meeting. She responds without any mention of her earlier text, telling me to be at some restaurant that I've never heard of, this Saturday, when the sun goes down—giving me just under two days to prepare myself.

Her refusal to acknowledge what she just knowingly put me through infuriates me, and because I'm so mad at her, I consider not showing up to the meeting. But, I have to remember that this isn't about her. And if I don't do this, I'll keep feeling stuck, and I can't stay stuck. I have to keep going. I have to carry on. Then maybe I can stop crying, lay down my head to rest, and find peace when I am done.

A knock on my window causes my heart to jump. I had been so wrapped up in my own thoughts I hadn't noticed Bash returned with Aidan.

I open my door and climb over to the passenger side as Aidan takes my place in the driver's seat. Bash gives us both a nod, as he gets back into his own car.

"I'm gonna take you to the hospital," Aidan says as Bash leaves.

"No! Please, that's not necessary."

"Well, I'm not entirely sure you don't have a concussion, and those are serious."

"I don't have a concussion."

"How do you know?"

"Because I've had one before, and this is… different."

"Different?"

"Yes."

"So where do you want to go then?"

"I don't know." If he takes me home, I'll have to explain to my parents why I'm coming home such a mess. Also, he would have no way of getting home himself unless he took Nightrider back to his house, which could just end up complicating things further.

"You know," he glances at me, "you can stay over at my place if you need to. It wouldn't be any trouble."

"Are you sure?"

"Of course."

"I'm sorry, Aidan," I say quietly as we pull out onto the road.

"There's nothing to be sorry for," he says firmly.

"Did Sebastian tell you about what happened?"

"He told me enough. I won't make you talk about it if you don't want to."

The rest of the ride we spend in silence. The pain in my head has gotten worse, making me dizzy and confused. No, no, it's making me *dazed* and confused. I don't realize we've arrived until Aidan opens my door. I get out of the car, but when my feet touch the ground I sway and begin to fall forward. Aidan catches me and holds me up, helping me to the house.

"Whoa," I say, stopping us right before going inside, "is that a bike? It looks really nice."

"Oh, yeah, Noah got it for me. He dropped it off a few hours ago. I should probably take it in now. God knows it'll get stolen out here if I don't."

Once getting me inside, Aidan goes back out to bring the bike in, and I sit down on the couch. I then hold my head in my hands as I feel him sit down next to me.

"Wren, is there anything I can do?" he asks softly.

I pick my head up from my hands. "Have you any pain meds?"

"Yeah, anything else?"

"It's cold," I blurt out, suddenly noticing the chill air inside the house.

"I know, our heater doesn't work. I'll get you a blanket. And now that I think about it, you're only in shorts and a tank top, do you need any other clothes?"

"No, it's all right."

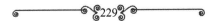

As he goes to get the supplies, I text my parents, telling them that I'm staying the night at Lena's so they won't wonder where I am when I don't come home. Good thing we have school off tomorrow, or they would be suspicious.

I briefly consider calling Violet, but then think better of it.

As Aidan is coming back over, there is a hard knock on the front door. He opens it immediately, apparently already knowing who's on the other side.

"Noah, this is not a good time."

"I know," a loud, and slightly slurred voice says. "That's why Bash told me I might need to check in on you."

The door is blocking my view of him, but I am very curious to see what he looks like. I consider getting up, but my legs feel like lead and moving seems to not be an option.

"And did he know how jacked up you were when he told you that?"

"Is she in there? You know I want to meet her." Is he talking about me?

"No, go away."

"Is Mom home?"

"No."

A few more things are said, but I can't make them out.

Finally, the door slams shut and Aidan comes back to me with a pill— which I take gladly—a blanket, some antibacterial stuff, and a wet wash-cloth.

"You know you could have brought him in," I say. "I wouldn't have minded."

"I didn't want to."

I nod and grab the blanket.

"Hey, where is your jacket anyway?" he asks, watching me wrap it around myself. "I could have sworn you were wearing it when you left earlier."

"Kate stole it," I answer, adjusting the blanket—it's surprisingly soft. I want to say something about the necklace, but I feel guilty about it for some reason…

"Are you serious?"

"Deadly," I respond under my breath, my hand involuntarily coming up to my neck, feeling where she had ripped it off.

"We'll get it back," he promises, and I can tell he means it. Of course, he's still talking about the jacket, though. "And until then, you can have

mine." He takes off his leather jacket and gently places it around my shoulders.

I want to say something in return, but the image of Kate sinking her teeth into my skin attacks my brain, making bile rise in the back of my throat.

"Do you mind?" he asks, kneeling down in front of me and taking my wrist in his hand, turning it over. "It needs to be cleaned."

I nod my head and he brings the washcloth to my skin, brushing it over the bite mark. It stings for a moment, but then the discomfort subsides, leaving a light cooling sensation of relief.

"I can't believe what she did to you," he murmurs.

"Me neither, I want to punch her face in," I say, sounding a little more bloodthirsty than I mean to.

His eyes meet mine with amusement. "I'd like to see that."

"And I wouldn't mind doing the same to Bianca."

"Why?" He looks puzzled all of a sudden. Perhaps Bash didn't tell him everything after all.

"No reason," I cover—there's no need to tell him about her part in all this now. "I didn't mean that. I'm just upset that her 'emergency' message wasn't as serious as I thought."

"Oh yeah, I forgot about that. What was it about again? The whole thing still confuses me a bit."

"It confuses me too."

The puzzled expression remains on his face.

"Are you two still going to the dance tomorrow?" I ask, changing the subject.

"As far as I know."

"Oh, I hope you enjoy yourselves."

"Me too, but school dances are never really what people make them out to be."

"Still, I bet you'll have fun."

He gives me a weird look, and I avert my attention to the walls of the room. "Is it just us here?" I ask suddenly. I know he told Noah their mom wasn't here, but I just want to make sure.

"Yeah." He sets the washcloth aside and stands up. "It's just us."

"Good," I respond without thinking, immediately regretting ever having opened my mouth.

"How's your head?" he asks, politely ignoring my comment.

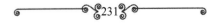

"Not great."

"Hopefully the pain pill will take care of that soon. But, if you decide you want to go to the hospital, just let me know. In the meantime, want me to get you an ice pack?"

"No, I just want to rest here."

"Let me at least move you to a bed. There's no need for you to sleep on this old couch. It's hard as a rock."

"I don't mind."

"We don't have a guest room, but you can use mine. I'll stay out here."

"No, you should get your own bed. I can handle the couch, trust me."

"I never said you couldn't."

"Good, then it's settled."

"You're very stubborn. You know that?"

"Yes, it's one of my best traits."

"Well, you must be tired. I'll let you get some rest."

"No, I'm not tired yet."

He smiles down at me.

I go to smile back but the throbbing in my head causes me to grimace instead. "Distract me until the pain pill kicks in," I plead.

"Ok, what would you like me to do?"

"Anything."

"All right," he sits beside me, "it might help if I distract you by making you talk to me."

"Aidan," I groan, "I thought you said you wouldn't do this."

"I didn't say *what* you had to talk about."

I shake my head but decide to do as he suggests. Not knowing how to start, I begin with the one thing that, no matter my mental state, really makes sense to me: music. I go over the entire *Appetite For Destruction* album, song-by-song, coming up with detailed theories on what they each mean and what life lessons they hold. Aidan remains silent, leaning forward toward me with his head slightly tilted.

My theorizing turns into me going on about what life is all about and how meaning can be found and how it can be lost. Soon, I'm just winding further down a dark philosophical road, saying whatever comes to mind. I ramble on until I somehow circle back to the ideas of the time it takes when you're all alone, with no one to call your own, and how you can never stop trying. Then I begin humming "My Michelle" and the events of this evening come coursing through me and out of my mouth. While I gloss over many details—specifically any ones that have to do with Bianca—I get out most of the story. When I'm done, I feel stiff and constricted, like there are invisible ropes around my entire body holding me in place and threatening to squeeze me to death if I say too much.

When I can't find it in me to speak anymore, Aidan takes over, saying it's his turn to tell me things. I am thankful for this intervention and as he begins talking, my displeasure melts away.

For the next hour, I sit there with my chin in the palm of my hand, without saying a word, listening as he tells me story after story. As time goes by, I expect him to grow tired, but he doesn't complain and each story is told with just as much energy as the first. He's got a true talent for it.

Just as I'm beginning to feel drowsy, he stops talking and looks over to the corner of the room. I follow his gaze and see an old record player sitting on top of a small, slightly slanted table.

"Another thing Noah brought back with him," Aidan explains when he sees me staring at it. "No idea how he got it, but it's very old—from the 60s. Don't think it's been used for a long time."

"That's kind of sad."

"Yeah, I bet it used to be played a lot, though. Back then people would dance to these things all the time."

"I wonder what it would've been like. Back then, I mean."

Aidan stands up and walks over to the table where he begins going through the drawer underneath it. He takes out a record and places the needle down on it.

"What are you doing?"

Without answering, he comes back over to me and extends his hand down to me. It takes me a moment to realize what he's saying.

I shake my head and my mouth opens to protest, but no sound comes out. Instead, my hand places itself in his, the leather jacket slipping off my shoulders as he pulls me up to him. That's when I notice the song—an old 60s track, "Sittin' On The Dock Of The Bay".

"This isn't really a rock song," I say, making a face.

"Not everything in life is a rock song, Wren."

I laugh and lean in closely, whispering to him with a small smile. "Yes it is."

He returns the smile but as we stand looking at each other, his expression becomes more serious. Slowly, his hands move down to my waist and mine come up to his shoulders. I can feel the energy from his body

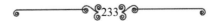

exchanging with mine. It's like I'm in some sort of dream. I don't remember the last time I danced with someone for fun.

Is this real? We begin moving together and the truth becomes clear.

Soon I'm not thinking at all, I'm just moving with him—each step happening effortlessly. But I feel grounded in his arms, present, not floating away. I'm right here.

"Wren," he says quietly as we sway forward and back.

"Yes?"

Unexpectedly, he dips me and brings me up again. Where did he learn this?

Then my feet leave the ground as he lifts me, spinning us around. He brings me down slowly, my body brushing against his... but we're just dancing. It doesn't count.

"There's something I want to tell you."

Out of nowhere, I begin to feel almost in and out of consciousness, a lazy drowsiness taking over.

The song begins to fade and he does one last dip, leaning me very far down—almost to the floor. That's when all my strength leaves me and my bones fall soft.

"Woah!" Aidan holds me up and then sets me down on the couch. "I'm so sorry, I never should have made you dance—"

He kneels over me and I look up at him to see his green eyes staring back at me, his messy hair appearing darker in this lighting than its usual dusky caramel color. Dusky caramel? Is that even a real color?

I reach a hand out and run my fingers through his hair, then moving them to his cheek and tracing all the way down the side of his jaw. It's no more intimate than what we just did, but he freezes—eyes wide.

"Sorry," I mumble, dropping my hand quickly.

"No, it's..." he shakes his head. "I..."

He goes to say something else, but I accidentally cut him off by collapsing backwards on the couch, unable to stop myself.

"She took my necklace," I mumble.

"Your what?"

"My necklace, the pendant—the one you gave me." For some reason, a tear falls from my eye as I say this.

I can vaguely make out a pair of green eyes staring down at me from above as the world around me fades to black.

***

I wake surrounded by pillows with a soft blanket laying on top of me and a leather jacket laying under me. It takes me a second to gather my surroundings, but I quickly remember where I am and why I am on a couch that really is as hard as a rock. I sit up and look at Aidan who is seated across from me in a chair. He's sleeping, with his knees curled up and his head lying on his arms, lips slightly parted.

I don't want to disturb him, so I decide to leave. I take the blanket I'd been using and lay it over him, then going on to argue in my head about taking or leaving the jacket. I mean he did say I could have it for now... Lastly, I write a note to him and quietly go to my car, driving to my house.

It's strange, really, but as I drive back, a deep aching feeling in me won't leave me alone. Though I suppose this isn't the first time I've felt this—it seems I have a lot of negative repeating patterns that I can't get a hold of.

Once at home, I spend the rest of my Friday held up in my room. And tonight is probably going to be the same because while I usually love Fridays—especially Fridays where I don't have school—tonight is the night of the Spring Formal.

Everyone was able to find a date: Bianca and Aidan are going together; Lena patched things up with Rose; Ella's going with Rob I think; and even Eric is going with someone at another school. Everyone has someone—everyone but me, obviously.

I consider going to the Formal for a few seconds. I almost go too, I do. But something stops me. All of a sudden, going seems like the worst idea I've ever had.

I know I should be happy for Aidan that he's there with someone, yet I don't feel that way. Not even a little bit. This is probably just because he happens to be going with Bianca—a person that I am still extremely mad at. It's not his fault though. I never bothered explaining to him what her part was in my unfortunate misadventure at the studio.

Rather than going, I sit at home alone in the dark singing softly to myself and watching *Dirty Dancing*. So this is what it has come to. I'm going to be alone forever.

After an hour, I turn off the TV and go upstairs. I check my watch and it's only nine o'clock. Man, I want this stupid night to end already. I should have gone to the dance, at least it would have given me something to do.

I go into the bathroom and place both hands on the counter, leaning forward toward the mirror. I bet Aidan and Bianca are having a great time together, meanwhile I'm here doing nothing for nothing so I guess that's what I get.

If I'm so miserable, why can't I go to the Spring Formal? No one has chained me down or forced me to stay here. No one even said I couldn't go, except for the school librarian who said I couldn't have a ticket because of some overdue books I've still got; but no school official could ever really stop me if I really wanted to get in. The only person stopping me is me.

Damn it to hell.

That's it, worst idea or not, I'm going to that damn dance.

***

It doesn't take long before I'm sitting in my car right out front of the school gym. There's a huge banner hanging over the doors that says Spring Formal in big letters, like they're trying to alert the aliens and heavens above that Sunrise Heights High has a great high school dance going on down here.

I hop out of my car, now wearing a *Keep The Faith* tour shirt and Aidan's leather jacket—you know, high school dance attire—and walk up to the admissions table.

As I get there, I realize I'm not ready.

I quickly turn around and walk away, this time going behind a tree so that I can hide out until I come up with a plan to force myself in. I'm standing here behind the tree, staring at the gym from afar, when I see Ella sitting across from my hiding spot on a bench with her chin in her palm. I don't even stop to think about it, I just come right out from behind the tree and walk over to her.

"Wren?" She seems pretty taken aback by me being here. "My God, were you behind that tree?"

I ignore her question and sit down next to her on the bench. "Why are you sitting out here alone?"

"Because I can. Why are you here? Aidan told me you weren't coming. Have you been hiding out here this whole time?"

Please, she's acting like she's never seen somebody skulking behind a tree. Also, she's clearly upset, being alone out here. Maybe her date ditched her. I don't see Rob anywhere nearby.

"Want to hear something crazy?" I ask. I'm feelin' pretty crazy tonight, and I've got a lot of crazy things to say right now, so getting some of it off my chest might be good.

"No. Why were you hiding?"

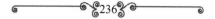

I continue on. "Sometimes I just look out at the sky trying to find out what it all means, thinking that maybe someday I'll get an answer."

"What are you talking about? Wren, you're not making any sense."

She's still touchy from that time I threatened to rip out her ribcage, but I keep going anyway. I want her to understand, so bad. "Now I just need an answer about what I'm supposed to do. I'm trying to carry on, you know, but it's getting harder. I mean, how do you carry on if you have nothing to carry on *for*? At the same time though, I'm starting to think that maybe I have found something to carry on for—but I just can't say for sure." *Last night, what did that dance even mean?*

"Wren, I don't know what you're talking about."

"Nothing. It's nothing." I finally stop, realizing that it's no good. Ella's not going to understand.

I wish her a nice rest of her night and get up, walking back over toward the entrance to the gym. I'm pretty sure it's too late for me to get a ticket now, so I sneak in the backdoor and make my way into the corner of the gym. There are hundreds of flashing lights repeatedly pounding me in the eyes and people dancing everywhere. The girls are all pretty and done up in fancy dresses, and there are plenty of guys dressed dashingly as well.

All of a sudden I can't breath so well anymore. I peer through the crowd, trying to see if I can find someone—anyone I know. It's just masses upon masses, a sea of moving bodies swaying and thrashing together. As the tide comes in I'm swept away, carried out into the water to get lost beneath the waves. My heart beats so fast now, like a rabbit when a wolf has cornered it. Then, through the bodies I catch a glimpse of a surprised face staring back at me. Suddenly, my heart calms and I can breathe once again.

His hair isn't combed back like most of the other boys, it's still just as messy as always, but there is something else different about him. Perhaps it's that he's in a tux.

Aidan makes his way through the crowd in my direction and begins talking as he reaches me, but I can't hear a damn thing over the crowd. He notices and takes my hand, pulling me outside.

"What are you doing here, Wren?"

"Good to see you too, Aidan."

"That's not what I meant. I just thought you said dances weren't your thing."

"Well maybe I decided to give one a try."

"Oh."

This isn't the welcome I had hoped for.

Just then, Bianca pops out of the gym and comes over to interrupt us. She's wearing a nice sparkly dress and has her black curls tied back in a high bun with a few loose ringlets to frame her face. Now that I am aware of their connection, it is very easy to see the familial resemblance between her and Sebastian; they have the same dark curls, pale complexion, and nice bone structure.

Looking at her, I wish I had dressed up too; dressing up can be fun. It's nice to look nice. I don't look nice.

"What are you doing here?" she asks me as soon as she gets to us.

"People keep asking me that tonight but I seriously don't have a good answer for you."

"You don't look dressed to be here."

"You know, you should probably just take this back," I say, turning to Aidan and beginning to shrug off the jacket.

"Wait, is that yours?" Bianca asks, as her eyes grow wide when she looks at Aidan.

But Aidan isn't looking at her. "I'm not taking it. I said you could have it, and I meant it."

I lift the jacket back up over my shoulders and cross my arms.

"Still," Bianca begins, "you should probably take it off anyways. It doesn't fit—"

"Yeah, ok, I didn't come here for fashion advice."

"Then why did you come?" she inquires, her large eyes narrowing again as she focuses back on me.

"I don't know," I say, unsure of how else to respond. "This is a mistake."

"All right then. Aidan, would you take me back inside?" she asks, directing her attention toward him. "We could be missing out on a good song."

"No, wait." I reach forward and grab her arm. "Aidan, would you mind giving us a moment?"

"Ok, I guess I'll go get some drinks or something," he says, clearly confused.

"Sounds good," I respond without breaking eye contact with Bianca.

Once he's out of sight, I move us over to my original hiding spot behind the tree.

"What are you playing at?" Bianca demands, yanking her arm free from me.

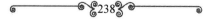

"We need to talk."

"About what?"

"Don't you freaking 'about-what' me. You know *exactly* what I'm talking about." The rage I had been forcing down begins to spill out.

"I understand why you would be upset."

"You don't seem to understand crap. What was going through your head when you decided to trick me into getting stuck in that studio? Really, I want to know, because for the life of me I can't figure out why you would think putting me in that situation would ever be a good idea. And when Kate—who's an actual psycho, by the way—pitched you this plan, you didn't even think to question it? I know you know there's something wrong with her so don't pretend to be more ignorant than you already are."

"I thought it was the only way to help you realize that you're not really ok. That you haven't—"

"You mean the only way to get me to see that I need to meet with Seth. And the only reason you even want that is so you can appease him—not so that I can get closure. I'm not sure what you see in him, but man he really must have a hold on you."

"View it as you will," she straightens up and crosses her arms, "it was necessary."

"Do you even know what happened to me? Kate freaking bit me! Ya ever been bit before, Bianca? Her goddamn teeth sunk right into my goddamn wrist!"

Shock fills her eyes, but I can't tell if it's real or fake.

"And you know what? You are all so obsessed with showing me I haven't moved on, but really you're the ones who can't seem to move on. So do me a favor and get a life so you can stop ruining mine."

"I never meant for it to be taken so far, I swear. I had no idea any of what happened to you was going to happen. And I'm sorry. I know you don't believe me, but really, I am. And I also want to say thank you, for—you know."

"No, please do enlighten me."

"I was so surprised when Aidan still wanted to take me to the dance. I mean, I know if he knew, he wouldn't want anything to do with me and I didn't think about that until I had already sent you that message. But you could have easily told him so I expected that you would and that he would hate me, but he doesn't—which means you didn't. And if you hadn't told him, I thought Sebastian would have; he really chewed me out for that one. Perhaps the reason you didn't tell him is because a part of you has already forgiven me."

"Oh God." My eyes roll to the back of my skull.

"It may not seem like it now, but perhaps this was all meant to be so that we could end up where we are now."

"I haven't even met with Seth yet."

"Regardless, I hope you will accept my thanks."

I turn away from her and head back toward my car. "I didn't do it for you."

I get in the car and start to pull out of the parking lot, but as I begin to move forward, someone steps in front of my path, stopping me.

"Aidan? What are you doing?" I yell out my window at him. "You trying to make me kill you?"

He comes around to my side, a clear frown on his face. "No, I'm just trying to figure you out. What is up with you?"

"Nothing."

"You keep saying that but—"

"Hey! Aidan, are you coming back?" Bianca calls after us, her voice higher than usual. Perhaps she is worried that after our conversation I will all of a sudden decide to spill everything.

"You better get back to your date."

"Man, Wren, I never wanted to go to the dance with Bianca!"

"Then why did you?"

"Because—" he stops himself. "It doesn't matter. But last night…"

"Last night?"

"Yes, and…"

"And?"

He shakes his head and looks away. "Never mind. Forget it."

He walks away from me and I take off, driving myself back home where I try and fail at getting some rest.

***

In the morning, I decided to put up posters in my room while also putting the Spring Formal as far out of my mind as possible. I figure I have until the sun goes down (when Seth set the meeting for) to kill time, so I might as well make use of these posters I've collected this past year. I've got everything—posters of movies about mystery, pirates, kings, dead poets, cowboys, space, superheroes, and music. (I guess I kind'a went through

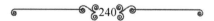

all my money on these, but it's definitely worth it). I also print pictures of my favorite characters and bands and paste them all around my bed's headboard.

I wonder, if I were a fictional character, what would people think of me?

I think about starting on some homework, but my mind is buzzing too fast and I can't concentrate. My English essay is just going have to write itself later.

After five hundred hours of pacing up and down my room, it's time for me to head to the restaurant. I may not have my leather jacket for this showdown, but I do have my cowboy boots—and that's better than nothing.

***

As soon as I walk in, I can feel his presence. It's cold and heavy, taking up all the air in the room. He shouldn't make me nervous at all. I've punched him before; I would have no problem doing it again.

Still, this place is eerily empty and deadly silent.

I spot him in the darkest corner, and take my seat on the other side of the table from him. It's only been a year since I've seen Seth, but he seems even bigger now—more menacing.

"Wren," he smiles, flashing his white teeth, "how good to see you."

"Cut the crap, Seth. Why am I here?"

"You say that as if you have something better to do."

"Maybe I do."

"Yes, I suppose your dwindling career as a little ballet star is pretty demanding."

I wince. "Did you really just call me here to insult me?"

"No, no I'm—I actually just want to say…" I wait for him to find the words. "… that I apologize. You know, for making things a little bit difficult for you. Not to say that you weren't a pain in my ass, because you were."

My mouth hangs open slightly for a moment before I shift in my seat and look down at my hands. After a moment of silence I look back up and see him frowning slightly at me.

"I'm not sure what to say."

"Well a 'thanks, I'm sorry too' might be a good place to start."

I roll my eyes and his frown deepens.

"All right, well, anyway, I have something of yours." He reaches beside him and pulls out my jacket—the one Kate stole.

"How did you get this," I ask, taking it from him; the moment my hand touches the leather, I feel a bit more whole. Even still, while I know it's mine, it almost seems like a completely different jacket.

"From that girl that took it of course—Kate."

"What about a necklace?" I ask hastily. "Did, did you get that too?"

"What necklace?"

"Uh, I don't know—just a necklace."

"Wren, there was no necklace."

"Never mind," I say, glancing back down at the jacket. "I wasn't aware you were so familiar with Kate."

"I'm not," he scoffs. "But I have my way of finding things out, so it didn't take long for me to find out about what she did."

"Yeah, she's a real peach. I bet you two get along great."

"Actually, I feel complete indifference toward her."

"That's not exactly how I would explain my feelings for her…"

"Then you'll be happy to hear I've taken care of the matter. Kate won't be bothering you any longer."

"Huh? What did you do to her?" This conversation just keeps getting more and more surprising.

"You're welcome. And I did nothing—nothing that you need be concerned about. Just know that she won't be going to Sunrise Heights High anymore."

"She's transferring?"

"Yes."

"How did you pull that off?"

"It wasn't that hard."

"That really doesn't count as an answer."

"You see, girls like Kate, they always have secrets—generally dark secrets. And if you know where to look, and you dig deep enough, you'll find something."

"You blackmailed her?"

"Blackmail is a harsh word."

"Why? I mean, what do you stand to gain from this?"

"Can't I simply do something out of the kindness of my heart?"

"I'm not entirely sure you have a heart."

His eyes harden, but the corner of his mouth turns up. "None of that matters. What happened in the past doesn't matter. All that matters is that you're here, now."

"It matters to me. You kissed me, for Christ's sake! And then practically burned the building down around me! And got me—"

"Keep your voice down, Wren!"

"Whatever. I still can't quite understand why you want me here so bad, after being so dead set on sending me away not that long ago."

"You did that to yourself. But, now, I figure your… punishment has gone on long enough. It's probably time for you to get back to where you're supposed to be."

"You mean back at the studio again? With you? I'm not going back there. To tell you the truth, I'm not even focusing on that—on dance anymore."

"What the hell does that mean?"

"I'm in a band now and—"

"Oh right. You, working with a band?"

"Just a high school band but yeah, sort of. Is that really so hard to believe?"

"I'm just surprised is all. I heard something about it from Bianca, but I thought there was no way it could be true. If you couldn't handle being part of a dance studio without letting your emotions get the better of you, I don't know how you'll handle being in a band. What songs do you guys do?"

This guy is asking to be hit. "At this point in time we're working on 'November Rain'."

He almost spits out his drink. "'November Rain'? Is that a joke? There's no way you could ever pull that off. Trust me, I know music and that isn't for you."

I'm really wishing I hadn't agreed to meet him here. I want to get up and walk out so bad, but I feel trapped, like I can't move or anything.

"What makes you an expert on music? And it's actually going pretty well, we're going to put it in the lineup for the concert were planning for." It's not exactly a real concert, but I'll still call it that.

"Ha! I doubt it. What do you even know about rock? Seriously, Wren, you're always so ambitious and think you can do all these things but it never goes the way you want it to. In the end, something always goes wrong."

He's basically telling me right to my face that I'm a screw-up who doesn't know anything—bastard!

"All I'm saying is you need to learn—"

"Well fortunately for me Seth, I don't give a damn about anything you say or think."

His eyes turn cold, like those of a reptile, as he stares me down from across the table.

"You know, you really shouldn't be so rude, Wren. Attitude doesn't look good on you. I'm just trying to help."

"I find most times someone says they're 'just trying to help,' in actuality they mean to do the exact opposite."

"Always with the insolence."

"Always with the being a dick."

Hot anger flashes across his face, but he quickly regains his composure.

"So what? You're going to try and put on this stupid concert out of spite?"

"No, you have nothing to do with any of this. I'm doing it because I want to."

He shakes his head and looks up at the ceiling. "This is stupid."

"You can slam me against the wall and strangle me, I'm still going to do the damn concert."

He stands up and leans across the table toward me. "You can sit here and mouth off as much as you want, it doesn't matter. You're still just that stubborn girl who's too headstrong for her own good, and I know you're going to fail, no matter what you do, one way or another."

He turns and begins to walk toward the exit, but he only makes it a few feet before he pauses and looks back at me. He opens his mouth to say something, but I interrupt him.

"Oh don't leave all mad Seth, just leave."

His complexion reddens. "Someday, you'll wish you had been more agreeable with me." With this, he walks out of the restaurant.

What a goddamn asshat.

CHAPTER 24

I'LL BE HERE FOR YOU

AIDAN'S EYES OPENED and immediately darted to the couch across from him. It was empty.

Where is she?

Just as he was about to jump up from his chair and search the house for her, he spotted a folded piece of paper sitting on top of the record player. Aidan read over the note a dozen times, feelings of disappointment and sadness filling him more each time. After last night, after everything that had happened, he'd hoped that she would still be there. That she would've stayed, but she didn't. She was gone.

Of course, he couldn't really blame her; it made sense she'd be anxious to go home, considering what she had been through at the hands of Kate. Oh God—Kate. The name alone nearly made him shake with anger. When Bash had first told him what happened, he'd suddenly been struck with a desire for some very… violent actions. It took everything in him not to act on those desires, and if he had not had Wren there to take care of, he was sure he would've. But he did have Wren.

And when she finally passed out from exhaustion, right after telling him the rose pendant he gave to her had been stolen; Aidan knew he wouldn't be able to leave her side even for a moment. Sure, his blood practically boiled when he'd heard about the necklace, but looking down at her innocent face, he just couldn't leave.

But now she was gone, and he could feel the hot anger returning in full force—what would he do about it? He also realized he was hurt that she had left. For some reason, he really wanted her to still be there. But Aidan didn't understand this, and now his chest felt heavy and tired. But he felt certain of one thing: there was *no way* Kate would get away with what she'd done.

Amelia suggests I begin drawing more, and it turns out it's actually very relaxing. I'm able to get things out of me that you can't when using words. That seems to be a big thing for me—saying things without having to actually say anything.

At the moment, I'm using graphic pencils to sketch out a pirate ship in the middle of a storming sea.

"I've been struggling with my temper," I comment to her while continuing to sketch out the ship. Honestly, that's putting it mildly. Just this morning, I wanted to cry because I felt so angry.

"Let's try something. What is something you like about the world."

I set down the pencil and look up from the drawing. "Free will."

"Free will? Ok, so I want you to focus on that and write something out for me."

"Write what out for you?"

"Anything, I just want you to try letting go of your anger as you write it and let the words flow out, whatever they may be."

All right, let's do this thing. I can be calm and flow.

I'm angry about the world—with my life. And while so much has happened since then, I still dream of drowning, sinking to the bottom of the river in the car with Lena, watching her die. And then I think of what would have happened if I had just burned to death that night in the studio. Maybe I should take my more recent sufferings as a blessing—as a distraction, a distraction from Aidan and everything else.

I try to say I don't care, but you know what? I do care. Just not as some people may want. Sometimes I'd like to run away from everyone and everything—to get away from the hands that feel like they're grabbing me all over, holding me down helplessly and violating me from the inside out. Still, I know now I can never give up on the world, not as a whole at least, no matter what people do to me or what they take from me. I think there is so much worth saving in humanity, even if just for the feeling of music in your soul or the feeling of your partner in a dance... and even if I was the last person still fighting on Earth, I would keep going till the end of my line.

I won't back down. It's my life and everyone can bite me.

"Ok," Amelia begins after looking over what I wrote, "it starts in a good place and then we end off with 'everyone can bite me.'"

"Yes, I guess so, huh."

"But, moving on from that, I think we should talk about Aidan. You've never brought him up, to me at least."

"No."

"Wren, please—"

"No."

I take my drawing and writing home with me and look it over again. Seeing what I wrote a second time makes me realize just how freaking crazy it sounds. Seriously, it doesn't make any sense and sounds like the ramblings of a madman. What's wrong with me?

I set the papers aside and wander downstairs to get a snack. Using all my energy to stay in a calm state of mind has made me hungry.

Before I see them, I can hear Cara arguing with someone from within the kitchen.

"I don't understand—orange juice is not superior to root beer. In fact, I don't even see how the two are connected. Can you just go get your sister now?"

"No! Not until you admit that orange juice is better!"

I walk in and find her sipping from a cup of what I'm going to assume is OJ, with Sebastian standing against the fridge. His tired eyes lighten faintly as he sees me.

"Finally," he says. "Can we go somewhere more private?"

Cara pouts at this but I give her a look, and she promptly stalks out of the kitchen.

"This is good," I say, moving toward the fridge. He doesn't move from his position in front of it and strangely stares at me.

"May I?" I point behind him, and he moves out of the way, his cheeks flushing.

I take out some strawberries and turn back around to face him. "So what's up?" I offer him some of the berries but he shakes his head.

"I haven't seen you since... that night. And I thought I should check in and see how you're doing."

"That's kind of you, but I'm doing just fine."

"Really?"

I nod vigorously, sticking a strawberry in my mouth.

"Well, it's been a few days, and I haven't heard anything from you."

"It's only been three days. And it's not like we really talk much outside of band rehearsals."

"Is a 'hey, I'm fine' too much talking for you?"

"I'm sorry, I didn't think of it."

He taps his fingers on the counter, leaning over it. "Yes, it seems you don't think of a lot of things."

"If you wanted to know so bad, why not just pick up your damn phone and call?"

"Would you have even picked up?"

"Bash, why did you come to see me if you're just going to be a jerk?"

He sighs heavily and places a hand on the back of his head. "I apologize. This isn't what I intended."

"It's ok." I hop up on the counter and grab another strawberry.

"And I don't mean to pry but I've got to know, what are you going to do about Kate? She's dangerous and, given her behavior, has a strange, obsessive fixation on you."

"She doesn't care about me—it's Aidan she wants. And as it turns out, Seth already took care of that."

"Seth what?"

"He said he took care of it."

"What did he say, *exactly*?"

"I don't remember, just that he got her to transfer schools."

"You don't believe him, do you?"

I stay silent, tugging at the hem of my overalls.

"Christ, Wren." His fist flies up to his forehead. "Seth is a powerful guy, in some respects, but he doesn't have *that* kind of power. Besides, why would you ever believe a thing he says? What could he possibly be getting out of this?"

"Even if it's not true, what am I supposed to do? Blackmail her myself? That's not the type of person I want to be. Though I did tell her she was messing with a son of a bitch—so maybe I should follow up on that."

"We'll figure out something. Also, when did you find out about all of this?"

The air in the room changes, becoming darker and less friendly.

"When I met with Seth."

Without warning, Bash slams his hands on the countertop and I flinch. "You met with Seth? I hope you realize how stupid that was. He is at least as dangerous as Kate, if not more so."

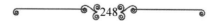

"I'm aware of that, Sebastian. Believe me, I am. But I knew what I was doing and—"

"Did you? Did you really?"

"Despite what you may think of me, I am not stupid. And the next time you question my ability to make decisions for myself, you can get out of my house."

"Is that what you think I think of you?"

"You haven't given me much else to go off of."

"I know you're a capable person," he says in a strained voice. This is clearly a bit hard for him to say. "You're one of the strongest... if not most stubborn, people I've ever met."

The strawberry I just placed between my teeth falls from my mouth and into my hand.

"Ok, I should go now," he says hastily.

"No, I don't want there to always be this awkward tension between us."

"Then what do you want between us?"

"I want to be friends."

"Friends..."

"Yeah, but like friends that don't only hang out to talk about super serious things like psychos and blackmail."

"Then I have another question for you, if we're going to be talking about 'other things'. Why do you look like you just got back from a day at the farm?"

I look down at my overalls and let out a small chuckle.

"Why do you look like you just got back from a casual funeral?" I ask, looking at his black jeans, shirt, and jacket.

"And just what exactly is a 'casual funeral'? I'm not familiar with the term."

"Like if a person was only mostly dead and they came back to life but wanted to have a funeral anyway."

"Ah yes, one of those." He laughs and for a moment he seems relaxed, but then he goes back to his serious self. "Hey, there was something else I came here to talk to you about."

"Lay it on me," I say, leaning back on my elbows.

"I, uh, was wondering if you could accompany me to this family dinner thing. It's for my parents mostly, and it's really stupid, but it's important to my family. If I don't show up with anyone—well it would just make it less weird if I had someone with me."

"When is it?"

"My house, next Sunday at six-thirty."

"Who's gonna be there?"

"Extended family and friends of the family—that type of thing."

"So Bianca will probably be there."

"Yes, probably."

"Well, she doesn't bother me anymore," I say, jumping down from the counter. "So I'm in."

"Great. Should I pick you up here around six-fifteen?" he asks, moving to the front door.

"No, I'll drive over myself."

"Ok, just promise me something."

"What?"

"That you won't show up in overalls."

"Very funny."

He smirks and steps outside, then pauses as if he's debating something.

"I know you don't want to hear about this anymore," he finally begins, "but you need to know that even if Seth really did do exactly as he said, he's going to expect something in return. He will find a way to use it against you, and I can't say what that will mean, but I can say this—he will come for you."

I take a deep breath. "So you're saying I should be worried?"

"I'm saying you should be ready."

A part of me almost looks forward to Bash's weird dinner party, but the week leading up to it proves to be difficult.

Band practices for the concert are more tense and awkward than they've ever been. Each time I find myself getting out of there as soon as we run through the "November Rain" number rather than watching the rest of the songs like I usually would.

I don't know what changed, but something is different about Bash, and it's making me incredibly uncomfortable. It gets to the point where I wonder if he even still wants me at the dinner party anymore.

But it doesn't end there. The tension between Bianca and me is at an all-time high since everything that happened. When I try to talk to Lena, she always has an excuse for why she needs to be doing something else. This has been going on for a while actually, but it still hurts like hell.

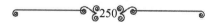

Aidan is also acting strange, like he's keeping his distance. Most days he won't even look me in the eyes. This doesn't just make me uncomfortable; it makes me downright miserable.

The one good thing is that Seth actually did what he said he did; Kate does not show up to a single day of school, meaning she is likely transferring. However, I am not as happy about this as I thought I would be. In fact, I feel as though all the happiness has been drained out of me, leaving me filled with the cold heartbreak of pure loneliness. And all the while, the possibility that my trouble with Seth has only just begun hangs over me like a black cloud.

***

Finally, it's Sunday. The clock strikes six-thirty before I'm ready and soon I am running late. To make up for lost time, I let Cara pick out my outfit as I hurriedly pin my hair up in a twist. It's a little messy but I don't think it matters much.

The outfit Cara chooses is a royal blue lace dress. Not having enough energy to care, I don't complain, quickly slipping it on and heading out the door—but not before grabbing a jacket. I should have grabbed my own—I've got it back now—but I didn't. I took Aidan's, which I would have returned to him, but he's been acting so strange lately that there hasn't been a good time to do so.

I arrive, as expected, about a half-hour after the start time. It's a very nice house, not as nice as his cousin's, but still nice. In fact, I didn't really pick up on it that time I drove over here in the middle of the night, but it's a lot fancier than I would have expected it to be considering how close it is to—well, it's just closer to Aidan's neighborhood than I remembered it being.

I follow the sign on the front door that directs me to the back gate, leading me into the backyard. Once I get there, turns out I don't actually see much of Bash for most of the time. He just raises his brows when he sees my outfit and then introduces me to a few people. As he is talking to some of his relatives, I wander off to explore the yard. It's huge, with a large garden area and a separate place for tables, chairs, and food. As I'm giving myself a private tour, I spot Bianca chatting with Ella at the dessert table. She looks very pretty but there's something a little off about her facial expressions—like she's in a particularly bad mood. For this reason, I decided to steer clear of her, heading deep into the garden.

I find a patch of roses and stand in front of them, focusing on the one rose at the edge with blackened petals that are beginning to fall off and die. I stretch my hand out to touch it but before my fingers reach it, the sound of laughter causes me to stop. It sounds very familiar. I search through the garden and just as I am about to give up and return to Bash, I hear it again—this time closer. I whip around a corner and see two people sitting on a bench, one of which is Lena.

"Lena!" I call to her and she turns to me.

"Wren!" She runs up to me. "I've been looking for you all over the place."

"I haven't been hiding." I look past her at the person she had been with, but his back is facing toward me so I am unable to make out who he is. There's something about him…

"Yes, well, I have someone who wants to speak with you."

"Actually, I was hoping that you and I could speak." I have so much to talk to her about, and we haven't spent much time together recently. "What are you doing at Sebastian's dinner party anyway?"

"I don't know who Sebastian is, but I was invited here by Bianca. Apparently she wants to get to know something or me better. And as for us talking, perhaps later."

"Please, I feel we haven't hardly spoken to each other since—"

"Later, Wren. I promise. But I think you should talk to him first," she urges, looking over at the man sitting on the bench.

My eyes focus in on him and for a split-second, I think it might be Aidan, but I quickly realize it's not, meaning there's only one other person he could likely be.

I nod to Lena and walk over to him. He remains motionless as I sit beside him.

"You're Noah, aren't you?"

He turns toward me, and I can instantly tell that my assumption is correct. Though his face hasn't been clean-shaven in a few days, he's got the same messy, dark hair, and bright, emerald green eyes—the same sculpted features and jaw line.

"Yes, I'm Aidan's brother," he replies, his eyes quizzically looking over me. Another difference to note, his voice is a bit huskier.

"What do you want?"

"Wow! You really just get right down to it."

"Would you like me to ask you how your day was first?" I joke. I'm

not usually so forward with strangers, but I feel like I sort of know him already.

"So feisty—I see why Aidan likes you." He finally takes his eyes off my face and looks down at what I'm wearing. "And I see you've got my jacket. Of course, I gave it to Aidan earlier this year."

"Uh, yes, I, well—"

He chuckles, his green eyes twinkling. "Relax, Wren. If you're wearing it, it must be because Aidan wants you to be." My mouth opens to respond, but he's already moving on. "Did you come here with anyone?"

"I came for Bash, though it seems like everyone I've ever known is at this damn dinner party."

"Hmm, that can be awkward. Of course, I'm on the other end of awkwardness—being only familiar with Sebastian and his parents."

"You don't know Lena? You two seemed like you were relatively familiar."

"No, I only just met her. She thought I was Aidan for a moment and then we began talking. I told her that I was looking for you, so she helped me try and track you down. It was taking a while though. We were about to give up when you found us."

"Do you always keep your back turned to the person you're trying to find?"

"Sorry, I guess that was a bit rude, but I wanted to see if you would also mistake me for Aidan."

"Well, I didn't; so are you going to tell me what you're here for?"

"I came for Aidan and to work some things out with Sebastian. He's the one who got me a plane ticket to come here, actually."

"So Bash is good friends with you too?" I already know the answer, but I want to see if I can get some more back-story from him.

"In a way. I'm the one who introduced Aidan to him. Now I'm just here trying to settle some scores while I still can."

"What do I have to do with any of this?"

"Sebastian told me you were here, and I thought it would be good to meet you—that's all."

"Ok, but how do you even know who I am?"

"I may not have been around much lately, but I do still check in on my brother. He's told me about you and I must say, you live up to every expectation."

"You should 'be around' more often."

"I haven't been doing so well, which is why I've kept my distance. But I'm trying to change all that. I'm trying to show him I care."

"That's why you got him that record player, and that bike?" I ask, thinking back to the one I saw outside Aidan's house.

"Yes. I wish I could give him a car, but at least now he doesn't have to walk everywhere. Should make his trip downtown to work easier."

I stay silent.

"I know that you may not think very highly of me—*I* don't think very highly of me—but just know that I really do want what is best for my brother."

"It doesn't matter what I know. Will you be there at the upcoming concert?"

"I'm going to try."

"It would mean a lot to him."

"I know. It's difficult, trying to find the balance between what is right and what's not, when it comes to the ones you love. You always want to be with them, but sometimes it's hard to say if that's what's best for them"—my pulse begins to pick up—"and if you keep too far a distance for too long, they'll eventually move on. Maybe that's a good thing. Maybe it's not."

I stand up quickly.

"Are you all right, Wren?"

"I'm—I have to go. Sorry."

I turn from him and race out of the garden. I need to leave this place for a while. I want to get away.

"There you are!" Bash yells, running up to me. "I thought you left."

"No. But I do think I need to leave now."

"You can't leave yet."

"I have to." I push past him and continue walking until Bianca blocks my path. Luckily, Ella doesn't appear to still be around.

"The vanilla cupcakes are quite good, aren't they? I made them myself," she boasts.

"Yeah, delicious." I try to side step her but she moves with me.

"Did you meet Noah yet? Noah Grey—Aidan's brother? I don't see him right now but I just spoke to him not that long ago."

"You know Noah?"

"More like I know of him. Very handsome, don't you think?"

"Yeah."

"You look like you've seen a ghost. What's the matter with you? I figured that after having Kate taken out of your way you would be much more relaxed. I, for one, am very glad Kate is gone." The way she says 'taken out of my way' makes me uneasy.

"Trust me, so am I. Still kind'a can't believe Seth did that."

"Did what?"

"Took care of the Kate situation."

"He didn't take care of anything."

"Um, what do you mean?"

"Exactly what I said, silly."

"So he's not the reason Kate is gone?"

She raises an eyebrow at me in disbelief.

"Then what is?" I push. Sometimes talking to Bianca can really suck all the energy out of you.

"Why don't you ask Aidan?" she scoffs.

"If you're trying to say this has something to do with him, I would appreciate it if you would just say so outright."

"You really don't know?"

"If it was Aidan who did it, how could Seth possibly have known to take credit for it?" He literally told me outright that he was the reason I was now "safe".

"I may have told him. But I don't feel like going into any of that right now."

"Oh, Bianca." My hands clasp behind my neck. "Just tell me what happened, god damn it. You owe me that much."

"I don't understand you and Aidan or what weird thing you two have going but I don't think it's—"

"Bianca…"

"Fine. But I'm not the only one who could be telling you this, Sebastian knows too. I told him a few days after it happened since he kept asking me about it and wouldn't leave me alone. He can be very annoying."

"Bash knows?"

"Yes, after you left the Spring Formal, Aidan told me he had to go somewhere, and I didn't want to be left alone so I said he could use my car and I'd leave with him. But we didn't take my car there because we walked to a nice restaurant near the school and had dinner there before coming straight to the dance. We had a very special time to tell you the truth—"

"Get on with it."

She glares at me and walks us over to a more private part of the yard. "To get back to my house to get the car, he practically had to drag me all the way there because, in case you didn't know, he's a very fast runner and I couldn't hardly keep up—I don't think he let go of my hand for even a second, it was… ok, ok, I'll get back to the story. As soon as we got the car, he drove us straight to Kate's address. He banged on the door so hard I thought it might come crashing down—good thing no one else was home—and when she finally opened up, he told me to stay outside while he went in. I heard some awful yelling at first but then things got quiet, and that's when I started to worry. But just as I was about to go inside myself, Aidan came out the door with your jacket in his hand, he looked angrier than I had ever seen him, and we got back in the car. It was scary, honest to God, but it was also kind'a—never mind. As we were driving back he said that he didn't want you to know about the whole thing. He said all you needed to know was that Kate wouldn't bother you anymore. And I don't know what he told Kate, but I could tell that he knew, without a doubt, that she wouldn't ever be coming back. You really don't know any of this? I mean, he said he didn't want you to know about it, but I assumed you two told each other everything. And even if he didn't tell you, I figured Sebastian would."

I try to clear my head to stop myself from being overwhelmed by all the information that was just dumped on me.

"Seth gave the jacket to me, saying he got it back from Kate."

"Why does that jacket even matter, I see you've found a new one." She disdainfully looks over my attire and I glare at her in response, prompting her to reluctantly continue. "I said I would get it back to you, so Aidan gave it to me, but then Seth saw it and said he would give it to you at the meeting instead."

"What about the necklace? The rose pendant?"

"Uh, yeah, about that… I sort of put it on, for… safekeeping. But then I forgot about it and a few days later, Sebastian noticed I was wearing it and made me give it to him. That's about when I told him everything."

So Bash has my necklace? Man, the more I hear of this story, the more questions I seem to have.

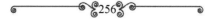

"As for what happened with Seth, I'm sorry. I didn't realize it at the time, but I guess he found the whole thing to be a great... opportunity."

"And you didn't think it suspicious that Seth was so curious?"

"Maybe slightly, but I didn't think much of it."

"Damn, the amount of times you have knowingly, unknowingly, and nearly screwed me over is amazing."

"Excuse me?" she reproaches. "You should be *thanking* me—I didn't have to tell you any of this."

"You know what, Bianca? I want to be your friend, I really do, but don't talk to me again until you figure out how to have a full, coherent thought that doesn't revolve around yourself."

I don't wait to watch her reaction unfold; I get out of there in a hurry. I'll have to deal with Sebastian later. But later comes sooner than expected when I find him waiting in front of the back gate.

"You are acting very weird tonight. Even weirder than usual."

"You're weirder than usual. Let me through," I insist.

"No," he deadpans.

"I swear, Sebastian, I will knock you out of the way if I have to." I'm starting to think maybe there's more to what he knows than what Bianca even told me.

"Prove it."

"I'd prefer not to."

"Then tell me why you're so eager to get out of here."

"For a lot of reasons."

"Whoa there, don't get too specific on me."

"Please, I can't do this right now," I plead. Usually I wouldn't resort to pleading, but I'm feeling rather desperate at the moment.

He squints slightly and folds his arms, refusing to move. "Did Bianca say something to you?"

"Just get out of the freakin' way, Bash. Or I'll move you myself."

"Let me see you try."

"Really? At your parents' dinner party?"

He shrugs. "There's no one back here right now."

"I'm serious, I just want to go home." And then maybe a bit farther after that...

"You can go after you tell me what the hell is up with you."

This boy won't quit.

"I can go whenever I decide to."

"Not if I stop you first."

"Is that so?"

I attempt to slip by him but he catches my arm, holding onto me tight. I turn on him and try to pull my arm free, but I just end up pulling us both to the ground. "Son of a—"

I fall on my back with him on top of me. As soon as we hit the ground, I swiftly shove him off.

"You knew," I say, jumping to my feet and leaving him in the dirt. "You knew and you didn't say anything."

He props himself up on his forearm and stares at me, a look of horror and confusion on his face. Still, he must know what I'm talking about.

"How could you do that?" I ask.

"I didn't think it was a big deal."

"You knew I was scared of what Seth was going to do to me. This whole week—what would have happened if I had kept on believing that I owed him? And then if he came to collect—"

"I wouldn't let that happen. Believe me, I would never—and Aidan didn't tell you either—are you going to be mad at him too?"

"Aidan doesn't even know Seth exists. And besides, that doesn't have anything to do with *you* not telling me, and you know it. Why didn't you just tell me?"

"I don't know."

I take my bottom lip between my teeth and nod, turning away from him. "And that's not all of it, is it?"

"What?" He sounds scared.

"Why do you know so much about Seth?" I just want to see if he will tell me the truth.

"I met him through Bianca."

"But why do you *know* so much about him?"

"Because..." he takes in a deep and almost shaky breath; he clearly doesn't want to be saying what he's about to say. "Because I did him a few favors, in exchange for some money so I could get Noah a plane ticket out here."

"What favors, Bash?"

He doesn't respond.

"You were the one watching me in the aquarium," I say for him, remembering the dark stranger from the field trip. "And at the football game." I'm not sure how I know this, but all of a sudden, I do. The pieces are coming together.

He appears surprised I came to the conclusion so quickly, but nods apologetically. "I knew it was wrong, but I needed the money if I was going to save up enough to get Noah to come here. I didn't want to, it just seemed like the best way at the time. Then he wanted me to do more favors, but I declined. He became really angry, but I still said no. So I pretty much broke off all contact with him from then on, but, of course, Bianca stayed with him..." he trails off.

"Did you know about the trap for me at the studio?"

"No! Not really... It's complicated."

"Don't worry, I can keep up."

"Bianca always had little plans and power plays going on, some of them revolving around you—but the day you saw me coming out of her house, I was trying to convince her to leave you alone. After that, I thought she was done, but then I heard something about you and Kate and the studio. That's why I came to get you."

"You were a little bit late on the whole rescue thing."

"I really am sorry, I thought you would be fine at—"

"Fine," I whisper with a small laugh, in spite of myself. "Where's the necklace?"

His face goes slightly pale.

"Bash..."

He reaches into his jacket pocket and slowly pulls something out, holding it in his fist before reluctantly letting go and dropping it into my already-stretched-out hand. It's my pendant.

"Before you ask, I know I shouldn't have kept it from you. I don't know why I did. I don't know why I did any of this. It's just... Wren I've always liked you!" *What is he talking about?* "Well not always, but I have for a long time and I didn't want you to know that Aidan did what he did because... because I just thought—I thought—"

"Thought what, Bash?"

"Wren, I'm sorry. Are you going to be mad at me forever?"

I clasp the delicate silver chain around my neck and pause a moment. "No. I don't think I have the energy."

I open the gate and begin to walk out.

"Wait! Where are you going?" he calls after me.

"I have no idea."

I know what it's like to be angry. I remember wanting to rip someone's throat out with my hands and watch as the blood ran down out of the open wound and soaked the ground around them. Maybe it was a fleeting feeling, maybe it wasn't. All I know is it still scares me to this day, and it's what I should be feeling right now—given my general history—but it's not.

All I feel is an intense desperation coming from deep within me. Earlier this week, I thought that something in me had died; now I think maybe something in me has come alive.

I walk straight past Nightrider and begin running, picking up my pace until I'm in a full-out sprint. I keep running until I find myself staring down a familiar street. In the distance, I can see him sitting on the brick wall out in front of his house. When he notices me, he immediately jumps down.

"Wren? This isn't a good time."

"I don't give a damn what time it is, Aidan," I say, now standing in front of him.

"I need you to go."

I roll my shoulders back and cross my arms. "Make me."

"You know I'm not going to do that."

"Then you're stuck with me."

"Wren—"

"I know what you did. With Kate, I mean."

"You do?" He takes a step back.

"Well, not really. But sort of. I want to know why."

"Why I did it or why I didn't tell you?"

"Both." I jump up on the wall and sit forward.

"I wanted to tell you the truth, I still do, I just—I can't."

"You can tell me anything."

He begins pacing back and forth in front of me. "Not this. It scared me, Wren. To see what I was willing to do—what I could do. It scares me."

My brow furrows but I don't say anything.

"And the truth is, I don't know if I'm ever going to be able to tell you why I did it or why I can't tell you."

"It's ok."

"Is it?" He stops and faces me. "Because I'm not so sure."

"What do you want me to say?"

"I don't know. I don't know anything," he says, arching his neck back and pressing his palm to his forehead.

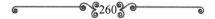

"Well, I don't know anything either."

"You know what I did, kind of."

"Not really."

"But a little bit."

"Yes, a little bit. Only because Bianca told me."

"She said she wouldn't do that."

"And you believed her? Come on, this is Bianca we're talking about."

He hardly seems to hear me. "Doesn't it bother you?" he asks.

"What? That you were able to get rid of Kate? No. If you hadn't, that would mean that Seth had, which would not be good."

"You don't—wait, who is Seth?"

"It doesn't matter, and if he hadn't done it, I would have done it myself."

"I told her if she ever came near you again, I would kill her."

He what? "Oh," I manage to keep a blank face, "I see."

"Don't you understand, Wren? I threatened to *kill* her. And I meant it."

"I understand." My face is still blank.

His brows furrow as he looks at me and shakes his head. "Not much gets to you, does it?"

"We both know that's not true." My voice comes out breathy and restrained at the same time. "Though perhaps I just don't get as bothered as you."

"Oh really?" He moves closer and leans forward, placing a hand on either side of me on the wall—his face only a few inches from my own. "Are you bothered now?"

"Bothered isn't exactly how I would explain it." I hold his gaze for a little longer and then lower my focus to the ground.

He gently puts his thumb under my chin and lifts it up so my eyes are level with his.

"It's so strange," he murmurs, "I only met you about eight months ago but I feel as though I've known you forever—and yet, it also feels like I only met you yesterday."

Before I can respond, he takes hold of my arm and lifts it toward him. "You're still wearing the jacket?"

"You're just now noticing? You should take it back." He's still holding onto my arm.

"It looks better on you." At this, he pushes back the sleeve over my wrist and examines the fading bite mark. "How does it feel?"

"Like a psychopath sank her teeth into my skin. But,"—his touch is very soft and careful— "uh, but it's gotten better."

"Good. If you don't mind me asking, why did she bite you?"

"Because I said 'bite me'."

We both stare at each other for a moment before bursting out in laughter. Once we manage to stop, I slide off the wall and stand up, making the distance between us even smaller.

His eyes suddenly find the necklace lying below my collarbone. "I wasn't sure if you even liked that thing," he says, cocking his head slightly. "I don't think I've ever seen you wear it."

I almost begin laughing again, but there's a serious look on his face that stops me. I swallow and pause, my breath catching up to me. "I like it very much," I say quietly.

After a moment of awkward silence, something comes to me. "I know things have been strange lately. And I know we both don't know much, but I need you to know one thing," I begin, looking up at him. "No matter what you do, I'm right here. I'm *always* right here."

CHAPTER 25

THE FORGIVEN

It's been a few weeks since the weekend of Bash's party and things have been getting better. Things are still a bit awkward between Bash and me and I've thought a lot about what he told me—how he feels about me—but I don't think he meant it. Not really.

It just doesn't make sense.

As for today, last Friday, the last day of the school year, I told Aidan that I would drive him up to the cabin his brother is staying at, so that's what I'm going to do.

I was reluctant at first, even after my talk with Noah, only because he hasn't always been the best to Aidan, but Aidan tells me that after a very long and hard heart-to- heart, they've been getting along better—putting their struggles behind them. So I think this trip means very much to him.

The car ride is actually a lot of fun, though the trip out there is quite longer than I expected. Aidan tells me he could do the driving (he really likes Nightrider), and I tell him that no one gets behind my wheel but me. During our journey there's a lot of arguing about which bands have the best concerts, which superheroes would win which fights, who's the best guitarist of all time (I think we both know who that is by now), and what *Star Wars* movies are the greatest. Seeing how much things have recently changed between us, this lighthearted banter feels amazingly normal.

After two hours of driving and one more to go, we decide to make a pit-stop and sit on the back of the car while we watch the sun set on a grateful/ungrateful universe.

It's absolutely breathtaking. The air is so peaceful and fresh and the warm pink and orange glow of the sun creates a feeling unlike any other.

"Hey," I say, turning toward him, "you got any advice that will help me some sunny day?"

"Course, you gotta take your time. You know, don't live too fast or anything," he answers with a wink.

"Ok, and it should be something I love?"

"And preferably that you understand."

I can't help but smile. Inside things are the best, especially when they have to do with music. "This is really nice, we should do something like this again sometime."

"Like go somewhere?"

"It doesn't have to be far, just somewhere cool that we can hang out at. Maybe at a time when we don't have to worry about taking you to your brother's cabin."

"Yeah, that'd be great. You know, my house is only a few miles from the harbor. The docks down there are really fun to explore."

"That would be awesome. I've been to the beach of course, but I don't think I've ever gone all the way down to the docks."

"Then it's settled."

I nod and look out at the setting sun.

"Wren," Aidan hesitates after a few moments of silence, "can I ask you something?" His voice is suddenly a bit deeper and more serious.

"Shoot."

"Umm—never mind, it's nothing," he falters and breaks eye contact.

"You can ask me anything."

"Why do you like Guns N' Roses so much?"

I can tell quite obviously that this isn't what he meant to ask, but I go along anyway. "For so, so many reasons. But," I squint, "there's something about his voice that I connect to—I can feel it in me when I listen."

"Like you're not so alone when you hear it."

I nod as I look over to see him leaning back on the car and looking out at the sunset as well.

"So, I know we're friends, but are we good friends now?" he asks all of a sudden a few minutes later.

"We better be," I respond.

"Who's your best friend?"

I almost say "You," but I stop myself just in time—I don't know why, admitting he's my best friend shouldn't be hard, but for some reason it feels more personal than that. *More personal, what the hell does that mean?* "I don't really have one right now. I used to have someone that, excluding my sister, I connected with more than anyone."

"Who?"

"Her name is Violet."

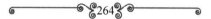

"What happened?"

"I'm not sure how to explain. Just, some things aren't meant to last, I guess."

"No, that's crap."

"Oh," I raise one eyebrow at him, "is that so?"

"Yeah, it is. Because you never give up on the people you care about. I mean, take you for example, I'd never just give up on you—even when you are a stubborn pain in the ass."

I turn toward him and he's still staring up at the sky, biting his bottom lip.

"Hey," I say and he looks toward me, "I care about you too."

"No need to be such a sap," he chuckles lightly, though I can tell there's something he's still hiding.

"You started it," I respond with a shrug. "Can I tell you something?"

He nods and looks at me intently.

"Actually…" *Maybe this isn't the best idea.*

"No, don't back out on me."

I can't find the words. Goddamn, why can't I ever find the words?

"Until you can tell me, I'm going to ask you something else. What were you doing when you showed up at my doorstep that night out of nowhere and then left? What were you going to tell me?"

"Who says I was going to tell you anything?"

"Aw come on, we both know you had something to say."

Son of a bitch. "Well, actually that's what I was just trying to talk to you about." Actually, that's not what I was just trying to talk to him about—because it's not what I was going to tell him at his house—but it's still something he ought to know about me. "I was kicked out of my old dance studio."

"That's what you wanted to tell me?"

"Yes?"

"How did it happen?"

"I was blamed for… something I didn't do."

He nods thoughtfully and looks out at the setting sun.

"You… you don't have questions?" I ask, confused. "You believe me?"

"Yes, of course. I mean, I have questions, but of course I believe you."

I stare at him, somewhat staggered.

"Can I tell *you* something now?" Aidan asks, leaning back with a hand behind his head.

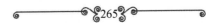

I nod, and I am already captivated by what he's about to say.

"I know it's not the same, but I was also kicked out of a school before."

"You were what?"

"Yeah, I know, I seem way too perfect to have ever be kicked out of anything, but it's true."

"When? From where?"

"Well, technically it's happened more than once. Quite a few times, actually, but the worst one took place here, the first time I lived here. I had already gotten expelled from one school for skipping too many classes, and at this next one, I got into a fight with a kid over my brother. He was saying things about him that I didn't like—most of which were true—but I picked the fight anyway."

"Oh, man. Who won?"

"Huh?"

"The fight. Who won?"

"Oh," he smirks, "I did. Though that didn't matter when it came to getting kicked out. And this was all right before I moved back to Kansas and—"

"Wait, *back* to Kansas?"

"Yeah, well not back to the same city but—"

"When were you in Kansas the first time?"

He smiles at me and lets out a small laugh. "That's where I was born, Wren. Wichita, Kansas."

"*Wichita*," I repeat to myself. "I don't know why I didn't know that."

"Because I never told you. I don't usually talk about the places I've lived."

"Where else have you lived?"

"You really want to know?"

"Of course," I say as I lay back on the car and prop myself up on my elbows so that I'm level with him.

We continue to sit on the back of my car, dusk turning into pitch-black night as Aidan tells me the story of all the different places he's moved to and why he moved to them. He starts in Kansas, and then things get complicated as he explains the journey to Lafayette, Indiana, and then to Texas, followed by Saint James, Louisiana, Sunrise Heights, and Kansas once again, and back to California.

"How about we listen to the radio?" I ask once he's finished. This is the type of conversation that should be followed by some good music.

"Yes, I'd like that very much."

Where do we go now?

Later that night, I drop Aidan off at his brother's cabin. It takes a little while for me to get his butt out of my Nightrider because he keeps asking me if I'll be ok driving back by myself. He even tries to convince me to spend the night at the cabin, but I tell him I've got something I've got to do. Since what he said to me about Violet earlier, I haven't been able to stop thinking about it. I need to talk to her, tonight. And I need to do it alone.

Once he does finally get out of the car, rather than going inside, he turns right around and ducks his head back in through the open window.

"What now, Aidan?" I groan.

His eyes sparkle even in the dim light of the moon and his expression is one of unfamiliar seriousness. "Wren, I never wanted to go to the dance with Bianca. Do you know why?"

I stare at him for a moment.

Before I can think of how to respond, he lifts his head out of the window and walks inside the cabin without looking back.

The ride home is lonely, and a storm begins to brew—something not common for West Coast summers. Come to think of it, we've had a lot more storms this year than usual.

I'm still thinking about what Aidan said when I get to my house and pick up the phone to dial her number. It rings a few times and I almost hang up, but then she answers.

"Hello? Wren?"

"Hey, Vi."

"It's so late. Where are you?" Her voice is distressed but calming at the same time.

"Can I come over?"

***

I look up at the dark, now-completely stormy sky as I run to her door. *Wow, that cold, black cloud really is coming down.* I knock, completely soaked by the rain, and wait. I close my eyes and let the water pour over me, tasting the drops that fall on my lips.

Violet opens the door and stares at me, her brows furrowed. "Come in, please."

I step inside and she leads me to the windowsill. We sit down on it, and I look outside at the raging storm, rain running down the glass panes like heavy tears.

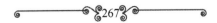

"Wren…" Violet pushes with a pleading undertone to her voice. I shift my focus from outside to her eyes.

Unsure of where to begin, I start. "I've had a really strange year."

"Me too."

"To be honest, for most of it, it kind'a felt like I was livin' on a prayer."

"Why? I want to understand—I want to know what's been going on."

"I've got all these changing seasons of my life, and I don't know what to do with them or where they're takin' me. I feel I've got to make it my own way, but I can see the storm getting closer and I'm not ready to get my head out of the clouds—"

"Is that some sort of elaborate metaphor-lyric mix-up? You know people don't understand when you talk like that."

"I'm lost, Vi, and I don't know where to go or if I'm ever gonna get there."

"Start at the beginning, and we can go from there."

"I can't."

"Try." Her voice is firm, patience wearing thin.

"I'm—I'm not ready."

She breathes in, pausing for a second before putting a hand on my shoulder and leaning her head in closer. "Then why did you come here?"

"I just—oh, Violet, can you forgive me?"

"Forgive you? For what?"

"For everything. I know that fire didn't only affect me—it hurt you too. I'm the one who destroyed your relationship, I'm the reason you quit dancing, I—"

"You give yourself too much credit," she finishes for me. "I know you're not the one who started the fire. And I know what kind of a person Seth really is."

"What?"

"I was upset when I first questioned you, I wasn't seeing things straight. You've just never really given me a chance to explain this to you."

"Still, I'm not good like you; you deserve better. I make things difficult and—"

"Sure, things after the fire were… difficult, and life has been complicated, but it was a whole lot easier when you were by my side. And I think you know that, so would you just shut up?"

"But I'm down *all* the time, and I won't let myself bring you down with me. I don't even have a reason for being this way anymore, it just is."

"No. I know some part of you knows that's not true, or you wouldn't have bothered coming here. Besides, nothing just *is*. Like you've always told me, you always got a choice, maybe not to all of a sudden feel better, but you can choose to keep fighting. So don't give me this crap about taking me down just because you're a little wayward right now—it's nothing you can't get through. And yeah, it's hard, but I'm with you. So, as far as this forgiveness stuff goes, I think we both forgave each other a long time ago—even though we didn't know it. But I swear to God, sometimes you are the most dramatic person I know, and if you disappear again and all of a sudden leave me hanging here... You're not going to do that, are you?"

"No," I say softly.

"It's late now, but I'd like if we could get together again sometime soon. If you think you can handle that."

"Are you free next Saturday night? Some people I know are going to perform at the Mainstreet Club—I'm gonna do the first song with them. There's fliers for it all around town"

"I'll be there."

After leaving her house, I walk through the park near my house. On the way back home, I watch the birds fly above me, running after them until I can no longer see them.

Some time last year, I decided I was a changed person, a person not worthy of the love or friendship of someone such as Violet. I was tainted, through and through, blinded by a damaged self-image. It didn't matter what anyone said, whether they liked me or hated me, I hated myself. A crushing guilt followed me everywhere I went; the abuse from Bianca or Kate or Seth all made me sick because a part of me felt that maybe I deserved it.

And the fighting, just to stay alive, seemed never ending. It still does. As I fight them, I am also fighting myself. But I can't live in-between forever. I must make a choice, to give in to them or to myself. Or perhaps there is another choice to be made... So where am I going? What am I going to do?

I'll be damned if I can't find out.

CHAPTER 26

HOUSE OF THE SETTING SUN

Aidan ignored the roars of protest as he pushed his way through the crowd and out of the club. He knew how important this concert was for the band, for him, but he *had* to find her—even if it meant leaving a few songs early.

Something was wrong. He could feel it.

He began running through the streets, desperately searching for her. It was possible that she had gone home already, but something told him that she was still here, somewhere close…

It was an unusually windy night for the middle of May, and the farther away he got from the club, the more panic he felt.

Where could she be?

The streetlights flickered above and the wind blew his hair in his face, making it nearly impossible for him to see. Then, just as he was about to turn around, from the corner of his eye, he caught a glimpse of a bright emerald green gown down a dark alleyway.

But the relief that washed over him was short-lived, for as he turned toward the alleyway, he noticed something else—something that proved the sinister feeling had been true.

She was not alone…

"You think anyone's seriously gonna be there?" Rob asks, twirling the microphone in his hand as was his habit.

We just got done running through "November Rain" for the third time today. It's a bit rough and now everyone's stressing about the concert and its turnout. We don't even get a rehearsal in the club, and I'm not sure we get a real sound check either, so that just adds to the stress. But there isn't much time for stressing—the concert is in three days.

"We put up enough damn fliers, there better be some people there," Aidan sighs.

"Yeah, we hung up like a bazillion," Tommy adds.

"It's never going to work." Sebastian shakes his head. "No one's going to come."

"Hey, everything always works except for when it doesn't," I say.

"You're not wrong..." Aidan mumbles, looking to the ceiling.

"That doesn't mean anything," Sebastian states, crossing his arms.

"Oh my sweet child, you have much to learn." I pat him on the shoulder and he rolls his eyes.

"And our single has fifty-five thousand views already," Tommy smiles. "Clearly the public loves us, so I bet there will be loads of people in the audience. If anything, there will be too many."

I still can't quite believe that their music video has that many views after being out such a short amount of time, but it does.

Just then, my phone buzzes. There's a message from Eric saying he'd like to meet me at the Ice Cream Shop diner tonight to talk.

We go through "November Rain" a few more times, to be sure we're prepared for tomorrow, and afterwards the guys invite me to watch a movie, but I tell them I have to meet someone.

"Before you go..." Sebastian says, catching me by the arm as I open the garage door to leave.

"Yes, Bash?"

"Can I talk to you?"

I look down at the rest of the band members, all of them are watching us. Rob and Tommy look away immediately, but Aidan is staring hard at Bash's hand that is now holding onto my shoulder.

"Sure, but not now. I really do have to go."

Reluctantly, he lets go.

I leave and head over to the Ice Cream Shop, texting Eric that I'm there. Then I order two sundaes and wait.

He shows up a little while later and his expression is one of forced pleasantness. I begin playing with the rubber band on my wrist.

"Sorry, your sundae is a bit melted," I say as he sits down.

"That's all right. I suppose I didn't come here for ice cream anyway."

"You said you wanted to talk to me about something."

"Yes, I did. You see, Wren, you have been one of the kindest people to me this year, and I have come to think of you as a friend. I mean, I know we used to be friends back when we were little, but I feel like we've just recently reconnected, if you know what I mean."

"I do."

"That's why I wanted to tell you myself that I won't be staying at Sunrise Heights High next year. My family is moving to San Francisco this summer, and I'll be going to a school there. We are probably going to begin moving sometime next week."

I stare at him, unblinking.

"Wren?"

"I… wasn't expecting that."

"This place, I just don't think it suits me."

"I understand." I understand exactly. My fists clench. "It's because of people like Bianca and Kate."

He hesitates. "It's the area as a whole—"

"No, it's because of people like them. Because they can be so cruel, and stupid, and—"

"You're angry."

"Yeah, I'm angry."

"You don't need to be. This is for the best. It really is, and I'm ok with it."

"Well I'm not."

"Oh Wren," he sighs, "you've done more for me than you know." *Obviously I did not do enough.* "And this isn't the only thing I wanted to talk to you about. I heard from Aidan that you will be doing a concert soon. I'd love to come see it." I didn't know Eric and Aidan talked.

"It's not a real concert."

"Still, I want to go."

By the time he leaves, I can't tell if I feel better or worse. Oh, no, it's definitely worse. I rest my head on my arms and think about where to go now—a question that never gets answered.

As I'm about to get up, "Knockin' On Heaven's Door" begins playing throughout the diner. I look over to the jukebox and see Lena coming toward me.

"You like this song, right?" she asks, sitting down in front of me.

"Umm, yeah, it's awesome."

"I was told I might find you here, you weren't answering your phone, and I wanted to talk to you. To really talk to you."

I don't say anything, waiting for her to continue.

"Why didn't you tell me about your concert? I had to find out from Eric."

"I don't know, I just wasn't sure you would want to…"

"Why would I not want to go? Anyway, it doesn't matter—that's not what I came here for."

"Then what did you come here for?"

"We haven't really spoken to each other lately. At first, it seemed like you were avoiding me and then later I was the one avoiding you. And I know you tried to reach out to me at that dinner party, but, again, I was sort of trying to stay away from you. Even now, I'm not completely sure why, I just—"

"It's ok." She's probably avoided me because she blamed me for what happened. And I got to say, I don't blame her for blaming me.

"No, it's not ok. And what's worse is after the crash, I never really thanked you."

"Lena—"

"I wouldn't be *alive* if not for you. And I never thanked you, not really. I never even really thought about how the whole thing might have affected you."

"I'm all right," I assure her.

"Good. Well, that's all I wanted to say," she gets up and leaves before I get a chance to say anything else.

I continue to stay seated a little longer. While I'm sitting here, I suddenly take hold of my necklace, smoothing it over in my hand.

I'm glad Eric and Lena will be coming to the show, but I still leave the Shop far more upset than when I came to it. I didn't even finish my sundae.

I think I need to get away from this place for a while. I think I need some time on my own—all alone.

I think I need to leave Sunrise Heights.

I've started to take my idea of heading off somewhere by myself more seriously. In fact, I've given it quite a bit of thought and have concluded that after the concert—directly after—I'm leaving. I don't know exactly how long I'll be gone, but maybe all of the rest of summer.

I mean, I do have a fair amount of money saved up from that failed bookstore job I had last summer, so I pack up a suitcase and pitch the idea to my parents—sort of—by telling them Violet invited me on a road trip. They're just happy that I am seeing Vi again, so they agree to it.

I feel a little bad about this, but I need to get out of this town for a while. There's something here that's messing me up, that I need to get away from.

I got to be on my own, and how exactly I am going to survive on my own for a few months, I'm not sure. But I'll figure it out—even though it probably means living out of Nightrider most of the time.

Cara's been warning me against it, she can tell something is up, but I assure her it's all going to be all right. Even still, I'm pretty sure she can see through me—at least to some extent.

Sometimes it really annoys me how smart she is. She's probably right to try and deter me from leaving, but I'm going to go through with it anyway. Tonight is the night of the concert. I don't exactly have time to second-guess myself. Hell, I'm already packed! There's no going back now.

At least that's what I say to myself as I slowly come down the stairs and find Cara waiting for me at the bottom.

"You're leaving tonight still?" she asks, watching me grab my leather jacket and put on my boots.

"Yep."

"Why did you curl your hair? You never curl your hair."

"Yes, well today I felt like it," I answer, pushing my loose ringlets out of my face as I stand up. *Hmm, maybe I ought to leave cowboy boots at home tonight.*

"Can I come to the concert?"

"No, sorry kiddo." *Where are my heels? I could have sworn I owned a pair.*

"Why?"

"I just would rather you not." *Oh, there they are!*

"How come?"

"Because," I slip on the heels and stand up, "you ask too many questions." *Jesus these are freakin' uncomfortable.*

"That's not it. Also, it's not all about you, I know Aidan is going to be there and I want to see him perform too."

"Cara, please, I just want to do this by myself."

"What about your parents?" my mom asks as she comes over to us.

"No, please no, mom."

"Must you wear that jacket with that outfit?"

I look down at the dress I chose and nod. It's long and emerald green, with a fit that holds tight to my slim figure on the torso and fans out in a mermaid style toward the bottom. It is perhaps a bit much for the occasion, but I didn't end up using it for the Spring Formal, and if I don't wear it now, I may never get the chance again.

"All right, honey, we hope you have fun. But we expect pictures, from both the concert *and* your trip, and you'll have to tell us all about it when you get back."

"Ok."

"How about just take me?" Cara asks again.

I give her a warning look and she pouts. "Ok, fine. But whenever you get back, you have to do something special with me again."

I hug her tightly. "Deal."

Then I step out the door.

***

My heart thumps loudly as I enter through the back door of the club. I'm running late, so I skip backstage and go straight to where I hear all the noise.

It's very loud and dark out in the audience as I walk onto the small stage and over to the piano. The band is already set up and ready to go. I can feel my hands shaking.

People quiet down a bit once I take my seat.

Why did I say I would be the one to introduce them?

I see Seth there, standing toward the back, and he's brought Bianca—I thought they were broken up, guess they're back together—along with a number of other awful people I used to know. A load of people I had hoped I'd never have to see again. But it doesn't matter. They can't stop me.

"Hello everyone," I say, looking out at the audience. There's over a hundred people here, more than I expected for a local band's debut concert. Guess Tommy and Bash did better with marketing than I thought they would. "I'd like to introduce you to this band and get you to really know who they are. In order to do that, I'm going to start us off with a song you may or may not know."

The stage lights are kind of blinding, but I can still make out Violet in the crowd along with Eric and Lena. I've never had any friends come to a show of mine before, but they're smiling and it makes me smile. I also see a few other people I recognize, including Ella. I even see Noah there, and I know how much that means to Aidan. I continue scanning the audience and see that Seth still hasn't left. *I can't let it get to me; I'm so close.* I focus all my willpower and let go of my nerves. I let myself feel the moment.

I look to Aidan and he smiles and gives me a small nod.

"I would dedicate it to all the people that try to make you feel like you're not enough, like you have something to prove to them, but I'm not—because it doesn't matter what they think. This is for all of you who feel like you don't have anyone. Like you're the only one. So I do hope you enjoy it. It's a song very close to my heart, and I think you'll all understand why it's so special. This song, a little something called"—I stare straight at him as I continue—'November Fucking Rain'."

As soon as my fingers touch the keys and begin playing, everything else disappears. It's all a blur afterwards. Blinding lights, a cheering crowd, band mates yelling and high-fiving each other. That's the thing about a song like "November Rain"; it'll really get people going.

I sort of remember hugging Aidan and the rest of them. Then I step down from the stage and as I walk through the audience, through everyone, to watch the rest of the show, what I've held inside of me no longer seems so important.

I exit the club a bit early, put on my jacket, and wander down the street. The wind has picked up and the streetlights flicker, casting flashing shadows on the pavement. I think perhaps I should've stayed and finished out the performance, but I just got a feeling—one that pulled me out here. I'm not sure what the feeling meant, but I want to find it. I want to find it before I leave. So, I continue wandering around, taking in the night's fresh air and enjoying the sense of freedom that comes with it.

As I begin to travel down an alleyway, I hear a voice whisper somewhere behind me, inviting another feeling I don't often experience: fear. When I look back, I don't see anything.

But the voice returns, sending shivers down my spine. I think I might be in danger…

"Wren," I hear it say, this time louder. They're taunting me.

I continue looking into the darkness, unable to make out anyone.

"Come out already," I demand, walking in the direction the voice appears to be coming from.

Just then, a dark figure emerges from the shadows and I run into it. I stumble back a foot and look up, shocked to find Seth looking back down at me.

"That's quite the dress—not one I would recommend walking around at night in," he says in a low voice. "By the way, the show is still going on."

"Yes, I know. I was just getting some fresh air. Where is Bianca?" I don't see her anywhere.

"Not here."

"Oh."

"So this is what you want to do with your life now?"

"I'm not sure what I want to do with my life. I don't think I'll really know for a long time."

He moves closer. "But you still won't take my offer? Even after what I did for you?"

I shake my head slowly, involuntarily moving back a step.

"That was a lie. You didn't do anything. And besides, I told you, no matter what I do from now on, I'm done with that part of my life."

"But is that really such a good idea?"

"I guess I'll find out."

"Things—" he begins moving even closer, "—things are just so different now."

"I know."

"Don't you ever miss it? The way it all used to be?"

"You're freaking insane if you think I miss anything about you or that goddamn hellhole you call a dance school."

"You make everything so, so difficult."

"Don't give me credit for what you've already done."

He sneers and takes another step. At this point, there's only about a foot of space between us. I could back away, but I stand my ground, refusing to move.

"Maybe I should have let you burn in that fire."

I look up at him, my eyes boldly searing into his. "Maybe you should have."

He leans down and I can feel his breath on my neck.

My boldness is slipping. "What are you doing, Seth?" I whisper, resisting the urge to turn my head.

"Do you know why I've done the things I've done to you?" His voice is low, a growling whisper.

When I don't answer, he moves closer, his lips brushing the side of my ear as he says, "Because I want you."

"Want me?" My voice trembles as I speak.

His hand pushes my hair back from my face. "I *care* for you."

And then I snap out of it, removing his hand from touching my face. "'Care for me'? '*Care for me?*' All you've ever done is hurt me!"

"Shh. Stop fighting."

"You've done this to me once before, I won't let it happen again."

"But you will. You want to—"

277

"No, this will *never* be what I want."

"You don't know what you want." With this, he grabs me and brings his lips down upon mine.

This is all just a horrible nightmare. It has to be.

My hands hit against his chest, but he doesn't budge. I can't go through this again, I—

Suddenly, Seth is pushed off me, forcefully. He stumbles back, and we both look at the person who is now standing between us, some of my nerves immediately disappearing.

"What is going on?" Aidan's tone is harsh—no, it's more than harsh—it's threatening.

Oh, thank God. I've never been happier to see anyone.

"None of your business," Seth spits and moves to step around him.

Aidan shoves him back and steps forward. "I don't think you want to do this."

If I didn't know Aidan, I would be afraid of him right now.

Rather than answering, Seth returns the shove, even harder this time. And while Aidan is tall with a fairly muscular build, Seth is even larger.

Aidan stumbles slightly and Seth turns on me. His cold eyes have a dangerous fire burning behind them as he stares down at me. But there's something different about his gaze this time, something more worrisome. It's a look I've never seen before, and as he stares into me I can see the flames dancing.

He shifts his focus from me to look at Aidan and then back again at me. Within a split second this all happens, whatever was holding him back breaks.

But Aidan isn't paying attention to Seth right now; he's looking at me. He's about to ask if I'm all right. I shout something, though I can't really hear myself, I think it's a warning. Aidan switches his focus and reacts, faster than I would have thought possible, catching Seth's fist and simultaneously throwing a punch.

It strikes Seth in the face perfectly and sends him falling back.

As soon as this happens, Aidan turns back to me. "What did he do to you?"

I can't answer; I can't say anything.

"Wren, what did he do?" He's yelling now.

Then, somehow, Seth is back on his feet. I want to warn Aidan again, but it's too late. I don't even have time to react as Seth tackles him to the

ground and climbs on top of him. I immediately move to tear him off Aidan, but as I grab his arm he hits me—perhaps on accident, perhaps not. Either way I can taste blood.

I can tell he thinks this will stop me as he turns his attention back to Aidan who yells at me to get away. But suddenly I don't have control over what I'm about to do next.

I jump Seth, catching him completely off guard, and we roll on the hard ground until I end up on top of him. As he looks up at me his expression is one of shock. I raise my fist and he shuts his eyes, but it never makes contact with his face. Instead, I let it drop onto his chest, my fingers curling around the fabric of his shirt. When he looks up at me again, he seems almost more shocked than when I first pinned him.

"Don't you ever touch him again!" I scream. "Ever!"

"Wren!" I hear someone call behind me.

I look back and Seth goes to push me off him but I quickly take hold of his shoulders and slam him back down. I know I'm not really stronger than him—in fact, when it comes to muscles, I know he's *much* stronger than me—so I'm not sure why it works, but it doesn't matter.

"You understand that? Do I make myself clear?" I ask, my voice lower this time. Before he can answer someone grabs me from behind and lifts me off him.

He quickly gets to his feet and stares at me as Aidan pulls me away.

Aidan continues saying things to me but I can hardly hear him. My focus is solely on Seth.

"You try this again and I will *hurt* you," I promise him.

He just keeps staring at me, unmoving, as I'm pulled farther away. Then I feel Aidan take my hand and we begin running.

We don't stop running until we make it back to the backstage of the club.

My chest is moving rapidly up and down as I try to calm my ragged breathing and Aidan's hands cup the sides of my face. Luckily, at the moment there's no one here but us.

"Are you ok? Jesus, what were you thinking tackling him like that? He's twice your size!"

"I'm fine," I reply quickly. "How are you?"

He moves a hand up from my cheek to my forehead and then down to my bottom lip. "You're bleeding!"

"Good," I mutter looking down at my hand, opening and closing my fist.

"What?"

"What?"

"I don't think you know what you're saying right now. If I didn't know better I would say you were drunk."

"I'm not."

"I know. I just want you to be careful."

"When have I not been careful?"

"Tonight. When you decided to leave early by yourself to go for a stroll down an alleyway and run into some psycho. I mean, why didn't you just wait for the show to finish? It's lucky I left early to go after you when I couldn't find you inside."

My brows furrow at the thought of him leaving early for me. "I'm not sure, getting some air just seemed like a good idea at the time."

"And did it 'seem like a good idea' still when you got cornered in that alleyway?"

"You're going to blame me for that?"

"No, of course not! I just—" He stops.

"Just what?" I ask quietly.

"Hope that you're ok."

"I'm fine, I just didn't expect… *him* to be here tonight."

"You knew that guy?"

I'm barely hearing his words. I can still taste blood in my mouth. It doesn't worry or frighten me though—it makes me want to destroy something. It feeds my hunger, my appetite for destruction. This is the part of me that makes me fear only one thing: myself.

My body heat rises and my pulse quickens.

"Who was he?" My eyes snap toward Aidan as he grabs my hand. Even as my pulse continues to race, I can feel the anger inside me disappearing until it dissolves completely and I am left with a new feeling.

I break eye contact and stare at the cracks running along the floor. "Seth." My stomach is squeamish just saying his name, but there's no point in keeping this from him anymore.

"Wren, I need you to tell me exactly who Seth is. I need you to tell me what he did." His voice is deadly serious. "I need you to tell me everything."

I take in a shaky breath and look back up at him. "Ok."

CHAPTER 27

NOVEMBER STORM

"Oh God, Wren. I'm so sorry," I hear Aidan say.

I just told him... everything.

Once again, I went into a sort of flashback state as I went through it but, suddenly, I'm out of my head and back in my body. And my body is... sitting on the floor. I don't remember how we got to the floor, but we did.

And I'm crying. *When did I start crying?* My face is hot and wet, I don't want Aidan to see me this—

Before I can finish my embarrassed thought, I feel a pair of strong arms wrap around me as he pulls me to him. Despite being caught off guard, I don't fight it, letting him bring me in close. I rest my head against his chest—which is hard beneath the softness of his shirt that is now becoming slightly damp from my tears.

I have never allowed myself to be this vulnerable in front of anyone. Yet I feel a strange sense of comfort and something else—safety.

Aidan lets me cry for some time, just holding me—a sense of mutual understanding passing through us. He doesn't move except to run a hand through my hair, sending tingles running down my back. Finally, there are no more tears. And all the pain fades until the only thing I can feel is the soft rise and fall of his chest.

A sigh escapes my lips and he lifts my chin up to look at him, I'm staring into an endless sea of green. "Are you all right now?"

He's very warm, and his scent is—I need to stop.

I pull away from him, sitting up and feeling colder all of a sudden. "Yes."

I hope I don't look like the mess I feel like.

As soon as I assure him I'm ok, he sits back and appears to be thinking hard about something. The concern on his face is now mixed with fierce anger. I've never seen Aidan this way. There's a dangerous intensity in his eyes combined with a cool collectedness that only makes him more intimidating. He stands up almost calmly and looks down at me.

"So, after everything he did to you, he blamed you for the fire and because of it, your entire life was ruined," he states back to me, like he's going over the facts of a court case.

"Well, yes, sort of... but—"

"Wren, I need you to stay here for a moment. I have to do something."

"What are you talking about? Aidan, where are you going?"

"Stay right here, and don't move until I come back."

"No, you're going after Seth, aren't you?"

"I need to do this."

"Do what? Fight him again?"

"Please, just trust me."

At first I want to argue with him more, but then I nod my head—a silent promise to do as he said. And then he walks out the back door once again and into the night.

I don't know how much time passes as I sit there on the floor before the door flings open. But it's not the backdoor; it's the other door that connects the backstage area to the hallway leading to the stage.

"Where in the hell is Aidan?" Bash hisses as he comes into the room. "And Wren where have you—oh." He stops as soon as he sees me on the floor.

I would stand up but I feel like I'd probably fall back down. I think Bash can see this because he kneels down next to me. "Wren, what's happened?"

Thank God I'm all out of tears.

"I'm fine, Bash. Everything is fine."

"You're eyes, they're red."

"You should get back out there to the concert."

"I'd love to, but it's a little difficult to do that with the lead guitarist missing. After you left, we only played a few more songs and then he left—telling us to just 'take a break' until he got back. But he's still not back."

"Sorry, I think he'll be here soon." In truth, I have no idea when he is going to be back, but seeing as he told me to stay here, I can only assume it won't be long.

"Well, we took a break for a while, but there's only so long you can do that. So now we're just trying to entertain the audience in any way we can—Rob is going to do some a cappella and Tommy has done more than a few drum solos. So we need to start up again before they scare everyone away. We could have just ended the show, really, but there's one more important song we're supposed to play."

"I see."

Still kneeling on the floor, he scoots a little closer to me. "Since we're waiting, I'd like to talk to you now."

"Now? But don't your band mates need you?"

"They can get on without me for a bit."

"All right, what is it?"

"I want to tell you I'm sorry. I know that what I did was wrong; and what I said, the night of the dinner party, was selfish—for multiple reasons."

What is he saying? It doesn't make sense, but at the same time I can tell he's being sincere.

"I'm confused, I don't know exactly how I feel—but I know that I feel *something*. I swear I wish I didn't. But I do." There's no way this is really happening. "I also know that you deserve more of an explanation for all of this, and for everything, but obviously we're limited on time at the moment. Perhaps tomorrow?"

"Bash, I'm leaving for the rest of the summer. And I'm leaving tonight."

"Oh… That's all right. This can wait."

"It can?"

"I suppose it has to. But things are more complicated than they seem. And I want you to understand, now, that Aidan is my best friend and I never want to do anything that could hurt him."

"Why are you telling me this?" I know they're best friends.

"I just want him to be happy. I want *you* to be happy."

"Ok, and this means?"

He laughs a little. "I think you'll see soon enough if you can't already." He stands up and moves back toward the door he came in through.

"Wait," I say, standing up as well, "you're leaving?"

"Yes, to make sure the audience isn't leaving. I will see you later, Wren."

As soon as that door shuts, the one behind me flings open.

"Aidan! I—" Anything I was about to say gets dropped as I take in his appearance.

There's a light cut on his lip, making it slightly swollen, and there's another on the bridge of his nose. He's also got more serious-looking cuts above his brow and across his cheekbone, along with a darkened eye—more scuffs than what could have come from when Seth tackled him. Then I notice his hands and see his knuckles have been thoroughly banged up.

"What the hell happened to you? You *did* go and get in a fight with him!"

"It doesn't matter." He slams the door behind him. "People are going to believe you now. Everyone will know the truth."

"What are you saying?"

"I've got the proof. No one's ever going to question you again."

"How do you have proof?"

"I forced him to confess. It's all right here, recorded," Aidan says, lifting up his phone.

"How did you get him to do *that*?" I know Seth, and admitting his wrongs is *not* something he does. Ever.

"Well, we did sort of get into a fight… After I tracked him down, I wasn't sure what was going to happen. All I knew was what I wanted to get from him. At first I thought maybe I'd talk to him, but as soon as I saw him, I knew talking things out wasn't an option."

"So you started a fight."

"He recognized me right away, and from there the fight just sort of broke out mutually."

"It looks like he got some hits on you."

"Yeah, well, you should see *him*." Aidan smiles faintly at what appears to be the memory of hitting Seth. This is the first time I've seen him smile since leaving the concert. "Don't worry, he's still alive. Though if I ever see him around again, he probably won't be."

I always knew he was tough, but being able to take on and beat an opponent like Seth who's even larger and more muscular… it makes me curious just how much skill and strength Aidan must have.

"Anyway," he continues, "that part isn't what matters. What matters is that people are going to know the truth now."

The door at the front of the room bursts open once more, this time with Bash, Tommy, and Rob all coming through.

"There you guys are! I thought maybe you'd dropped off the face of the earth," Tommy exclaims. "And—whoa, what happened to your face man?"

"I'll explain later," Aidan promises, "right now we've got a show to finish."

"Oh thank God," Rob sighs. "People were leaving—there's only so long Tommy can perform drum solos before everyone goes insane."

Aidan nods and then turns to me. "Think you can make it through listening to one more song?"

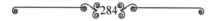

I go back out into the audience, pushing my way to the front of the crowd, and watch as the band takes the stage once again. Aidan apologizes for the delay and tells us that they've got one last song to perform. Even with a black eye and cuts all across his face, he looks like he was born to be up there.

"This is a very special song," he says, gazing out over the audience. "It's for someone I know." His eyes find mine and he winks. My heartbeat picks up and a warmth spreads through my body. "Someone that is very important to me."

Then he looks to his band mates and nods, kicking off the song.

Just before the first note, I somehow know what is going to be played.

And then, the sound of "Sweet Child O' Mine" fills the club. While at first people appear to be annoyed by the delay, everyone goes wild as soon as they begin to play.

They sound amazing, this might be their best song yet—they must have been practicing for quite some time.

It's perfect. And watching Aidan…

I'm in love with this song. I love everything about it.

But then, why do I suddenly feel so sad? The soaring happiness I had now feels as though it's been crushed. New tears begin streaming down my face as I look up at him playing onstage.

Everything is changing, yet everything is the same. I have to get out of here now! I have to leave Sunrise Heights before I change my mind.

The song comes to an end. Once again, everyone is cheering.

With blurry eyes, I force my way back out of the crowd and out of the club. I suck in a deep breath of fresh air as soon as I reach outside, taking hold of the rose pendant and smoothing it over in my hand. *Where do I go now?*

"Wren!" I hear a voice call out from behind me.

I flip around to see Aidan standing before me.

"What are you doing leaving again like that? Didn't you like the song?" His voice is concerned, maybe even hurt.

"I loved the song, Aidan, I just—I couldn't help it. I…"

"Listen, Wren, I know tonight has been crazy—so much has happened—but there's something I want to say. I tried to tell you the night you stayed over—the night we danced."

"What is it?" I'm trying desperately to hold the tears back now.

"I have to go back inside, but—"

"Please, tell me."

"Not now," he says with an urgent undertone, "later tonight. Can you meet me on the docks at the harbor?" *Damnit.* "You know, just like we talked about."

"Aidan, I would, but I can't."

"What do you mean 'you can't'?"

"I'm leaving. Tonight. I'm going to be gone for a while…"

"How long?"

"I'm not sure, maybe a few months."

"A few months!"

"I'll probably be back after that—"

"Probably?"

"I know it's sudden, but I just feel like I need some time away from this place, some time on my own."

"Why?"

"I don't know."

"That's not good enough."

"What? 'That's not good enough'?"

"I just don't understand."

"Neither do I—that's why I have to do this." *These things I feel—it scares me.*

"And you have to do it alone?"

My mouth opens, but no answer comes out.

Instead, I hear the club doors open as someone else comes out of them and up to us.

"Wren, there you are! You had me worried, is everything all right?" Violet asks, placing a hand on my shoulder as she gets to me.

Aidan stares at me another moment, my words still caught in my throat, and then he walks back into the club without looking back.

My chest feels like it's going to tear in two.

"What was that about?" she asks once he's gone.

"Nothing." *Only that I just screwed up everything.*

"And what happened to your forehead? And your mouth?"

I deflect her questions with one of my own. "What did you run out here for?"

"I thought it was weird when I noticed you leave the first time, but this time it looked like there was something particularly wrong."

"Did it?" I say mindlessly as I begin walking in the direction of my car. Violet walks with me. "I'm just trying to help you."

"Well, don't." And then I get an idea. "Hey," I grab hold of her hand, "come on."

I'm pretty sure I can feel her roll her eyes, but she comes with me anyway.

"I want to know what's going on," she demands as we get to my car.

"Let's go for a drive. I can take you home after."

"No, really, what's going on?"

"I just want to spend some time with you," I say, getting in the car as she follows my action.

"Sure you do."

I reach into the back of the car to grab my change of clothes and I quickly slip into them, taking off the long green dress to get into jeans and a t-shirt. Then I switch out my heels for my regular boots.

Ah, it feels so good to be back to normal.

We head off down the road, and I notice her studying me.

"If you're gonna keep looking at me like that, I'm gonna drop you right back off at the club."

She doesn't seem to pay my words any attention. "You know, you seem different."

"I am different, Vi. It's been a while since we've really hung out. You're different too."

"I don't mean it that way, there's something else… I'm just not sure what it is."

"Right, well, you let me know when you figure it out."

"Are you going somewhere?" she asks, looking over her shoulder.

"Hm?"

"There's a suitcase, in the back."

"Yes, I'm going off tonight for a sort of road trip by myself."

"By yourself? I knew something weird was going on with you. And how long will you be on this 'sort of road trip'?"

I shrug. "Maybe the rest of summer."

"That is the stupidest thing I have ever heard you say, and *that* is saying something."

"What are you going on about, Violet?"

"Why are you doing this?"

"Because I just feel like it."

"Bullshit, what's the real reason? Does it have something to do with what you were doing outside the club when—"

"Look, I don't know ok?"

"I think you're running from something."

"Can we just enjoy each other's company now and focus on something else?"

"Ok, fine. But I know there's something going on with you."

We ride in silence for a bit until I suddenly get an idea.

"Hey, Vi, you remember when we used to hang out and I'd make you listen to rock music with me?"

"Of course."

"Remember 'Night Moves'?"

"How could I forget, Wren?"

"What about the 'It's Alright' song? It's been a while so I'd be surprised if you still know what that one is." It's true. We haven't listened to it since forever.

She makes a face and reaches into her bag, pulling out a cassette. Ha! Who even uses cassettes anymore?

I lean over a bit to take a glance at it and feel my heart jump a little when I see what it is. On a piece of old, peeling tape is the title *Wren's Playlist*. I must have given that to her years ago. She then puts it in, skips to number seven, and presses play.

We drive on down the road, no destination in mind, singing along to the song. We drive a long time, until the moon shines bright overhead and I finally take Violet home.

After this, I keep driving. I somehow know once I leave nothing will be the way it was. Things really have changed.

About an hour out of town now, I skip through my CDs, unsure of what I'm looking for. Nothing feels right, so I switch on the radio.

The song "Sittin' On the Dock of the Bay" is playing. I would laugh, but then I think I would cry.

My hand moves to switch the station but stops. I listen to it all the way through. Just when it ends and I think I'm safe, the next song comes through. It hits me so hard it hurts—like a shock wave through my entire body: "Sweet Child O' Mine". Of course. I look out at the stars and smile to myself, a tear falling down my cheek.

In one swift turn of the wheel, I spin my car around and begin driving in the other direction. I don't stop until I reach my destination.

I hop out of my car and walk down to the docks, my heart beating fast. It's midnight, so there's no one here. I knew it was a long shot from the moment I decided to come back. But I'm here now, I might as well enjoy the peacefulness of the docks at night. I walk along them slowly, looking up to the moon, surrounded by stars, and then down at its light shimmering on the gently moving sea. Maybe everybody does need somebody, I don't know for sure. But there's one thing I am certain of:

I'm not the only one.

Or maybe that means I do know the answer after all.

At the end of the docks, I sit down, hanging my legs over the edge, and stare into the water, running my fingers through it. The air tonight is warm, but the water is cool and I shiver even though I'm not cold.

I swing my legs back up on the dock and lay down, facing the sky. Just then, I hear it: the sound of music being played. It's an acoustic guitar, and it's coming from the other side of the docks, across the water. What a beautiful melody, I think I know the song.

I get to my feet and walk over there. It's a boy playing, I can make him out more clearly now. Wait, not just a boy—that's *Aidan* playing.

A part of me knew he was here—I could *feel* it—and now, there he is.

I come up from behind, stopping a ways back, just listening to him. The song he's playing is an old one, one from the King of Rock and Roll. Then, unexpectedly, he begins to sing. I've never heard him sing before—not once. I always thought he wasn't able to, but that's not the case. He can sing—better than I ever could.

I walk up beside him, and he practically drops his guitar, jumping up.

"Wren." Just hearing him say my name gets my heart to pick up even faster.

"Aidan, I—" he cuts me off, bringing his arms around me and pulling me into a fierce embrace. I freeze, but then my arms wrap around him, holding on tightly. We finally let go, standing back and staring at each other.

"I thought you left." His voice is a little breathless—soft, but with a slight huskiness.

"I did," I say, the corner of my mouth tilting up, "but then I came back."

"What changed your mind?"

I bite my bottom lip and roll my eyes—I think he knows.

He stares at me another moment, then breaking into a smile and looking to the sky.

"How come I've never heard you sing before?" I ask.

"Why? Did you like it?"

I nod, moving closer. "Play some more, please."

We sit down next to each other with our legs hanging off the side of the dock, just far enough not to be touching, and he starts the song again. His long fingers move across the guitar, almost delicately at first, and then I watch his mouth as he begins to sing and my stomach churns.

When it ends, I feel something changing inside me.

As he's looking out across the water, I closely examine his features, observing the different cuts across his face. There's a smaller one running along his jaw line that I didn't notice until now.

"Did it hurt?" I ask, referring to his fight with Seth. I kick myself as soon as the words leave my mouth. What a stupid question, of course it hurt.

But Aidan doesn't make fun of me. He simply sets his guitar down and looks at me. "It doesn't matter, it was worth it," he firmly assures me. "And I'd do it again."

I can't believe he got me the proof to clear my name. My breathing is becoming shaky. There's only one question left to ask.

"Back at the concert, what did you want to tell me?"

Unexpectedly, he gently takes my hand in his—sending sparks of electricity through me at his touch.

"I'll tell you," he says, still holding my hand, "but you have to lean in—closer."

My brows furrow, but I want to know, so I listen.

"Closer."

I come closer.

"*Closer.*"

"I *am* closer…"

I'm cut off by the intense fire in his eyes, which spark in the moonlight shining down on us. It's not the kind of fire I would see behind Seth's eyes; it's something else… it's brighter, stronger. Suddenly I'm so captivated by those eyes, I can't even remember who Seth is.

Aidan is all I can see. Everything that I am is connected to him—a sensation that starts out softly and grows more urgent until it's so power-ful, it scares me. Aidan seems to continue to scare me… but that's not the only thing he does to me.

I've never felt anything like this.

My chest is fluttering. I'm lightheaded, dazed, tingling—nervous. Then I can't think anything anymore—his lips are on mine.

Aidan's kissing me, and everything else in the world is gone.

Our lips move together, and somehow my hands are in his hair. My entire body is burning, wanting to be closer. I'm practically on top of him—

Suddenly, I pull back; my head is spinning. I look at him and his eyes are wide, staring at me in worry. We're both breathing heavily, trying to understand what just happened.

"I'm sorry—I wasn't thinking, I just—"

This time it's me who cuts *him* off, moving back on top of him and practically pushing him down on the dock, kissing him. He's shocked at first, but immediately begins kissing me back, pulling me to him and lifting me slightly before flipping us so I'm underneath him.

He leans down and whispers something in my ear, my heart jumps at his words.

Then his lips find mine again, and I can't think clearly enough to come up with a response. *Aidan is kissing me.* That's all that matters.

I'm kissing him.

This is all that's ever mattered.

WREN'S PLAYLIST

Careful, this stuff'll knock you off your feet

- Welcome To The Jungle
- Dust in The Wind
- Iron Man
- Simple Man
- Sweet Child O' Mine
- Back in Black
- Comfortably Numb
- Livin' On A Prayer
- Last Child
- My Michelle
- 18 And Life
- War Pigs
- The Unforgiven
- You Could Be Mine
- Without You
- Estranged
- More Than A Feeling
- The Zoo
- No One Like You
- Think About You
- Goodbye Stranger
- All My Love
- Enter Sandman
- Don't Damn Me
- Shoot To Thrill
- People Are Strange
- Don't Go Away Mad (Just Go)
- Paradise City
- Sweet Emotion
- It's My Life
- Love Hurts
- Crazy Train
- Take Me To The Top
- You're Crazy
- The Trooper
- Goodbye Stranger
- Child Of Innocence
- Wheel In The Sky
- Renegade
- Fade To Black
- Live Wire
- Out Ta Get Me
- Fear Of The Dark
- Miracles Out Of Nowhere
- Turn The Page
- Heartbreaker
- Somebody To Love
- Patience
- Night Moves
- Home Sweet Home
- Shadow Of Your Love
- Paint It Black
- Born To Be My Baby
- Shout At The Devil
- Bringing On The Heartbreak
- Heartbreak Hotel
- Nobody's Fault
- Juke Box Hero
- It's So Easy
- Nothing Else Matters
- Looks That Kill
- One Way Or Another
- Hair Of The Dog
- Rocket Queen

- Rock Of Ages
- Immigrant Song
- Always Somewhere
- Civil War
- Stairway To Heaven
- It's Alright (this one's hard to find)
- Locomotive
- Street Of Dreams
- Time For Change
- Knockin' On Heaven's Door
- Dream On
- You Belong With Me
- Smoke On The Water
- Don't Cry
- Mary Jane's Last Dance
- Still Loving You
- For Whom The Bells Toll
- Time For Change
- Wanted Dead Or Alive
- This I Love
- Come As You Are
- The Weight
- I Want To Know What Love Is
- Sittin' On The Dock Of The Bay
- I Need You
- Carry On Wayward Son
- Free Bird
- Can't Help Falling In Love
- Blaze Of Glory
- November Rain

WREN'S SONGS

"Something Big"- (unfinished)

Sometimes you feel like hitting
   everyone and watching as they
   fall down
Sometimes they hit you and you
   fall hard
Sometimes you wake up tired
   and just want to go back to bed
Even so, I can't find a place to go
   and lay my head
Something' big is coming, I can
   feel it now for sure
But I don't know what it is or
   why I should even care

"Make It Through"

If we could make it through,
   what would you say
The people, they all seem so
   happy
With their lovers and friends
Leaving you alone and broken,
   though it's not all as it seems
Many are lonelier
Than all of your dreams

And when you feel like dying,
   don't give away your hope
I'll be standing by your side until
   the end

How you've been so lost there's
Something to be said
It can seem like you're the only
   one
Still looking at the people
   laughing away their pain
Thinking you're not the same

If there's just one thing you
   wanted
You just want to feel better
As you slip farther away, know
   it's never too late
Your heart has never been one
To be ruled by fate

So tell me
Where will you go now
After you fall down
It might take a while
But all I want
Is for you to be free

"Home Again"

Making it home again no more
Been through Heaven and Hell
   as the years roll over
I can't stand to see you go by
I'm here to keep you safe alright
But you can't see how you give
   me pain
Take it and leave me in the rain

If there's something you need
from me
Know I'll always be there
If that's what you want then I'll
make it right
I must give in a little longer
It's ok, I'll be there soon
You won't have to make it
through

"Out Of This Place"

I'm getting outta here, whether
you like it or not
Try and stop me
I wanna see you try
Don't worry, if you can't feel my
anger
You will

Touch me again and I'll kick you
in the face
Do it one more time
I want out of this place
You think I'm so freakin'
helpless
I know your arrogance makes me
sick
I used to care
Now your name's just one to
cross off my list

They talk about peace and crap
like that
I'll talk about peace when I'm
finished
I move forward

You pull me back
It was a fun while it lasted
But now I'm done with this track

You think of yourself as an asset
Really you're just an Asshat

No more running, I'm here to
stand and fight
I'll take down whatever comes
my way
Alright
You think I can't
I'm gonna punch through your
throat

Screw you

"If Only"

It hurts so bad now
Oh I know
I'll tell you tomorrow, if I'm still
around
Take it slowly, and it's gonna be
ok
There's no need to be afraid

Making it alone never felt so
lonely
I'd like to know what happens
next
Oh if only

Something's broken inside me,
please get it out
I'm bleeding through my heart

But I can't find the knife
I'm filling with doubt
Why won't you help me out
What's wrong with me

Making it alone never felt so
  lonely
I'd like to know what happens
  next
Oh if only
Baby

I would take you with me, but I
  know you wouldn't come
I'm running out of freedom here
So give me a chance before I'm
  done
If it all comes down to it, I think
  I'll slowly drift and die

Making it alone never felt so
  lonely
I'd like to know what happens
  next
Oh If only
Only

"Take It Down The Line"

I'm kicking down the wall
It's banging in my mind
You'd like to trap me here
But I haven't got the time

Come over to my side
I'll show you something new
I'd promise to be gentle

But I know that won't please you

I hit you to the ground
Before you can go knocking me
  around
The night is closing in
Why can't I get away

If your feelings bother you
Why don't you take 'em down
  the line
I can take them for you but you
  won't ever be mine

So I've gone a little too far
No one's to be blamed
I've got a lot of problems
Maybe too many to be saved

"No One Can Help Me Now"

No one can help me now
I'm lost forever
Alone for eternity though that's
  not what they say to me
If I'm going then I just want to
  be gone
While they won't let me go, no
  one will bring me up
So then I'm drowning on my
  own
Too far to tell you what I need
I am just lost inside my dreams
You know if it's true than this
  must be
Be the end of me
N' I'm takin' this in stride

But there's nowhere left to cry
And there's no way to get out
  now
No matter what I do
We always end up right back
  here
All alone oh
Why'd you have to leave me
There was something great here
Now it's dead and gone
So what am I to do
If I really can't have you
Oh no one can help me now
Guess I'll have to make it on my
  own
'Cus no one can help me now
We take it all alone
No one can help me now
It's all passed away
Oh no one can help us now
Maybe we'll find our peace
  someday

"What You Don't Mean To Me"

Honey you can't see
What you don't mean to me
'Cus I've moved on but you're
  still here
Why are you still here
Try and keep me under control
It's too bad
But I don't work that way no
  more

You never wanted me anyways
You know it's true

I'm fighting for change and you
  won't let go
I ask you what you need
But your answer isn't me
N' you never wanted me
  anyways

Things are gettin' crazy now
I'm picking up my pieces
You don't want my love
Good, you're not getting it

If my time is up
I'm taking you down with me
If you don't let me go
I'm gonna stab you through the
  heart
Trouble is rounding the corner
Turn your head, I'll kick you
  down
Try it, I can do this all day

Untitled work: suggestions needed

Tell me your hidden sorrows, n'
  I'll make it ok
Give me a place in your heart,
  and don't look back today
The past is gone and so it will
  remain
Sometimes people are there for
  you,
And sometimes only the winds
  of shadows can be blamed
If you don't give me your hand
  now, I'll be lost out here
  forever now

Searching for somethin' that I'll
never find
So don't take that away from me
'cus I can't love without
anyone to be mine
If I am the only one, then what
does that make you
If I'm the only one

Isn't there another place,
someday we'll find another
way
The rains are coming down hard,
telling me not to cry this time
But no one told me this would be
and I won't fall away and die

FINAL GOODBYE

Don't ever let anybody tell you how to be. Live life your way.

ABOUT THE AUTHOR

Julianna Morgan has no experience to put in her bio, but that won't stop her from creating one. She attends Emerson College in Boston where she lives with her two roommates, though her heart lies in the West with her family back in California. She has been a dancer her entire life, spending all of her summers away from home at ballet summer intensive programs, and planned to become a professional at it before deciding to go to school for film. Along with dance, her passions are art, piano playing, drawing, not following rules, music (especially rock), movies, getting into trouble, acting, trying to understand the line between reality and illusion, and writing. *Rocket Queen* is her debut novel and she is not certain what to do with her life now that it has been published, though she plans to continue writing for as long as she's alive, however long that may be.

You can get in touch with Jules over email—julsballerina@gmail.com, or on Instagram @julianna.morgann. You can probably find some other ways, too.